The
Duplicate
Bride

The
Duplicate
Bride

NEW YORK TIMES BESTSELLING AUTHOR

GINNY BAIRD

Preview of *Accidentally Family* Copyright
© 2020 Sasha Summers

Entangled Publishing, LLC
10940 S Parker Road
Suite 327
Parker, CO 80134
Visit our website at www.entangledpublishing.com.

Amara is an imprint of Entangled Publishing, LLC.

Edited by Heather Howland
Cover design by Bree Archer
Cover art by KrisCole/GettyImages
Interior design by Toni Kerr

Print ISBN 978-1-68281-522-9
ebook ISBN 978-1-68281-521-2

Manufactured in the United States of America

First Edition October 2020

AMARA

ALSO BY GINNY BAIRD

THE HOLIDAY BRIDES SERIES

The Christmas Catch
The Holiday Bride
Mistletoe in Maine
Beach Blanket Santa

THE CHRISTMAS TOWN SERIES

The Christmas Cookie Shop
A Mommy for Christmas
Only You at Christmas
The Doctor Orders Christmas
A Glorious Christmas
A Corner Church Christmas
His Christmas Joy
Noelle's Best Christmas

For John

With many thanks to my publisher, Liz Pelletier,
and editor, Heather Howland,
for the support and opportunity!

CHAPTER ONE

Hope Webb turned the final page in her novel and sighed. Real love. The predestined kind.

If only she could live it and not just read about it.

Unfortunately, every time she thought she'd found her happily ever after, the relationship crashed and burned. Even if she *was* prone to making bad picks, as her neighbor, Iris, said, she'd learned from her mistakes. The next guy she fell for would be totally into her, so the situation would be mutual. No crashing and burning allowed.

She cradled her open book against her chest, reclined in the frayed rope hammock, and let herself sink into a relaxed haze. Now wasn't the time to think about her abysmal dating history. It was summer break. It had been months since she'd had time off work, and the peace was desperately needed.

A warm breeze riffled the flouncy hem of her yellow sundress where it rested against her pale thighs. Her favorite surfboard-patterned traveler tumbler sat on the plastic table beside her, loaded with iced chai.

Heaven.

Apart from the yapping of her neighbors' Chihuahua, who'd apparently set his sights on a squirrel, and the sound of Iris cheerfully singing "Age of Aquarius" while tending her adjoining garden, things were tranquil in her Durham neighborhood.

Her cell phone buzzed.

She tugged down the brim of her floppy sun hat, determined to ignore it. That had to be Principal Carson texting again. She'd already uploaded her grades. *Check.* Done the last-day walk-through of her classroom with the school VP. *Check.* And turned her laptop in to the district's IT center for its annual refurbishing. *Check.*

Check, check, check.

School's out for summer.

Buzz-buzz, buzz-buzz, buzz-buzz.

Hope set her jaw. This was probably about summer school. Principal Carson had tried to get her to teach again this year, but she'd turned him down. She'd never been good at saying no—to anyone, really—but she was frazzled. Burnt out. And she badly needed a break from unruly students, complaining parents, and mountains of paperwork. Her job had its positive aspects, obviously, and she loved her students. But they were much easier to appreciate in September than in June. Besides that, she had her sister's wedding to attend in their old hometown of Blue Hill, Maine, and she was leaving for it next week.

Jackie was marrying rich bachelor Brent Albright after a whirlwind courtship. Back when she and Hope were in high school and living in Blue Hill, the entire town had gone into a tizzy each time the Albright clan arrived for their annual summer stay.

Everyone in their friend group had been dying to meet the gorgeous Albright boys—especially Jackie, who'd dreamt of getting swept away into a life of privilege and luxury.

She met Brent face-to-face for the first time at a wedding she'd organized in Boston. It had, apparently, been love at first sight.

Buzz-buzz, buzz-buzz, buzz-buzz.

The vibrations escalated, causing Hope's phone to dance on the flimsy plastic table.

This was no longer texting territory; a call was coming through. Which made her wonder if it was Principal Carson after all. He had a strange aversion to phone calls—especially when he was begging favors.

"I think that's your phone, child," Iris called helpfully from above her bright red begonia hedge, which in these postage-stamp-size yards stood only ten feet away.

If Hope didn't love the stocky older woman as much as she did, she might have scowled. "Do I have to answer it?"

Iris laughed, her brown eyes sparkling with mischief. "They're just going to keep calling if you don't."

Iris was skilled at delivering unsolicited—and uncannily accurate—advice, as well as plates of calorie-rich cookies. The woman loved to bake, which would have been great if Hope had inherited her mom's fast metabolism. But no. She gained weight just *by reading* high-fat recipes. Not that she'd ever turn down all the goodies Iris brought by.

Hope lowered her sunglasses and peered at Iris, the warm afternoon light kissing the woman's deep brown skin.

Iris gave her a sunny grin, and Hope groaned.

"Ugh, *fine*."

That's when things became eerily quiet. So quiet she could no longer hear the breeze sifting through the trees overhead or the low droning of honeybees by the honeysuckle-laden back fence. Even the dog had stopped barking, having scampered around the side of the building. The only sound breaking the silence of the humid afternoon was the steady *clip-clip-clipping* of Iris's garden shears.

A really weird sense of foreboding blanketed Hope.

She snatched up her phone and saw the missed call was from her twin sister, Jackie. Her heart lurched as she stared at the barrage of text messages her sister had sent before the call, each one more frantic than the last.

> *Please call me.*
> *Desperate emergency.*
> *SOS*
> *Where are you???*
> *Ahhhh. Is your phone on vibrate???*

She nearly dropped the phone as it buzzed again, then scrambled to answer it.

"Jackie?" she asked in a near panic. "What's wrong?"

"OMG. *Hope*." Jackie sounded on edge. "Where have you *been*?"

"Um, busy." Hope flipped her book shut and set it aside. "What's going on?"

"It's the wedding!" Jackie wailed. "*Such* a disaster."

"Oh, no."

"Oh, yes! The Martin wedding is totally falling—"

"Wait." The wedding her sister was working on? *That's* what the crisis was about? Hope flopped back into the hammock. "I thought you were talking about *your* wedding."

"Huh?" She envisioned her sister's brow creasing below her wispy dark bangs. "How can I possibly think about myself at a time like this? The Martins are counting on me!"

Hope sucked air back into her lungs. Naturally, she'd assumed Jackie had been talking about her own wedding, and naturally, she'd been wrong. Her sister might be a phenomenal wedding planner, but she was terrible at making her own wedding a priority.

"You scared me," Hope said. "I thought there was something seriously wrong. Like you and Brent were having trouble or something."

"There *is* something seriously wrong. Mrs. Martin got into a fight with Emile Gastón."

Hope closed her eyes. "Who's Emile Gastón?"

"Only the most brilliant caterer in Boston, and Mrs. Martin had the gall to tell him his crème fraîche was a 'flopé.'"

"Maybe it was?"

"That's not the point. The point is I thought I had things all sewn up, but, now that the catering's blown, I'm going to have to start over. And this is a double mess with the wedding going off in Nantucket. Do you know how hard it is to get anything done in Nantucket at the last minute?"

No, but obviously her sister did. "I thought the

Martin wedding was still a few weeks away?"

"That's why everything has to be set before my big day and the honeymoon. Brent and I will be in Bermuda right up until the Thursday before the Martin wedding. So I can't just leave for Maine with the logistics dangling."

Any second now, she'd be subjected to another lecture from her sister on how hard weddings were to arrange.

"You have no clue how challenging this is!" Jackie began, right on schedule. "Lining up the venue and the food and the band to show up at once. The invitations have already gone out, and the RSVPs are pouring in—"

"What about your assistant? Can't Rachel take things over for you?"

"The stakes are too high. If I don't handle this myself, it won't get done. And anyway, Mrs. Martin is insisting that *I* fix this."

Hope rubbed her forehead. "I'm sure you'll find a replacement," she said, trying to soothe her. When there was silence at the other end of the line, she added, "For Emile. The caterer?"

"Hopie…"

A sinking feeling settled in her stomach. Jackie never called her Hopie unless she was asking for something huge.

"I'm really in a bind here. I can't possibly pull everything together by tomorrow."

As in, the day Jackie was scheduled to drive from Boston to Blue Hill to meet up with her fiancé and his parents and grandparents, as well as her and Hope's mom. The rest of the wedding party was due to arrive Monday, which was when Hope had planned to show up.

"I'm sorry, Jackie. I know you're in a tough spot. I wish there was something I could do."

"Yeah," she said slowly. "About that… Remember when we were kids and we pretended to be each other? No one could tell us apart, sometimes not even Mom…"

Hope's heart thumped, and alarm bells rang wildly in her head. "Uh-uh, no way," she said, catching her sister's drift. "That is not happening."

"I can pay for your new ticket and the rental car?"

"No, Jackie, just *no.* You can forget about it!" She lowered her voice, remembering she was outdoors and that Iris was within earshot. "I am *not* playing you. Okay? Not during your own wedding week."

Iris looked up from trimming her begonia hedge. "Everything all right, child?"

"Oh, yeah! Fine! It's just my sister. Nervous bride." She waved Iris's concern aside and hissed quietly into the mouthpiece, "Are you out of your ever-lovin' mind?"

"No. I'm thinking plenty clearly. Thanks."

Hope tightened her grip on her phone, unable to believe what her twenty-eight-year-old twin was suggesting. Jackie had to have majorly lost it to suggest a plan like that. Hope had to find a way to talk her down from this ledge.

"I'm sure if you explain things to Brent," she said, "he'll understand."

"It's not Brent I'm worried about," Jackie rasped quietly. "It's his grandmother." She dropped her voice a notch further. She was probably in a public place. "I didn't tell you this before because it's embarrassing, but I don't think the woman likes me."

"You've met her?" Jackie hadn't mentioned this. "When?"

"She and her husband live in Boston. Brent and I had lunch with them, and well…she gave me the eye."

"Which eye?"

"*The* eye. You know, where it looks like someone's peering straight through you? She kind of squinted at me, appraising-like, and asked how long I'd been in love with her grandson."

Hope gasped. "What did you say?"

"*Forever.* What else could I say? Brent took my hand and told his grandparents we're a great match. I mean, we've talked it out and have plenty of good reasons for being together, so we are. His grandfather toasted us with his congratulations then, but Granny just dabbed her lips with her napkin and mumbled something about rushed nuptials and haste making waste."

"Well, that was unnecessary," Hope snapped, affronted on her sister's behalf. Even if the engagement had been short, Brent's grandmother could have at least been gracious about it.

"I *know*. The family's already doubting me, and nobody's giving me a fair chance. Here's the thing—Brent's grandma is like the *queen* in that family. So, if she doesn't like me, then maybe the others won't, either."

"I'm sure they'll all love you once they get to know you," Hope said. Jackie was so outgoing and fun. Meanwhile, Hope was on the quieter side—except for when she was commanding high-energy students. She was a rock star at getting preteens to behave in the classroom, which was one reason she loved her job. The other was summer vacations—when she wasn't being coerced into teaching summer school.

"If I arrive late to my own wedding week, Grandmother Margaret's going to pounce," Jackie persisted. "She already hinted that she thought I was unreliable and might not make it." She adopted a high falsetto, imitating the older woman. "*With your very busy schedule, are you sure you can squeeze in one more wedding?*"

"That's awful! It's almost like she was daring you not to come."

On the other side of the hedge, Iris huffed, and Hope suspected very strongly that she was listening.

"Or warning me off, right?"

"Totally. How did Brent react?"

"He lowered his eyebrows and just said, '*Grandmother.*' Grandpa Chad gave her the elbow. Brent apologized to me later, claiming his grandmother's 'so sweet' deep down, but the jury's still out on that one." Jackie's tone verged on desperation. "I wouldn't even be asking if it weren't so important," she said. "Grandmother Margaret is out to sabotage this wedding. I can just feel it."

"So then, have Brent talk to her."

"He has!"

"And?"

"He wouldn't tell me what she said, so it must have been pretty horrible."

Hope's protective instincts surged to the fore. Even though she and Jackie had been born only minutes apart, she took her role as the big sister seriously. "Brent's family sounds awful."

"It's just the grandmother, honestly. Grandpa Chad seems okay. I haven't met Brent's parents or siblings." Jackie was silent for a moment, and then she sniffled. "I'm sorry…sorry I even suggested it. I was just thinking if it was only for *one short day*, it would be like old times. A little game, but for all the right reasons."

Hope rolled her eyes. She knew where this was going. "What about Brent?"

"What about him?"

"Uh, surely he'd know if it was me and not you."

"He's the *groom*. I doubt he'd even notice."

Wait. "What's that supposed to mean?"

"It means he'll be distracted. Wedding-week jitters and all that."

"Since when do guys get 'wedding-week jitters'?"

"Come on, Hopie. Don't be sexist."

She suspected there was more to this story than *wedding-week jitters*, so she waited Jackie out, shooing away a honeybee that tried to settle on the lid of her tumbler of iced chai. The drink sat on a flimsy plastic table with one bent leg, purchased at a thrift shop, like just about everything else in her cozy duplex. Student loan payments still ate up most of her salary.

After a long pause, Jackie finally caved. "All right, here's the thing. Brent and I haven't exactly spent a whole lot of time together. Especially lately. He's had his travel, and I've had—"

"Let me guess," Hope said deadpan. "The Martin wedding?"

"Yes!"

Unbelievable. "Well, maybe you should have considered getting to know Brent better before committing!"

"Please don't yell at me. I feel a migraine coming on."

"You and me both."

Jackie groaned. "Okay, fine. I get it. It was a lame idea." Next, she said wistfully, "But it kind of *would* have been like old times. Do you remember opening night of *The Sound of Music*?"

The memories of being seventeen and in their junior year of high school flooded Hope. "You were cast as Maria," she said. "But then you came down with that stomach flu."

"You were my hero," Jackie said. "You came to my rescue."

"It was easy. I'd been helping you rehearse for weeks. I knew all the lines."

"You stepped in that night in my place, and nobody was the wiser. Not even Mom."

"It helped that you were better by the next…" Hope's words trailed off when she got the parallel Jackie was making. "This is different, and you know it."

"Yeah." She blew her nose. "We probably couldn't have pulled it off, anyway."

Hope sighed, trying to imagine herself in Jackie's shoes. What if Brent Albright really was Jackie's Prince Charming? Shouldn't Hope do everything in her power to support the marriage? Her sister's luck in the man department hadn't been much better than hers, and here was a guy who'd offered Jackie her very own happily ever after.

Loads of people had problem in-laws, but those in-laws becoming a problem before the wedding really wasn't fair. She wanted to help her sister—she really did. But impersonating her twin wasn't the right solution.

Then, Hope got a brilliant idea.

"Okay," she said, deciding. "Here's what I'll do. I'll go up to Maine a day early, but not as you—as me."

"What good will *that* do?" Jackie asked weakly.

"I'll explain that you've had an unavoidable delay and that I'm there to help with preparations in your place."

Jackie thought a moment before answering. "I guess that could work."

"Honesty's the best policy."

"Usually."

"*Always.*" If the Albrights were so heartlessly unforgiving that they wouldn't cut Jackie this tiny bit of slack for a business emergency, maybe Brent's family wasn't worth marrying into. She'd reserve judgment about the groom. People could choose their friends, not their families. "But, before I go, you'll need to contact Brent to let him know there's been a change in plans."

"All right. I will." Jackie heaved a breath. "And thanks, Hopie. You're the best."

She sounded exhausted, and she wasn't the only one. Hope was drained by the conversation, too. And now, she had to pack.

She ended the call and swung her feet down off the hammock. Scratchy dry grass prickled the bottoms of her bare feet and poked up between her toes.

"Sounds like more than nervous-bride troubles to me," Iris commented from beneath her broad straw hat.

"The wedding's just hit a little wrinkle." Hope stood, gathering her book and drink off the table. "But it will all get ironed out. I'm headed up to Blue Hill early to help."

She smiled with more confidence than she felt, not knowing what kind of welcome she'd receive in Maine, but she was determined to give this her best try. She'd always been there for Jackie, and now wasn't the time to let her down. Not when she was under so much stress.

Iris gave her a motherly smile. "Jackie's lucky to have a sister like you."

"Thanks, Iris. I'm lucky to have her, too."

Hope walked toward her back door, and Iris cheerily brandished her garden shears.

"Well, safe travels! Good luck ironing everything out."

• • •

Brent Albright sat on the patio of his grandparents' Blue Hill home, watching the sky take on a purple-orange hue as the sun set over the deep blue water. His dad, Parker, relaxed in the Adirondack chair beside him, and a low fire crackled in the stone firepit nearby.

As many times as he'd been here, Brent never got tired of the view. The three-story white clapboard house had a covered wraparound porch facing the bay. Manicured bushes and fragrant flower gardens hedged its lush lawn.

When the tide was low, a private pebble beach rested at the bottom of the worn wooden steps leading down to the blackish sands. When it was high, like it was now, the beach was swallowed up by undulating waters.

Brent sipped his scotch, savoring its smoky warmth in the chill of the evening. Even in June, it got a lot cooler here at night.

"When is that bride of yours scheduled to arrive?" his dad asked above the low hum of crickets and the brisk evening breezes wafting off the water. His dad was in his late fifties now, with his shortly cropped hair graying at the temples. For eons, Brent had thought of his dad as ageless, but the years had finally begun to creep over his features.

"Sometime tomorrow afternoon."

"Can't wait to meet her."

"She's excited to meet you and Mom, too."

Brent swirled the booze in his glass, wondering when his own excitement would kick in. When he and Jackie had made this bargain, it had seemed reasonable. Astute. Now, Brent worried that he'd been kidding himself.

His dad drained the rest of his glass and shot him a curious stare.

"You know I'm not one to go meddling in your business…" he began.

"No," Brent said a tad more defensively than he

intended. "That's Grandmother's job."

His dad frowned. "She seems to think this hasty marriage has something to do with your taking over Albright Enterprises. Any truth to that?" he asked, tilting his tumbler with the question.

Though Grandpa Chad had made it clear he'd be more comfortable ceding control of his luxury hotel corporation to a married grandchild, he hadn't specifically made this a condition of Brent assuming the reins.

Still, it had been obvious that Grandpa Chad viewed Brent's older brother, William, as his next top choice should Brent continue what his grandfather had deemed his "reckless bachelor lifestyle." William had always been more focused and settled, and it had been tough walking in his perfect shadow. Brent had taken longer to get his feet on the ground.

He'd run through various jobs in green energy and banking before scoring this Albright Enterprises slot. And, once he took over the family business, his new position wasn't something he could bail on easily. Yet he was confident that he could handle it.

After he'd become engaged to Jackie, Grandpa Chad had shared that confidence, too.

"I'd hate to see you rushing into anything," his dad said when Brent didn't answer. "On account of professional ambition."

"It's not that at all," Brent said firmly. "Jackie and I make a great team."

Love would come later.

He hoped.

"What ever happened to that girl you dated right

after college?"

"Amanda?" Brent asked, thrown. His dad hadn't asked about his old girlfriend in years. Amanda Robbins had been the first—and only—woman to break Brent's heart. Afterward, he'd promised himself he'd never let that happen again.

Brent was proud of the fact that he'd been successful so far.

"I have no idea. I'm guessing she's married by now."

"And that other gal... Sheryl, was it? Sheryl Bryce? The attorney in New York?" His dad thoughtfully tapped his chin. "Then there was Wesley, the extremely talkative one."

Brent frowned. "What are you getting at?"

"Just that life is long, son. When you're choosing a life partner, it's important to choose carefully."

"I *have* chosen carefully."

His dad's forehead rose. "After three months?"

"You told me yourself that three minutes was all you needed to know that Mom was the one for you."

"Yeah, that's true." His dad chuckled. "The moment I looked into those pretty brown eyes, I was a goner."

Brent had heard this tale a billion times, but he indulged his dad in the memory.

"We were in a creative writing class together," his dad went on, "and Elsa sat beside me. I'll never forget the way she smiled. Just as beautifully as she does today."

He finished his drink and set the glass on a table beside his chair. "I don't recall a lick of that first lecture," he reported with a grin, "but I did ask for her number. It took me nearly the entire semester to work up the nerve to call her…"

"Then, she asked you out first," Brent finished.

His parents had a ton in common, and both had set their sights on New York. His dad now ran his own literary agency, and his mom was the managing editor of a home and garden magazine. They still lived in the same upscale Brooklyn neighborhood where Brent and his siblings had grown up, but Brent's childhood summers had been spent right here in Blue Hill.

His dad gave him a thoughtful look. "It's pretty awesome stuff, marriage with the right person. I just hope that Jackie's the right person for you."

"She is, Dad," Brent said, but way deep in his heart there was a shadow of doubt. He couldn't compare his situation to what his parents had, though. These were different times, and he was his own man. Besides that, he was thirty-two, not some kid, so old enough to make up his own mind.

His dad shared a warm smile. "I'm glad to hear you say that."

CHAPTER TWO

The voice on the GPS commanded Hope to turn left in fifty feet onto a gravel country road. For the past several miles, she'd driven across one-lane bridges, over inlets, and beside the stunning banks of Blue Hill Bay. Across the slow-rolling waves, she could just make out the hazy outline of Cadillac Mountain. Lobster boats trolled the glistening waters, and sailboats glided along, billowing winds caught in their colorful spinnakers.

When she'd lived here as a teen, Hope had never really appreciated the beauty of Blue Hill. Then again, she and her family had lived in the more… *modest* part of town near the coffee shop where her mom had worked. Basically, nowhere near this ritzy stretch of private homes on secluded waterfront acreage.

The audio directions announced that she was approaching her destination in another twenty feet. She searched the left-hand side of the road, but there were so many blueberry bushes between her and whatever lay on the other side.

There. Up ahead. An ivory flag covered in four-leaf clovers hung proudly from the mailbox at the end of a driveway, sporting the name "Albright" in gold-bordered green letters.

That was…fancy.

She slowed to a stop and glanced down at her white slacks and sleeveless top, worried that she'd underdressed. She wasn't exactly used to hanging with high society, but at least her outfit was coordinated. Her navy sandals matched her clutch purse, and her gold hoop earrings went with the small heart necklace that she always wore on a chain around her neck.

Her hair, though…that was a mess. She'd straightened her dark waves with a flat iron before her flight, but the whipping winds in the convertible Jackie had rented had undone her effort.

She twisted her hair up in a clip and frowned at her reflection in the rearview mirror. Still disheveled, but passable. She'd run a brush through it later when no one was looking.

More blueberry bushes bordered the drive as Hope rounded a bend, tiny fruit clusters weighing down spindly branches. She'd always loved the color of ripe blueberries, but the season wouldn't peak until later in the summer. Some of the small orbs were already deep blue, while others held a reddish tinge, bordering on purple—

A figure appeared in front of her in the drive, and Hope slammed on her brakes. Tires squealed and rocks scattered as the convertible skidded to a halt.

The woman spun toward her. A wicker basket dangled from the crook of her arm, and a long blond braid tumbled past one shoulder from beneath a floppy hat. She looked to be in her fifties. Could this be Brent's mom?

She shoved her gear stick into park and cut the engine, her pulse pounding.

"Jackie," the woman said with a stunned smile. "Close call. You almost hit me!" Despite her casual jeans and checkered shirt, the woman's enormous rock of an engagement ring glimmered in the bright light, and silver bangles jangled on her wrist. "I'm Elsa Albright."

So, she *was* Jackie's future mother-in-law.

Eeep.

That's all Hope needed—for the Albrights to think of the Webbs as reckless drivers. She hoisted herself up in the seat so she could speak over the top of the windshield. It was odd that Brent hadn't told his mom about the change, but maybe he hadn't had time.

"I'm *so*, so sorry, Mrs. Albright. And, actually, I'm not Ja—"

"Of course you *aren't*." Elsa skirted around the two-seater and popped open the passenger door, hopping right into the car. "Nobody's used to navigating this narrow driveway." She set her blueberry basket on the floor and leaned toward Hope.

"And *now* a proper introduction and a hug."

Oomph. Elsa squeezed Hope so tightly a burst of air escaped from her lungs.

"I'm so thrilled to finally meet you."

"Mrs. Albright—"

"Elsa, please." She tucked a lock of Hope's hair behind her ear. Then, she latched on to Hope's chin, turning it from side to side. "Aren't you *pretty*? Every bit as pretty as Brent said."

Wait. "No—"

Elsa stopped her by patting her cheek. "No false modesty, now. Haven't you heard?" Her brown eyes twinkled. "Brides are *supposed* to be beautiful."

No. No, no, no. "I'm not—"

"What's all the commotion out here?" a woman's voice demanded.

Hope whipped her head around to see a stern older woman bulldozing her way toward them with her chin held high. From her haughty demeanor, Hope guessed she was the grandmother.

She rammed a hand loaded with gemstone rings against the driver-side door and sneered. "I see you decided to join us."

Gah. *This* is what Jackie had to deal with for the rest of her life? "Actually, I—"

Margaret's blue gaze was as cool as ice. "I'm surprised you could work us in."

"Brent's told us *all about* how busy you've been," Elsa inserted nervously. "With that Maupin wedding?"

"Martin," Hope said, dazed. This was *not* going the way she'd expected. She was under siege from all sides. At least Brent's mom seemed nice enough, but Grandmother Margaret definitely wasn't the warm-and-fuzzy type.

Far from it.

Elsa gave a short laugh, trying to downplay the situation. "Believe it or not, Margaret here thought you'd prioritize *that* wedding over this one." She rolled her eyes like the idea was absurd, and Hope wanted to melt through the floor.

Jackie needed to show up and *fix this*.

"Now we know that's not true, hmm?" Elsa grinned at Hope. "Here you are!"

"*There* she is." A dark-haired guy in a black polo shirt and khakis ambled down the drive.

Hope nearly swallowed her tongue. Brent

Albright was gorgeous as a teen, but as a man? She couldn't breathe. In addition to the rugged-yet-refined-man thing he now had going, he walked with an easy stride that implied he was in command of his *completely* flawless body.

His smile, though…that's what stole her breath away.

"Hello, sweetheart," he said, gently nudging past Grandmother Margaret.

Hope's breath hitched when she saw his unbelievably hot mouth dropping down toward hers. Wait. Was he going to kiss her?

"Brent!" she gasped, abruptly turning away. She could *not* kiss her sister's fiancé.

No matter how exciting that had momentarily seemed.

He stumbled forward, his lips landing awkwardly on her cheek while his hands grasped her shoulders.

Hope's world turned upside down, and her heart thundered as the pressure of his kiss lingered, his scent washing over her. He smelled like sand and sea and pine…and she had to resist wrapping her arms around his neck and yanking him into the car.

She broke into a sweat. *This is* not *happening. I am not attracted to Jackie's future husband!* This was so incredibly twisted.

Not as twisted as Brent thinking she was Jackie, though. Shouldn't he have some gut-level instinct about the woman he loved and was about to marry?

"Sorry about the display." His whisper tickled her ear, and tingles raced down her spine.

Not good. Not good at all.

He shot a glance over his shoulder, meant for

only her, and Hope got his meaning. They were playing the loving couple for his grandmother's benefit. But why was it an act anyway?

She had to tell them she wasn't Jackie now. Now, before it was too late. Her sister must not have gotten in touch with Brent, but Hope could explain things.

"In truth, I'm…er, not…" She tried to speak, but she got caught up in Brent's heady stare. He had very dark eyes, maybe the darkest she'd ever seen. And, ooh, how they sparkled in the sunshine. "What I mean is…"

Desperate to regain her footing, she wrenched herself free of Brent's gaze and turned to Elsa, who sat beside her in the passenger seat.

Brent's mom's immediate acceptance of her—no, *Jackie*—made her heart pound harder.

Elsa was trying so hard to be warm and welcoming, despite that fact that Hope had nearly flattened her in the driveway like a blueberry pancake.

Hope was at a total loss over what to do.

She'd told Jackie that this was impossible.

That she would no way in a million years impersonate her.

It was unethical and wrong.

And yet, she'd been helplessly cornered and suddenly had nowhere to turn…

An unnerving silence filled the air. She bit her bottom lip and peeked at Grandmother Margaret.

Sure enough, the older woman gave her *the eye*.

Hope prickled with agitation. How dare Grandmother Margaret judge her sister as not being good enough for Brent? That's pretty obviously what she'd thought when she'd first challenged Jackie not to show up here. Now, she was being just plain mean. Acting surprised that she'd make time for her own wedding.

Jackie *was* making time; she was just running late. Through no real fault of her own.

Hope didn't like deception, but she hated the idea of some condescending snob dissing her family even more. Grandmother Margaret had cast really harsh aspersions on Hope's own flesh and blood: her precious twin sister—her *baby* sister, if only by a few minutes. The sister who was always getting herself into messes and who relied on Hope to get her out of them.

Jackie's words came back to her like loudly blaring sound waves in her brain.

Just for one day…for all the right reasons…

Then there was Iris's voice, topping everything off.

Jackie's lucky to have a sister like you.

She tightened her fingers around the steering wheel, worrying that she was getting in over her head. But, if she could help Jackie by making inroads with Brent's tricky family, she should, right? It still seemed wrong that Brent couldn't tell her and her twin apart, though. That made her question his relationship with Jackie and what exactly was going on between them.

But that was for the two of them to figure out, not her. All Hope had to do was serve as sort of a placeholder for the next twenty-four hours until Jackie got here. Maybe, during that time, she'd be able to make progress with the grandmother.

A girl can dream.

"Sweetheart?" Brent gave her another devastating smile, and, for an instant, she couldn't think straight or even recall where she was. "I was saying that we should head back to the house."

"Right," she answered, realizing she'd slipped away.

She wanted to confront them all, she really did, but she was overwhelmingly outnumbered. Taking the easy way out sounded more and more tempting by the second.

Besides that, it really *was* just for one day. Would *kind of* be like old times…

And seriously, how much could go wrong?

A lot, if she was being honest with herself.

She grew lightheaded in the summer heat. A lie of omission was still a lie, but it could be a *white lie* if it was due to good intentions. Somewhere between Elsa's startling welcome and Margaret's evil eye, she'd lost her way. Then, when she looked at Brent again…she found it.

Grandmother Margaret shot her one last snooty look, then made excuses about going to get the mail.

Something snapped inside Hope, and that cinched the deal.

Nobody got the best of the Webbs. She and her sister might not have been raised with money, but they'd grown up proud. The Albrights were *lucky* to have Jackie joining their family. Hope planned to make them aware of that.

Yep. She was going to do this.

Brent looked over the sports car she'd picked up at the airport in Boston. "Nice wheels." A dimple deepened in his left cheek, and Hope's stomach flipped. "Ready to come inside?"

If he was half as great as he seemed, he'd make the very best husband for Jackie. It was her sisterly duty to make sure their wedding *happened*. This is what the Webb family did. They stood together when times were tough, and times probably couldn't get any tougher than the ones Brent's grandmother was prepared to dish out.

Hope nodded and put the gear shift in drive, her hand trembling at the thought of what lay ahead. One full day of pretending to be Jackie.

But she could do this.

Of course she could.

It would be just like opening night at *The Sound of Music*.

All she needed to do was avoid getting too close to Brent.

Because, even though he'd only kissed her on the cheek, that kiss had rocked her world.

And that *definitely* wasn't right.

Not when he was six days away from marrying her sister.

• • •

Brent helped Jackie from the car, noting that she looked prettier than ever. She'd always been a great-looking woman, with her sweet brown eyes and that gorgeous brown hair, but there was something different about her now.

Maybe the Maine air had given her cheeks that pink tinge. Or maybe it was from the pressure of meeting his family. He frowned, concerned that his Grandmother Margaret had been unfriendly. He was *not* going to let her negativity ruin this week for him and Jackie.

Even though he and his fiancé weren't exactly *in love*, he wanted to believe that they'd get there eventually. He had every reason to love Jackie and pretty much no reason not to. He just wasn't there yet.

In other circumstances, he might have worried about rushing things, but knowing Jackie viewed their upcoming marriage the same way helped alleviate any guilt.

"I'm going to clean up," his mom said, heading toward the house, holding her berry basket. "I'll see you kids later. There's fresh lemonade in the kitchen. Help yourselves."

Jackie nodded her thanks, then opened the trunk with her key fob.

Brent dug out her meager carry-on in surprise. "Just one?" He'd never known her to travel with less than two suitcases—at a minimum one checked bag and a carry-on. That wasn't counting the oversize bag she claimed as a pocketbook.

"I, er…" She dropped the key into her purse, which was also awfully small. In fact, it nearly fit in her hand. "Decided to pack light."

Her bag was so lightweight, he had no idea how she'd managed to squeeze multiple pairs of shoes into it. She never traveled with less than five pairs. "There's always a first time." He grinned, but she didn't return it. Man, she was on edge, and he couldn't blame her. He had such a big family compared to hers, and she was probably concerned about making a good impression.

He leaned closer and took her hand, trying to reassure her. "Everything will be fine," he whispered, giving her fingers a gentle squeeze.

"Yeah." She stiffened and awkwardly tugged her hand away. "Sure."

His heart sank. He had to do better. When he'd joined the others in the driveway, the tension between Jackie and his grandmother had been overwhelming. Maybe he could ask his mom to have a word with Grandmother, since she and his mom were close.

Jackie turned toward him, wearing a puzzled expression. "You didn't get my last phone call, did you? I mean, er…my voice message? Or maybe my text?"

"Actually, I've kind of misplaced my phone."

She blanched. "Misplaced?"

Luckily, he had a good idea where to find it. It was probably under a sofa cushion in the den, where he'd been watching the soccer match with his grandpa yesterday afternoon. He'd been so distracted he hadn't realized it had gone missing until now.

"Jackie," he said slowly. "Is something going on?"

She hesitated a beat. "Um, yeah, it is. Was."

Her eyebrows knitted together, then she shook her head. She wore her hair up, but a few strands framed her face, making her look even prettier than usual. How would she react if he reached out to touch those loose strands?

"What I mean is," she said, pulling him back into the conversation, "I wanted to update you on my travel plans because I was running late."

"You got here just in time." He reached for her hand again, right as she moved to adjust her hair, which really did look different the more he stared at it. "Wait," Brent said. "Did you cut it?"

"It?"

Brent laughed at her blank expression. "Your hair? You look different."

"Do I?" She scrunched up her lips, evidently thinking. "Oh, right! Yeah, I did. In layers."

She plucked a clip from the back of her head to demonstrate, and a dark, wavy mass tumbled to her shoulders.

His heart jolted in a weird way.

Maybe it was a jolt of surprise, but he didn't think so.

Whoa. This is news.

"I got this new style for our wedding," she added, doing a little swish of her bangs. They accentuated her dark brown eyes, making them look even bigger. "Do you like it?"

Brent's pulse thrummed in his ears.

This reaction definitely isn't normal.

She beamed up at him, and his neck warmed.

Neither was that.

"It's…" Brent's throat tightened. "Very nice." He didn't know what was happening here, but his fiancée was having an unusual effect on him. Not an unpleasant one, either. It couldn't seriously be just the haircut. Or could it?

"Where are we going?" she asked as he led her down the flagstone path.

"To the carriage house," he said, remembering that they'd discussed these arrangements.

"Ah," she said, sounding like she knew, but the question in her eyes said she didn't.

"It's where you're staying with Meredith, your mom, and your sister until the wedding, remember?" He studied her. "The main house is full up, but the carriage house is really nice. I'm pretty sure we talked about this?"

"Oh yeah. The *carriage house*," she said on a breath. "Of course."

Brent caught a whiff of her perfume, which reminded him of lilies of the valley. It was a pleasant scent but different from the one with more citrusy undertones that Jackie normally wore. "You smell nice," he said as they reached the carriage house and he held open the door.

She stepped past him with a blush. "Thanks. You do, too."

Jackie glanced around at the kitchenette and mini dining room that joined a cozy seating area with large sliding glass doors overlooking the bay. A woodstove stood between a rustic dining room hutch and the back of the sectional sofa, which was positioned to have a view of the water.

"The master bedroom's in the back." Brent pointed through the kitchen. "Full bath is down this hall." He indicated the passageway that included a washer and dryer. Next, he motioned to a set of stairs off the living area. "A small den with a pullout couch is that way, and the bedroom with twin beds is on the other side of it."

Jackie didn't try to hide how impressed she was. "It's fabulous."

If she thought the carriage house was nice, he

couldn't wait to show her the rest of the place. He'd grown up exploring every part of the property with his siblings, and he knew he took the beauty of it for granted. Seeing it through new eyes would be fun.

Brent set down her bag. "You should all be comfortable here. The fridge is stocked with snacks and drinks, but meals will be up at the main house. When you're ready, I can show you around?"

Her gaze landed on a wrapped loaf of banana bread that sat beside a covered plate of homemade cookies on the counter.

"Those are from Grandmother Margaret. I told her you wouldn't eat them, since you're so strict about your diet, but she wanted to have them here for the others anyway."

"That's really sweet of her." Jackie blinked. "And unexpected."

"She has her good side." He shot her a wink, and she blushed—again.

He'd never known her to be much of a blusher before, yet here she was, his *blushing bride*. He repressed a grin at her unbearable cuteness. Though he and Jackie didn't have what he'd call an *ardent* relationship, she was causing some odd "stirrings in his soul," as Grandpa Chad would say. He ached to take her in his arms and kiss her like he meant it. In fact, he found that he'd unconsciously taken a step toward her.

Jackie backed away, breaking the spell, and glanced at the door. "I'll meet you up at the house in a few minutes, okay?"

"Oh. Yeah, sure." Great. Now he was crowding her. Had he completely forgotten what their arrangement was? Just because his brain was strangely scrambled in her presence, that didn't mean she felt the same way. Her infrequent kisses were quick and cool. He was out of his mind to think they'd suddenly be passionate. "Take your time."

He couldn't explain his out-of-the-blue magnetic attraction to her. Jackie definitely wasn't acting like herself, but neither was he. She was probably nervous about meeting the rest of his family, but what about him? Maybe he was getting stoked about their marriage after all? Yeah, that had to be it. It would be awesome if he and Jackie could really make this work.

Except she'd have to be into him, too.

And, at the moment, he wasn't getting that vibe. The vibe he was getting was more like she was eager for him to go away.

He was probably overthinking it. Hopefully.

"I can't wait to meet your mom," he said, stepping outside. "And your sister, Hope."

"Hope!" Jackie exclaimed, like he'd just shouted *fire*. "Right!"

Then she slammed the door, leaving Brent standing there stunned.

CHAPTER THREE

Hope, a nervous wreck, called Jackie. She didn't know how she'd let this happen, but she had, and it was too much.

"Jackie Webb, here. Thanks for calling. Please leave your number at the beep, and I'll get back with you."

Argh.

She was just about to send a panicked text when her phone rang.

"Sorry," Jackie said. "My phone was in the bottom of my bag, and I couldn't find it." She paused a beat, then asked in a breezy way, "So. How's Blue Hill?"

"Horrible." Hope's gaze snagged on the panoramic view out the sliding glass doors. "Beautiful." She heaved a breath. "*Messy.*"

"Those are quite a few conflicting adjectives. What's so horrible about it?" She gasped. "Grandmother Margaret?"

Hope stared down at the homemade goodies. "She supposedly has her good side."

"I…see?"

"She baked me banana bread. I mean, not me—you. Or, all of us. And cookies, too."

"Let's hope they're not laced with arsenic."

"Ha. Ha."

"So," Jackie asked, "how did everybody take the news about my delay? I sent Brent a text message, but he never answered."

Hope turned away from the windows and began pacing. "That's because he didn't get it."

"What?"

"He's lost his phone."

"Oh, no. Then, it's a good thing you're there to explain things."

Hope fell silent, twisting a lock of her hair around one finger. "Um, so, about that…"

"Yeah?"

"Everybody here thinks I'm you."

"What? Why?"

Hope grimaced. "Because when I got here, they kind of assumed it."

"And you didn't bother to *correct* them? Hope!" she exclaimed, her voice rising. "What about all that *stuff* you said? 'Honesty's the best policy'?"

"It is." She didn't know why her sister sounded so upset. Jackie was the one who suggested the plan to begin with.

"Then, how did this happen?"

"I don't know. One minute, I was driving the car—"

"The rental?"

"Yes. And the next, I was nearly running her over."

Jackie gasped. "Grandmother Margaret?"

"No. Brent's mom."

"Is this some elaborate joke? You're setting me up for something, right? A big punch line." She laughed nervously. "Okay. I'm ready. Sock it to me."

Hope braved it. "Brent believes it, too."

"What?" Jackie's voice became a soft murmur.

"That you're me?"

"Yeah."

The line went silent. Hope let her sister process that news without interruption.

"Okay, all right," Jackie finally said. "This isn't so bad. Let's think this through. You haven't kissed him, have you?" she asked in an accusatory tone.

"Brent? No! What kind of sister do you think I am? I mean, it was awkward. Trying to avoid it."

"It shouldn't be *that* hard," Jackie grumbled. "Brent and I aren't much into PDA. He's not the type."

"Er…that's good." For Hope, at least.

"Just try not to be alone with him."

"I wasn't planning on it."

Through the phone, Hope could hear her sister drumming her fingernails. "Maybe we can make this work."

"I'd rather not," Hope said. "What about Mom?"

"Oh. I forgot to tell you. I just heard from her that she's coming up tomorrow instead of today. Something about car trouble. She's already let Elsa know."

"Well, that's something. So, Mom won't be an issue because you'll get here first."

"Hopie, about that…" Jackie said, and Hope's stomach sank. *Not again.* "I was just about to tell you…the Martin wedding has hit another hurdle."

"What?"

"The Bridal Bouquets Boutique had assured us that two hundred and forty-two miniature bonsai trees were on order, but now there's been a holdup in the delivery date."

"Who needs bonsai trees for a wedding?"

"Apparently, the bride, Gwyneth, does. She's honeymooning in Hawaii, and the outdoor reception is thematic. Each mini bonsai was supposed to be the centerpiece on a guest table."

The entire notion seemed ridiculous, but Hope decided not to say so. Instead, she homed in on Jackie's veiled message. "So what are you saying, Jackie?"

"Well, I was going to ask you to pass along the message, but since that's no longer an option… It's just *one more day*. I'll be there by Tuesday for sure. Way before Meredith," she said, mentioning her best friend.

"You mean she's not arriving on Monday with the others?"

"She was supposed to, but then she got this fab opportunity to appear on a morning cable show. I, of course, urged her to take it. She'll be there Tuesday afternoon now, sometime after the tea party. But I'll be arriving first."

"And Mom?" Hope asked pointedly. "You just said she's coming tomorrow."

"Oh, right. Maybe try to minimize contact? And, whatever you do, don't let her look you in the eye." Apart from the twins and their mother, few people knew that Hope's eyes were slightly larger than Jackie's. It was one way Ava had been able to tell her girls apart when they'd attempted that twin-swap game as kids. Hope's birthmark was another big tip-off.

Her pulse whipped into overdrive when she realized what Jackie was insinuating. "Jackie, no. I can't do it. There's no way—"

"But sweetie. You already are—and that's on you. Besides, it's only another day."

Only another day, Hope repeated in her head, reflecting that a mere twenty-four hours didn't seem that long in the course of a lifetime. The lifetime of happiness she could help deliver to her sister by ingratiating herself—as her twin—with Brent and his family.

Even to her, this sounded a little messed up, but Hope hung on to the fact that her motives were good. She sighed in resignation. "What am I supposed to do?"

"Act natural. Be yourself. Only, not as you…as me."

This hole that the two of them were digging just seemed to keep getting deeper. Was it possible to explain things to Brent and his mom if she confessed she was actually Hope and not Jackie? What about Grandmother Margaret? The revelation would only prove her suspicions right.

"This is starting to get complicated."

"It shouldn't be too, too bad," Jackie assured her. "Starting tomorrow, there will be lots of activities to keep you busy, including the cocktail party for arriving family before dinner.

"Then Tuesday, there's the morning meeting with the wedding coordinator. I won't be able to make it in time for that. Later that day, there's the ladies' tea and croquet party," she mused. "And the men will be sailing. So, that should give you a nice long break from Brent until I show up to relieve you, hopefully by three o'clock."

Hope's mind tripped back through the itinerary, her thoughts snagging on one detail. "Tuesday morning I'm meeting with the wedding coordinator?"

"Yes, Eleanor Bell."

"What am I supposed to do there?"

"Just look at her schedule and say everything looks great. I already gave my input earlier, and Meredith helped me with suggestions."

Hope drew in a breath, starting to feel calmer about the situation. "Okay, that doesn't sound too bad. It will just be me and her, then?"

"And Elsa, of course. Mom insisted on being there, too. Grandmother Margaret also elbowed her way in."

Hope groaned. "Nice."

"You're the best for doing this. The very best."

"Not really. I was kind of ambushed," Hope said. "And you know that thing you said about Grandmother Margaret giving you the eye?"

"*No*. She did that again?"

"In spades."

"And yet, she baked us banana bread. Hmm."

Hope eyed the suspicious baked goods. "Precisely why I am going to wait and let *you* eat it."

"Funny. You know I don't eat carbs."

"Yeah, yeah. I know."

"Well…?" Jackie inquired with unmasked interest. "What did you think?"

"Of?"

"My groom-to-be."

"He, um…seems really nice."

"Smoking hot, too, right?"

Hope's face warmed. "I didn't particularly notice."

"That's probably for the best," her sister said. "Given the circumstances."

"Oh, um," Hope said, just now thinking of it. "There's one little thing. You're going to have to cut your hair."

"What?"

"Brent commented on my haircut. He likes it."

"I hadn't even considered that. Are you still wearing it like you did at Debbie's wedding?"

"Yeah. I can text you a photo if that would help."

"Okay, great. I was going to get my hair done before coming up there, anyway, and I've already moved my appointment—twice."

"So, see you Tuesday?"

"The day after tomorrow. Totally promise. I'll shoot you a text when I'm on the way."

• • •

Hope strode toward the main house, gathering her courage. The itinerary seemed easy enough, but maybe she *should* just tell everyone the truth. The longer she kept this up, the harder it would be. What if she slipped up? What if they figured out she wasn't Jackie and decided to call off the wedding because of Jackie's lying sister? The one who already almost ran over the groom's mom? Jackie would *never* let Hope live that down.

"Well, hello," a man's voice boomed from beside the firepit situated on the patio. The middle-aged guy with salt-and-pepper hair resembled Brent, but his smile-creased eyes were lighter.

He set down the bundle of twigs and logs he'd gathered on the stone patio and dusted his hands on his jeans.

"You must be Jackie," he said, extending his hand. "It's so great to meet you." His collared button-down shirt was rolled up at the sleeves, and its crisp white color matched his bright grin. "Parker Albright," he said, clasping one of his hands over both of theirs as they shook hands. "Welcome home."

Hope blinked. "Pardon?"

Parker released his grip. "Brent tells us you grew up in Blue Hill, at least in part."

She tried to paste on a friendly smile but worried that it looked fake. "That's right. My sister and I lived here with our mom during our junior year of high school."

"Ava, yes. Elsa and I look forward to meeting her tomorrow."

"I'm sure she's excited to meet you, too."

"You've already met Elsa, I hear."

If by "met" he means "nearly ran her over." "Yes. She's great."

His eyes twinkled in a kind way, like he was on her side. "And Grandmother Margaret." He motioned Hope forward. "Come on, let me show you up to the house. Elsa left lemonade in the kitchen for you and Brent."

Parker led her up some brick steps to the enormous covered back porch. Square white columns supported the roof above it, and strategically placed rocking chairs tilted lazily in the breeze.

There was even a porch swing at the far end, and planters filled with ferns and flowers were everywhere.

"This place is gorgeous," she said as Parker held open one side of the large French doors to let her inside.

"We enjoy being on the water, especially in summertime."

They walked into an opulent room that Parker called the den. Cream-colored walls housed teeming bookshelves, and a sturdy roll-top desk sat in one corner. A dry sink serving as a bar stood in another, and oriental rugs blanketed the hardwood floors.

The flat-screen TV directly ahead of them had a set of matching loveseats on either side. Brent stood in front of one of them, flipping up its seat cushions and checking underneath.

He looked up when he heard his dad and Hope enter the den. "Hey there." Brent paused, steadying a sideways-turned seat cushion in his hands. "You get settled in okay?"

"Yeah," Hope answered. "The carriage house is beautiful."

Parker excused himself through a side door that led to what looked like a library. "I'll leave you two to the lemonade," he said with a grin.

Based on Jackie's initial impression of Grandmother Margaret, Hope had guessed Brent's family would be equally monstrous. She hadn't expected warmhearted Elsa or Parker.

She turned her attention back on Brent as he shoved his hands down into the framing of the loveseat, obviously searching for something.

Her heart lurched when she realized what it was: his phone.

"I'm sure it's around here somewhere." Concentration furrowed his brow. "I had it yesterday, and I was sitting right, aha." He reached for something.

She didn't think twice. "Wait!"

One second she was by the French doors, and the next she'd rammed into Brent and flung her arms around him, pinning his upper arms to his solid torso.

They were muscular arms, too. Unnervingly masculine. And strong.

So strong, Brent could probably break out of her hold if he wanted to. But he didn't appear eager to pull away. Mostly, he seemed intrigued—or maybe amused.

One dark eyebrow arched, and Hope's pulse fluttered. Not good. Not good at all.

"Um… What are you doing?"

She stood there, helplessly looking up at him with her right hand clasping her left wrist, as she held his solid build against her.

From the corner of her eye, she spied Brent's cell phone resting on the loveseat frame, where he'd dropped it in surprise. It lay faceup, showcasing a text alert from Jackie.

Emergency delay…

Brent tried to see what she was staring at, and Hope yelped. "Brent!"

"What?"

"Your phone." Wrong thing to say, because he turned to glance at it. In one lightning-fast move,

Hope released his arms and pressed her palms to his cheeks.

"Well, hey there," he said, grinning.

Wrong result. Wrong. Wrong. Wrong.

Hope bit her bottom lip, and her mind spun furiously. His cheeks were stubbled with five o'clock shadow and really sexy feeling. Hope swallowed hard.

Think. Think. Think.

"Yes?" He leaned toward her, and Hope's heart thumped. At least she had his full attention and he wasn't glancing at his phone. Unlike Hope's last boyfriend.

Wait a minute. What was she doing? Making comparisons. *Now?*

She snatched his phone from the couch and held it behind her back. "I don't want you to look at it."

"What? Why not?"

Yeah, why not? "Because," she said, scrambling for a good reason. "This week is supposed to be about us, remember? Not cyber communications." She added a play pout for good measure.

"Wow," he said, looking her over. "You've changed."

"It's our wedd...wedding," she said, slightly mangling the word. "Shouldn't we be all about each other?"

Brent's eyes danced. "Absolutely. And here I thought it was only me."

"Only you?"

"Who feels this ramped-up attraction between us." He brought his arms around her and drew her close.

Hope's pulse shot through the roof and she nearly dropped his phone. *Oh no, I'm feeling it. Maybe a little too much.*

She broke away and beelined to the French doors, swiping open his phone under the guise of looking out over the water.

There. The message! She quickly hit delete and closed the app.

She spun back around with a sweet smile on her face. "Maybe I should put this away for safekeeping, hmm?"

"But what about arrangements? We have family coming in."

Boy did they ever, and Hope couldn't wait for Jackie to get here. "Yes. But until then, this can just be about the two of us together—without interruptions."

Brent's eyebrows knitted together. "What if someone needs to reach us? The violinist or the caterer? The photographer or—"

"That's what we hired Elaine for," she said, congratulating herself for remembering the wedding planner's name.

Brent cocked his head. "Eleanor, you mean?"

Or not. "Yes, her." Hope had never been great with names. Which was why she gave her students assigned seats—in alphabetical order.

"What about your sister?"

"What about her?"

"Won't she need to reach you?"

"Her schedule's all set," Hope said with a wave of her hand. "She'll be here the day after tomorrow."

Brent gave her a blank look. "I thought she was

coming tomorrow with everyone else?"

Gah. *Think fast*... "Stomach flu," she blurted out.

"Oh no."

"Twenty-four-hour kind. Or maybe food poisoning. She's not sure."

"That's too bad. I hope she's better soon."

"Yeah. Me, too."

He seemed to consider her for a long moment, then sighed. "Okay, then. Fair's fair," he said, extending a hand toward her, palm up.

Hope stared down at his open hand and then back into Brent's eyes, trying not to get lost in their swoony darkness. "Huh?"

"I love the idea." One half of his mouth turned up in a grin, and Hope's stomach flipped. "No cell communications for either of us until Tuesday."

"Tuesday?" Hope asked weakly. "What?"

"You'll need your cell for your meeting with the wedding planner, but until then..." He wiggled his fingers.

"Wait—"

"Nope. No arguments." His dark eyes twinkled. "It was your idea. This will give us time to really get to know each other. One on one, like we've always talked about."

Get to know each other? What?

Panic buzzed in Hope's brain like some annoying insect. It was so loud she could barely hear herself think. What kind of marriage arrangement had her sister gotten herself into? Clearly a very casual one, if he could be so easily convinced that Hope was her sister.

Brent stared her down. "Your phone, Jackie.

Hand it over."

"*My* phone? No, I couldn't…can't… The Martin wedding." Not to mention keeping in touch with Jackie.

"Isn't that what assistants are for?"

"But, I…er…*oh*…" Hope stared up at Brent as he waited patiently for her to extract her phone from the back pocket of her slacks.

She moved as slowly as she could, tugging the device from her hip pocket and taking her sweet time passing it over. That's when she spied it: a brand-new text from Jackie.

One more thing—

Brent plucked the phone out of her fingers.

"Two can play at this game," he said, holding it high.

Hope jumped for it, but he just lifted it higher, which was pretty easy for him to do, since he had a good five inches on her.

"Brent. Wait," she called, springing up in the air again and again, until she realized it was useless. Sadly, that was more exercise than she'd gotten in a month, and the entire episode left her winded. "We…really…should discuss this."

"We already have." He grinned and crossed the room to the roll-top desk.

"You can't put my phone in there," she said, aghast. "Your Grandpa Chad might find it. There might be messages…er, photos. Things we wouldn't want your granddad to see." Who knew if that was true, but she assumed her sister and Brent had been intimate. They were getting married, after all. Maybe they'd exchanged sexy texts or pictures.

"Really?" Brent appeared intrigued.

Or maybe not?

"I thought you didn't believe in that sort of thing."

Her cheeks burned hot. "Oh, um…I don't."

Brent pursed his lips. "Anyway," he said. "I'm not putting it in the desk."

He reached over the top of the piece of furniture and removed a painting of a sailboat from the wall, revealing a concealed safe.

She watched wide-eyed as Brent deftly worked its big silver dial, turning it to the left, then to the right, then to the left again, until it clicked.

He swung open the door and deposited Hope's phone on an interior shelf.

Other items crowded the safe's interior—most of them looked like small velvet sacks.

"Family jewels?" she asked lamely.

He chuckled. "Yeah." He motioned with one hand, and Hope understood what he wanted her to do: hand over his cell phone, so he could stash it away with hers.

"Brent, honestly. Don't you think—"

"Fair's fair. I won't have mine; you won't have yours."

Don't panic. It was only until Tuesday, and by then Jackie would be there. She reluctantly handed over Brent's phone, and he placed it in the safe beside hers.

Maybe she could sneak in here later and get her phone back. But how? She wasn't any good at safecracking. Besides that, as far as she knew, this whole place was wired. Loaded with hidden security cameras everywhere.

She scanned the den, feeling paranoid. Also thinking that she needed to stop streaming so many cozy mysteries in her spare time.

Brent shut the safe, returning the painting of the sailboat to its place above the desk.

"Now," he said. "How about that lemonade?"

CHAPTER FOUR

Brent handed Jackie her drink, sensing that something was off. Something had definitely changed about her; he just couldn't put his finger on *what*.

"Oh, thanks." They stood in the upscale kitchen, which gleamed with marble countertops and stainless steel appliances.

"This kitchen's so pretty," she said, glancing out the large window above the farm-style sink that overlooked the rose garden. "So much natural light."

"Yeah." He sipped from his glass. "It just got updated last year. My brother Derrick helped with that. He's got a very good eye for detail."

"I can't wait to meet Derrick. I forget, but I know you mentioned it—is he bringing a plus-one?"

He chuckled. "If Derrick had his way, he'd bring a *negative*-one."

Her eyebrows knitted together. "What?"

"Long story," he answered, "but I can sum it up in one word: Olivia."

"Ah." Her face registered understanding. "Ex-girlfriend?"

"Ex-*wife*. Big blowup?" He studied her features. "Don't you remember?"

She sucked in a breath. "*Olivia*. Of course." She took a big gulp of lemonade and set down her glass. "I'm sorry. I'm just a little…preoccupied."

"No worries. No one's going to be saying anything to Derrick about it, anyway. The topic of Olivia is strictly off-limits."

"My lips are sealed. I am sorry, though. Sorry about Derrick."

"He's twenty-nine," he said. "He's got his whole future to get over it."

"Yeah, well…" She lifted her glass toward his, and they clinked them in a toast. "Here's to that."

Brent studied Jackie's outfit, noticing for the first time she wasn't wearing her usual spiky heels. "I know you packed light," he said. "Any chance you remembered your running shoes?"

"Sure. I always—" She hesitated. "Why?"

He gave her a hopeful smile. "Well…I thought we'd go for a run tomorrow morning."

She blanched, which was not the reaction he expected. Jackie loved running and was freakishly obsessed with maintaining her daily exercise routine. So much so that she didn't understand why he didn't pop out of bed ready to run a marathon every morning. But in an effort to show he'd make a good life partner, he'd decided to give it a try.

"Oh, you know what? That sounds really, really good, but— Aren't you going sailing?" She looked a little panicked.

"Not until Tuesday." He eyed her. "The day of your tea party? Remember?"

She slowly sipped her lemonade but said nothing. He knew she wasn't thrilled with the idea of high tea and croquet—a "suggestion" Grandmother had made that he suspected Jackie agreed to out of fear. If he'd had his way, she would have been out on the boat with him.

"In any case," he continued, "Mom always makes

breakfast around nine. Simple stuff like muffins, yogurts, and fruits... I thought if we head out at six—"

"Six?" Jackie gasped. "In the a.m., you mean?"

"Yes. It's beautiful here in the mornings."

"I'm sure it is. But...isn't that a little early?"

Not based on the schedule she usually kept, but she did seem tired. The drive and the Martin wedding must have taken a lot out of her. "How about we start at six thirty and only do half the usual run? An easy two-and-a-half mile jog sounds pretty good to me."

Her mouth dropped open. "What?"

He didn't know if he should laugh or be disappointed at her shocked expression. "Why are you so surprised? I know at least *that* much about you. If you don't work out every morning before breakfast, you're 'impossible' the rest of the day."

When she stared at him, he added, "Your words, not mine."

"Yup."

"So then...let's do this. Together."

"Together, right," she said, swallowing hard.

He frowned and watched her drain her glass of lemonade. She was completely out of sorts. He'd have to think of a good route that might cheer her up while also showing his willingness to be the partner she'd wanted, romantic or not.

"Would you like more lemonade?" he asked.

"Nope. No, thank you," she said, still seemingly uncomfortable.

Maybe she was still getting acclimated. New place, new faces. Maybe a tour of the house would help. He took her glass and deposited it with his in the sink.

"Let me show you around."

• • •

Hope followed Brent through the foyer to the living room on the other side of the front hall. Like the kitchen, it, too, had a bay window overlooking the front lawn. A gorgeous baby grand piano was situated beside it.

How had she gotten roped into running two and a half miles at six thirty in the morning? By the guy who can't tell one twin from the other, but weirdly recalls one of them's obsessive exercise routine? It was just her luck that Brent had latched on to this detail.

Unlike her sister, Hope got her exercise through meditation. On her futon, while holding a nice cup of tea or something, and streaming 1990s sitcoms on her laptop.

Brent slid open a set of paneled doors dividing the living room from the library, which contained more loaded bookshelves. This room had apparently once had dark-paneled walls, which were now painted a creamy white like the rest of the house inside. Large windows afforded views of the bay, and others looked out on the side yard, which included a boxed-in herb garden.

She surveyed the rows and rows of books, knowing she could get lost in here for days. There was a selection of nonfiction topics, from sailing to marine life and gardening…to history, geography, and travel. There was also a fab collection of fiction. Her gaze lingered on the romance novels, and she couldn't help but wonder who read them. The Albrights all seemed so literary. "This is a fabulous room."

"Yeah, perfect for those of us who know how to enjoy some down time." Brent's eyes danced, and she guessed that he was teasing her, because Jackie almost never took time off.

"I enjoy my downtime," Hope protested on her sister's behalf. "I have lots of hobbies."

He set his chin. "Name one."

"I…um, enjoy photography."

"Uploading photos from your weddings to Instagram hardly counts."

"Says who?"

He surprised her by taking both her hands in his.

"I know you work hard," he said. "Extra hard on everything."

She stiffened automatically, then willed herself to assume a relaxed pose.

"There's nothing wrong with being a perfectionist," she answered, trying to ignore the fact that Brent's grasp was steady and strong. Warm and affectionate.

And, *oh nooo*.

He made her heart pound.

"On the job? Maybe not. But at home? I'm hoping you'll learn to unwind a little." He stared into her eyes, and these really sexy crinkles formed around his, making him look so, so attractive. "That's what we talked about. This marriage being good for both of us. No sense waiting until Saturday for the perks to begin."

Her panic spiked as Brent drew nearer. He really was an okay guy. A great guy, who cared about his bride-to-be and put her happiness first. But that bride-to-be wasn't Hope. It was Jackie.

She jerked back, breaking out of his hold.

His brow creased. "Is there something—"

"PDA," she spouted. "Not here. Not now." She dropped her voice in a whisper. "Anyone could come in at any minute."

He laughed and raked a hand through his hair. "True." He gave her a devilish grin. "Maybe I'll sneak out to the carriage house later."

"No, don't."

Brent cocked his head.

"I mean, with so much going on and our wedding day being just a week away, don't you think it would be good to wait until the wedding night?"

His dark eyes sparkled. "I've always known you were an old-fashioned girl; I just didn't know how old-fashioned."

"Ha. Yep." Hope grinned tightly, her face burning hot. She was desperate to change the subject. Thankfully, her gaze landed on a set of oars mounted over the hearth.

"Those belonged to Grandpa Chad in college," Brent said, following her gaze. "He was on the crew team."

"Oh?"

Brent appeared puzzled. "You don't remember me telling you about that, either?"

Hope bit her lip. It was so easy to trip up with this subterfuge; it was like there were snares laid at every turn.

"We won the championship that year," an older gentleman boasted, ambling into the room through the side door that led to the den.

The gray-haired man wore a vest under a suit coat with a tie, even though it was mid-June, and expertly tailored slacks. He extended a hand. "So nice to see you again," he said, giving her hand a warm squeeze.

"You too, Mr. Albright."

"Now, please." He shot her a generous smile. "Chad will do. Or, better yet…" He paused in thought. "Why don't we try Grandpa?"

"Oh, how sweet." Hope released his hand, touched. "Of course."

"You'll be my granddaughter-in-law soon enough," Chad continued. "Might as well dispense with the formalities."

She appreciated Brent's grandfather's generosity of spirit in welcoming Jackie into the Albright family—she only wished his wife shared it.

"I understand you've met Parker and Elsa?"

"Oh yes. They're awesome."

"Margaret's fairly *awesome*, too," Chad said with a knowing grin. Then he leaned forward and whispered, "She's just good at hiding it."

Hope giggled, relieved to know that Grandpa Chad was apparently in her corner. Parker and Elsa seemed to be, too. Or, really, in Jackie's corner.

Even if Grandmother Margaret was positioned against her.

Chad patted his vest pocket as if searching for something. "I think I left my evening cigar in my desk drawer. I best go find it before mealtime."

When Chad left the room, Brent turned toward her. "What do you say? Would you like the rest of the tour?"

• • •

Brent took Hope to the second floor, which held four lavish bedrooms with four-poster beds and fireplaces, each with a private bath. He only allowed her a brief peek at what he called the bridal suite before quickly shutting the door.

"Wouldn't want to spoil your anticipation of the wedding night."

Hope tried not to think about wedding nights and Brent in the same sentence. She couldn't wait for Jackie to get here and free her from this awkward predicament.

"Some things are best left to the imagination," she said lightly. Which was a terrible choice of words, because they only caused her imagination to run wild—and straight into some insane fantasy world where she was the one marrying Brent and not her sister.

"What's on the third floor?" she managed after a pause.

"Come on. I'll show you."

Hope followed him up a back staircase, her knees wobbling. She'd told Jackie she'd avoid being alone with Brent, and she hadn't done a very good job of it so far. From here on out, things would change. She'd make up excuses about needing to rest before dinner, and then make it a point to only see Brent in a crowd.

She hoped he'd been joking when he'd hinted at sneaking down to the carriage house later. Maybe, as a precaution, she should lock the door.

The third floor contained an area Brent called the playroom toward the front of the house.

There were three bedrooms across the hall, and each had a dormer window facing the bay. The center room had been shared by Brent and William when they were kids. Brent was staying there now, and Hope spied his unpacked suitcase through an open closet door.

She went to the dormer window and peered out at the breathtaking view. Elsa and Margaret were having a conversation near the firepit. Each held a glass of lemonade as Elsa gestured with her free hand. It almost looked like the two women were arguing about something. It couldn't be easy being Margaret's daughter-in-law.

"How long have your parents been married?" she asked Brent.

"Thirty-five years. Why?"

"I was just thinking. That's an awfully long time to be married."

"I don't believe it's felt long to them." Brent shared a soft smile, and for a moment he looked sentimental, like he admired what his parents had. "They really love each other."

"Naturally." Hope gave a self-conscious laugh. "Most married people do."

"Don't worry," he said seriously. "It will come along for us."

"What, love?" Hope asked, thunderstruck. She

couldn't be hearing this right. She just couldn't. Jackie had mentioned she and Brent had been slightly estranged lately. Still, they had to have developed deep feelings for each other in spite of that, right? What kind of deal had her sister signed up for? She took a giant step backward. "Wait—wait a minute. Are you saying that you don't *love* me?"

Brent raised his hands. "Whoa, Jackie... I'm so, so sorry. Really, I am. I didn't mean that to come off as—" He stopped talking, his hands falling to his sides. "Hang on. Are you saying...? Are you in love with me?"

Hope stared at him wide-eyed, her brain churning wildly. She knew Brent and Jackie's engagement had been rushed, but she'd assumed that was because they'd fallen head over heels for each other.

Obviously, she'd been wrong.

"It doesn't matter," she said, because she honestly didn't know the answer. "What matters is why we're doing this in the first place."

"I thought you wanted to? I mean..." He raked a hand through his hair. "You accepted my proposal."

Jackie had never shared those details. Why had Brent even bothered to propose if they weren't in love? What could he possibly have said?

Let's give this a shot and see if we actually fall for each other someday?

They might have had better odds spinning the roulette wheel in Vegas.

"I'm sure I was overwhelmed," she said, unable to hide her skepticism.

Brent hung his head. "I could have done things better, I suppose."

She frowned, not liking where this was going. "Better than what?"

"Writing it on a cocktail napkin."

Hope's jaw dropped. "You proposed on a *napkin*?"

"Oh, right. Like you could forget the huge fight that caused. But that was only initially. We were at that charity event, and you were constantly on your phone. It was the only way I could get your attention." He paused to study her. "We laughed about it...later?"

"I'm sure it was *hilarious*." She snagged a tissue out of the box on the nightstand and dabbed at her suddenly misty eyes.

He studied her, his brow furrowed. "Wait a minute. Are you saying you don't remember?"

Now she was in it. Time to dig herself out.

"Of course I *remember*. What girl wouldn't? It was all so *romantic*." She crumpled up the tissue, feeling stupidly sentimental.

She didn't know what she'd imagined for her sister, but it hadn't been a will-you-marry-me-on-a-napkin proposal. Jackie deserved better than that.

"You're right, and I was wrong. So, if you want me to try again..."

Brent squared his broad shoulders, and Hope realized with horror that he was about to get down on one knee. She had to stop him.

"Wait."

"Wait what?" he asked, looking up.

"This has gone all wrong."

"Apparently," Brent said with a frown. His gaze fell on her left hand. "Grandmother Margaret's ring.

You're not wearing it."

Uh oh. How hadn't she thought of that? Jackie would be wearing an engagement ring. The thought that it had come from Grandmother Margaret gave her the shivers.

"Grandmother Margaret's ring," she said stoically. "That's just it."

Brent watched her expectantly as she continued.

"The woman who can't stand me. So, what kind of great wedding juju does that bring?"

"It's a family ring," he said on a sigh. "Grandmother Margaret never wore it. It was given to her by Grandpa Chad's mother. That's an Albright diamond—very special—and the emeralds around it are flawless as well. I'm sure Grandmother never would have given it to me if she honestly didn't approve—"

"Ah, but you proposed before I met her, didn't you?"

"Sure, but not with the ring. That came later. You know that."

"Before or after I met your grandparents?"

Brent narrowed his gaze. "Want to tell me exactly what's going on here? Because if you're getting cold—" He stopped short, and the blood drained from his face. "Don't tell me that you've lost it. It's a family heirloom."

"I haven't lost a thing." Hope self-consciously rubbed her ring finger. "I'm just…having it sized." There. A perfectly logical explanation. Really, she ought to be commended.

"Sized? But I thought it fit perfectly?"

Ack. "When my hands get soapy, it slips off," she

improvised. "I didn't want to take the risk of mis-placing it. Or, or…having it go down the drain."

"I wish you'd said something sooner. I know a very good jeweler in Boston. He could have rushed the refitting."

She was painting herself into a corner. She had to find a way out of this, and fast. "I'll have it back really soon. Maybe even sooner than I think. If it's ready in time, Meredith will bring it up when she comes." Better yet, Jackie would be here on Tuesday wearing that ring.

Hope was going to have to find a way to contact her and let her know about all the crazy stuff that had been going on. But she needed to extract herself from this conversation first.

"In any case, it's fine." She hadn't meant to, but she'd let her exasperation slip.

"You're still not happy with the ring, are you?"

"I just feel awkward about it after that thing your grandmother said when I got here."

"Oh? What thing was that?"

She met his eyes. "Your grandmother said she was surprised to see me. I guess she was amazed I'd made the time."

Brent sighed. "I'm sorry."

"Does she know?" Hope asked, the thought occurring to her. "That we're entering into a loveless marriage?"

"Of course not. I wouldn't break your confidence. Our reasons for getting married are nobody's business but our own."

She pursed her lips, dying to know. "And what reasons *are* those, exactly?"

He eyed her. "We're both at the right age, compatible. We get along, share good laughs."

"That sounds like the makings of a friendship, not a marriage."

"The best marriages are based on friendship. You said so yourself."

"So then, why not wait? What's the big rush?"

"Well, there's Grandpa's business…"

It only took Hope a second to put it together. Brent was taking over Albright Enterprises after his and Jackie's honeymoon. She knew that he was changing jobs and that this would be a step up. She'd never guessed that this hurried wedding had anything to do with his career bump.

But, apparently, it did.

He met her gaze. "Look, we've already been through this. If you've changed your mind, please just tell me. All these questions are kind of freaking me out."

She couldn't believe it. This was a marriage of convenience, pure and simple. But what did Jackie have to gain? Oh yeah, right. The life of privilege and luxury she'd always wanted.

Although, Jackie wasn't exactly poor nowadays, so why had her sister sunk so low? Didn't she believe herself capable of achieving more? Of finding a man to really love her?

There's no way this was just about him being an Albright.

Brent shoved his hands in his pants pockets and shook his head. "We can call this whole thing off right here and right now, if that's what you want."

"*No.*" Hope's throat constricted at the thought.

She was here to save Jackie's upcoming wedding, not trash it in less than two hours. "That's not what I want," she said, breaking a sweat. "I just think I... need to lie down."

"What? Are you getting sick?"

"Just a small headache." She grimaced. "I felt a twinge of it earlier but forgot to take something for it."

"Maybe you should rest before dinner?"

"That's what I'm thinking, too."

"We're not done with this discussion," Brent said. "There are things we need to talk out."

"Yeah, of course." She massaged her forehead and winced. "Later." Like Tuesday, when her sister could deal with the fallout on her own.

"Sure." Brent gave a worried frown and motioned for her to descend the stairs before him. As she did, she turned and glanced over her shoulder.

"Do you think I could borrow your laptop for a bit?"

"Not now, you can't," he replied. "Staring at a screen is the last thing you need to do with a headache brewing." And then, seeming to read her, he added, "I'm sure the Martin wedding is doing just fine without you. No doubt Rachel has it all under control. Why don't we see how you're feeling after dinner?"

Hope's stomach soured at the thought of having to sit around that table with Grandmother Margaret watching her like a hawk. It was bad enough when she thought Brent actually loved Jackie. Now that Hope knew that he didn't—and that Jackie didn't really love him—it would be even harder to keep up the ruse. She *really* needed to talk to her sister. Somehow. Posthaste.

"My stomach's a little queasy," she replied honestly. "I'm not so sure I'll be able to make dinner tonight."

Brent paused on the stairs. "You really are feeling miserable, aren't you?"

"I'm sure I'll be better by tomorrow."

"Maybe we should call off that run?"

Yes. "That might be a good idea. Just until I'm feeling better."

"Okay. We'll go Tuesday."

"Right. Or maybe even Wednesday."

When they reached the foyer, Brent looked her over one last time. "Get some rest."

Hope nodded, desperate for some alone time. So she could freak out all by herself over her sister's pending *marriage of convenience.*

What on *earth* had Jackie done?

CHAPTER FIVE

Brent, his parents, and his grandparents sat at the dinner table. Two of the chairs with place settings were empty.

"I was hoping her headache was minor," Brent said, "but it's apparently not." He worried about the misunderstanding they'd had, thinking he might have caused it.

He took a bite of his food, distracted momentarily by its savory flavors. The rosemary-sage rub his dad had used had been made with fresh herbs from the garden. "This lamb's delicious, Dad. Thanks for cooking." Which Parker was prone to do occasionally, flexing his culinary muscle.

Grandmother Margaret scrunched up her face, digging into her own dinner. "I would think not eating would make her headache worse."

Elsa nodded. "I'll make up a plate for Jackie. Brent can take it to her after dinner."

"What was the holdup with the mother again?" Grandpa Chad asked, eying the empty seat beside him.

"She's had a car emergency," Brent explained. "Something about a faulty starter. She expects to have her car back tomorrow."

"They have car rental places in Bangor, I hear," Margaret said.

"Perhaps she prefers not to rent, Mother," Parker cut in. "And anyway"—he shrugged—"it's only one more day. She'll get here with the others."

"We look forward to meeting Jackie's sister," Grandpa Chad said.

"When she gets here, of course," Elsa added. "We hope she's feeling better soon, too."

Grandmother Margaret picked up her wine. "Are they normally sickly? The Webb girls?"

"Margaret," Chad reprimanded in low tones, and Brent's neck steamed. What was it with his grandmother? Her finding fault with Jackie had begun in Boston and hadn't let up since.

She turned to her husband, wearing a smug look. "It's a relevant question. We Albrights are all of sturdy stock. There will likely be babies in the mix one day."

Now she was carrying things too far, mentioning kids when that was a sore point between him and Jackie. Not that his grandmother knew anything about that. Though sometimes it was like she had a weird sixth sense.

Brent set his napkin on the table and scraped back his chair.

"You know what?" he said, standing. "I'm suddenly not very hungry." He headed for the kitchen, leaving the others looking stunned. While Brent was all for respecting his elders, he didn't need to let one of them drag his fiancée through the mud. "If you'll excuse me, I think I'll take Jackie her food now, while it's still hot. I'll save mine for later."

His mom started to stand to help him.

"Keep your seat, Mom. I'll get it."

"You're sure?" she asked.

"Yeah, thanks."

As Brent left the dining room carrying his still-full dinner plate, he heard low whispers behind him. A few of them sounded cranky, and he guessed his dad and grandpa were scolding Grandmother Margaret for her behavior.

Brent wasn't sure why Margaret had such an intense dislike for Jackie, but she certainly wasn't making this wedding week any easier. And it had scarcely begun.

• • •

Brent cut across the back lawn, carrying the eco-friendly food-storage container holding Jackie's dinner. He still felt terrible about their talk this afternoon and how it ended. He'd thought that he and Jackie had a mutual agreement and that both of them had decided this marriage would be great for their careers. Not exactly terrible for them personally, either.

Now, he found himself questioning the basics of the arrangement they'd made. He'd told himself he wasn't being selfish—more like equitable. It wasn't only his career that would benefit from this union; he could help her advance hers, too. But he'd obviously missed something very important. He'd failed to see the cards laid right out in front of him.

It had taken Jackie coming to Blue Hill for him to see her softer side, the vulnerable part of her personality that was obviously crushed by this marriage of convenience. Just because things had started out that way didn't mean they had to end there. It might be last minute, but it wasn't really too late to make a change. To really try to do this right and work on them forming a real—and loving—relationship.

Then Brent could prove to his family, once and for all, that Grandmother Margaret's speculations were wrong. He could also prove something critical to himself—that he was capable of opening up his heart again. After Amanda, he'd had only casual relationships and, despite his good education, fleeting forms of employment.

He'd always been afraid to take chances, which was one reason he'd had such difficulty cementing a career. When you decided to pick one thing and stick to it, you were making a commitment. Up until now, Brent hadn't totally been a commitment kind of guy.

But he was ready to change all that now.

He was making a bold move in taking over Albright Enterprises.

He also wanted to make an honest effort with Jackie. Because the cold truth was, if Brent couldn't give his heart to the woman he intended to marry, then he shouldn't be marrying at all.

Dusk closed in, and a dark purple curtain hugged the water as night creatures chirped and hummed. Soon the stars would come out with moonlight glistening against the bay.

He found himself wishing he could share all that with Jackie. That it could be just the two of them with a couple of glasses of wine on the deck of the cozy carriage house, which had a pretty outdoor gazebo accessible from the deck and on the far side of the hot tub.

That gazebo was also a great place for watching sunrises. While he'd never considered it before, sharing sunrises with Jackie suddenly sounded like such a perfect plan. Which was obscenely mushy and so *not* like him.

He didn't have a mushy bone in his body. He was rock-solid through and through—tough enough not to need anyone that badly. He'd learned his lessons about "needing" from Amanda. But, suddenly, Amanda seemed so long ago, and he found himself wanting to move forward.

He knocked at the carriage house door, wondering if he should come back later, but then the door cracked open the tiniest bit.

He could see just a sliver of her face, including one big brown eye.

"I'm sorry to interrupt," he said hoarsely. "I hope you weren't sleeping."

"No. Just resting my eyes."

"I brought you something to eat. This lamb dish of my dad's is the best."

She slowly pulled back the door, accepting his offering.

Brent saw she'd changed into athletic shorts and an oversized T-shirt that said "Dancing Queen" in bright pink letters with a small pink tiara above the script. It was undeniably offbeat and cute, and he'd never seen it before.

"Thank you."

"I—" Brent awkwardly cleared his throat. "I mean, I know now's not a good time… But later?" His forehead rose with the question. "Maybe we can talk?"

"Yeah, um, sure."

"I hope you feel better in the morning."

"Thanks. Me, too."

"And Jackie?"

"Yeah?"

"I wanted to let you know—I don't blame you for what you said earlier. About the ring…the way I proposed…all of it."

"We made a deal," she said solidly. And still, her lips trembled.

Brent was starting to see it was a rotten one at best. "Yeah, well. Deals can be amended."

"I'm not sure what you're saying."

"I'm glad that you came clean with me. Because, you know, I don't think it's too late to make things work."

She toyed anxiously with the food container, tilting it in her hands. "Too late? No, of course not. We have…until Saturday."

"Then, hopefully, the rest of our lives."

Jackie blinked up at him, and Brent's heart pinged. He could read the doubt in her eyes—the hurt and confusion, too—and he hated himself for making her feel this way. But he was already formulating a plan to make things better.

Even if he couldn't convince Jackie to fall head over heels in love with him by the weekend, he could at least give her a good start in that direction. He could do this thing. Become the sort of guy Jackie could really care for. And he was determined to pull out all the stops to make that happen.

"Just give me this chance, and I promise you, I won't let you down," he said, growing more confident by the minute. He was great at tackling challenges and could do almost anything when he put his mind to it. "By this time on Saturday, you'll be crazy about me."

• • •

Hope stared down at the dinner container in her hands.

What had she gotten herself into?

What have I gotten Jackie *into?*

So much was going on here, Hope could barely keep up. First, she'd learned about that terrible marriage of convenience idea and her sister's decision to settle. Next, Brent's saying that he's going to do better and change all that so he and Jackie could really make things work. And the look in his eyes when he'd left the carriage house... Whoa. He seemed seriously on board with making that thing about Jackie falling in love with him happen.

Hope peered out the window up the path as Brent rounded the corner by a bayberry bush. She told herself not to panic so she could think straight. Maybe she shouldn't have lost it in the main house with Brent when they'd had that discussion, but then, maybe in some unexpected way, her getting emotional had been a *good* thing.

It had to be her reaction to that horrible proposal on a napkin and the whole stupid marriage of convenience scheme that had set him off and got him thinking. And now, he was determined to really try and develop a better relationship with Jackie.

Okay then. The big mess that she'd made since she'd gotten here wasn't really such a huge fiasco after all. She'd helped her sister, in fact. In a major way. Whew.

Delicious smells tempted her, and Hope peeked into the food container, ravenously hungry. The lamb looked tasty, but there was so little of it. At least there was a big helping of veggies. It would have been even better if the meal had included something starchy, like an enormous baked potato with butter and sour cream. Just the thought made her stomach rumble.

She set the food container on the counter and reached into a cabinet for a dinner plate, taking a few deep breaths to calm herself.

This is great. Things are super. Perfectly fine.

When Jackie got there on Tuesday, she'd find Brent a new man. Someone who was all about romancing his bride. Surely that wasn't a *bad* thing.

On the contrary. Only good could come of this situation. Totally great things.

All she had to do was find a way to warn her sister about what was going on so she wouldn't be caught off guard by Brent's new agenda.

She needed that laptop.

• • •

Hope could see the upper two stories of the main house from the front stoop of the cottage. She waited patiently until the last interior light went off on the second floor.

It took Brent longer to turn in on the third floor,

and she wondered what he was doing. She hoped it wasn't using his laptop, because she was counting on that still being in the den downstairs.

Finally, his bedroom light switched off, too.

Hope set the mug of herbal tea she'd been drinking on the stoop railing and grabbed the flashlight she'd found in a kitchen drawer.

She flicked it on to step off the stoop, and gravel crunched beneath her shoes. While it was doubtful anybody could hear her, she still needed to be careful, as she'd noticed a few open bedroom windows upstairs.

She edged her way up the path, the flashlight's bright beam trained on the ground while moonbeams swept against the wraparound porch.

Cool breezes rippled off the bay, causing gooseflesh to rise on her bare arms and legs. *Brr. Chilly.* She should have worn her sweatshirt. There was no bothering with that now. She was already halfway to the house and needed to keep going before she lost her nerve.

A few dim lights resonated from inside the kitchen.

Through the dining room window, she spied a glimmer of light streaming in from the connected room: the den. Hopefully nobody was up late watching television or reading in the library.

As she cut across the back lawn and approached the rear porch, she was relieved to see that the TV beyond the French doors was turned off. The den appeared empty, with only one small light burning on an end table. Shadows crept into the den from the darkened library on its right side, indicating that room was deserted, too.

Hope gathered her courage and climbed the brick stairs.

Then she stepped onto the wooden porch—and it *creaked.*

She froze, her heart pounding. During her stealthy approach of the house, she'd forgotten to check Brent's bedroom window upstairs to see if it was open, but she suspected it was.

She counted to twenty, her pulse thrumming in her ears.

There. Up ahead. She spotted it.

Brent's laptop lying on the coffee table, exactly where he'd left it.

Now, all she had to do was sneak into the house, log onto her email account, and send a quick message to Jackie.

Yeah, right. Assuming Brent's computer isn't locked with a password or anything.

She squared her shoulders, determined to forge ahead.

A trickle of sweat ran down her left temple as she pressed the door open. Just a small bit at first, and then widely enough for her to slip through it, shutting it at her back.

"Jackie. Hi. I thought I heard someone in here. What are you doing?"

Hope's chin jerked up, and she saw Elsa watching her from the doorway to the dining room, dressed in a checkered bathrobe and holding a tall glass of milk in one hand.

"I…er….um." Hope frantically scanned the laptop and met Elsa's gaze. "Was just feeling a little queasy, so I thought I might find some ginger ale?" She gritted her teeth, trying hard not to look guilty. "I didn't want to wake anyone."

"Oh, you poor thing." Elsa waved her toward the kitchen. "Come with me. We'll get you some soda crackers, too."

Hope hesitated about following her. Maybe she could still finagle using Brent's laptop later, or even sneak it back to the carriage house with her when no one was looking. "Uh, right. Okay." She clutched her stomach dramatically, then said, "Thank you."

Elsa reached into the pantry, producing a box of crackers and a small bottle of ginger ale. Next, she grabbed a glass from the cupboard and added ice to it before pouring the soda in.

She arranged the crackers on a plate and then handed it to Hope along with the drink. "Maybe you should sit for a minute?" she said, indicating one of the two blue-and-white gingham checked chairs situated in front of a bookshelf holding cookbooks.

The tiny table nestled between them held ship's-wheel coasters.

"I'm sorry your stomach's feeling sour." Her brow rose with the question. "Were you able to eat any of the dinner Brent brought you?"

"Oh, yes. I did, actually. It was so, so good." She took a sip of soda. "Thanks."

Elsa drank from her milk as Hope nibbled on a cracker. "I know this family can be a bit overwhelming," Elsa said. "When I first met Chad and Margaret, I was just like you. A great big ball of nerves."

"I'm not exactly—"

"Jackie." Elsa's dark eyes glimmered. "It's o-*kay*

to feel anxious about your wedding day. After all, it's a big deal."

"Yes, yes it is."

"But it will be just like it was with me and Parker." She sighed. "Love will see you through."

Hope choked on a sip of her drink and started coughing.

Elsa patted her back. "Are you all right?"

"Yeah. Mmm-hmm." Hope took another quick swallow of her drink, and the bubbles burned all the way down. "I was just thinking about how lucky Brent is to have parents like the two of you."

"You're lucky, too, I hear. Brent's told me a little about your mom, and she sounds great. So creative. She's a performer?"

"Um, sort of? As a hobby, I mean. Just don't get her started."

Elsa laughed in understanding. "Hobbies are good. We all should have more of them."

"Yeah."

"What are yours?" Elsa asked earnestly.

Hope figured it didn't hurt to share this much. "Well, I really love to read."

"Me, too." Elsa smiled. "Which genres?"

"Romance, truthfully?" she admitted.

"I love romance. All kinds. You probably saw some of my collection in the library."

"I *did*," Hope said, loving that she had this in common with Brent's mom. "We have lots of the same books."

Elsa's eyes held a devilish gleam. "Grandmother Margaret reads them, too."

"Nooo…" Hope laughed.

Elsa giggled in reply. "So does Grandpa Chad."

"Ha. That's amazing."

"I know." Elsa nodded like they were friends, and Hope was appreciating this conversation so much. "They really are a pair."

"It's great when the right people find each other," Hope said, speaking from the heart but not thinking.

"Like me and Parker," Elsa shared. "And you and Brent."

In some ways, Hope found herself wishing it *was* her and Brent. His mom was so special. It was impossible not to like her and to want to have Elsa like her back.

"I can't wait to meet your family," she said. "Brent says that Hope's a schoolteacher. Such a worthy job." She studied Hope in the dim light. "Are you sisters close?"

"We're not as close as we used to be." Hope found it spilling out of her against her better judgment. Elsa was just the sort of person you wanted to share things with. She was probably dangerous to sit next to on a plane. "We were, though, as kids, yeah. Pretty inseparable."

Elsa's face registered understanding. "Relationships go through cycles like that—even our most precious ones."

The woman's compassionate nature made Hope wonder about what her home life had been like growing up. "Do you have brothers and sisters?"

"I was one of three girls," she answered. "The youngest."

"Are you all close?"

"We are." Elsa smiled. "Denise and Molly will be

here on Saturday with their husbands, so you'll get a chance to meet them then. A few of Brent's cousins, too."

"It's nice having a family-only wedding."

"It's your and Brent's day. It's important for you to have the kind of wedding you want. Small and intimate."

"What was your wedding like?" Hope asked.

Her voice took on a wistful note. "Really beautiful. Parker and I were married in a cathedral. Washington Cathedral."

"Nice."

"My father was still working as a diplomat back then with lots of Washington connections. Parker and I were right out of college, and our group attended, too. But most of the five hundred guests were honestly our parents' friends."

"I've never been to such a big"—Hope stopped herself, remembering she was Jackie, who coordinated large wedding parties all the time—"gathering for any of my personal friends," she corrected. "I mean, I've been hired to help run the big ones. But that's different."

"That's right," Elsa said as if remembering. "Your cousin Debbie was married last year."

"In October, yeah."

"How large was her wedding?"

"Definitely larger than mine, but not nearly as big as yours. I'd say around a hundred and fifty people."

"William and Sofia's wedding was that size and held right here in Blue Hill."

"This is getting to be quite the wedding location."

"It's the perfect spot for tying the knot, especially with someone you love."

Hope's grin tightened.

"We had such a great time at William's wedding," Elsa continued, "that Margaret said she wished all of her grandchildren could be married here. Parker and I were so happy to hear that you and Brent decided that was the right idea. Chad and Margaret were thrilled, too."

Elsa paused before continuing. "I don't want you to worry about Margaret. Once she understands how much Brent loves you, she'll love you, too."

"And in the meantime?"

"Don't let her push you around." Elsa leaned toward her with a confidential look. "Margaret respects others who hold their own."

Hope wondered how she was supposed to do that without becoming rude to the older woman. She supposed she'd have to use diplomatic skills. That must be Elsa's trick. She'd come from diplomatic parents, after all. "Thanks for the tip."

They both stood, sensing it was bedtime.

"And thanks for the ginger ale and crackers," Hope said when Elsa took her dish and glass. "They really helped." She smiled at the other woman. "Our talk did, too."

Elsa set their glasses and the plate in the sink, then wrapped her arms around Hope. "You're going to be my daughter soon. I hope we can be friends."

Moisture burned in Hope's eyes as she returned Elsa's hug. While she had a solid relationship with her mom, Ava had never exactly been motherly. Elsa was so genuinely warm, it made Hope want to melt into her.

She could sense what a good mom Elsa must be to her children. The cool thing was, she seemed open to welcoming one more.

"I'd like that," Hope said with a sniff.

Elsa patted her back. "So would I."

After their embrace, Hope started to turn, and Elsa picked up a pink-and-white box that had been sitting on the counter. It looked like a pastry box, and its swirly emblem said "Sugar Sweets."

"Late-night snack?" Hope asked her, joking.

"No." Elsa laughed, and then she lowered her voice. "I'm just getting things ready for tomorrow." Her eyes darted to a lined bread basket that rested by the stove. There was an empty cooling rack beside it. When Hope didn't understand, Elsa stepped toward her and popped open the lid on the box. "My world-famous blueberry muffins," she whispered. "But, shhh… This is our little secret."

Hope giggled at Elsa's revelation. "But the blueberries?"

"Oh, I pick them all right," she confided. "I'm just not much of a cook. So, most of what I gather we use on cereal and such. None of the others really pay much attention to volume."

She nodded to a mason jar of dark-colored jam by the cooling rack. "That came from Sugar Sweets, too."

Hope grinned, liking Elsa more and more. So, Brent's mom had her sneaky side, hmm.

"Don't get me wrong," Elsa told her. "Margaret's a really wonderful mother-in-law, but in some ways she's a tough act to follow. She doesn't bake, though, so somehow early on that became my territory." She shrugged. "Unfortunately, I don't make much more than a mess in the kitchen."

"Oh, Elsa. You and I have a lot in common." Hope reflected on the goodies in the carriage house. "So, the treats in the carriage house?"

"Also from Sugar Sweets."

"I thought Brent said they came from his grandmother?"

"Oh, yes. She asked me to produce them. *So*, produce them I did."

Hope chuckled, and Elsa began placing blueberry muffins on the cooling rack, so in the morning it would look like they'd been resting there after coming out of the oven.

"And, in all these years, Grandmother Margaret's never guessed?"

Elsa gave her an impish grin. "Please don't tell her."

"I wouldn't dream of it."

• • •

Hope hurried toward the carriage house, clutching Brent's laptop to her chest with one hand while guiding her way with the flashlight in the other.

Everything was going to be okay the moment she emailed Jackie.

What a great and kind thing she was doing for her sister in helpfully paving the wave for her arrival. She'd converted Brent into a loving fiancé. Or one that aspired to be loving, anyway. Plus, she'd made friends with his mom. Still, Jackie couldn't get here soon enough.

She entered the carriage house and strode to the farm table in the kitchen.

Then she set down the laptop and pulled out a chair.

An instant later, she stared at a darkened screen.

The battery on Brent's laptop was completely dead.

CHAPTER SIX

Brent woke up feeling energized. There was nothing he loved better than having a clear objective. Marriage of convenience or not, he didn't need to wait for love to find them. He could go out there and make it happen. The way Jackie now fell into his gaze gave him fresh hope.

She'd never looked at him like that before. Like he could be her "somebody special." Not because they were pretending, but because they didn't have to. That's what he wanted with her—a real relationship, in which they both understood each other because they shared things together and knew each other's hopes and dreams.

He arranged a single pink rose in the small bud vase on the breakfast tray he'd fixed for her and decided to take out to the carriage house. He'd served her things he knew she would eat, like a hardboiled egg, some yogurt, and a slice of melon. Even though she normally didn't eat carbs, he'd also included a dry piece of wheat toast, just in case she was still feeling off and needed it to settle her stomach.

He wished she could try some of his mom's incredible blueberry muffins, but he wanted to respect her dietary choices. He lifted the tray off the counter as his mom breezed in from the front hall.

"There you are." She noticed his tray. "Taking something to Jackie?"

"Yeah, I thought I'd check on her."

"I hope she's feeling better."

"Yeah. Me, too."

Grandpa Chad appeared in the kitchen next, straightening his vest by tugging at its bottom flaps. Brent had noticed his grandpa's clothing becoming a little snugger lately, but he supposed that came with his grandmother's cooking.

"You got a phone call early this morning," Chad said, addressing Brent. "Or, rather, your fiancée did. Her sister, Hope, called to say she's coming late."

"Late?" Elsa asked. "Oh no. Again?"

"Said something about not being able to reach Jackie's cell phone and it ringing straight through to voicemail."

Brent instantly regretted locking her phone away. "Ah, yeah. Right."

"Is something wrong with her phone?" Elsa asked Brent.

"We just made a little pact," Brent said, "to put technology on hold."

"Oh, how sweet."

"But impractical, it seems," Chad informed them. "Hope was a bit frantic about not being able to reach her sister."

"Of course." Brent nodded at his grandpa, then started toward the hall. "I'll have Jackie give her a call."

"Did Hope say what's wrong?" Elsa asked with concern.

"Just that her flu bug's holding on," Chad answered. "She was hoping it was a twenty-four-hour ordeal, but now she's worried she should give things a little longer. Considerate of her, really. Not wanting to infect the rest of—" He stopped short as Jackie barreled in the front door, nearly slamming into Brent.

Brent gripped the breakfast tray tighter and stabilized its teetering coffee carafe.

Jackie stared up at him, looking all fresh-faced and completely healthy. Only, what was she holding?

Hang on—is that my laptop?

"Brent. Oh, hi." She nodded at Grandpa Chad, then peeked around him and into the kitchen. "Morning, Elsa."

"Good morning," Elsa said. "Feeling better?"

"Yes, much. Thanks." Jackie's gaze swept the tray in Brent's hands. "What's this?"

"I was just bringing you breakfast. In case you still weren't feeling well."

"That's so nice of you." She closed the door behind her and smiled at the others. "But I'm happy to eat in the dining room with everyone else."

She peered up at him through her dark lashes, and Brent's heart thumped. Her new haircut really did suit her, and her form-fitting sundress showed off her curvy figure. Which was a bit curvier than he remembered, but that wasn't a bad thing by any stretch.

"I hope you don't mind," she said, holding up his laptop. "I borrowed this last night because I remembered something I need to tell Rachel…"

She continued with some details about the Martin wedding, but Brent found himself swimming in her pretty brown eyes.

She swapped out his computer for her breakfast

tray, then went on to explain. "The only thing is your battery's—"

"Dead. Yeah, I know." He shook off the temporary spell she'd cast over him. "I left the charger in my hotel room in Manhattan, but I've already ordered another one."

"Hope called," Grandpa Chad said. "She's apparently still not one hundred percent and will be one more day."

Jackie blanched. "What? Oh, no. You mean she can't make it till Wednesday?"

"Such a shame for her to miss the tea party and croquet," Elsa mused.

"You should probably give her a call," Brent said. "Let me go grab your phone—"

"Good idea," Elsa said. "You can call from in here. We all want to know how she's doing."

Jackie's dark eyes widened. "Uh, actually? The call can probably wait until after breakfast."

"Are you sure?" Grandpa Chad asked her.

"Yeah, yeah. It's fine.

"Here, let me take that," Elsa said, relieving her of the breakfast tray and carrying it into the kitchen. "We'll set you up with a place at the table."

• • •

"Morning, everyone," Hope said, taking the seat where Elsa deposited her food.

Fortunately, there were heartier-looking treats on the table, like those luscious-looking muffins she'd seen last night, an elegant fruit and cheese platter, and a serving dish of fried bacon and sausage links, which rested by Parker's elbow.

A couple of covered casseroles sat on the sideboard, and Hope guessed from what was on Grandmother Margaret's plate that those contained hash browns and some kind of heavenly-looking egg and cheese casserole.

"We normally don't eat this heavy first thing in the day," Grandpa Chad explained, "but it's going to be busy with so many people coming in, so Margaret wanted us to keep our strength up."

"Elsa makes all the baked goods," Margaret announced.

Elsa pursed her lips, avoiding Hope's eyes. Was that a smile the older woman was trying to hold back?

"She does a great job of it, too," Parker said proudly.

"Stays up late sometimes to do it," Grandpa Chad added.

"Yeah." Brent laughed. "She claims she's a midnight baker. Right, Mom?"

He glanced at Elsa, who just said, "Um-hmm."

Hope wanted to laugh but held it back for Elsa's sake. It was fun sharing a secret with Brent's mom. And it honestly didn't matter to her what was homemade or store-bought. She was starved, and everything looked—and smelled—delicious. She expectantly glanced around, trying to figure out what the procedure was, but the serving style appeared pretty casual here.

Brent took his empty plate to the sideboard, and Hope got up to join him.

"Should I just help my...self?" She slunk back

into her chair, when all eyes turned on her.

"You're eating cheese now?" Brent asked with a grin, and Hope held her breath. Darn Jackie and her spartan low-fat life. No wonder she was a whole dress size smaller. She dieted and exercised, neither of which sounded like tons of fun.

"The eggs are loaded with cheddar, I'm afraid," Elsa said apologetically.

Margaret waved them all off. "She's got her hard-boiled egg."

"I, uh… Yeah. It's just that…" Hope stared down at her paltry breakfast, then over at Brent as he heaped browned diced potatoes and onions on his plate. "Those potatoes smell *wonderful*."

"What?" Brent asked in joking tones. "You're eating hash browns now, too?"

"Oh, for heaven's sake," Parker said. "Let the girl eat what she wants."

Elsa leaned toward her with a whisper. "You might want to watch the potatoes, though. Grease on top of yesterday's queasies…" Her forehead rose. "May be a bad mix."

"Oh. Oh, right." Hope wished she'd concocted some other imaginary ailment than a migraine involving nausea. But it was tough getting out of that now.

So she daintily sipped from her water glass and said, "Could you please pass that great-looking blueberry jam? I thought I might put a very small bit on my…dry toast."

"Here you are," Margaret said, handing it over, badly tilting the crystal serving dish loaded with jam so that its small spoon nearly jettisoned toward the table.

Hope lunged for the glass container, righting it quickly to keep the gooey blueberry goodness from spilling over the rim of the dish and onto her plate. Although, at this point, she was so hungry she could probably lap it up with her tongue.

At least there were extra treats back at the carriage house. She'd have a huge snack later if she couldn't get enough to eat here. In the meantime, she was determined to make an ally out of difficult Grandmother Margaret. Even if the effort nearly killed her—and it probably would.

She startled the older woman by gently patting her arm. "I'm so glad you're joining in the wedding planner meeting tomorrow. Things just wouldn't be the same without you."

When Margaret stared at her in surprise, Hope added, "Thank you."

Margaret dabbed her lips with a napkin and said, "Yes, of course. Glad to do it."

As she lowered her arm, Hope noticed a gorgeous charm bracelet on her wrist. It contained five dangling sterling silver hearts inlaid with individual heart-shaped rubies.

"That's so pretty," Hope said, admiring the jewelry. "How long have you had it?"

"Thank you," Margaret said primly. "My mother gave it to me when Parker was born. There was only one heart charm on it then."

Hope made an educated guess. "The other four are for your grandchildren?"

A slight smile cracked through Margaret's stern veneer. "Why, yes."

Hope smiled as warmly as she could. "I think that's a beautiful keepsake."

"It is beautiful, and I do intend to keep it." She exchanged an insiders' glance with Chad. "That is, until Sally gets married."

Brent chuckled at this. "You could have a long wait, Grandmother."

"She'll find the right one," Elsa said with confidence. "He just hasn't come along yet."

Parker's blue eyes twinkled as he addressed Brent and Hope. "She just hasn't gotten 'lucky in love' yet, like you kids."

"Everyone *gets lucky* in time." Grandpa Chad chortled, and Grandmother Margaret swatted him.

"Mind your manners, husband."

"What did I say?" He gave her a look of utmost innocence, and everybody laughed.

• • •

A short time later, Brent deftly worked the safe's combination in the den.

"So?" Hope asked, wondering if their cell-phone sequestering was over. "This is it, then? All bets are off?"

He popped open the safe, extracting only one of the phones: hers. "I wouldn't say 'off.' How about 'on hold temporarily'? Just so you can touch base with Hope to make sure she's all right. And yes, okay. While you're at it, you might as well check in with Rachel about the Martin wedding." He handed Hope her phone. "Afterwards, we can put it away again. Even if it's just for twenty-four more hours. I can live without mine if you can live without yours."

"Sure I can," she said, not wanting to act like it was a big deal.

She glanced down at her phone, noting several alerts on the screen. Her battery was also nearly dead. Although the reception was perfect, she decided to fib about that so she could step outdoors. "I'll just step outside and make those calls."

"You're welcome to stay here."

She pulled a face. "Reception."

"Ahh, gotcha." He seemed to think on this too long. "Although, I've never had—"

"Be right back," she said, striding to the door.

"Good, because I've got a fun plan for this afternoon."

Hope turned on her heel. "Plan?"

"Just a little surprise. You'll see."

She nodded and walked outdoors, taking a seat in one of the Adirondack chairs by the firepit. The view of the water was gorgeous from here. Then again, this entire place was phenomenal.

There was a slew of text messages on her phone from Jackie, but rather than take time to read them, she called her sister instead.

Relief surged through her when Jackie answered on the first ring. Then, her sister hurled an accusation. "Where on earth have you been, and why aren't you answering your phone?"

"It's a long story, all right?"

"Let's hope it's a good one. I started worrying when I couldn't get through, so I had to call the landline."

"I know. Grandpa Chad told me."

"Okay, good. So you got the update."

"You're not coming until Wednesday? Seriously?"

· "Afternoon, okay? I'll make it in time for the clambake." When she didn't answer, Jackie continued. "Eleanor will fill you in on the whole itinerary in the morning."

"What about Meredith? Isn't she coming tomorrow?"

"Oh, *yeah*," Jackie said, like she hadn't considered this. "Oops. I kind of forgot about that part, but don't worry. I'll talk to her. Fill her in."

"You mean she'll know?"

"She has to. Otherwise she'll figure things out. She *is* my bestie."

"I don't know if I can fool Mom. What if she figures things out and blabs?"

"She can't. You'll have to finesse it."

Hope blew out a hard breath, agitated with Jackie for putting her in this position. She was equally annoyed with herself for not stopping this whole thing the moment it began. What had started out as *one short day* had suddenly morphed into three, and Hope couldn't decide who she was more furious with: Jackie or herself. "This has to be your last delay. I mean it. Things with Brent are becoming challenging."

"Challenging how?"

"He's locked away our cell phones."

"Then how are you on it now?"

"It's only temporary. We're going to put my phone back in the safe until tomorrow when I get off."

"Safe?"

Hope lowered her voice. "Brent's very serious about making things work."

"Oh." Jackie sounded surprised at first, then curious. "Is he?"

"Why didn't you tell me, Jackie? Tell me that this is a *marriage of* ahhh"—she froze in horror as Grandmother Margaret rounded a boxwood hedge. She held clippers in her hands and wore garden gloves—"*made in heaven.*"

"What on earth are you talking about?"

"I just want you to be prepared. For a *very romantic* wedding."

Jackie sounded totally confused. "Naturally it will be romantic. All weddings are."

"Yes, yes, that's true, especially for couples who are *in love.*"

"Hope. Is there something you're trying to tell me?"

Margaret sternly strode toward her, then pivoted and began clipping roses from the flower garden. Even with her back turned, Hope could tell Brent's grandmother was listening with her eagle ears.

"Will you look at the time," Hope said. "I'd better run. I'm so sorry you're still sick and hope you feel better soon." She dropped her voice into a whisper and hissed, "*Super soon*, okay?" Then she clicked off and peered at Margaret.

"I take it that was your sister?"

"Yeah, she's doing a little better and is hoping to be here by Wednesday."

"Wednesday now? Oh, dear. She's going to miss the tea."

"She feels terrible about that." Hope forced a smile. "But she'll be here for the boil."

"Boil?"

"Er…bake. Clambake."

"We wouldn't want your sister to miss that."

"No."

"Or any of the rest of it."

Hope swallowed hard. "Most definitely not."

Margaret stared at her a long while and seemed to be deciphering something. "You know," she said, briefly glancing toward the house. "My grandson has a very big heart."

"Oh, yes. Very big. Big, big. *Huge.*"

Margaret locked on her gaze, and Hope held her breath, her heart hammering against her rib cage. "You won't break it?"

"No, I…couldn't—wouldn't dare."

Margaret clipped another flower, grasping it by the stem. "Let's hope not," she said, returning her attention to her flower gathering.

CHAPTER SEVEN

Brent helped Hope into the canoe he'd carried on
the roof of his SUV away from town and over a one-
lane bridge.

Several others launched kayaks from the same
small inlet.

"Canoeing. Who knew?" Of course, she'd suspected that when she'd seen the boat strapped to the top
of his vehicle, but Brent had been very cagey about
what they were actually doing today, until he'd pulled
over and parked in the shade in a nearby spot.

"Wanted to surprise you," he said with a crooked
grin. "I hope it's working."

"Consider me surprised." Hope climbed into the
wobbly craft while Brent steadied it in his hands.
They both wore bulky life vests, making it hard to
maneuver gracefully with the canoe bobbing back
and forth. She felt carefree and daring and more
than a little excited about having this adventure with
Brent.

Although she'd told Jackie she'd try not to be
alone with him, this wasn't exactly breaking her
word. There were tons of other people around,
including more vessels out on the water.

Brent joined her in the canoe, hoisting himself
inside it with one deft move and seating himself on
the other bench. He looked really great today in a
red T-shirt and khaki shorts that showed off his
muscular thighs.

If Hope had known they were going canoeing, she might have dressed more sporty. But Brent had said she was fine in her sunflower-patterned halter dress and sandals. At least she'd brought along a big sun hat. Plus, before leaving the house, he'd suggested she apply sunscreen.

"My brother Derrick built this," he said, his eyes roving over the canoe's sleek lines. "You won't find too many more like it: hand-crafted out of wood."

She perused the canoe again, marveling at Derrick's talent. "That's impressive."

"There's a boatbuilding school nearby. He's one of their instructors."

"I can see why."

He picked up one of the canoe paddles that he'd set on the floor next to an old-fashioned picnic basket with a flap lid. "You might want to hang on while I push us off. Once we clear the shore, it will be smooth sailing."

"Or paddling, as the case may be," Hope said lightly, and Brent laughed.

"Yeah, that." His eyes sparkled, and she dropped her chin, embarrassed to be enjoying his attention.

He was trying so hard to take her on a fun date. And it was working. Only not on the person he thought she was—his fiancée, Jackie. How could Brent so easily believe she was Jackie? Hope had puzzled through it a dozen times and hadn't arrived at a good answer.

This only proved what she suspected from the start. Brent didn't really know her sister. And Jackie only surface-level knew him. What a messed-up situation. But Jackie could have helped with that. If she'd gotten to Blue Hill on time like she was supposed to, it would be her in this canoe now, not Hope.

So Hope shouldn't feel guilty for having a good time. It was a harmless picnic, after all. And out in the open, in the middle of broad daylight.

Brent settled back on his bench and dipped his paddle into the water before stroking it back toward his hip in a practiced rhythm. Soon, they were gliding over the water.

Hope glanced at the second paddle on the floor, feeling she should do her part. "Want me to help?"

"Naw." He grinned, and butterflies flitted about in her belly. "Just sit back and enjoy the ride."

Sunshine glistened across the waves, and gulls called overhead in the nearly clear blue sky. The temperature was warm but pleasant, and a gentle breeze blew around them, riffling Hope's hair beneath her sun hat. She had to hold it on at one point when the wind kicked up.

She settled in to enjoy the view of the shore as they moved away from it. "Look. There's your grandparents' house!" she cried, spying the big white house with the cozy carriage house located alongside it, divided by the garden hedge.

"Yeah, it looks a lot smaller from here." He smiled and steered them to the right and away from the house.

"Where are we off to?"

"Someplace special," he promised. "You'll see."

She was almost sorry that Jackie was missing this. Selfishly, though, she secretly savored Brent's company. She knew he wasn't *her* groom. But it was awfully fun to get caught up in the fantasy. And that's all this was, honestly. A fantasy that would be over soon.

How depressing.

"You've never told me certain things about yourself, you know," Brent said after a pause.

"Oh yeah?" Hope asked, sensing she needed to tread carefully. "Like what?"

He quirked a grin. "Your favorite color."

She laughed in relief, having expected something deep and meaningful. "That's easy," she said, smiling back at him. "It's blueberry blue."

"Not any ol' blue?" he teased. "But blueberry blue?"

"No other blue will do," she proclaimed.

He surveyed her features. "When did you decide that?"

"When I was a kid living in Blue Hill."

"Then I'm glad that you're back here in summertime, so you can be *awash* in your favorite color."

Hope giggled at the twinkle in his eye. "What's yours?"

"My what?"

"Don't play cute with me," she said with a saucy air because she was enjoying their light banter. "Your favorite color."

"Haven't got one."

"That is so not fair. And *so* not true."

"I'm serious. I like all colors equally."

"Nobody likes all colors equally."

"Okay, then. Blueberry blue."

"Shut up." She rolled her eyes. "You made that up."

"I do love blueberries. My mom makes the best muffins. It's too bad you can't eat them."

"Oh, I…could make an exception." Hope bit her lip. "To be polite."

He shot her an amused look. "One muffin's not going to hurt you, anyway. You're perfect just the way you are. Besides that, we're going running in the morning."

"Ha," she said, kind of hoping he'd forgotten. "Yeah."

"Okay," he said, relenting. "It's red. My favorite color is red."

"Red?"

"Sure. Like the Boston Red Sox." He kept paddling with ease. "Now you ask me something."

"Like what?"

"Anything in the world."

"Are we, like, on 'favorite color' level, or can I ask for the den safe combination?"

Brent belly laughed at this. "You can ask, but I'm not telling. After we're married, though?" He shrugged. "We'll see."

"Okay, fine." She squared her shoulders. "I'll ask." It took her a couple of minutes to think up the question. "What were you like as a kid?"

"Oh…pretty perfect."

"Maybe I should ask your sibs?"

"True." He repressed a grin. "They might dish."

"So, there *is* dirt on baby Brent?" She envisioned a miniature version of him playing outdoors and making mud pies, and she nearly snorted.

"I did *not* make mud pies."

Hope gasped. "But, how did you know—?'"

"Probably because I can read your mind."

Eeep. Thankfully, he was wrong about that.

"I mean it, though. Seriously."

"Wild guess. And anyway," he said nonchalantly. "You told me you and your sister used to do that when you were little."

"Uh, right." Hope's heart sank. So, Brent and Jackie had engaged in some discussions about their childhoods, and here she was, thinking her conversation with Brent was unique. "I bet you got a kick out of everything else, too."

"Would have if I could have."

"What do you mean?"

"We never finished that conversation. You took that call. About the Martin wedding."

"The Martins. Oh, *yeah.*"

"You know," he said seriously. "It hasn't always been about them. You had that other wedding before. What was the bride's name? Covington?"

"Hmm. I think so?"

"This Maine air must be doing you good if you've already wiped that."

"Well, it was stressful…all that wedding planning."

"I know." He gave her an earnest look. "Which is why it's good you're finally relaxing." He dipped his hand into the water and flicked a fine spray of chilly droplets toward her. They speckled her bare arms and cheeks.

"Hey!" she yelped, but she was laughing. She stuck her hand in the water and cupped at bit of it in her palm, flinging it in Brent's direction.

He chuckled as the splatter landed in the center

of his T-shirt. "Bull's-eye."

Hope grimaced. She hadn't meant to get him *that* wet. "Sorry."

"It's okay," he said. "I'll dry."

"You never really answered my question."

"You first."

"On what?"

"How about the kid thing?"

She sucked in a breath, wondering how much to share.

"What games did you like to play, for example?" He steered them toward a cove. "Bet you planned weddings for your dolls."

"Would have if I could have, but our mom didn't believe in us having them."

"Weddings or dolls?" he teased.

"Dolls, you goofball." She splashed him again, and he laughed. "We did have this old chess set, though, and all of the pieces looked like people. I used to marry those guys off to each other when my mom wasn't looking." Which was true. Hope had always imagined having a two-parent home with a big family. Sort of like the one that Brent had.

Brent chuckled. "How creative. Did Hope play with you?"

"No, she wasn't into that stuff," she said, speaking really of Jackie. "She was all about setting the scene. Always drawing stuff."

"Any schools in the picture?"

"Ha. But, no. Although we *did* play school." Hope couldn't help smiling. "The two of us, I mean. Me and—Hope."

"I'm guessing *she* was the teacher."

"Hope. Yeah. Definitely. Yes, she was."

"So, what did your mom say when she found her chess pieces missing?"

"Oh, she never noticed. Mom's not much of a chess player, to tell you the truth."

"Are you?"

"Used to be. I was on a team in school."

"That's pretty fascinating."

"It was fun. Chess is so much like…" She stopped because she was about to say math.

"So much like…?" Brent asked, leading.

"Puzzles," Hope answered. "And I love working puzzles."

"Seriously?" He grinned. "I didn't know that, either. I like puzzles, too. Especially those insane thousand-piece ones. You know, the sort it takes you all of Christmas vacation to work?"

"*Yes*," she said, knowing just what he meant. Now she was curious. "What did you play as a kid?"

"Video games."

Hope giggled. "Nothing else?"

"Besides thousand-piece puzzles?"

She playfully huffed.

He glanced out over the bay. "When my family came here in the summers, our parents had a strict rule about limiting technology." He shot her a teasing stare. "Sort of like you and I are doing now. It allowed us to have more time outdoors.

"We went sailing a lot with Grandpa. One year, we got a bocce ball set and played on the back lawn. During our high school years, it was cornhole."

"I *love* cornhole."

"Do you really?" he said, sounding pleased. "So

do I. We'll have to play sometime."

"Great."

"Anyway," he continued. "Other than those things, on rainy days, my brothers and sister and I played games indoors. Old board games that our parents used to play when they were little, like Clue and Monopoly.

"Grandpa Chad also taught us to play poker. Although, honestly? Grandmother was better at it." He lowered his eyebrows. "She's got the world's best poker face."

Hope laughed. "Yes, she does."

"Give her some time. She'll come around."

"What makes you so sure?"

"My mom talked to her."

Hope thought back to seeing the two women talking by the firepit and wondered if that's what they'd been discussing. "I love your mom. She's really great."

"Yeah, I know. I'll keep her. But Jackie?"

"Huh?"

"I'll also keep the rest of them, too. Things will work out—you'll see. I'm feeling more and more optimistic about, well, pretty much everything. Aren't you?"

It did seem like they were making progress. Starting to engage as a couple for real.

And that seriously messed with her head.

Given that she was pretending to be her sister.

But now wasn't the time to have doubts about her well-intentioned impersonation. She wasn't doing this for selfish reasons, but in an effort to help Jackie. And, in a big way, she already had. She'd formed a connection with Elsa and had been accepted by Parker and Chad. She just had to break through to Grandmother Margaret, and Brent seemed sure she would.

"I'm excited about meeting your mom," he said. "It's great she'll be here later today."

Hope worried about that and keeping up the ruse but knew she'd have to deal with that situation when she came to it. "Yeah. I know she's excited to meet you."

"What's she like? Your mom? You never talk much about her."

Ooof. "That's because she's...different?"

"What do you mean?"

"A little eccentric." She grimaced. "Marches to her own tune, so to speak."

"I'm sure any tune will be fine with me."

"Watch yourself," she joked. "You don't want to encourage her to sing."

"That would be a problem, would it?"

"Oh, yeah," she answered, grinning.

Brent grinned, too. "I'll consider that fair warning."

It was a beautiful day on the water with occasional sailboats passing by. One loud speedboat tore by at a clip, towing a water-skier, and Brent had to work to stabilize the canoe during the resulting onslaught of waves, which sent Hope giggling as she clutched onto her hat.

"You think this is funny, huh?" he asked. "It won't be so cute if we capsize before lunch."

"I'm sorry," she said, stifling another chuckle. "I just can't remember having so much fun."

"That's because you don't make enough time for it," he informed her sagely.

"I know you're right." She exhaled. "It's good to relax."

"Speaking of that…" Brent said, navigating the canoe into a sequestered spot in the cove beneath a canopy of trees. "Are you ready for lunch?"

Brent opened the picnic basket and pulled out a chilled bottle of pinot grigio, cranking its twist cap. "Wine?"

"I'd love some," she said, feeling giddy in spite of herself.

He located the wineglasses in the basket and passed them to her to hold so he could pour.

He must have noticed her scanning the contents of the basket. "Everything's low-fat but healthy," he said. "I brought nuts, fresh fruit, veggies…"

"Is that cheese I see in there?" she said, lusting after it. "And a loaf of French bread?"

"Just a little for me. It's okay if you don't want any."

"Oh no. I mean, yeah. Just a tiny taste would be good. I mean, I have to keep my strength up and everything. In light of the wine," she added creatively.

"You're right about having something solid in your stomach with the alcohol," he agreed. He finished filling their glasses and capped the wine, returning it to its chilling sleeve in the basket. "I brought some of Grandmother Margaret's chicken salad, too. It's really good and made with almost no mayo."

Hope's stomach ached from hunger. "Sounds delish."

"Would you like to enjoy our wine first, or are you ready to go ahead and eat?"

"Eating sounds great."

"Okay," he said, toasting her glass. "Then let's get to it. Cheers."

"Cheers," she said, taking a grateful sip of wine.

Brent passed her his glass to hold and pulled a small container out of the basket. "I forgot about this, but you probably won't want it." The small glass jar contained an orange shredded mixture dotted with red bits. "It's Grandmother's famous pimento cheese."

"Oh, yum. I mean, I would love to taste it. Maybe on a very small piece of bread."

He started to prepare her plate, cutting off a slim sliver of bread from the loaf.

"Okay, not that small," she said. "Maybe a bit larger."

He tried again with a second piece, but it honestly wasn't tons bigger. "You know what?" Hope said like she'd just thought of it, because she had. "Why don't we split the loaf?"

Brent's eyebrows rose. "Split it? Are you sure?"

She needed him to hurry this up, because she was about to start drooling at any second. She'd barely had any breakfast, and then Brent had whisked her away for this adventure shortly after that. So she'd never had time for that snack. "Yes, please."

He tore what was left of the French bread in half and handed her portion to her.

It took all the strength she had not to sink her teeth into it. Immediately.

Without butter. Or cheese, even.

"I kind of like this new healthy appetite of yours," he said with a chuckle, continuing to fill her plate. "Maybe now I won't have to eat dessert alone?"

She'd eat ten desserts at the moment. "Don't push your luck," she said instead. Jackie was going to *kill* her. "A little more chicken salad, please?"

Brent looked up. "You can have anything you want. You're the most beautiful woman in the world to me."

She was unnerved by the compliment because she'd enjoyed it. And this made her feel squirmy. Brent was looking at her the way he should have been looking at her sister.

Stop and live in the moment.

All this was *great* for Jackie. She and Brent were becoming close.

By proxy.

"So, yes or no to the pimento cheese?" he asked, unscrewing the container's lid.

"Yes. Please."

"On the plate or crackers?"

"Ooh, we have *crackers*?"

Brent chuckled. "Maybe you've been no-carbs for too long."

She grinned. "That's just what I was thinking."

"Right, well, you'll want to be careful easing out of it." He handed her the plate, looking worried. "You don't want to overdo it right away. You could shock your system."

"You're right," she said, nibbling absently on a pimento cheese–loaded cracker. "Mmm, this is heavenly." She paused in thought while Brent filled his own plate. "I thought pimento cheese was a southern thing?"

"Grandmother grew up in Atlanta."

"How interesting. I didn't know that."

"She also has a weakness for pralines." Brent winked, and she laughed, unable to imagine Margaret having any weaknesses at all. "We all have our downfalls, I suppose. What are yours?"

"My weaknesses, you mean?" she asked, sampling some of the chicken salad, which was delicious.

"Yeah, those." He dug into his food, apparently hungry, too. That made Hope feel about a billion times better. She hated chowing down alone, which was why Jackie was no fun to eat with. While she admired her sister's resolve, Hope had no clue how she lived that way.

"Maybe I haven't got any." She adjusted her hat. "Weaknesses, that is."

"Hmm. Maybe not."

"How about you?"

"Oh, I've got plenty."

"Is that so?" She knew her tone sounded flirty, but she didn't care. She was having fun, and this was totally innocent besides. Just a picnic between friends. With wine. On the water. And he was maybe the best-looking guy she'd ever seen.

She took a long swallow of wine before asking, "Such as?"

"I'll let you in on a secret, but you have to swear you'll take it to your grave."

She laughed. "I swear."

He sipped from his wine with a Cheshire cat grin. "I'm abysmal at wardrobe."

She found this impossible to believe. She'd only been here two days, but each time she'd seen him, Brent had been dressed impeccably, even in a casual way.

"It's true." He held up his hand. "I only order online, and when I do, I copy the outfits on the models exactly."

Hope snorted wine through her nose and had to grab a napkin. "Do *not*."

He pointed to his T-shirt, shorts, and shoes, and named a well-known outdoors store. "Spring Catalogue. I even bookmarked the URL."

She hooted. "Brent."

"What I was wearing yesterday?" He named another high-end cyber store. "Last summer's sale. I bookmarked that page as well."

She was cackling so hard she nearly spilled her wine. "You have to stop," she said, catching her breath. "There is no way you only order online. What about your business clothes?" In his line of work, she was sure he had several nice suits.

"Believe it or not, there are stores where one can walk in and have an entire professional ensemble put together—*and* tailored."

She sighed happily. "So, on your own, you're a total fashion fail?"

He nodded. "Exactly opposite from you." He studied her sundress and sandals. "I like the new look—I really do. It's perfect for this week and summer."

Hope ducked her chin, embarrassed yet pleased by another compliment. "Thank you."

He raised his glass to hers. "Here's to learning to

relax, new hobbies, and summer."

"Here's to all of that, yes." She clinked his glass with hers. "And here's to an excellent picnic. Thanks so much, Brent. This has been the best."

. . .

They finished their lunches, chatting about "dream vacations." Brent had several places he wanted to visit, and he was stoked to learn Jackie had many of the same locales on her travel bucket list. It did his heart good to learn that he and his fiancée were so much on the same page.

"Ooh. And Bora-Bora," she added excitedly after devouring her last bite of the chocolate tart that he'd packed for dessert. He was glad he'd brought enough food for the two of them. He'd never seen Jackie eat this much, but he was glad she wasn't worrying about things like that now. It was their wedding week, after all, like she said. It was good for both of them to loosen up a bit and chill.

"I've always wanted to go there, too," he told her, not wanting this fun excursion to end. He realized they should get going shortly, because the day was wearing on and the tides would be changing soon. But he was having such a great time, he wanted to give their adventure a few more minutes. "We can drop in on Bora-Bora on our way to Australia."

"Tasmania and New Zealand, too," she said with a dreamy gleam in her eye. The thin gold chain around her neck held a delicate gold heart pendant, and Brent commented on the pretty accessory, which he'd never seen her wear before.

"Oh, thank you. I've had it for a while."

"It suits you." He knew he shouldn't ask, because it might have been a romantic gift from another guy, but curiosity got the better of him. "Where did you get it?" Though he wasn't normally the jealous type, the thought of her loving anyone else somehow brought his cool-tempered blood to a slow boil.

She fingered the dangling piece of jewelry. "Maybe we should keep this conversation moving forward?"

"We *are* moving forward," he teased. "I'm just kind of wondering from what?" *Or whom*, he thought, feeling a lead weight in his stomach.

"If you must know." She straightened her spine, looking sassy. "I got it from somebody special."

"Figured as much." Brent's neck burned hot, and she tilted her chin at his expression.

"It wasn't from another guy, if that's what you're thinking."

"What?"

"I gave it to myself for Valentine's Day two years ago." She shrugged and then said, "I deserved it."

"I'm sure that you did. Do."

She sighed, gazing out over the water, and Brent saw the sun had lowered in the sky quite a bit since they'd started out. They really needed to head in soon.

And yet, he couldn't bring himself to break the moment.

"I guess I never told you about my dating past?" She asked this in an off-kilter way, almost like she couldn't authentically remember.

"Past boyfriends, no."

She started to speak and then thought better of it. "Maybe we shouldn't go there now."

"You don't have to unless you want to. I honestly didn't mean to make you uncomfortable."

"I'm not uncomfortable, really. It's just…" She bit her lip in thought. "I grew frustrated, I guess. Tired of the pre-holiday dump thing, so I—"

"Hang on," he said, stopping her, because this he had to hear. "What 'pre-holiday dump thing'?"

She stared at him in surprise. "You know, that thing coupled-up people sometimes do. A big holiday's coming up. Maybe it's Thanksgiving and an opportunity to meet each other's families. Or Christmas, and expectations loom *high* for a big, amazing gift." Her eyes widened dramatically on the word "high," and Brent couldn't help but chuckle.

"Ah, I see. So, to prevent any disappointments, there's a breakup instead?"

"Which is seriously *such a disappointment* in its own right."

"I'm sorry," he said. "Those guys were utter jerks."

"It wasn't just them." She rubbed her heart pendant. "I did my fair share of dumping, too."

"Then it looks like I dodged a bullet. A pre-wedding dump could be the biggest dump of all."

Jackie's cheeks colored.

"Oh, wait. I didn't mean…" He hung his head in shame, then peeked up at her. "That wasn't how it sounded. I hope you know that I would never do that to you. I would never let you down on our wedding day."

She stared at him a long moment, and he wondered why there was so much sadness in her eyes. "You're really pretty wonderful, you know that?"

That was unexpected. "Um, thanks. So are you."

"And the necklace?" She sniffed. "I gave it to myself because I wasn't sure if anyone would ever…"

Her chin trembled, and Brent reached for her, leaning forward and rocking the canoe.

"Hey," he said, steadying her smooth shoulders in his hands. "There will be lots of great Valentine's Days ahead. I promise." She viewed him doubtfully, and Brent's heart ached. "You and I didn't know each other last February. But we're changing that now. We're getting married. *Married*, Jackie," he said hoarsely. "And I'm determined to make this work. You do believe I'm going to try?"

"Yes. Of course."

"And you'll try, too?" He searched her eyes when she didn't answer. "I'm not asking for a miracle… Because the funniest thing is, I feel like one's already happened."

He inched closer, dying to kiss her, because the moment felt so right.

"Brent, I—"

Then both startled at the sound of Jet Skis roaring by.

Three teens were out joyriding and kicking up some serious wake. Jackie jerked back, and Brent tried to steady her, but their erratic movements sent their canoe rocking wildly as roiling waves crashed toward them, one after another.

The canoe teetered back and forth, and Jackie

gripped its sides with white knuckles.

"Don't move." He snatched up a paddle in a vain attempt to stabilize the canoe, but it was already too late.

The canoe capsized.

CHAPTER EIGHT

Cold. Cold. The water was so cold—and murky. Brent sank abruptly, then bobbed back up, propelled by his buoyant life vest, his shoes momentarily making purchase with the muddy bottom.

He encountered Jackie on the surface of the water, splashing and flailing her arms around. The water temps here in June stayed in the forties and fifties, and already his skin was feeling tingly numb. He had to get Jackie out of the water, or they risked hypothermia.

"*Argh!*" she hollered. "It's *freezing!*"

She lunged for a bobbing paddle and clung on tight, then grabbed the second one as it floated by. Her wet hair was plastered to her head, and her teeth chattered.

"Yeah, yeah, I know." He flipped the canoe back over, following the safety protocol. *People first. Things later.*

Their picnic basket drifted away, followed by Jackie's sun hat, which was turning in lazy circles in an eddy. Brent pushed the canoe toward Jackie and relieved her of the paddles, tossing them into the canoe. "Let's get you back on board, and I'll take us home."

"My hat!" she cried, seeing it caught up in a new swell and spiraling away.

"We'll grab that on our way out of the cove. That picnic basket, too." He grimaced. "It belongs to

Grandmother."

He tried to give her a boost into the canoe, but she sagged in his arms. Out of the blue, Jackie laughed. Then she started laughing harder. So hard that she couldn't manage to haul herself into the boat.

Brent tried helping her again and found himself laughing, too. He was sure that both of them looked like drowned rats, but still, they needed to get out of the water right away.

He got a better idea, deciding to get himself into the canoe first and then hoist her aboard. "All right," he said, extending his hand. "Let's try this."

He gave her a firm tug upward and caught her under her arms, lifting her into the canoe. She scrambled toward the far bench, shivering and gripping her elbows with her arms crossed in front of her.

"I'm so sorry about this," Brent said above the nip of the wind.

"It's not your fault. The canoe kind of just… flipped."

He frowned when she shivered again. "You're freezing."

"I'll be all right."

Brent's heart pounded at the distressed look in her eyes. The sun had sunk lower, and it had grown later than he'd originally thought. "I'll get us back as soon as I can."

"Maybe I can help?" she asked, lifting one of the paddles.

He nodded, knowing the sooner they got back the better. Besides that, moving would help get her core body temperature back up. "I won't fight you on that this time."

He motioned for her to turn around, and she spun on her seat so they both faced westward with him positioned behind her.

"All right," he said. "Let's get going. We can grab our stuff as we move along."

He caught a floating cloth napkin drifting past. Next, he scooped up the bobbing empty wine bottle.

The tide had begun ebbing already, with the mudflats hugging the shoreline becoming more and more exposed.

The farther the tide went out, the harder it was going to be to bring them ashore without things getting very messy.

Jackie nabbed items that had come from their overturned picnic basket from the other side of the canoe.

Each of them was careful not to rock the canoe again as they propelled themselves out of the cove, grabbing what they could as they went along.

Brent snagged the soaking picnic basket by its handle.

Seconds later, he plucked Jackie's soggy sun hat from the water.

He handed it to her, wincing as she shook it out while giving another shiver. Her pretty sundress clung to her like a glove, and the damp fabric was likely making her colder.

"I'd offer you my jacket if I had one," he apologized. Unfortunately, his clothing was just as soaked through as hers.

"Thanks," she said, dipping in her paddle and

stroking it back in a practiced move. "I'd probably take it."

He smiled at the humor she displayed in the situation, noting her skill with the paddle.

"Hey, you're pretty good at that."

Then, she overreached, and the craft listed.

"Ahh!" Jackie yelped, and Brent's heart hammered.

"A little more gradual next time," he said. "Try holding your paddle steady and stroking it back like so."

He gave a demonstration with his paddle, and she made a fumbled next attempt.

By the third time, she got it.

She peered back at him and grinned. "And there you thought I was so great at this."

"You're doing fine."

The wind picked up as they pulled farther out into the bay.

Brent scoured the shoreline, calculating an obvious three-foot drop in the tide.

They'd never make it back to where he'd parked his SUV without having half a mile of muck to wade through.

His grandfather's dock extended farther out into the bay. Even with the tide receding, if they got there quickly enough, they might just make it in time.

Someone in the family could give Brent a lift to pick up his SUV later. Since he lived so close by, Derrick was probably at his grandparent's house by now.

"I think we need to head that way."

When she looked at him questioningly, he

explained. "The water level's dropped a lot. I'm not so sure we'll make our launch point."

Her dark eyes rounded. "What?"

"But we can make it to my grandparents' house. It's much closer to where we are. Plus, they've got a deep-water dock. Um…when the water's deep, that is."

"Then why didn't we launch there?"

He shrugged. "I wanted to take the scenic— Watch out."

She whipped her head around to see they were approaching an anchored lobster trap and Brent was attempting to steer them around it.

She focused her effort on her paddle, managing to help him circumvent the bobbing buoy marking the trap.

They rounded a bend and had to paddle harder, since they were aiming toward shore and now were working against the very strong tide.

Their canoe struggled along, lurching a few feet forward and then one foot back.

"This is nuts."

"Keep going," he encouraged. "We'll make it."

"At least I'm feeling warmer."

She was being such a trouper about this, and it had become a disaster of an afternoon.

Well, not a total disaster. The first part of it had gone okay, and he'd loved the fun conversations they'd had. He'd also liked learning about that necklace. Even though he was agitated at the thought of other guys not treating Jackie well, at least that was in the past.

At last, they approached the stretch of land

where his grandparent's place was located.

He spotted the carriage house first, then the roofline of the main house beyond that.

"Almost there," he told her.

Then he groaned when he saw the bottom steps to the dock hanging two feet above the open mudflat below it.

"Yikes," she said. "These crazy Blue Hill tides."

Their canoe ran aground with a *bump*, wedging itself into the mud.

"No worries," he assured her. "We'll make it."

She shoved her paddle into the mud, and it stuck like glue.

"Yeah," she asked with a worried frown, "but how?"

• • •

Brent jumped out of the canoe, and mud splattered up against the side of it.

Hope stared down, aghast to see he'd landed in the muck ankle-deep.

"Come on," he said with outstretched arms.

She freaked. "You're expecting me to jump into *that*?"

"Not into that." He nodded toward the ground, taking slogging steps closer. "Into these."

She frowned at his outstretched arms. "You're going to carry me?"

"Unless you have a better idea."

The truth was she didn't. Hope knew from living in Blue Hill that mudflats could be disgusting. Certain folks made their living by digging for bait in these fertile fields.

Some of the bloodworms found here could be more than a foot long, and she didn't want to step on any of them.

"Wh—what about you? Don't those worms bite?"

"Not if we move fast enough. Besides…" He glanced toward the steps to the dock, then back at her. "It's less than fifty feet, and I'm wearing water shoes."

"Right."

His water shoes were more like open sandals, which left him vulnerable to attack from whatever lurked beneath the surface. So she couldn't leave him standing there forever.

She stood unsteadily, remaining in a crouched stance, and the back end of the canoe wavered. The nose of the canoe was still waylaid in the mud.

Brent gripped the side of the vessel with one hand and told her to slide her arm around his neck.

When she did, he reached behind her bent knees with his other arm and swept her into his embrace.

Her heart pounded as the hem of her damp dress dangled below her. His wet T-shirt had partially dried, and the warmth of his body seeped into hers, with his broad shoulders breaking the bite of the wind tearing off the water.

He took a giant step forward, then another, each motion creating a weird sucking sound.

She stared back at their waylaid craft. "What about the canoe?"

"I'll grab some waders and come back for it."

She frantically scanned the sticky, dark area

ahead of them, watching for any movement or strange divots. Mudflats also contained "honeypots," deep holes that could sink a person's foot quickly. If Brent got sucked into one of those, his chances of a bloodworm attack would be higher.

He was obviously aware of this, too, because he moved extra carefully, testing the weight of each new spot before fully setting down his foot.

Hope's gaze swept to the left, and her heart stopped.

A ghoulish-looking creature wiggled out of the muck, and it was headed right for them.

"Brent. Run!"

Her panic spiked when he did just the opposite.

In fact, he stopped walking to stare at her.

"It's a big one. Huge. *Huge*, huge."

"I'll go faster," he said, picking up his pace but not exactly running. Their increased speed caused more mud to fling and muck to fly as he hustled them toward the dock.

"Grab onto that railing there," he said, "and I'll give you a boost."

She did, and once she was secure, he lifted himself up onto the wooden steps and out of the mud next.

"Whew, that was close," she said, breathing hard.

He chuckled. "A big one, huh? With fangs?"

"How would I know about fangs? I wasn't about to let it get *that* close."

They reached the top of the steps to the dock, and there was another long flight of stairs ahead of them, scaling the cliff to the back lawn of the main house.

Hope thought she heard the sound of laughter and happy chatter lightly threading through the air. "Oh no, has the party started?"

Brent checked the angle of the sinking sun.

"Might have by now." He eyed her from top to bottom and pursed his lips. "I hope that's not dry-clean only."

Hope goggled down at her dress, which was pockmarked with mud.

Even her heart-pendant necklace was coated with sludge.

She wiped the small jewelry piece with her fingers, then looked up at him, wide-eyed. "You mean I'm going to have to meet the rest of your family looking like this?" she asked, mortified.

"We could always make another run for it?" His forehead rose, causing Hope to belly laugh. Then, she laughed again at the sheer absurdity of the situation. It was a warming laugh, too, one that filled her heart and smoothed out the rough edges of her soul.

Despite being capsized with Brent, she'd had the very best time with him. She wouldn't have changed any of it for the world—not even this.

He must have been thinking the same thing, because he stepped toward her.

"Thanks for coming on a picnic with me. I'm sorry that it ended badly."

He was so near she could feel the heat of his breath against her lips.

"It didn't end badly," she barely managed to say.

Brent cradled her face in his hands and gazed into her eyes.

Time, space, and reason slipped away.

"No," his tone grew husky, and he drew closer. "It didn't."

His lips brushed over hers, and heat flooded her face. She wanted his kiss so badly, but she couldn't give in. He was Jackie's fiancé. But still, it didn't feel like it was Jackie he wanted to kiss. It was *her*.

Hope's resolve weakened, and she tilted up her chin.

"There you are!" a woman shouted.

Hope stared at the precipice in alarm.

Ava Webb stood at the top of the steps, wearing dangly ostrich feather earrings and a glittery gold headscarf knotted on one side. Her chin-length auburn hair shone extra brightly in the sunlight, and she held a cocktail glass in one hand.

Hope gaped up at her. "Mom?"

Ava gave amused smile. "*What* have the two of you been up to?"

Brent greeted her with a grin. "Hello, Mrs. Webb. It's so great to finally meet you."

• • •

Hope climbed the steps with wobbly knees, Brent right behind her.

She'd nearly kissed him. Or at least he'd almost kissed her.

And oh, how she'd wanted him to.

What a horrible sister I am.

On top of her guilt attack, now she had to face her mom while pretending to be Jackie.

"Why Jackie," her mom said, scanning her outfit.

"Your dress is a mess."

Hope grimaced, avoiding her mom's gaze. "Tidal surge."

But what was still surging inside her were her emotions, turning all topsy-turvy at the thought of what she'd nearly done.

What she'd ached to do with Brent: kiss him until his lips turned blue.

"Brent Albright," he said, shaking her mom's hand. "Welcome to the wedding."

Ava considered his muddy clothing. "Looks like you two had an adventure."

He grinned at Hope, and her heart skipped a beat. "We did. Sorry," he said, waving at Derrick. "I need to grab my brother."

A guy in boat shoes, shorts, and a collared shirt approached them in brisk strides. Derrick Albright had a fair mix of his parents' features, with Parker's dark hair and blue eyes. He was ruggedly handsome in a rough-hewn way and was almost Brent's height—a little shorter.

"You must be Jackie," he said with a bright smile. He chuckled good-naturedly at her appearance. "I'm guessing the hug will have to wait?"

"If you don't mind," she said, chuckling, too.

She shook Derrick's hand and introduced her mom, who exchanged pleasantries with the youngest Albright brother before excusing herself to refresh her drink.

Before she stepped away, she pulled Hope aside and whispered, "Is everything all right?"

Hope laughed self-consciously, freaking internally that her mom suspected something. Though

Jackie and Hope had fooled her a couple of times by swapping places as kids, Ava had gotten better at detecting their subterfuge over time.

"Uh-huh, great." Hope glanced toward the garden path when her mom tried to meet her eyes. "I just need to go and grab a shower."

Ava started to say something more, but—mercifully—Elsa called her away with a wave of her hand. "Oh, Ava. Come on over here and meet Brent's grandmother." She stood on the porch with Parker, Chad, and Margaret, who'd just joined the group.

"Delighted," she said, putting on her posh-people airs. She murmured softly to Hope before retreating: "Catch you later."

Derrick perused the dock area and the marooned canoe at the base of the mudflats. "A little boating trouble?"

"Yeah, just a tad."

Hope nodded in goodbye. "I'll see you both in a bit."

• • •

Hope stepped from the hot shower feeling like a new woman. She'd also calmed her nerves regarding her mom detecting her identity. Ava loved the idea of high society, so she would easily be caught up in the swell of schmoozing with the monied Albrights.

As long as she didn't hang around Ava too much—or sit across the table from her—everything would probably be fine.

The situation between herself and Brent caused

Hope greater concern, because she secretly worried that she was falling for him. She was starting to learn things about him. Things that he'd never told Jackie because she'd been so distracted by her own life.

Hope could picture those Albright summers, with Brent and his brothers and sister playing board games in the den. Or maybe poker with their grandparents around the kitchen table, while Grandmother Margaret displayed her card shark ways.

It had only been Hope and Jackie growing up, and they'd never really played family games. They definitely hadn't played cornhole or owned a bocce ball set. It all seemed so fun and nostalgic, and it helped Hope understand Brent a little better.

This was probably why he was working so hard on their relationship now…or, really, his relationship with Jackie. While the marriage of convenience had started as a sham, once he believed he could get Jackie to really love him, he began having bigger dreams.

Dreams that probably involved the sort of home life he'd grown up with.

The sad thing was, Hope was beginning to have those dreams, too.

Dreams of creating a family with Brent, just like the great one that he'd come from. She called herself up short with a swift mental kick. *Stop now. Don't be stupid.*

It didn't matter that she loved Brent's great sense of humor or that he got her jokes when she teased him back.

What mattered was that she was making progress

on *her sister's* behalf.

Great progress. Really huge.

Her budding relationship with Brent and his family would only benefit Jackie in the end.

So, everything was awesome.

It was okay to feel conflicted by her attraction to Brent, because he was a really great guy. Thoughtful, funny, and handsome. Just the sort of person she might have picked out for Jackie if she could have.

By the time she got out of the shower, the entire tiny bathroom had steamed up, enveloping her in its warmth as she cloaked her body in a plush towel and wound a second one around her head.

She was glad that private picnic was behind her so she could focus on other things. Like being in very public company with Brent. As long as she could avoid being alone with him again, she wouldn't have to worry about slipping up and doing something dangerous like kissing him senseless.

Her mind started to wander into fantasies about what that would be like.

Then, she ran the tap water cold in the sink and splashed it on her face.

She really had to get a grip on this "crushing on Brent" nonsense. That was not what she was here to do. She was supposed to be helping Jackie.

Which she was. 100 percent.

Hope pressed open the bathroom door and nearly jumped out of her skin.

Ava stood in the laundry area, swiping through some data on her phone. Her partially drained drink rested on a cocktail napkin on top of the dryer.

"Mom."

Ava glanced up. "Oh, hi, sweetheart. Have a good shower?"

"Yeah, uh. The best." She quickly dropped her gaze to her mom's phone. "What are you doing?"

"Just looking up that video from Debbie's wedding."

"Not the karaoke one?" Hope asked, horrified.

"Yes, that's the one. Oh wait," she said. "Look at this."

Ava smiled, staring down at her phone, then flipped it around so Hope could see. "This is that Halloween pic from when you and your sister were in the sixth grade and you both dressed as witches. Daring me to guess which *witch* was which."

Ava narrowed her eyes, and sweat swept Hope's temples. "Want to tell me what's going on?"

"Nothing."

"No?" Ava stared down at Hope's leg. "Then what happened to your birthmark?"

Hope made a desperate attempt to deflect her mom's accusatory stare.

"I...er...laser surgery?"

"Laser? That sounds extreme," her mom said, sounding like she didn't buy it. "Wasn't that dangerous?"

"No. Not really." Hope adjusted the towel so it dropped a little lower, covering that spot on her outer thigh. "I just thought...Bermuda...bikini... honeymoon... You know." Hope attempted to move past her in the narrow space. "If you'll excuse me, I'd better go and get dress—"

"*Daughter?*"

She halted at her mom's accusing tone.

"*Where*—exactly—is the actual bride?"

Hope's stomach clenched. There was no avoiding her mom's stare now, because she'd latched onto Hope's gaze and was hanging on tight. "I can explain—"

"I knew it. Just knew it. *Knew* that something was wrong." Ava's cheeks flushed with annoyance. "You and Jackie can't be doing this again. Not now. Why?"

"It's a long story, all right?"

"So? Abbreviate it."

Hope pursed her lips, knowing she was going to have to spill the beans. Also knowing she'd have to find a creative way to convince Ava not to.

"I think I'd better make us both some tea," she finally said.

CHAPTER NINE

Ava arched an eyebrow, waiting for her to begin.

Hope set her mug on a side table, her hand trembling. She hadn't been big on deceiving her mom, just like she hadn't meant to start pretending to be Jackie in front of the Albrights. "It's sort of hard to explain," she started.

Ava sipped from her tea. "I'll bet."

She and her mom sat in the cozy seating area by the sliding glass doors overlooking the water. They couldn't stay here forever because the rest of the Albrights were expecting them to come up to the main house for drinks.

Hope cinched the belt on her terrycloth robe, stalling. "It was all so sudden, Mom. Jackie had this wedding thing."

"The Martin wedding?"

"Yes."

"I've heard all about it." Her mom shrugged. "Well, not *all*. But enough to know your sister's been stressing over it—majorly."

"That's just it. Things *have been* stressful. All the way around. She had this last minute problem with the caterer—"

"Oh no. Emile Gastón?"

Hope blinked at her mom. "How do you know about Emile Gastón?"

"*Darling*, everyone knows about Emile. Everyone who is anyone. His name is *legend*."

"Meaning you read about him in one of your society magazines." For someone who was supposedly so Zen, her mom spent an awful lot of time pining over how the other half lived. Hope questioned, for the first time, if this was where Jackie got it from.

Ava shifted in her seat. "Maybe."

"Anyway. The point is, Jackie had this delay. Stuff she had to get under control before leaving Nantucket."

"I'm following but not understanding."

"It was only for a day," Hope babbled. "She asked me to come here as her, but I said *no*."

"You apparently didn't say it firmly enough."

"I did so! I'd planned to explain that Jackie was delayed by that big Martin wedding. Jackie meant to be up-front about the whole deal, too. She even texted Brent before I got here, but he never got it. He'd lost his phone in the sofa, and by the time he found it the whole ball of wax had started rolling."

"And you didn't try to stop it?" Ava shook her head. "I don't know what on earth possessed you, Hope. Pretending to be Jackie. Even around Brent." She paused a moment to consider this. "That's a little odd, don't you think? That he wouldn't know the difference?"

"Yes, that's just it." Hope latched on to the opening her mom provided. "Brent didn't know Jackie very well at all."

Her mom blinked. "Then why are they getting married?"

"Long story." Hope waved her hand. "Marriage of convenience."

"*What?*"

"I know it sounds bad, but both of them agreed to it, for whatever reasons."

Ava frowned. "I'm really disappointed in your sister." Then she thought better of it, glancing out at the view. "Although if she had to marry somebody, one of the Albrights wasn't a bad pick."

Hope rolled her eyes. "What I'm *trying* to explain is my motivation in all this. It's only for the good and all about helping Jackie."

Her mom tugged at the knot on her headscarf. "When I saw you down on that dock, it looked like you were helping yourself to the groom."

"Mom, no. It's not like that. Brent and I… What I mean is, because he believes I'm Jackie, I'm actually helping her and him build a better relationship. Brent thinks there's a chance now for him and Jackie to be authentically happy. He's started working on that, too."

"Isn't that supposed to be your sister's job? Getting to know her future husband?"

"Yes, but…she's not here. She'll be here on Wednesday before—"

Ava gasped. "*Wednesday* now? When did that happen?"

"I just found out today. She's had another snafu with the Martin wedding."

Her mom inhaled a deep breath and released it. "What you're doing is wrong, Hope. Mostly to Brent, but also to his family. I want you to march out there and tell them all the truth."

"But I *can't*." Her heart hammered. "It's already too late."

"It's never too late to do the right thing."

"Tell that to Grandmother Margaret."

"What has Brent's grandma got to do with anything?"

"A ton." She seized this angle. "It's all because of her that this happened, anyway."

"Your impersonating Jackie?"

"*Yes*." Hope nodded, attempting to lure Ava in. "She doesn't like our family."

Ava's eyes flashed. "What?"

"Doesn't think we're good enough."

Her mom huffed. "Well. She's got another thing coming."

"I know, right? It's totally insane. We Webbs are every bit as worthy as that stuck-up old woman."

"Of course we are. We've always been." Ava briefly studied the ceiling. "We did actually live on the other side of the railroad tracks downtown, but still, that doesn't mean anything. We're good people. Hardworking and hon—" She cagily eyed her daughter. "Hardworking, anyway."

"I know this looks bad," Hope begged, "but you didn't see the 'eye' that Grandmother Margaret gave me."

"Which eye?"

"That appraising eye. Sort of like this." Hope did her best to imitate Grandmother Margaret's cold assessment of when she arrived.

Ava sank back in her chair like she'd been physically shoved.

"That doesn't look very friendly," she said with a scowl.

"It wasn't. Mom, here's the truth. I didn't come

here planning to pretend to be Jackie. I was going to explain about her work problems and see if I could help out with things until she arrived. But then, Grandmother Margaret and the others ambushed me in the driveway. Elsa was there, but she was actually nice. Grandmother Margaret, though… She couldn't wait to say how surprised she was that I'd turn up for my own wedding."

Her mom gasped. "How *crass*."

"Yeah, exactly. Very rude. And then, Brent showed up, and somehow everybody thought—I mean, just assumed—I was Jackie, and with Grandmother Margaret staring me down in her super unfriendly way, I didn't know what to say."

Ava set down her mug. "Does Grandmother Margaret still think this? Is she dead set against the marriage?"

"She's not one hundred percent behind it, I can tell you that."

"Well." Ava set her chin in an indignant manner. "That's not really her business, is it? The ones who decided to get married were your sister and Brent."

"My thinking, too."

Her mom studied her fingernails, which were painted a shade of burgundy bordering on deep purple. Scarily, it kind of matched her lipstick. "I still don't like what you're doing, but I'm beginning to understand it. But Hope"—her eyebrows rose—"how long can you keep this up?"

"It's just until the day after tomorrow, and tomorrow's going to be busy. The guys won't even be around for most of the day. They're going sailing."

"That's something, at least."

Hope grasped this ray of light. "So, you'll help me? You won't spill my secret?"

Ava pursed her lips. "Now, I didn't say that."

"Mom, please. It can't all unravel now. Imagine the huge blowup that would happen if everyone found out that I'm Hope, not Jackie. It would ruin the wedding. They'd probably call it off." Hope frowned, then said sourly, "Which is just what Grandmother Margaret wants."

Her mom sighed, but Hope could tell she was caving, so she decided to heap on a little sweetener. "And this wedding has to go on. It's going to be so beautiful. Just perfect. And the minute Jackie gets here, she'll know it's true. She'll be so, so happy about the change in Brent, and now the two of them will have a chance. A real chance at their happily ever after, and the reception's going to be great. There might even be a chance for singing."

"Yeah?" Ava's face lit up. "That could be fun."

"Oh yeah, absolutely," Hope said, nodding vigorously. "And you know what you've always said. That you want to sing at your daughters' weddings."

"I do actually have a song picked out." She grinned. "Because I was hoping."

"Perfect! No guarantees, okay?" Hope rushed to add. "This is Jackie's wedding, so totally her call. But I'll certainly put in a good word and suggest it."

"Would you, Hope? Aww. That would be so nice. Really."

"You've got it, Mom."

They sat there in silence, staring at each other, as what they'd just agreed to sank in.

After a few moments, Ava said, "We've been

down here awhile. You'd better get dressed. I'll go back to the main house and hold down the fort."

"Thank you." Hope stood and gave her mom a hug. "Just maybe don't play that video."

"Which video?" her mom said all innocent-like.

"That one from Debbie's wedding."

"But, you said—"

Hope pulled away and pasted a smile on her face. "I mean, not yet. No guarantees, remember?"

Her mom patted her cheek. "Sure, sure. No problem."

• • •

Hope dressed as quickly as she could, her head pounding. She had to rejoin the others before her mom made a mess of things—by either accidentally outing her as Hope or playing that karaoke video from her cousin's wedding. She scooted up the garden path, spotting Ava standing near the firepit. She held out her phone and had captured Parker, Elsa, and Chad's rapt attention.

Elsa nodded politely while Parker stared gob-smacked at the small screen, his arms still loaded with tinder for the outdoor fire. Meanwhile, Chad swirled his drink and took another long swallow. Intervening now would be pointless. Ava was already showing off her singing skills, which honestly weren't great.

But maybe this would work to Hope's advantage. If her mom had already launched her crusade to sing during the wedding, that would become her focus, and she'd be less likely to throw a monkey wrench into things by revealing the secret that could upend everything.

So, Hope decided to leave well enough alone. She stole quietly toward the main house and slipped in through the front door. She found Grandmother Margaret in the kitchen, cutting vegetables for a crudité tray. She'd tied an apron around her waist and wore a pale blue cardigan, which brought out the color of her deep blue eyes.

Margaret glanced up from the cutting board, where she chopped carrots and celery. "If you're looking for Brent, Derrick's taken him to collect his SUV." She held Hope in her gaze an extra moment. "I hear you had quite an adventure."

"Yeah." Hope produced a little laugh. "Memorable for sure." She perused the kitchen, which still managed to appear pristine, even as it was evident there was a meal in preparation. Something baked in the oven, and a couple of pots simmered on the stove. "Can I do something to help?"

"Dinner's pretty simple," Margaret said. "Oven-fried chicken, mashed potatoes, and collard greens."

"I love collard greens," Hope said, thinking she'd recognized their distinctive scent.

"Do you, now?" Her eyebrows rose. "I always found them hard to come by in Boston. Of course, now with farmers markets and produce services, things are changing. It's a greener planet, I suppose. In more ways than one."

Hope grinned at Margaret's attempt at humor. "It could get greener."

"It could indeed. That's one reason Chad's so pleased with Brent taking over Albright Enterprises.

He's proposed so many green initiatives. Brent's very special."

"Yes." Hope felt her cheeks color, so she changed the subject. "Can I prepare the mushrooms and radishes, maybe?" she said, seeing them washed and ready to cut on the counter.

"That would be great, if you don't mind." She nodded toward a drawer by the sink. "You'll find extra aprons in that drawer."

Though Hope didn't normally wear them, she didn't want to break protocol in Margaret's kitchen, so she selected a fun one that contained a blueberry appliqué. Of course. "This is an amazing kitchen. What a great place for baking."

"Oh, I don't bake often," Margaret answered. "But I do love to cook. Full dinners, lunches, yes. I also don't mind a big country breakfast once in a while. But I've never had much patience for timers and ten-minute cookies. That's Elsa's purview."

"She does a really great job of it, too," Hope said, guarding Brent's mom's secret. Then, she recalled she was Jackie and not big into carbs—although she was actively working to change that impression. "I mean, her muffins look so good. I can't wait to try them." She hesitated before adding, "I normally don't eat much bread, but I've decided to make an exception for this week. There will be wedding cake, after all."

Margaret handed her a small knife and another cutting board, then returned to her task of mixing a vegetable dip with a whisk in a pretty pottery bowl. She seemed to be looking at Hope in an odd way, which made Hope feel self-conscious. "Jackie, dear?"

"Hmm?"

"I know."

Hope's heart beat a million times per minute. "Know?"

"Don't think I don't have eyes and that I can't see it."

The knife came down so hard on the far side of the radish Hope nearly nicked her finger. She kept chop-chop-chopping without looking up, perspiration forming at her hairline. Was it possible Margaret had figured her out?

"I saw you, Jackie," she said softly. "You and Brent."

Hope raised her eyes to Margaret's, not understanding.

"I was up in my bedroom earlier, grabbing my sweater, and…" She tilted her head to one side. "He was carrying you through the mudflats."

"Oh, that." Hope's cheeks heated as Margaret continued.

"I may be in my seventies, but I haven't forgotten." She gave a wistful sigh and stared at the ceiling. "Young love. All those outrageous things we do."

Hope sent down her knife to listen.

"Oh yes," Margaret said, reading her expression. "Chad and I had our adventures, too."

"Yeah?" Hope asked, utterly intrigued.

Margaret placed her bowl on the counter, whisk still in it. "I was a flower child."

"You?"

"Product of the sixties." She smiled. "Chad and I went out to San Francisco. I wore a flower in my hair."

Hope blinked. Of all the things Margaret might have told her, she definitely hadn't expected this. "Was this after college?"

"Before," she corrected. "We ran away to be hippies, which drove our parents nuts. My parents more than his. Chad just had his father, and his father was pretty laid back."

"And your parents weren't?"

"Oh, *no*. Very conservative. They didn't approve of my choices or of Chad." Grandmother Margaret actually *giggled*. "He had long hair then and hadn't yet made his way, but I knew he would. He was always very smart and talented."

"Was his dad in the hotel business, too?"

"He owned a gas station," Margaret supplied evenly and without judgment. "Chad worked there in high school, and that's how we met. He checked my oil and washed my windshield."

Hope chuckled, trying to envision this scene based on how Chad and Margaret were now.

"When the glass cleared," Margaret went on, "he gave me the most unbelievable grin, and well…that was kind of it for me."

"That fast? Really?"

"The heart wants what the heart wants," she explained. "Sometimes it takes longer to discern our heart's desire. At other times?" She shrugged. "We can know in an instant."

Hope recalled Brent's lips brushing over hers, and she grew weak. "Yeah."

"You're probably wondering why I'm telling you this," Margaret said with an earnest gaze. "It's because I'm afraid I owe you an apology." She set her chin before continuing. "When we met in Boston, I got such a different impression of you. I'm sorry I didn't understand. Perhaps I hadn't given you enough time…but I didn't really feel that you loved my grandson."

"And now?" Hope asked, growing lightheaded.

"I can just look at you and tell."

Heat burned in Hope's cheeks. "Is it that obvious?"

"Obvious isn't a bad thing. You are getting married."

Oh, but they weren't, and how that made Hope's heart ache. Whatever was going on between her and Brent, it was bound to end badly. At the very least, horribly for her.

Jackie, on the other hand, was in for a pretty great marriage. But was this marriage really meant for Jackie? She and her sister were so different, she couldn't help but wonder.

"Thank you for confiding in me and for your apology," Hope said. "I'm afraid I owe you one, too." Margaret's brow rose, and she continued. "You're not the only one who misjudged. While I knew you loved your family, I guess I didn't understand how much."

"I would do anything for my son and grandchildren."

"Yes, I'm sure you would."

It was the tender sort of moment that called for a hug, but Hope wasn't sure how Margaret would take it. Instead, Margaret showed her by pulling her briskly into her arms. "Welcome to the family," she said with a stiff embrace.

Heat prickled Hope's eyes as she returned Margaret's hug. She felt horrible now for not giving the older woman the benefit of the doubt. When she'd bad-mouthed Brent's grandmother to her mom, she'd never in a million years have expected this turnaround.

It was clear that Grandmother Margaret really loved her family. And when she'd intuited that something seemed off about Brent and Jackie's marriage, she'd actually been right.

"Hel-lo?" a male voice called from the hall. "Grandmother?"

They turned toward the foyer, where a tall man with a mop of short brown curls stood beside a gorgeous dark-skinned woman.

"William," Margaret said happily. "And Sofia. Oh, my dears. Please come here and meet Brent's fiancée. *This* is the lovely Jackie."

Before Hope could process that shockingly positive introduction, Sofia raced toward her with a warm hug. She had dark brown eyes, delicate features, and a tiny diamond stud on the right side of her nose, but otherwise wore no jewelry beyond the simple wedding band, and—okay—a pretty huge rock of a diamond solitaire engagement ring on her ring finger. "Jack-ie. Oh. So happy to meet you."

William hugged her next. Within his chiseled face, he had Parker's exact nose. His medium brown eyes were a shade lighter than Brent's. "I hope it's okay if I call you sis?"

Hope laughed. "Only if I can call you bro."

William chuckled, and the others smiled, making Hope feel like she'd just scored a point with Brent's family. More points. Extra credit.

What an incredible service she was doing for her sister.

William thumbed over his shoulder at their suitcases. "I'm sorry we're late," he said to his grandmother. "We had a little holdup on the road."

"Holdup?" Margaret asked worriedly, but Sofia rushed in.

"It was nothing, honestly. We just had to stop more often than normal." She shrugged. "Blame me for drinking too much coffee."

"Sofia's a very prominent attorney in New Haven," Margaret told Hope.

"I don't know about the prominent part," Sofia answered.

"That's how we met," William offered. "Sofia works with Sally, and Sally introduced us."

"Your sister, Sally?"

"That's right," William said. "The two of them were in law school together and now help run a women's law practice."

Sofia grinned. "Sally said her brother and I were perfect for each other, and naturally…" She gazed at William, and Hope caught the warm affection between them. "She was right."

"How sweet." She remembered what Jackie had told her about Brent's older brother. "And you're a college professor there?"

"Economist, yeah."

Hope reflected on Brent's business background and the notion of Sally being a lawyer. It was interesting that Derrick was the youngest male and also the "creative" among them. They all seemed to be great people. Her sister was lucky to be getting these in-laws.

"You have such a wonderful family," Hope said to Margaret.

"And now you're joining us," the woman said so warmly that Hope wanted to cry. Really cry, in big, hard, jerking sobs, which she was about to break into at any minute.

"Grandma. William. Sofia. Woo!" The front door swung open, and a cute blonde with long wavy hair bounced through it, dropping two heavy carry-on bags with a *thud*. She scuttled into the kitchen, beelining for Hope. Curvy and effervescent, Sally was on the shorter side compared to the rest of them. "And *you* must be Jackie."

"Sally," Hope said, returning her hug. This was such a huggie family. "Great to meet you."

Sally *squeed* at Sofia next. "Girlfriend," she cried, hugging her, even though they'd apparently seen each other only hours ago. "How was your drive?"

"Good, and yours?"

"Okay." Sally stifled a yawn. "I got that brief turned in before leaving."

"Great, thanks," Sofia said.

"Fortunately for me," William supplied, "school's out for summer."

"I know just what you mean." Hope bit her tongue when the others eyed her curiously. "I mean, I…er…remember those days."

"It's so exciting that you're a wedding planner," Sally said, taking Hope's hand. "I can't wait to hear all about it."

William stared around the kitchen and then

peeked into the dining room. "Where are the others? Out back?"

"All except for Derrick and Brent," Margaret said. "They've gone to run an errand but will be right back."

"What time is dinner?" William asked.

"Something smells…delicious." Sofia covered her mouth and looked like she wanted to gag. Hope scanned the others' faces, but apparently no one else had noticed.

"Not until eight," Margaret said, answering William. "Why don't you all go and settle in while Jackie and I carry these refreshments outdoors. Oh my," she said, turning to Hope. "Where are our manners? Nobody's fixed you a drink."

"Did I hear someone call the bartender?" Chad asked, striding into the kitchen. Then he welcomed his grandkids to Blue Hill and offered Hope her beverage choices.

CHAPTER TEN

"There you are, big brother," Sally said, giving Brent a kiss on his cheek when he joined her, Jackie, and Ava by the firepit. William and Sofia were there, too, and his parents and grandparents sat on the porch.

He grinned at his baby sister, who appeared upbeat. Brent found this remarkable, as she dealt with heartrending tragedies day after day. Most of her cases concerned divorces. Sometimes Brent wondered if that was why she herself seemed shy of marriage.

"Sal, good to see you."

"We were just chatting with Ava about karaoke," Sally filled in.

Ava turned to Brent. "That's right. You haven't seen the video."

"Mo-om," Jackie muttered, doing an embarrassed eye roll.

"I don't mind seeing the video," Brent said.

Jackie leaned toward him and teased, "It's the hearing part that matters."

Brent repressed a grin, glancing over at Jackie, who'd dressed in a pretty skirt and top. She'd washed her hair, which flounced about her face in wispy layers. It was funny—Brent had never really paid much attention to Jackie's hair before, but now all he wanted to do was run his fingers through the soft waves. He'd clearly missed a lot about her. Her heart necklace glimmered in the firelight, and he wondered why she'd waited until this point in their relationship to wear it. Or had she worn it before, and he'd never noticed that, either?

It was a disappointing possibility.

And something he intended to rectify this weekend.

"Sally was just telling us about Grandmother Margaret being a concert pianist," Jackie said, redirecting the conversation. "Does she still play?"

"Not as often as she used to," Sally said. "Although she played a lot when we were little."

Brent remembered that being one of the best parts of their Blue Hill summers. The sound of his grandmother's sweet sonatas wafting up to his bedroom as he drifted off to sleep.

"She used to play late at night," Sally explained to Jackie and Ava. "Her music filled the whole house."

"All the way up to the third floor," Brent agreed.

Sally smiled. "It helped when we had our windows open and the windows were open in the living room, too."

"What a marvelous place to vacation," Ava said, her gaze sweeping the lawn. She admired the expanse of the house, staring up at the three dormer windows. "You children slept up there, then?"

"That's right," Sally answered. "Those times were so much fun." She frowned. "I really miss them."

"Miss them?" Ava asked. "What do you mean?"

"Once we all got into college and started developing our own summer plans, with jobs and such, it was harder for us to get together. This is the first time since William's wedding," Sally said, sipping from her drink.

"How long ago was that?" Ava asked.

Brent smiled and took a swig of his beer, recalling the happy day. "Two years ago this summer."

"My!" Ava exclaimed. "This is getting to be quite the wedding locale. Was it a small wedding like this one?"

"Much bigger," Sally replied. "Sofia's from a large family, too, and has eight nieces and nephews. She's the youngest of four girls. She and William also have tons of grad school friends. So…" Sally lifted a shoulder. "The wedding list grew quickly."

"Did everything go okay with getting your SUV and the canoe?" Jackie asked Brent.

"Ahh, yes. That reminds me," he teased, thinking of the specimen he'd saved. "When Derrick and I hauled it out of the mud, we had a run-in with the swamp monster you saw earlier."

She gasped. "Oh no."

Brent chuckled. "Hang on. Let me just go and get it." He set his bottle on a table and traipsed toward the dock stairs.

"Brent, wait!" He turned back to see she'd paled. "Do you really think that's necessary?"

"Oh, yeah," he said, stifling a chuckle. "Absolutely."

Minutes later, he returned with the gnarly twisted stick that had been poking out of the mud, right alongside the set of tracks Brent had left behind him as he'd carried Jackie toward the house.

Sally wrinkled up her nose at the icky specimen. "What's that?"

"Something much more harmless than a bloodworm."

"A stick?" Jackie asked with surprise, and then she burst into laughter. "Oh boy."

"Maybe someone will let me in on the joke?" Ava asked.

"Time to eat, everyone. Come inside." The group glanced toward the porch, where Parker and Chad were getting to their feet. Margaret stood by the French doors with Derrick beside her.

"Sure, Mom," Jackie said as they strolled back inside. "I'll tell you at dinner."

• • •

The meal passed pleasantly enough, and Hope was glad that the tension of her being here was easing. Much of this had to do with her and Margaret's earlier talk in the kitchen.

She never would have guessed about Brent's grandmother being a former hippie — or a concert pianist. The two things seemed so at odds with each other. Then again, Grandmother Margaret herself appeared a contradiction.

She was so stoic and stiff on the one hand. On the other, it was just like Brent had said. She really did have a heart of gold. Hope was touched that she'd finally opened up that heart to her — and, by extension, to her sister. Jackie was going to be *so pleased* by how everything had gone.

Really, that was the only thing that kept her participating in this terrible charade.

Derrick ended another rollicking tale about his boatbuilding school that had the whole group in stitches. After the laughter subsided, he asked Hope,

"When is your sister arriving?"

"Not until Wednesday, sadly, but Meredith will be here tomorrow."

"Meredith is *Jackie's* best friend," Ava supplied, placing undue emphasis on the name. She shot a sly wink at Hope, and Hope slid down in her chair. Her mom was so proud of her secret, and also apparently pleased with her ability to keep it.

Just a few more hours, Hope tried to tell herself. Soon, it would be bedtime. Then, she'd only have one more day and a half to get through. Thankfully, tomorrow would be extra busy.

"That's great," Sally replied to Ava. "I can't wait to meet them both."

They'd just finished dinner and had moved on to dessert: a yummy shortcake with ice cream and strawberries.

"Just think," Elsa said. "By this time on Wednesday, we'll all be here. Our new immediate family."

"Except for Gavin," Parker corrected.

"He's Parker's best friend," Chad said for the Webbs' benefit.

Margaret waved her loaded fork. "The brother he never had."

"He was also the best man at our wedding," Elsa added.

"Gavin's the only nonfamily member at this family wedding," Brent said to Ava. "He really is like family, though. Uncle Gavin to all of us."

"How nice," she answered, taking a taste of her dessert. "Margaret," she said, "this shortcake is delicious."

"Oh, I can't take credit." Margaret smiled at her

daughter-in-law. "Dessert was all Elsa."

Elsa's cheeks reddened, so Hope jumped in. "Looks so yummy. Can't wait to try it."

Only Sofia looked less than enticed, covering her mouth with her napkin.

"Excuse me. Just one minute." She hurriedly left the table, and William watched after her with a worried look.

"Are you okay?"

"Yeah, yeah." She waved a hand and skirted toward the den. "Just need some air."

The conversation resumed with Sofia's absence becoming more and more pronounced, though everyone pretended not to notice.

Margaret admired the pretty purple crystal that hung from a long silver chain around Ava's neck. "That's so unique," she said. "Does it represent anything special?"

"Oh yes." Ava preened. "My chi. My aura's purple, you know."

Hope stared at her wide-eyed, but her mom didn't take the hint. She went on and on about how intuitive she was and about how she could sense things about people, particularly when they were *wrong* in how they interpreted others. Ava angled her body slightly toward Margaret as she said this, but Margaret just raised her eyebrows. When Ava offered to read everyone's tarot cards, Hope knew she had to stop this runaway train.

"I've never had that done," Chad answered. "I'm game."

"Sure," Derrick said. "Why not?"

"I've got a deck right here in my purse," Ava said,

reaching down toward the floor.

"Mom."

Her mom's chin jerked up. "Yes, Ho—holy moly. I almost called you Hope." Ava broke out in a titter as Hope's heart pounded like a kettledrum.

Elsa glanced around the table with a happy gleam in her eyes. "That probably happens to mothers everywhere. I sometimes mix up my boys."

Parker agreed. "Yes, but just the names, not the people."

"Oh. I'd never...mix up the people," Ava said with a bright flush. "Jackie and Hope are so distinctive. Neither one is anything like the other. In fact, they're *very* different. As different as night and day. Yin and yang. The moon and the—"

"Did you know that my mom's also into music?" Hope said to Margaret, abruptly interceding.

"No, dear." Margaret appeared intrigued and turned to Ava. "What instrument to you play?"

"Just my voice box." Ava splayed her fingers against her throat. "Right here."

"She's really quite good," Parker said.

Margaret smiled. "Oh?"

"We saw...*heard* a video," Chad said before drinking some more wine.

"Yes." Elsa smiled politely, then glanced toward the den. "Sofia's been gone a while. Maybe someone should go and check on her?"

"I'll go," Sally said, and then her phone buzzed in her pocket. Her face fell when she read the incoming number. "Yikes, I'd better take this. Could be important. Sorry."

Sally slipped toward the kitchen, and Hope

stared around the table, noting the men were energetically discussing their sailing trip, while Margaret and Ava were recalling several tunes relating to what they called retro music. Margaret was probably more thrilled than she should have been to learn that Ava was also a musician. But that was only because she hadn't yet heard her sing. Elsa started to stand, but Hope intervened.

"I can check on Sofia."

"Oh, would you?" Elsa sighed gratefully. "That would be very nice. I just heard the coffee beep and was about to go and serve it."

• • •

Hope found Sofia sitting on the back porch in a rocker, holding her head in her hands.

"Sofia?" Hope asked quietly. "Are you feeling sick?"

"A little," she mumbled, her voice muffled. "Mostly queasy."

"I'm sorry." Hope sat down beside her. "I know where they keep the ginger ale around here. Would you like me to bring you some?"

Sofia glanced up with a haggard look. "Actually, ginger ale sounds divine."

Hope walked to the kitchen through the hall so as not to disturb the others and prepared the ginger ale for Sofia, bringing it to her on the porch. She thought back to Sofia's behavior earlier, remembering that she'd been the only one not drinking wine at dinner. "Did this come on all of a sudden?"

"I think…" Sofia wryly twisted her lips. "More like two and a half months ago."

Hope gasped. "You're pregnant?"

"Please don't say anything to the others," Sofia whispered. "Nobody knows yet."

"Not even William?"

"Especially not William."

Hope surveyed Sofia's eyes, not understanding.

"We've been trying so hard." Her chin trembled. "And, well…last time." Moisture glistened in her eyes. "Things didn't work out so well." She took a tiny sip of ginger ale, staring sadly into her glass.

"Oh, Sofia. I'm so sorry."

"William really wants to be a daddy. He'll be a super one, too."

"I'm sure you'll both make great parents."

"Thank you. I hope we get the chance." She sniffed before continuing. "In any case, before… William was crushed. I don't want him to live through that a second time."

"He loves you. It's so obvious. Maybe he'd welcome the chance to go through this with you. And hey." She smiled when Sofia met her eyes. "Who's to say that this time things won't turn out perfect?"

"Brent told us you were pretty," Sofia said. "He never mentioned you're so nice."

"I'm not being nice. I'm being honest." The minute those words left her lips, Hope felt like the world's hugest fraud. But the sympathy she felt for Sofia wasn't manufactured. It was genuine.

Sofia heaved a sigh. "Maybe you're right about William. I don't know." She took another sip of her soda and studied the darkened horizon past the low-burning glow of the firepit.

"Don't worry about what you told me," Hope said. "I can keep a secret."

"That's good," Sofia said. "Because I wouldn't want to steal your thunder."

"My thunder?"

"Girl, this is your wedding week. The attention should be on you."

"There's never a bad time for happy news," Hope said. "But I understand your reasons for wanting to wait before telling your family."

Sofia considered her a moment. "But not about me waiting to tell William?"

"I didn't say that."

"No, that's true."

"It's a very personal decision," Hope answered. "And we've only just met. I wouldn't presume to tell you what to do."

"You never told me. I was asking for your opinion."

It honored Hope so much that Sofia would confide in her this way, and she badly didn't want to blow their new connection. "I'd say listen to your heart. The heart wants what the heart wants."

Sofia smiled. "Now where have I heard that expression before?"

"Grandmother Margaret," they both said together and laughed.

"There you are," William said, stepping through the French doors. "I was worried when you didn't come back." He stared down at the glass in her hand and then at the half-empty bottle of ginger ale on the table beside her. "Ginger ale?" His forehead crinkled with concern. "Sofia?"

"I'll go and see if Grandmother Margaret needs help with the dishes," Hope said, getting to her feet.

Then she left Sofia and William alone on the porch to discuss whatever it was Sofia decided her heart desired.

Moments later, she peered back through the French doors before entering the dining room. William had pulled Sofia out of her chair and into his arms, and both of them were crying.

Hope's heart swelled with happiness as she said a silent prayer that everything would be all right. For Sofia. For William. For the three of them.

• • •

Derrick left shortly after dinner, and Sally excused herself to go upstairs. When Brent and Jackie entered the den to look for the others, neither William nor Sofia were anywhere in sight. Only a dim light emanated from the partially shut doors to the library, indicating that Chad and Margaret were probably still in there reading.

"Things are pretty quiet around here," Jackie said. "It looks like my mom already headed back to the carriage house. Maybe we should call it a night?"

Getting some rest was probably a good idea, but Brent wasn't ready to leave Jackie yet. They'd barely had any time alone together since their picnic, and Brent wanted more private time with his bride-to-be.

"It's honestly not that late," he said, checking the mantel clock and seeing it was just half past ten.

"Are you maybe up for one more glass of wine?"

She hesitated a beat. "I don't know, Brent."

"It's really nice out on the porch this time of evening," he said. "As long as you wear a sweater."

"I'm afraid my sweaters are down at the carriage house."

"Then we can use one of these," Brent said, snagging a soft throw blanket from the back of one of the loveseats. He shot her a grin. "Come on. We never did have that talk you promised me."

"Talk?" Her forehead creased sweetly. "But we talked all afternoon on our picnic."

"I'm talking about the other talk." He teasingly lowered his eyebrows. "The one about our engagement?"

She gave a little laugh. "Oh yeah. That one."

"Look at it this way," he said. "This is our last night of freedom from the greater world before our cyber communications resume."

"And we get back our phones!" she said with an elated gasp.

Brent wasn't sure why it bothered him that she seemed so ecstatic about it.

He understood she had to stay on top of logistics for her business, as well as their wedding, but he honestly hadn't missed the nearly constant buzzing of text messages in his pocket. He'd kind of enjoyed the singular buzz he caught from staring into Jackie's gorgeous brown eyes. He'd never noticed how large they were or how captivating they could be before. Especially when she was looking at him—and appearing to adore him—the way she was now.

"Well, all right." She shared a shy smile. "One

little glass of wine probably won't hurt."

"I'll pour, and you reserve the porch swing."

He tossed her the blanket, and she caught it with a surprised chuckle. "Deal."

• • •

Hope sat on the porch swing with the blanket draped around her as whistling winds wafted off of the water. The nearly full moon was high in the sky with a smattering of stars in the inky background beyond it.

Even from here, she could hear the low crackling from the firepit as its embers burned low, casting wavering shadows across the patio and the lawn. This place was so cozy. Despite its size, it still felt like a home.

Brent stepped out the door holding two glasses of wine. "I'm sorry, I should have asked if you'd prefer red or white. I noticed you drank pinot noir with dinner, so I brought us more of the same."

"That's perfect, thanks." She accepted a wineglass from him, and Brent took a seat beside her on the porch swing. There was no escaping the fact that the setting was very romantic. "Do you want some of this blanket?" she offered as he settled in.

"Nope. I'm good, thanks. My thermostat runs high." He grinned, and her pulse fluttered.

"That's funny," she said with a laugh. "I'm always cold."

"Are you?" Brent's forehead rose. "I thought you told me the opposite."

Hope bit her bottom lip, realizing she'd made a

slip. Jackie was always on the warm side, likely due to the fact that she was racing around all the time. When she wasn't on her feet coordinating weddings, she was doing insane things like taking five-mile runs. Apparently.

"Right. That's right," she amended. "I do tend to run warm when I'm into my regular routine. But being up here has been so relaxing. I guess my metabolism's slowed down."

Brent chuckled at this. "No worries. We'll charge it back up in the morning when we take that run."

"Run," Hope replied nervously. "Right."

For a moment, neither one spoke as they both sipped from their wine.

After a bit, Brent broached the topic he'd evidently wanted to bring up. "I am sorry about that proposal, you know. I feel like a jerk about it."

"Brent, don't—"

"No, hear me out. You were right about a lot of things. It was definitely *not* romantic. More procedural than anything else."

"I *did* go along with it, you know."

"Yeah, I suppose both of us could have done better. Really thought this thing through."

Hope held her breath. "Are you having doubts now?"

"Far from it." His eyes sparkled in the soft light. "I'm actually starting to believe we made the right decision."

She considered the reasons for him and Jackie making their agreement in the first place. "Is taking over Albright Enterprises really that important to you?"

"Yes."

"Why?"

He set his chin and then surprised her with his answer. "William."

"William? I'm not sure I get it."

"Please don't misunderstand, because I deeply love my brother and he's never been anything but extra kind to me, but everything in life has come super easy for him."

Hope heaved a sigh, knowing she couldn't break her confidence with Sofia. "I wouldn't be so sure about that."

Brent sipped from his wine. "You could be right. There are always things that people don't know about each other. But on the surface, it's been a little tough living in my big brother's shadow. He was always more accomplished in school, always better at everything. Including knowing what he wanted to be from the start: a college professor. Then, when he met Sofia, he knew right away that she was the one. When the two of them found their first house, they bought it in an instant."

"William's decisive, you mean."

"Yeah, and focused. Where I've always been…" Brent swirled the wine in his glass. "A bit less so, I suppose." He looked up and met her eyes. "Until now."

Her heart pounded as he went on. "You make me feel something, Jackie. Something I wasn't even sure I was capable of feeling. I mean, anymore."

"Anymore?" she asked gently. "And so, there was someone?"

"A very long time ago."

"And?"

"The poets would say she broke my heart."

"Brent," she said, moved by his confession. "I'm sorry."

"You're probably wondering why I never told you this before?"

"You don't have to tell me now, if you don't want to."

"But, I do…" Brent took her hand. "You're different, somehow," he told her. "Different from how I imagined. I guess getting to know your bride is not such a bad idea after all."

"I'm sorry about your heart."

"Don't be." He captured her in his gaze, and Hope's heart stilled. Then, her heart skipped a beat when he continued. "You're helping put it back together. And not just in the relationship sense. I want to be a better man. Taking over Albright Enterprises used to be about proving myself just as capable as my brother, but now I want this for *us*."

A wave of guilt crashed over her. At the same time, she felt bathed in happiness—in a very twisted way. Brent was starting to get personal with her… very personal. But thinking she was Jackie. Which was all messed up and wrong. "Brent—"

"You don't have to say anything. I know I'm laying a lot on you." He stared into her soul, and Hope imagined her whole world changing. Wanted to hang on to these new feelings emerging between them and never let go.

"It's okay," she said, also admitting her truth, even though she predicted it would eventually shatter her. "You're helping my heart, too."

"Am I?" He gently squeezed her hand, and she couldn't help holding his a little tighter. The two of them felt so connected right now, and not in a fake way, but for real.

"Brent, I...I'm not sure what's happening between us."

A smile warmed his face. "Is it too much to hope we're actually falling in love?"

"That would be something," she said with a dreamy sigh.

His gaze washed over her, and oh how she wanted him to sweep her away. To some place far from here, where it was just the two of them, starting over from the very beginning. And without the complication of her sister's bogus marriage in the way.

"My heart's been broken, too, you know. A whole bunch of times."

"Oh no." Sadness filled his eyes. "Jackie, I'm sorry. Were these the pre-holiday-dumping guys?"

"A few of them, yeah. But not all. I've just never...you know." She dropped her chin. "Found the right one."

When she looked up at him, he said, "Some things are worth the wait."

Hope desperately wanted to believe that was true. Because she'd wait an eternity for Brent if she thought he could really be hers someday. "Yeah."

"What happened with those other guys? I mean, you don't have to tell me."

"It just wasn't...mutual," she said, finding it painful to admit it out loud. "Or maybe the word is *reciprocated*."

"Well, that's not really your fault. I mean, you couldn't very well force your feelings. I've been there, too."

She realized that he'd misunderstood her, so she explained. "No. I mean it was me who wasn't loved."

He gazed at her in disbelief. "What kind of idiots were these?"

This brought a shaky smile. "The kind who weren't completely into me?"

"Maybe we should be grateful for that." He lifted her hand to his mouth and kissed the back of it. "If one of them *had* been, then maybe you and I wouldn't have found each other."

He was making so much sense and being so sweet, it was only making Hope fall harder. And she'd been having a really tough time not falling for Brent as it was. She was sorry that he'd been hurt, too, and wanted to know what had happened.

"What about you? Was it only that one bad breakup?"

He laughed bitterly. "I was one and done after that."

"I'm sorry."

He turned away and looked toward the bay. "It was right after college, when I lived in New York. We dated for two years, and I thought it was going somewhere."

"Two years? That's a long time."

"Yeah, but I guess it didn't take."

"What happened?" She stared up at his rugged profile, so badly wanting to know. Mainly so she could help make it better, if she could.

"Truthfully?" He met her eyes, his eyebrows

arched. "She said she couldn't handle my family."

"Your family? You're kidding," she said, wondering if it had been about his grandmother.

"She said they were too intrusive. Especially Sally."

Hope 100 hundred percent wasn't expecting this. "Sally?"

He nodded. "Sal was in college, then, and not really wild about Amanda. I asked her why, but she never really had any good reasons, just said it was a gut-level thing. Sally's instincts have turned out to work well for her professionally. She never takes a case she doesn't totally believe in and says she can *read* all her clients."

"Like she did Amanda?"

"Yeah." He shrugged. "In any case, it wasn't just Sally. I think my mom wasn't so wild about Amanda, either, but she was too diplomatic to ever say that."

"Ahh. And Grandmother Margaret?"

"She never met her."

"What? In all that time?"

"Amanda wouldn't come home with me for holidays."

"I see."

"Anyway, none of that matters now." He squeezed her hand. "I've found someone so much better. My perfect match."

Brent was perfect. So perfect for somebody, and Hope was starting to think that was her and not her sister. She was the one he'd been getting to know and bond with, not Jackie. And yet, Jackie would be here on Wednesday, and Hope's little fantasy life, where she pretended she'd finally found a guy who was really into her, would be ended.

Brent checked his watch. "It's getting late. Are you ready to head back to the carriage house, or do you want to sit here a while?"

Hope wished she could sit there for *hours* with Brent, snuggled up against his warmth.

"I don't mind sitting," she said shyly. "For a little longer."

"Good." Brent reached over and wrapped an arm around her shoulders, tugging her close. "Neither do I."

Then, they sat staring over the water as Hope's mind spun and her heart ached, and she wondered what on earth she was going to do. She was giving her heart to her sister's fiancé, and it was seeming more and more impossible that she'd ever get it back without it breaking completely apart.

CHAPTER ELEVEN

Hope had barely opened her eyes when someone knocked at the door. She wasn't sure whether she was really awake or still dreaming. Maybe it was a woodpecker or something. *Yeah, that.* She groggily rolled onto her side, clutching a pillow.

Her mom was on the pullout couch in the lower-level den, and the second room in back with twin beds had been assigned to "Hope" and Meredith. She'd only been given the master as a courtesy, since she was the bride. Hope planned to square everything up when Jackie arrived and reconfigure the sleeping arrangements any way that Jackie wanted.

There was another light rapping sound, and Hope sat up in bed. Someone was out there. At— *what?* Hope squinted at the clock beside her bed. *Six in the morning?* It wasn't even light yet, was it? She trained her gaze on the window, seeing fine slivers of light peeking through the slanted blinds. *Who on earth?*

"Jackie?"

Hope sat up with a jolt. Brent? "Coming." She rubbed the sleep out of her eyes and grabbed her bathrobe, slipping it on.

"You're not ready?" Brent asked when she answered the door in a daze.

"Well, Captain Obvious. No."

Brent raised an eyebrow when she cupped her

mouth. "Cranky this morning?"

"Sorry. I…just don't wake up very well."

He frowned. "Since when? You've always been a morning person."

"Er…right." She tried to sound perky but still felt out of sorts. "Except for today."

"Don't tell me you're feeling sick again?"

"No, it's not that. I just need"—she turned back toward the kitchen—"coffee."

"Ah," he said, understanding. "Of course." Brent peered around the side of the building. "I'm happy to wait while you make some. I can meet you in the gazebo if you'd like." Then he added as an afterthought: "I suspect your mom's still sleeping?"

"*No, I'm not*," Ava moaned. Her mom sounded just as grouchy as Hope felt. Jackie was the only one of the three of them who could wake up with a smile. Ava and Hope both struggled.

"Okay." Brent backed away from the door. "See you in a few."

• • •

By the time Hope had made the coffee and changed into her shorts and tee, she felt more human. She'd washed her face, brushed her teeth, and downed a quick glass of water before joining Brent outside on the deck. "I brought two cups of coffee, in case you want one?"

"Thanks." He accepted the mug she gave him, and she sat beside him at the small table in the screened gazebo. "I'm sorry if I got you up too early."

"I'm sorry that I was such an ogre. Mornings and me? Bad marriage."

He laughed at the remark. "You're a very good actress, then, because I never would have guessed that from before."

She sucked in a breath, gathering her courage. Maybe she should tell him now. Let the whole sordid truth come out. Sure, he'd be ticked, but at least she would have come clean.

And to what end?

What would learning that she was Hope—and not Jackie—do to Brent and his family? They would all feel so deceived, and any headway she'd made on her sister's behalf would be totaled. Besides that, Jackie would be here tomorrow. So, what was the point in ruining things for everyone?

He stroked the back of her hand with his thumb, and she had to will her pulse not to thrum in response. Unfortunately, her will wasn't strong enough, and her heart began hammering anyway. "Are you worried about something? Because if it's about the wedding and today's meeting with the wedding planner—"

"No, it's not that."

"Then what?"

"I'm afraid, Brent," she said, her breath shuddering.

"Of what?"

"Everything."

"Baby," he said, and Hope's heart skipped a beat because he'd never called her that before. "Things might have started off a little rough, but we're getting there. Yesterday was awesome. I mean, really amazing. The picnic…the porch swing. Everything."

She sighed because she'd loved every moment of being with him, too. "Yeah."

He tugged at her hand, pulling her closer. "I thought that I knew you. I mean, not super well, but the big picture of who you are. And here I'm starting to learn that I never really knew you at all. That's probably what other people saw and why they said we rushed it."

"People? Which people?"

"You already know about Grandmother Margaret." He frowned. "But my dad questioned us, too."

"Parker?" A red-hot arrow blazed through her chest. "Oh."

"Honey, you have to look at it from their side. We've only been dating for three months." He raked a hand through his hair. "But suddenly it seems like…well. I can't imagine a time when I *didn't* know you. It may sound stupid, but I feel like I always have."

Hope's breath caught in her throat. "It doesn't sound stupid." She licked her lips. "Not, not at all."

"So, then…" His eyebrows rose. "You feel the same way?"

"Yeah," she said, unable to stop herself. "I do."

He set his palm against her cheek. "I can't wait to hear those words on Saturday."

"I…oh…" She tried to be strong and fight this tide, but it was *such* a losing battle. Every time she was this close to him, she only wanted to get closer. And then, he kissed her, and she didn't know which way was up or down or right or wrong.

Wrong, this is wrong. Very wrong.

She pulled back.

"Where are you going?" he asked, trying to follow her.

"We'd better get going. The time, and my meeting with the wedding planner."

He straightened, seeming confused. "Oh. Okay. All right." He looked…disappointed.

He wasn't the only one.

• • •

Good. Good. This is good. Hope was glad they were running uphill, because she needed to serve penance. *Ahhh.* What had she *done*? She'd kissed Brent—actually kissed him.

Not super deeply or anything, but still…she'd honestly wanted more.

How would she explain it to Jackie? Maybe she shouldn't; that would be the best thing. It might not go over so well with her dramatic sister that she'd begun falling for her fiancé.

Anyway, Jackie didn't need to be privy to every little detail. There were such things as TMI and oversharing.

"How much farther?" she pleaded, staying on Brent's heels as he scaled the mountainous terrain. He'd said this was a short run, but this last part had been practically a vertical climb.

"Almost there." He grinned over his shoulder. "I can't believe you never came here before when you lived in Blue Hill," he said, reaching the summit and extending a hand. "Let me help you up. You won't believe the view."

Hope let him tug her along, fighting the stitch in her side. She'd never been so out of breath. Her entire body would pay for this tomorrow. But then, she joined Brent on the flattop rock overlooking Blue Hill Bay, and she decided that the effort had been worth it.

"This is gorgeous," she breathed, seeing Acadia National Park and Mount Desert Island across the water.

"I'd hoped you'd like it." He smiled, his sunglasses glinting. "I was about to say 'selfie time,' but then I remembered about our phones."

She laughed, stunned to realize she'd actually been enjoying certain aspects of not having her cell phone. Like not being constantly reminded that Jackie was the one marrying Brent and that she was the imposter. "Yeah. About those?"

"We'll get them out of the safe as soon as we get back to the house. Though you've got to admit, it has been kind of nice not having all those interruptions." He tugged her up against him, and Hope pressed her fists against his chest.

"We really shouldn't—here."

Brent arched an eyebrow. "I wasn't about to suggest doing the naked mambo."

Heat seeped up her neck and into her cheeks.

"I was more hoping for a kiss." And he leaned in to do just that.

"Brent!" she cried suddenly.

"What?" he snapped, actually sounding agitated.

"Girl Scouts."

He stared at where she was pointing. A band of small girls in green uniforms and sashes headed their way, each one holding a walking stick.

"Great," Brent grumbled. He released her and looked out over the water. "Should be a great day for sailing. Nice for tea and croquet, too."

The Girl Scouts and their leaders hurried past them and onto a higher boulder for a better vantage point. After they did, Brent pushed his sunglasses on top of his head and surveyed Hope fully. "I get that you're nervous because things are changing so fast between us. But if there's something about me you don't like...that you're honestly not attracted to..."

She gripped his upper arms, and then she wished that she hadn't, as that only made her want to hold him closer. "It's not you—"

"It's me," he said, sardonically.

"I kissed you in the gazebo."

"Jackie," he said, setting his jaw. "Level with me. Because you're sending me really mixed signals... If you don't want to do this, then I'm good. I can take it if you're not as wild about me as I am about you."

Hope's spirits flagged. "That's not it," she whimpered. "I'm *totally* wild about you."

"Yeah?" he asked with a cockeyed grin.

"Yeah."

He searched her eyes. "Then what's the problem?"

"If I told you, you probably wouldn't believe me. What's more?" She lifted a shoulder. "You'd be mad."

"At you?" He appeared incredulous. "Doubtful." He held her tighter. "Try me?"

She pursed her lips. "What if I was...someone that I'm not?"

His forehead creased. "I'm not sure I follow?"

"The woman you got to know in Boston, Jackie Webb. She's the woman for you."

"It sounds a little weird referring to yourself in third person."

"Humor me."

"O-*kay*."

"I think it would be better if we could erase all this…everything that's happened these past few days."

He gave a worried frown. "And why would we do that? Jackie, listen." He pulled her closer, so close she could feel his heartbeat. "These past few days have been some of the best days of my life. And you know what I suspect?" He reached up and held her chin, diving into her eyes. "I suspect 'that woman in Boston' might not have been the right fit for me. But the woman I've gotten to know in Blue Hill is. Can't you see, baby? You don't have to pretend any longer."

"What?"

His hand slid into her hair. "It's you that I want—the real you."

"Me, me?" she asked on a breathy sigh.

"You, you." His mouth moved nearer, and her knees went weak.

"Tag! You're it!" A couple of Girl Scouts darted past them, chasing after a third one, and Hope nearly lost her footing.

"Whoa, there." Brent grabbed onto her elbows to steady her.

"Girls!" the scout leader warned testily. "I told you! No running!"

"That was close," Brent said, talking about Hope's near fall.

"Yeah, very," she said, meaning things in another way. This was so hard, and she was liking him so much. But he wasn't her fiancé; he was Jackie's.

"Hey." He placed his palm on her cheek and leaned toward her. "You okay?"

"Yeah, yeah. I think so." But honestly? In her heart she wasn't so sure.

· · ·

When Hope returned to the carriage house, it was after nine thirty. She and Brent had missed breakfast, and he'd had to dash off on his sailing trip, since he'd already been keeping the others waiting. At least she finally had her phone back. She needed to contact Jackie to fill her in on a few things.

Hope entered the kitchen just as her mom came in from the deck through the sliding glass doors. Ava was dressed prettily in a funky zebra-stripe-patterned jumpsuit with a huge crimson sash used as a belt. She wore chunky seashell earrings, a clamshell necklace, and strappy red sandals to complement the sash.

"Where on earth have you been?" she asked, noticing Hope's sweaty outfit. "It's nearly time for our meeting with the wedding planner. I was just heading over there now."

"I know, and I'm sorry. Brent and I went out for a run, but Eleanor hasn't arrived yet. I've just come back from the main house, and the downstairs was pretty empty."

"Have you heard from Jackie?"

Hope pressed a button on her phone, and a slew of texts appeared, a whole bunch of them talking about—Instagram? *What?*

"She wants me to take photos," Hope told her mom. "Document the meeting with the wedding planner."

"For the wedding album?"

"I think for social media," Hope said, continuing to flip through messages as she headed for her bedroom. "There's too much to read here." She glanced up at Ava. "I'll grab a quick shower and change and give Jackie a call before meeting you up at the house." She sent Ava a questioning look. "If I'm a few minutes late, do you think you can stall them?"

"Of course, hon. Of course."

Hope nodded in thanks.

When she turned away, Ava asked, "Are you feeling all right?"

Hope glanced back over her shoulder. "Yeah, why?"

Ava's eyes glimmered with intrigue. "Your aura's changing colors. Looks like it's turning pink." A smile crept onto her lips. "Are you sure *you're* not the one meant for Brent, and not Jackie?"

"Mom! How could you say that? Jackie will be here tomorrow! And, by that time, her aura will be even pinker than mine. Extra pink. Super-duper pink! Flamingo pink, probably."

Ava shared a doubtful look. "I suppose we'll see."

The moment her mom sashayed out the door,

Hope called Jackie. And, *ugh*. It went straight to voicemail. So, she decided to text her instead.

Scanned through your texts.
Will read in detail later.
Wedding planner meeting in a few.
Okay on insta. Username and password, please?
Can't wait to see you tomorrow.
Let me know when!

. . .

At a little past ten, Hope joined the others in the main house, where she found the meeting taking place in the dining room. She glanced around the table, apologizing for running behind schedule, encountering the one unfamiliar face.

"Jackie." A poised blonde wearing a business jacket with a fake gardenia pin on it held out her hand. "Nice to see you again."

Hope shook hands with her across the table. "Elaine."

"It's Eleanor." The wedding planner smiled tightly and glanced down at the tablet she'd brought along with her and which rested on the table. "I see we have both the moms." She perused Grandmother Margaret. "And the grandmother."

"It's Mrs. Albright, dear," Margaret said tersely, and Hope couldn't blame her. Eleanor didn't project the coziest vibe. In fact, she seemed a tad hostile. Hope was almost afraid to ask about taking snapshots, although she figured it would be safer to request permission.

"Oh, and you can call me Elsa."

"Ava," Hope's mom said, smiling slightly, but her smile didn't reach her eyes.

"Fine, thanks," Eleanor said, her gaze on her device. "First, let's start with the problems."

"Problems?" the rest of the women said together.

"Um…" Hope held up her hand. "Do you mind if I take some pictures?"

Eleanor screwed up her face. "Of the problems, you mean?"

"No. The meeting?"

Eleanor shook her head. "Shoot away," she answered, charging ahead with the details. "First we have the weather issue."

Hope peered out the window at the clear blue sky.

"Things are looking dicey toward the end of the week," Eleanor continued. "So, we should probably develop a backup plan for the ceremony."

"Weather, right." Hope tapped some notes into her phone and then snapped a pic of the group surrounding the table. Try as she might, she couldn't seem to catch Eleanor without wearing a scowl. Why was the woman so bitter? Wasn't wedding planning supposed to be fun?

"What about the back porch?" Margaret suggested. "It's nice and broad. Could probably accommodate thirty people. Especially if we moved furniture around and used the folding chairs."

"Good idea," Elsa agreed.

"It's a beautiful porch," Ava added. "Acoustics will carry very well from there."

Elsa appeared to appreciate this thought. "For the violinist, yes."

"I was actually thinking about—for me." Ava beamed around the table and then settled her gaze on Hope. "I'm afraid I let the cat out of the bag. Oopsies."

"Mo-om. I told you we'd think about it." Hope attempted to sound gratefully chipper but technically failed. "I haven't even mentioned the idea to Brent."

"It's just a little wedding tune," Ava told the others. "I've been practicing for weeks! Ever since I first heard about the wedding."

Hope decided to address this with her mom in private. This was tantamount to blackmail, and Ava knew it. Though Jackie honestly might not mind, it really needed to be her—and Brent's—decision.

"The porch could work." Eleanor nodded without looking up. "Assuming it's not windy."

Margaret frowned. "Oh dear. I didn't consider that."

"I thought the rain wasn't coming until Sunday?" Elsa leaned forward with the question, and Hope was glad somebody in the family had been watching the weather report. She would have typically checked it on her phone, and there was no television in the carriage house.

"These fronts can shift suddenly," Eleanor said, finally gracing them all with a look. "Especially this time of year. The forecast is looking dubious toward the end of the week. Anything could happen."

That's when Hope noticed something strikingly familiar about her. She'd seen those hazel eyes before, but they'd been shielded by heavy-framed glasses, and the teenager who wore them had light brown hair, not blond. Then, the realization clicked. "Lainie?" Hope asked uncertainly. "Lainie Fitch?"

Eleanor raised one pencil-thin eyebrow. "You can't say you didn't know until now."

"I, um…er. Sorry, no. I mean, yes, of course. It's just that you're very different." The Lainie Hope had known in high school had been extremely awkward and shy. She and Hope hadn't exactly been friends, but they'd been in a few classes together.

"You're not," she said pertly, and Hope felt the dig. That's when she remembered. Lainie'd had the most embarrassing "secret" crush on the president of the math club, but he'd had the unbearable hots for Jackie. While Hope had known Lainie a little and always been kind to her, very popular Jackie had likely never noticed her. They didn't share any classes and weren't exactly in the same social orbit. It was funny how they seemed to be now, with both of them becoming wedding planners. Although Hope imagined the schedule for coordinating nuptials in Blue Hill wasn't quite as demanding as setting them up in Boston, one never knew.

"Isn't this a small world?" Hope smiled around the table. "Lainie and I knew each other in high school."

"I knew who *you* were, anyway."

Lainie's tense smile caused Grandmother Margaret to bristle. "Weren't you the lucky one?"

Hope couldn't believe Margaret had rushed to her defense. At the same time, she couldn't make an enemy of the wedding planner. "We were both lucky," Hope rushed in, "to have gone to such a great school." She viewed Eleanor in what she hoped came off as an admiring fashion. "And look at you now, doing so well with your own business and everything."

"It's small but profitable." Eleanor nodded, and then she got back to business. "So, plan B is on the porch if it rains." She studied her tablet. "Worst-case scenario, we'll have to move everything indoors."

Elsa appeared worried. "That might be cramped, but it could work."

"Maybe we should have gotten that tent, dear," Margaret whispered into Hope's ear. "Do you think it's too late?"

"Is it?" she asked Eleanor, sure that Eleanor had overheard.

"There'll be an extra charge because this change is so last minute."

"Better safe than sorry," Ava said.

"Ava's right," Elsa agreed.

"All right," Eleanor said, speaking crisply. "I'll see to it." She studied her list. "The cake issue is next."

"What about it?" Hope asked.

"You wanted white chocolate whip, but the caterer says she can't make it."

Hope knew one thing. If Jackie had ordered a certain type of cake, she'd had hard evidence that sort could be made. Her whole life was wedding planning. "And why's that?"

"Because of the tiers," Eleanor explained. "The batter's too light to stand up to the weight. Only the top tier can be white chocolate. The others will have to be vanilla cake."

Hope didn't want to alter Jackie's wishes for her cake. White chocolate had always been her sister's favorite. She'd even asked for white chocolate Easter bunnies as a kid. "Well, maybe we should check out a different bakery?"

Eleanor blanched, aghast. "At this late date?"

"Or," Hope corrected quickly. "Maybe I could talk to the cake maker? See what accommodations she can make?"

"What about cupcakes?" Elsa suggested. "Those can be cute."

"Cupcakes for a wedding?" Margaret asked, appearing horrified.

"My niece had that done at her wedding," Ava informed the group. "They were set on a tiered stand and actually looked very nice."

Everyone's expectant eyes turned on Eleanor. "Cupcakes could work," she said, taking notes, and Hope panicked. Jackie had told her just to okay plans that were already set, not to change them.

"Wait. What about—"

"Do you have a better idea?" Eleanor asked.

"I, um…no." Hope wondered why Jackie had chosen Eleanor to coordinate her wedding. Then she recalled Jackie saying that Elsa recommended using the planner who'd handled William and Sofia's ceremony. Weddings by Eleanor Bell was also the only game in town.

"Okay, now." Eleanor heaved a breath. "About the flowers."

Hope massaged her forehead with her hand. Jackie had told her everything was all set. "What about them?" she asked, peering at Eleanor.

"We're going to have to make some changes there. The red roses you requested came in yellow."

"*Yellow?*" everyone asked at once.

"They're a very pretty yellow, though," Eleanor assured them. "It might already be too late to get in another shipment. The florist said she could try, but it will be down to the wire to secure the ninety dozen you requested."

"What?" Hope's jaw unhinged. "Ninety what?"

"Dozen." Eleanor eyed her evenly. "You were pretty insistent about that. One dozen for every day of your courtship with Brent."

"Oh, that's sweet!" Elsa said.

Hope quickly did the math, understanding that totaled over one thousand roses.

"Yellow can be good," Ava said.

Margaret backed her up. "It is summery. Nice for June."

"Is there no way to get them in red?" Hope asked. "Yellow is kind of a friendship flower." The others looked at her, and she continued. "Symbolizing, um, platonic love?"

"Then, what's the florist supposed to do with all the others?" Eleanor countered.

"Well, since it was the florist's mistake…"

"It wasn't her." Eleanor shook her head. "But her supplier."

"Oh."

"It's such a little detail," Ava whispered from Hope's other side. "Maybe just go with it."

"Fine, fine," Hope agreed, feeling like she was treading through heavy sludge. This was not going as she'd anticipated at all, and she was going to have a lot of explaining to do to Jackie.

"The caterer's good with the food order," Eleanor replied, finally delivering some positive news. "The tables, linens, and place settings are ready to go, too. The beverages and bartender have been confirmed, along with the officiant. That only leaves..." She flipped through her tablet. "The issue with the musician."

Hope's stomach clenched.

"She's not so sure she can play '*Eres Tú*'."

Hope's eyes widened in horror. Her mom had studied in Mexico in college, where she'd somehow heard the old seventies love song, which was an American pop classic, even though it was sung in Spanish. She'd wanted it sung at her own wedding, but her church's regulations hadn't allowed it. Hope and Jackie had grown up hearing their mom croon the old piece while badly mangling its high notes.

"I can't imagine how that got on the agenda," Hope said, glaring secretly at her mom. "We can just take it off."

"Oh, no." Ava raised her hands in protest. "Please, sweetheart, let's not."

"That's a beautiful song," Margaret said, as if recalling its high strains. "I haven't heard it in *decades*."

Shockingly, Ava took this as an invitation.

"*Como una promesa, eres tú, eres tú—*" she began singing, and Hope shouted.

"Mom!"

When everyone turned toward her, Hope softened her tone. "I mean, please. Stop." Then her forehead shot up as she scrutinized her mom. "You mean you got in touch with the violinist directly?"

"It's Nancy Carole," she explained. "She and I worked together as baristas in the old days. She was putting herself through music school then."

So her mom *had* gone behind Jackie's back. She'd essentially admitted as much.

"I certainly had nothing to do with this," Eleanor said sourly. "But, if you're insisting on this change, you might have to find another violinist."

"Well! She said it would be no problem." Ava shrugged, appearing haughty. "Maybe Nancy's not as talented as she thinks she is."

Hope couldn't wait for this meeting to end and the "fun" part of this day to get started. "No, no. We're good," Hope told Eleanor. "We can leave off '*Eres Tú*' and stick with the original plan."

"All right." Eleanor gave a few final staccato taps on her tablet. "Looks like we're all done. Thank you, ladies!" Then she stood with prompt efficiency and shook everyone's hands.

"I'll see you out," Margaret said, standing. Elsa decided to go with them, leaving Hope alone with Ava at the table.

"You and I are going to have to discuss the song thing," Hope said. "You know I said no promises."

But Ava's attention was still on the departing women and tightly focused on Eleanor. "I don't like her aura," she whispered with a grimace. "It's very brown."

CHAPTER TWELVE

Brent grabbed a line and helped Derrick hoist up the mainsail on his grandpa's forty-foot sailboat. His dad was at the tiller with Grandpa Chad seated beside him, and William scrambled around untying them from the dock. Within minutes, their sail caught the wind and they were moving away from the marina and into deeper water.

As much as Brent adored his baby sister, who was also an expert sailor, there was something special about being together with just the Albright men. He checked his watch, thinking of Jackie. Her meeting with the wedding planner should be done by now. Hopefully it had gone well.

The three brothers seated themselves on the bench on the starboard side of the ship as it listed port-ward, and they turned toward Long Island, one of the larger islands in the center of the bay. It was a gorgeous day, and the wind was just right.

"So, um," Derrick began from beside him. "This marriage came up awfully fast."

William leaned forward beyond him to address Brent. "But Jackie's awfully nice."

"Not saying she isn't," Derrick said. "I'm just asking…" He viewed Brent directly. "What's the big rush?"

"You married Olivia after six weeks," William replied.

"Yeah." Derrick shook his head. "And look

where that landed."

"I appreciate your concern, little brother," Brent said. "I really do. But Jackie and I are fine."

"So what?" Derrick persisted. "You didn't give her an engagement ring?"

"Of course I did. The one that belonged to Grandmother Margaret's mother."

"Yeah? Then where is it?"

William appeared interested in the answer to this question, too.

"She's getting it sized," he said, supplying the explanation Jackie had given him. "It was too loose, and she didn't want to risk losing it."

"It's a shame you two couldn't get that done before the wedding."

"Yeah, well. I didn't know it was a problem until recently." Brent flipped down his sunglasses when the sun glinted against the boat. "And anyway, it's not the engagement ring that matters for the ceremony. It's the wedding bands."

"You have them?" William asked.

Brent chuckled. "Tucked away for safekeeping, yep."

"Coming about!" their dad shouted. The captain and the men ducked under the swinging boom holding the mainsail as it swerved abruptly in the opposite direction, turning the boat the other way. Then, they were seated on the port side, the wind and the current tugging their vessel along as they sailed parallel to the land.

"Jackie's much more than meets the eye," Brent told his brothers when they were newly settled. "She's more than pretty. She's accomplished and smart. Sweet and thoughtful, too."

"I'll second that last part." William tugged on the bill of his hat. "She seems awfully sweet, I mean. Sofia took right to her, and Sofia's always been a great judge of character." He grinned broadly, patently alluding to himself. "Case in point."

Brent and Derrick guffawed.

"Yeah, yeah. Sure," they both said. Then the wind kicked up, its blustery chorus punctuating their happy banter.

• • •

After Eleanor left, Hope made up an excuse about being tired so she could go back to the carriage house and take a nap. Not that it was a lie. She fell into an exhausted sleep, dozing for more than two hours and completely missing lunch in the main house. She awoke feeling refreshed—and to a mild bubbling sound, drifting into the cottage through the screen door to the deck.

Hope found her mom soaking in the hot tub outside while applying a "Mother of Earth Mud Mask." It had mostly dried on her face, causing deep grooves and wrinkles where the mud had cracked.

Ava heard her approach and looked up from the paperback novel she was reading. "Oh, hi. How was the nap?"

"Really great, thanks." Hope took a sip of the coffee she'd brought out with her. Since she'd missed the midday meal, she'd snacked on some more of that delicious banana bread and had also indulged in a few of those yummy cookies. At least nobody was watching her carb intake at the carriage house.

Her mom sat up and set down her book on the folded hot tub cover, which had been slid back on brackets. Warm steam rose up around her as perfuming bubbles percolated nearby. Although she was in her fifties, Ava still had the figure of a thirty-year-old and wore a tiny red bikini.

She claimed she maintained her body through hard work, low carbs, and a StairMaster. Which Hope found admirable. Though she wasn't about to forgo chocolate and bread herself, she gave her mom credit for the amazing discipline she exhibited in at least one area of her life. In that way, she was a lot like Jackie.

"Did you reach your sister?"

"Not yet. I texted her but haven't heard back. I'll try again later."

"The sooner she gets here the better, in my opinion." She shot Hope a knowing look. "For all parties concerned."

Hope slid her phone out of her pocket, checking it again for any missed messages or calls. But there was nothing from Jackie, probably because she was busy wrapping up that Martin wedding and preparing to finally attend a wedding week of her own.

Ava sighed dreamily and ducked down lower in the water so it covered her shoulders. "*This* is the life. If I'd experienced this side of Blue Hill before, I never would have left it."

"Ha ha." Hope took a seat on a lounge chair on the deck, gazing out over the water. A large sailboat was trolling along, and she counted five men on board. A couple of them—a guy wearing a fishing hat and another in a baseball cap—waved their arms while shouting hello. A third man wearing sunglasses gave a slow wave, his smile sparkling, and her heart skipped a beat. She'd know that grin anywhere.

"Look," she said, standing. "That's Brent."

"What? Where?" Ava glanced frantically around, partially blocking her face with upturned hands.

Hope bounced on her feet. "Not here. There." She held up her phone, recalling Jackie's instructions to capture as much of the activity as possible on Instagram. What a stellar update this would be.

She otherwise wouldn't have been able to provide a glimpse of Brent's sailing trip, but now she could add this fun tidbit to Jackie's Instagram story. She loaded the Insta app and pressed the camera icon.

Wait. That's my face. Argh.

She angled her phone toward the water and began filming a video of the big boat sailing past. Afterwards, she'd post it to Jackie's story.

This was going to be so cool.

Brent spotted her on the deck and waved. With her free hand, Hope waved back. Then Brent surprised her and made an elaborate show of blowing her a dramatic kiss.

"Now that's smitten," Ava commented from beside her.

Heat warmed Hope's face as she tried to end the recording.

Wait. What? Noooo. Where did it go-oh-oh?

She fiddled with her phone, hoping it hadn't uploaded.

Ack, no. She'd just pressed "send to story." She had to take it down.

Unfortunately, Hope wasn't really great with Instagram.

She opened her Internet browser and ran a frantic search.

"What are you doing?"

"Just Googling something," Hope said, only briefly looking up. Gratefully, she found instructions on deleting the story seconds later. Whew. That had been close. If Jackie'd seen that, what might she have thought? That Brent was smitten, probably. Just like Ava said.

Her mom studied her a moment. "How do you intend to explain all this to Jackie?"

"I don't," Hope said with a relieved sigh. "I already deleted the upload."

"You uploaded that? To where?"

"Insta."

"You kids with your social media. Not everything has to be recorded in real time, you know."

"Tell that to Jackie, the wedding planner," Hope said. "She records tidbits from every wedding she coordinates, apparently. Unofficial glimpses into the prep. That's all before posting a few formal photos at the end."

"Hmm." Ava sank down in the water, letting the bubbles cover her shoulders. "It would be kind of fun to have an Insta post of me singing '*Eres Tú*.'"

"Mom. *Really.*"

"All right, okay." Ava scooted back up onto the hot tub bench once she'd checked to make sure there were no more sailboats carrying handsome young men drifting past.

Hope sat back in the lounge chair, attempting to couch things more tenderly. "Don't misunderstand. I'm sure that Jackie would be touched. But, the truth is, none of that's been settled yet. You know as well as I do that I only promised to put in a good word, not that it was a done deal, like you seemed to indicate during our meeting with Eleanor. Besides that, as far as I know, Brent doesn't even speak Spanish."

"There's an English translation."

"Mom."

"Perhaps something different, then?"

Hope lowered her eyebrows.

Ava huffed out a small breath and examined her nails, extending her hands above the gurgling water. "Maybe you're right. Maybe during the ceremony is not the most appropriate time." She looked up with a hopeful stare. "How about at the reception?"

"This isn't like Debbie's wedding," Hope reminded her. "With a hundred and fifty guests. This is a small, intimate wedding, Mom. A family-only thing."

"*I'm* family," Ava said, the hurt in her voice coming through.

Hope's heart softened toward her mom. As complex as she was, Ava truly only meant well. "Of course you are," she said. "And I'd kiss you if you weren't covered in dried mud."

"Yikes. I'd better wash this off. What time is it?"

"Three o'clock. Almost time for our tea party."

"Then I'd better get ready." Before she climbed from the water, Ava surprised Hope with an earnest question. "Do you think it's too late?"

"Too late for what?"

Ava appeared uncharacteristically timid. "For me to find what you have…" Her gaze drifted toward Blue Hill Bay. "With Brent? Or whatever it is he thinks he has with Jackie?"

Every time her mom hinted that Brent was falling for her instead of her twin, Hope felt worse. But also, twistedly, in a certain sense, better. Because, despite her best efforts not to, she found herself falling for him.

"I don't think it can ever really be too late. Do you?"

"I suppose not," she said, sounding resigned. "I had that once, you know. With your dad."

"Yeah?"

"It wasn't for very long, but—while it lasted—it was pretty awesome."

"I'm sorry, Mom. Sorry that all went away."

"I'm not." Her eyes shone warmly beneath that earth-caked mask. "Not sorry for any of it. And you want to know why?"

Hope waited.

"Because I got something wonderful out of it. Two somethings wonderful. You and your sister."

• • •

Afternoon teatime was much more fun than the meeting with Eleanor, owing in part to the fact that Grandmother Margaret served chilled glasses of sherry before the tea. She'd had tiny finger sandwiches and a variety of puff pastries and petit fours brought in as well.

A gorgeous spread had been laid out on the dining room sideboard and table, and everyone had filled small plates with goodies and carried those, along with their sherry glasses, onto the back lawn, where a croquet course had been established.

Only Sofia wasn't drinking, but nobody but Hope seemed to notice her slipping into the kitchen to fill her sherry glass with ginger ale instead of the alcoholic libation.

They divided into two teams, with Margaret, Hope, and Sofia playing on one side and Elsa, Sally, and Ava playing on the other. The midafternoon weather was absolutely perfect and sunny, with a warm breeze blowing off the water, causing everyone to hang on to their hats.

At Margaret's insistence, they'd all worn dresses and "bonnets" as she called them, and she kept a neat selection of them in her ample walk-in closet upstairs. When they'd convened for their tea party, she'd invited the other women to join her upstairs in her master suite so they could select a whimsical hat to wear. Hope was sorry that Jackie was missing this.

Grandmother Margaret smacked a ball with her mallet, ramming it through a tunnel of wire horseshoe-shaped hoops.

"Nice shot, Grandmother!" Sally cried, and the others all agreed. She turned to Hope with a sunny grin. "I saw the pic of the meeting with the wedding planner you put up on Instagram. How did everything go?"

"Oh, uh…really good. There are a few little hiccups, but nothing we can't work out."

"I think it's great that you're posting updates."

"Yes," Ava said. "She even got a video of the men out sailing earlier."

"Well, that's fun," Sally answered just as Hope gave Ava the side-eye.

"I know," Sofia said. "Why don't you get a pic of all of us wearing our hats?"

Margaret nodded happily. "That's a delightful idea. Here, hand me your phone. I'll get the rest of you, and then we can switch."

Hope's heart pounded. *No.* No, no, no. No. She could *not* give her phone to Grandmother Margaret—or anyone else, really. What if her contact list accidentally popped up with Jackie on it?

Sofia's face lit up. "Why don't we set it on a timer so we can all get in the photo?"

"Even better," Sally said with a grin.

"Great idea," Hope chimed in, flush with relief.

After some discussion, the group decided to prop the phone on the stone ledge of the firepit, securing it against a spare brick. Then they backed away and set up the shot with all of them kneeling or crouching down against the backdrop of the crystal-clear water.

"Okay, here we go. Ten seconds." Hope tripped the start button once the others were all in place, then raced back to scoot in among them. This was a cool idea and way more harmless than that stupid story she'd accidentally uploaded.

"Say cheese, everyone!" Sally called out.

"How about cheers?" Margaret quipped, and they all giggled just as the pic snapped. Seconds later, the phone buzzed and shook.

Hope lunged for it, worried it was going to fall

into the firepit.

But Sally got there first, staring down at its face with a puzzled frown. "Incoming call." She looked up. "But that's weird. Why does it say Jackie?"

Hope froze, momentarily paralyzed. Next, she tugged away her phone, wondering if she wouldn't have been better off leaving it in the safe. "It's, uh…"

Ava burst out laughing in the worst display of stage laughter Hope had ever seen. "Sometimes my girls do that. Call each other by the other's name." She giggled and sipped from her sherry. "Hope and Jackie can be very…" All eyes turned on her, and Ava appeared caught out. Still, she managed to pull things off with a dramatic wave of her hand. "… goofy that way."

"It's true. We are," Hope agreed hastily. "Super goofy. I'm sorry, all," she said, glancing around. "But Hope and I *don't really* go around switching names. This is my friend, Jackie. You remember, Mom?" She sent Ava a pointed look. "The one from college?"

"Oh yes. Right. Her." Ava took another swig of sherry. "You roomed together sophomore year. It was always so confusing."

Hope grimaced at the others and hustled toward the house as her phone continued to buzz, indicating an incoming call. "Anyway, I'll just tell her that now's not a good time."

"Maybe you should check on Hope?" Margaret suggested.

"Great idea," Hope said. "I'll do that, too."

As she departed, she heard Sofia say, "I need to run indoors. Can I get anyone anything?"

"I'll take a tad more sherry," Ava said.

"Yes," Margaret nodded, lining up another shot. "I'll take a touch more, too."

"Might as well bring the bottle," Sally said with a laugh.

As Hope neared the house, Sofia sidled up beside her, appearing worn. Hope's phone had finally stopped buzzing, but she intended to call Jackie back—the moment she could find a private place. "Are you okay?" she asked, worried that Sofia looked tired.

"Oh yeah, the fatigue is normal." Sofia smiled softly. "Normal is good. I just needed to get out of the sun for a few minutes and grab some more mineral water." Before they entered the den, Sofia studied Hope. "Thank you for what you said last night. I told William."

"I figured you had."

"He's so happy."

"Aww."

"We're both cautiously optimistic."

"That's wonderful, Sofia," she said, giving her shoulders an impromptu hug. "I'll hold good thoughts for all of you."

Sofia hugged Hope back. "Thanks, Jackie."

. . .

As Sofia disappeared into the kitchen, Hope cased the bottom floor for a secretive spot. Then, she spied the coat closet tucked under the stairs in the downstairs hall and decided that location was perfect. Nobody would think to look for her there. She called her sister and stepped inside it, lightly tugging the door shut as she nestled into the dark, cavernous space.

"Hope? Is that you?"

"*Jackie*," Hope whispered hoarsely. "What are you doing calling? I was supposed to get back in touch with you."

"You said you needed to talk."

"Yes, but I was going to call when I was free."

"So, what's going on now?"

"The tea party. You know the schedule."

"Yeah, right. So, what about the boat thing? What was that all about?"

Oh, no. Hope winced. "Boat…thing?"

"The story you uploaded, Hope."

"You saw that?" Hope asked, wanting to sink into the floorboards.

"And what was Brent doing?"

"Sailing."

"I mean, why was he blowing you a kiss?"

"I, er…it wasn't me he was blowing the kiss to."

"What?"

"It was his grandmother."

"Grandmother Margaret?" Jackie sounded befuddled. "But why?"

"She was standing right behind me on the deck," Hope improvised. "While I was filming, I mean. She waved to Brent, and he—"

"That's a little weird," Jackie said, sounding miffed. "I mean, I know he loves his grandmother and all, but still."

"I agree, which is why I deleted it. After I thought about it, I decided it looked…wrong."

"Okay, well. Whatever. Don't forget to capture

the other moments. I saw the one with Eleanor. Could you please try to get her to smile next time?"

"I'll, uh…try?" She drew in a breath. "When are you getting here tomorrow?"

"Uh, about that—"

A wave of dread crashed down on her. "Jackie, no."

"Hopie," she said, and Hope's heart thundered. "You don't understand. This wedding is a nightmare. Now the venue's pulled the plug."

"*What?*"

"The club where we were supposed to hold the reception has made an accommodation for a senior member, meaning the Martin party has been booted out."

"Wait a minute. Can they do that?"

"I guess they can do anything they want. It's the club owner's grandson who's graduating from high school. They're throwing some kind of huge family party."

There was a commotion in the den. The rest of the women had come back in the house.

Jackie was still babbling on about venues and rescheduling.

Hope rubbed her temple. "You can't possibly be saying you're delaying again?"

"I wouldn't if this weren't necessary."

"Necessary? What about *your* wedding?"

"I'll be there. I swear."

"Jackie," Hope said in low tones. "You can't keep putting me in this position. It's…difficult."

"Well, okay. I know. I'm sorry. But, at this point in time, what do you propose we do? Call the whole charade off?"

She thought of how Brent's family had come to trust her, and her heart ached. Margaret and Sofia had confided personal details about their lives, and even Elsa had let her in on her non-baking secret. When she thought of her growing attraction to Brent, Hope's heart nearly split open.

She couldn't possibly let all of them down and cause a big blowup days before the wedding. Jackie would be here soon enough, anyway. But would it be soon enough to keep Hope from falling harder for Brent and his wonderful family? She just didn't know.

"No. I don't think we should do that," Hope told her sister. "It's already too late."

"Okay, great. I think I can have everything settled by Friday."

"Friday? Are you joking?"

"I've already bought my ticket. I'll fly direct from Nantucket to Boston and pick up my rental car there."

"What time on Friday? Because there's a lot to fill you in on. I mean, seriously. A ton. Brent's not the guy you thought he was."

"What do you mean by that?"

"He's really trying, Jackie. Trying to be a good groom, despite this *marriage of convenience* you stupidly agreed to," she added with a hiss. She couldn't help but be irritated. She'd been doing her best to keep up this pretense without losing her heart to her sister's fiancé, but each day that passed, the situation grew harder.

Jackie gasped. "Marriage of convenience? Who

told you that?"

"Brent did."

"He admitted it? Outright?"

Hope wrapped a lock of her hair around her finger, feeling both sorry for—and annoyed with—her sister. "Why wouldn't he? He thinks I'm you."

"Oh yeah. Right. I kind of didn't want you to know that."

"So why did you do it, Jackie?" Hope sighed with frustration. "Why did you agree to this in the first place?"

"There were lots of reasons. Loads and loads, okay?"

"Like what?"

"Like… Hang on, Rachel has a question. *No*," Hope heard Jackie tell her assistant. "*Not the cream-colored ones. Dusty rose.*"

Hope rolled her eyes at the distraction, then snapped at Jackie, agitated. "Can you pu-leeze focus on your wedding for one fraction of a second?"

"I will. I promise. From the moment I get there."

"On Friday?" Hope asked wearily.

"Yes."

"You never answered my question. About your engagement."

There was a long pause on the line, then Jackie sniffled. "All right, it was Rodney."

"Rodney Campbell?" Hope asked, astounded. "Your ex? What has he got to do with anything?"

"Shortly before Brent proposed, I learned Rodney was getting married—to Elizabeth Yates, of all people."

"Who's she?"

"His former wife."

"I didn't even know that Rodney had one."

"I didn't, either." Jackie broke into sobs. "But he said he'd never really gotten over her and had never actually loved me."

Hope's heart sank for her sister. "Ouch. Jackie, that's terrible. You never told me."

"Of course I didn't tell you. I didn't have to because Brent proposed a few months later, and I thought, well, at least he's never been married before and comes from a good family. I mean…" She paused with hesitation in her voice. "They are okay, aren't they?"

"They're actually pretty wonderful."

"Okay, then. Please, pretty please help this go off."

"I don't know how much longer I can keep this up, Jackie. It's not only his family that's wonderful. Brent's pretty amazing, too."

"Uh-oh," Jackie said. "You aren't actually falling for him?"

"No. No, I didn't say that."

"Because, Hopie, I mean, really. You can't do that. Brent and I made this deal. He needs me, and I need him." She thought on this a moment. "Business-wise."

"So that's what this is all about?"

"I'm sure the love part will come along in time."

Hope was more confused than ever. When Jackie pointed things out in black and white, it was pretty plain that she and Brent had gone into this arrangement with similar expectations. Neither one seemed to have given a thought to finding real love.

"Maybe you and Brent are more alike than I believed."

"What's that supposed to mean?"

Then again, Brent seemed different now. He'd come around and was really trying to build a relationship with Jackie. Or with Hope *as* Jackie. It was impossible to know if he would have tried nearly as hard if the real Jackie had been here, instead of Hope acting in her place. Hope tried to sort things out, but she was a jumble of emotions. Nothing really made sense anymore. She just wanted the pretending to end.

"It means you need to hurry up and get to Blue Hill," she told her sister. "Whatever kind of arrangement you think you and Brent made—it appears the dynamics are changing."

"Well, don't let them change too much," Jackie warned her. "Just try to keep things steady until I arrive."

"That won't be easy—not with Meredith coming this afternoon."

"Don't worry about Meredith. I spoke with her, and she'll be fine."

"Mom knows."

"What?"

"But she's cool for now. She's promised not to tell."

"How on earth did you work that?"

"I'll tell you when you get here."

"Okay. I've got things all set. I should get to Blue Hill by around four in the afternoon."

"Be sure you get an economy hatchback like the one I reserved."

"No problem."

"And don't forget about the hair."

"Already cut it."

Hope bumped into a man's overcoat and pushed it aside. "So, what am I supposed to tell everyone?"

"I thought you already said that I was sick?"

"I also said you were doing better."

"Well then, say I've had a relapse."

Hope sighed.

"The wedding dress will be there tomorrow," Jackie informed her. "It's being delivered by special courier. Please check to make sure everything looks okay. The shoes, veil, and accessories are coming with it. And take photos. For Insta."

"All right."

"Actually, I can't wait to see them, too."

CHAPTER THIRTEEN

Brent rode back to his grandparents' place with Derrick in Derrick's SUV, with William driving ahead of them, chauffeuring Grandpa Chad and Parker. What a great moment that had been when they sailed past the carriage house. Jackie had been on the deck, and he'd happened to spot her. She looked adorable standing there, filming him on her phone, so he'd snapped a pic of her, which he'd sent her, along with a few others he'd taken on the boat. She hadn't responded yet, but maybe she hadn't seen his text.

He'd felt bad about becoming grumpy during their run this morning. Jackie had never been into public displays of affection, but seriously. It wasn't like the two of them were preteens. They were adults and getting married.

His thoughts drifted away to the honeymoon and an image of them walking hand in hand down the shore, with him in his swim trunks and her in her very tiny bikini. They could swim and play in the water, then come back for a nice lazy nap at their beachside bungalow in the afternoon. Brent found himself looking forward to that "nap" and spending time with his new bride. When there was nobody else around to distract—or disrupt—them.

Tires squealed, and Derrick's vehicle fishtailed sideways as a hard-hitting object rammed into them from behind. Derrick cursed and gripped the wheel, glaring back over his shoulder.

"What on earth?"

Brent spun in his seat to spy a dark blue European sports coupe with a bent grill and sagging front bumper. A dark-haired woman climbed from its driver seat, looking possessed. She stomped up to Derrick's driver's side window in precipitous heels, a fitted sweater top, and a very short skirt. Derrick rolled down his window.

"Excuse me," she said without preamble. "You just ruined my car."

Derrick sputtered a laugh. "I—what? You must be joking."

Her dark eyes narrowed, and her nostrils flared. Meredith Galanes. Brent had only met the woman once, and she was seriously wound tight. Very nice-looking, though, with her olive skin and long, springy curls spilling past her shoulders.

His brother ran a hand through his hair and glanced at Brent, as if to say *can you believe her?*

Derrick leaned into his steering wheel and peered out the window behind them. "I'm guessing you did some damage, too."

"Me? To you?" she asked, clearly astounded. She set one hand on her ample hip, accentuating her curvy figure. "It was totally your fault. You stopped on a dime."

"Sure. When you hit me."

"I hit you because you stopped."

Meredith ducked her chin to peek into the car, and she spotted Brent in the passenger's seat. "Oh, hi there. Happy wedding." She returned her attention to Derrick, apparently waiting on him to say something. Probably apologize, which—knowing Derrick—he wasn't about to do.

Brent noted that William had stopped up ahead of them, and now he, Parker, and Grandpa Chad had stepped from the car, curious to see what was going on.

"Uh oh," William said, walking toward them. "Looks like someone had a little fender-bender." He glanced at Meredith's car and then at her. "Ugh, that's too bad. That's this year's model, isn't it?"

Derrick shot William a disgruntled stare.

"You must be Meredith," Parker said, extending his hand. "Sorry about the unfortunate circumstances."

"Thanks. Nice to meet you," she said before sending Derrick a look that telegraphed *at least someone's apologizing*.

Derrick swung his door open so abruptly he nearly smacked Meredith's bare legs. Or perhaps that was his intention. He climbed from his seat and ambled to the back of his SUV. "Aha. Just as I suspected… There's a great big dent—right there."

"Derrick." Parker shook his head in disappointment at his youngest son's ill manners. "Let's just leave this for now."

"Leave it?" Meredith asked with alarm. "But what about my—"

"I'll pay for any repairs," Grandpa Chad said. "The accident happened on my property, after all. Meredith," he said. "Welcome." He gave her a sympathetic nod and shook her hand. "The curve in this drive can get rather tricky at times."

"Why, thank you," she said, seemingly avoiding

Derrick's prickly gaze.

"I'm William," their brother said, greeting her. "Brent's older brother, and that guy over there…" He motioned with his chin. "Is Derrick."

Derrick worked hard not to scowl. "Hello."

Meredith rolled her eyes. "We've met."

"It's more like we collided," he said testily. "When you rear-ended me."

"Oh, I…?" Meredith fumed. "Don't think so."

"Why don't we all go on up to the house?" Parker suggested. "I know Jackie and the others will be excited to see you."

. . .

Hope heard a weird screeching sound, like metal scraping against the drive, and she walked around the side of the house to see the men had returned from their sailing trip—and brought a wreck of a vehicle with them. A short, pretty brunette stepped from the damaged car, her gaze settling on Hope. "Jackie!" she cried, rushing forward.

"Meredith," Hope returned, wagering her guess had to be right. The women rushed toward each other and embraced. Then Meredith tugged at the floppy sides of Hope's garden hat. "Cute look. Where did you get it?"

"It's on loan from Grandmother Margaret."

"Hel-lo," the woman in question called, heading their way.

"Hi-ya," Ava rejoined. Sofia came next, accompanied by Sally.

Before they got too close, Meredith latched onto

Hope's shoulders and tugged her closer. "Just for the record," she whispered, "I don't agree with this one bit. Thank goodness it's just until tomorrow."

Which meant she hadn't gotten the latest update.

"Meredith," Grandmother Margaret crooned. "We're so glad you made it. Welcome to Blue Hill."

"I can't believe we've never met," Ava gushed. "All Jackie does is talk about you."

"I'm Sally." She shook Meredith's hand.

Sofia introduced herself as well, and then Grandmother Margaret said, "You might want to take your luggage down to the carriage house and settle in." She saw Derrick striding toward the back porch and caught him.

"Derrick. Be a dear and grab Meredith's bags from her car?"

He stared at his grandmother for a prolonged beat, then gave a tight grin. "Glad to," he said, shoving his hands in his pockets and striding toward Meredith's car.

"What's up with him?" Sally asked no one in particular.

"Maybe rough seas?"

The group of women turned and stared out at the peaceful water.

"Beautiful place," Meredith said to Margaret. "You can't beat the view."

The trunk of her car closed with a loud bang.

Sofia giggled. "Or the peace and quiet."

Grandmother Margaret arched her eyebrows, her gaze trailing after Derrick. "Yes."

All eyes turned expectantly on Hope, and she realized she should offer to accompany Meredith.

"Come on," she said brightly. "I'll show you where you're staying."

As they headed toward the carriage house, Derrick sauntered ahead of them, carrying two huge suitcases, with smaller tote bags and a daypack tucked under his arms.

Brent rounded the corner from the drive, accompanied by William.

"Hello, sweetness," he said, beaming down at Hope in her bonnet. "You look awfully cute in that."

Heat warmed her cheeks. "How was the sailing?"

"Awesome. Did you ladies have a nice tea party?"

"The best."

Brent gazed down the path at Derrick, who was struggling to open the screen door and hold on to Meredith's many bags. "Looks like somebody better go and help him."

Brent angled that way, but Hope stepped in front of him. "It's all right. I'll get it."

She dashed down the path and held the front door open for Derrick as Meredith took her time teetering down the flagstone path in her heels.

"Where would you like these?" Derrick asked once Meredith finally made her way indoors.

She glanced around the charming cottage and then at Hope.

"Can you please put those in the room downstairs?" Hope suggested. "Thanks, Derrick."

Derrick thumped down the wooden steps. A few seconds later, they heard the heavy thud of bags hitting the floor. A sliding door slid open and then shut with a *clank*, and Hope surmised he had departed via the deck.

She pursed her lips. "Hmm. He's normally not like that."

Meredith narrowed her gaze and studied Hope anew. "I can't believe you and your sister," she rasped. "How did you get yourselves into this?"

"It was all this really huge mix-up."

"That's what I heard from Jackie. But, seriously, Hope. You mean to tell me all of them believe it?" She gestured toward the main house. "Even the groom?"

Hope's face steamed. "*Especially* the groom, I'm afraid."

Meredith cocked her chin. "Uh-oh. He's not…? *You're* not…?"

"I've just been trying to hold down the fort, okay? I never meant for any of this to happen. I swear, Meredith, I didn't. In fact, when Jackie suggested it, I told her I wouldn't do it. Flat-out refused."

Meredith screwed up her lips. "Of course it was Jackie's idea. I love that woman to death, but she does get those wild card ideas." Her eyes widened at Hope. "Like marrying some guy she doesn't even love."

"I know," Hope said, sensing she was building an ally. "That's totally wrong, right?"

"Totally wrong," Meredith agreed. "I can't even see how she agreed to it."

"Do you know about Rodney?"

Meredith frowned. "Rodney-Schmodney, yeah. He is so totally not worth this kind of revenge."

"It's not just about Jackie," Hope said. "It's also

about Brent and his family."

"They seem very nice," Meredith said. "All but one of them, anyway."

"Derrick's fine," Hope assured her. "I'm not sure what his problem was earlier."

"O-kay."

Hope observed Meredith, her heart hammering. "There's something you don't know."

"What's that?"

"Jackie's not coming until Friday now."

"Friday? *What?*"

"It's the Martin wedding."

Meredith crossed her arms in front of her and began pacing the floor. After a beat, she met Hope's gaze. "Nuh-uh. I don't think that's what this is about."

"But the venue's been blown. Jackie just told me this after—"

"It's all a smoke screen." Meredith's dark eyes flashed. "Jackie's getting cold feet."

This was one thing that hadn't actually occurred to Hope before. Now, she wondered if Meredith wasn't making some kind of sense. "You mean, you think she's having doubts?"

"Jackie is a wedding planner, Hope. She arranges matches made in heaven all the time. Don't you think it might start to bother her after a while that her very own marriage is a sham?"

"I...um, maybe?"

Meredith tapped her chin. "I mean, I knew something was going on when Jackie got engaged so quickly, but she didn't spill all the beans until I was about to come here."

"That was a big can of beans."

"Yeah," Meredith agreed. "The hugest."

Both women sighed.

"Have you thought about telling them the truth?" Meredith asked. "The Albrights and Brent?"

"Thought about? Sure. Dozens of times. But the right moment's never exactly been there, and then there's Brent... He's so..." Hope shrugged, a helpless mix of emotions. "Just everything."

"Uh-oh. Oh, no. You've *fallen* for him?"

"No. Not totally. I've been...reining myself in. But, Meredith, listen. It hasn't been easy. Once he realized how upset I was about the marriage-of-convenience thing—"

"Wait a minute. How did he learn that?"

"We had this talk," Hope explained. "Shortly after I got here and after everyone had mistaken me for Jackie."

"Including Brent."

"Yes."

"So, go on. You had this talk..."

"Yeah, and it sort of spilled out of him about how this whole marriage was some kind of business deal. I was literally shocked and hurt, on Jackie's behalf, and I guess I didn't hide it."

Meredith's swift mind put things together. "So, Brent thought you were upset—as Jackie."

"Exactly. And after that? He seemed to change. I mean, really, really change. Not that I knew him before. But, based on what I learned about his relationship with Jackie, this became all new territory for Brent. He decided to try to do better, I guess."

"That's sweet," Meredith said. Then she frowned. "And a little sick, I suppose. Since he's trying to do better with you and not your sister."

"I know," Hope agreed. "It's horribly messed up."

"Okay," Meredith said, holding up her hands. "Here's what we're going to do. Preserve our loyalty to Jackie while trying to figure this whole thing out."

"Keep pretending, you mean?"

"Yeah, keep pretending. I mean, what else are we supposed to do? I've only just gotten here, Hope. I don't even have the lay of the land. Maybe once I do, I'll come up with a bright idea."

"That would be amazing. Thanks."

"You don't need to thank me," she said. "I'll probably need to have my head examined for this." She cagily surveyed Hope. "Who else knows. Anybody?"

"Just my mom, but she's promised to be cool."

"What a mess."

"You're telling me."

"Don't worry," Meredith said. "We'll get through this. It's just until Friday, and—in the meantime—maybe we'll figure something out."

• • •

At dinner that night, Brent kept trying to hold Hope's hand under the table. Finally, she just let him because it was becoming too awkward trying not to. Plus, people were starting to notice.

"You never answered my text," he said while the others were engaged in conversation.

"What?" she asked, feeling lost.

"I sent you some pics. From the boat?"

She bit her lip, panic seizing her, before she coolly worked her way out of it. "Ah yeah, those were awesome. Thanks!"

"How did things go with the wedding planner?" Parker asked from the head of the table. Hope was grateful for his interruption. She'd obviously messed up by not thinking Brent might try to text her. Then, there was that little business about her sister's mysterious recurring illness that she'd had to explain to the group. This was turning out to be a pretty unappetizing dinner, though the food itself was really good.

"Oh, fine," Elsa said.

Ava and Margaret echoed her sentiment. "Just fine."

"There were only a few little snags," Hope said, sipping from her wine.

"What kind of snags?" Worry creased Meredith's brow. Fortunately, she was seated at the opposite end of the table from Derrick, which was honestly to everyone's benefit. The tension between them was palpable.

"We had to make a few last minute modifications," Hope explained. "But everything will work out okay."

"Whatever you decided is okay by me," Brent said good-naturedly. "After all, you're the expert."

"She is an expert," Meredith agreed proudly. "And so great at what she does."

"Brent tells us you're a relationship adviser?" Parker inquired of Meredith.

"Professional matchmaker."

Derrick's eyebrows arched. "You mean that's a real job?"

"Derrick," Elsa admonished quietly.

"And what is it you do?" Meredith didn't quite mask the combativeness in her tone.

"I'm a boatbuilder."

Her eyes widened in feigned interest. "Ooh, you mean the 'boat in a bottle' kind?"

Derrick set his napkin down on the table. "Anybody else need more water?" he asked, standing.

"I'll take a little," Grandpa Chad said, holding up his glass.

After Derrick departed, Meredith glanced around and said sincerely, "I hope I didn't offend him. I honestly didn't know what kind of boatbuilder he meant."

William stroked his chin to disguise his smile, and Brent pursed his lips against a grin. If anyone was going to get the best of Meredith Galanes by insinuating she didn't have a real job, it wasn't going to be Derrick Albright. That writing was on the wall.

"It's all right, dear," Grandmother Margaret said. "We're sure you meant well."

"Who's ready for dessert?"' Sally asked suddenly.

"I am," Sofia said, easing out of her chair. "I'll come and help you serve it."

· · ·

As folks were clearing the table, Brent tugged Hope into the den by latching on to her hand. "Come here, you," he said. "We haven't had a moment alone all day."

"That's not true. We had our run." Her heart

hammered when she saw the predatory look in his eyes. The sad thing was, it made her spirit soar and her pulse pound harder, because all she could think of was being alone with Brent, too.

Brent pulled her closer, tugging her into the hall. "I would hardly call that private." He stroked her heart pendant with his free hand. "I'm glad you told me about this. It's so special."

Hope gazed up into his heady, dark eyes, and all reason went out the window. "Thanks," she said a bit too breathlessly. "So are you."

He gave her a lopsided grin, and her heart skipped a beat. Then she saw his hand on the door to the coat closet under the stairs.

"Brent?" she asked in low tones. "Wha-what are you doing?"

He held a finger to his lips and cracked open the door. In one smooth move, he pulled her toward him and into the dark, cramped space, shutting the door.

Hope felt like a naughty teenager, escaping from the others. She'd never tell Brent she'd been in here earlier today. No need to have him start thinking she had a thing for closets. Although, at the moment, she kind of did.

"This is nuts." She giggled as darkness engulfed them. "I can't see a thing."

"You don't need to see. Just feel."

His hands found her cheeks, and she sensed him hovering nearer. "Brent."

"Hmm?" His mouth found hers like a heat-seeking missile, his lips lightly grazing hers.

"Ooh, oooh…" She tried not to fall under his spell, but his kiss was sheer magic.

"Sweetheart," he moaned softly. "It's just you and me."

"That's what I'm afraid of," she murmured because it was true. As long as they were around his family or Meredith or her mom, she could keep up the pretense of being Brent's non-PDA fiancée. Enforcing the non-PDA part in private was pretty much impossible.

"Don't be," he whispered.

"But, I... You and I..."

"Are getting married," he said, and Hope's heart caught in her throat. Oh, how she wanted this to be real—with all her heart. She closed her eyes, willing all thoughts of conflict and Jackie away.

Even Meredith knew that Jackie didn't really love Brent. They'd had no business becoming engaged in the first place. It would have been different if he'd held her the way he did Hope now. But she suspected he never had.

He kissed her gently at first and then more firmly, increasing the pressure of his lips, and she had to hang on to his shoulders for fear her knees might buckle.

"Tell me you love me?" he said, and tiny shivers raced down her spine. Then he kissed her again, and those little buggers skittered their way back up her torso again, sending ricocheting sensation throughout her body.

She feared, at any second, she might faint dead away.

"Tell me." His voice grew husky, and her head spun. "Please say it, baby. Tell me that things have changed. Tell me how you really feel."

The words flowed right out of her mouth before she could stop them.

"I love you," she whispered, sliding her arms around his neck and hanging on tighter.

Brent tugged her up against him.

"That's pretty great," he growled. "Because I love you, too."

Then he covered her mouth with his, and there was nobody left in the world but the two of them.

• • •

Hope was miles deep in Brent's sexy kiss when a bright beam of light invaded their hiding space. Then the swath of light grew larger, bathing their heated faces in its glow. They jerked apart, and Hope realized she'd lost track of the last time she'd come up for air.

"My goodness," Ava said. "Here's to the bride and groom."

"Mom." Hope stared at her, aghast, straightening her hair. "What are you doing here?"

"Just hunting for the broom," she said, reaching past Hope's left shoulder and grabbing a broom handle. "Here it is." She nodded at Brent, who appeared positively mortified. "I'll just pretend I didn't see this."

She swung the door shut, but Brent halted its advance with his palm. "Maybe we should, um..." He motioned toward the hall with his chin.

Hope's whole body vibrated, so full of Brent's fire she couldn't stand it. Then reality dawned, and she was doused in icy-cold guilt. *How could I do this*

to Jackie? How could I? How could I? How could I?
What's more, her mom had caught her red-handed.
No doubt with her aura extremely pink.

Then again, she wouldn't be in this position if
Jackie hadn't thrust it upon her. What was her
sister's problem, anyway? Was Meredith right about
the Martin wedding being a smoke screen? Did
Jackie really have cold feet?

Even if she did, she owed it to everybody here to
face the music and sort things out. Hope was
annoyed by her sister's flippant attitude at skipping
out on her own wedding week. Things were so out of
whack in Blue Hill. She was falling for the groom,
while the groom was falling for her because he
thought she was his fiancée.

The entire ordeal made her head throb. But her
lips were throbbing harder from his kisses. How she
wished that she was his one and only, and not her
frustrating sister, who maybe didn't even really want
to marry him, anyway.

If things had worked out differently, in another
universe, maybe Brent could have been Hope's des-
tiny. What if she'd been the one working in Boston
instead of Jackie? Or what if she'd somehow met
him some other way?

If he had never met Jackie, would he have fallen
for Hope?

Did he really care for her as a person—not just
because she had Jackie's same dark hair and big
brown eyes? Okay, slightly larger eyes. But still.

"Jackie?" Meredith called, noticing her entering
the den. The others were seated on the comfy furniture and finishing up their dinner wine. "I was

looking for you earlier. Where have you…" Her voice trailed off when she noted Hope's flushed expression. Brent's neck reddened, too, and Meredith gave them a knowing look. "Oh."

"I think I'll call it a night," Grandpa Chad said, resting his hands on his knees.

"Me, too," Margaret said, preparing to leave with him.

"That's our cue," Parker said to Elsa.

Elsa smiled around the room. "Don't forget to turn out the lights."

Sofia yawned. "I'm beat, too." She glanced at William. "Honey?"

"That makes both of us." He took Sofia's hand. "Night."

Derrick and Meredith stared each other down. Finally, Derrick said, "I'm not tired."

"Me either," Meredith said.

"Oh yes, you are," Hope said, taking her by the elbow. That's all she needed—the maid of honor and the best man getting into a knock-down-drag-out fight before Jackie's arrival.

"Fine," Meredith said. "I could use some downtime."

Sally glanced toward the library. "I think I'll stay up and read for a bit."

Ava appeared helplessly lost. Her mom was such a night owl; she no doubt considered the lot of them party poopers. "Coming, Mom?"

Ava's gaze swept the room as Derrick flipped on the TV, turning to a sports channel.

"Uh, sure. Okay. Good night, everyone."

She and Meredith linked arms and headed out

toward the carriage house.

Hope gave Brent a shy smile. "See you tomorrow?"

"Yep." He grinned. "Can't wait." When she turned to go, he winked. "I'll text you later?"

Her face burned hot. "Yes, that would be—" Wait. "No, don't!" Brent texting her meant he'd be texting her sister's phone. "What I mean is, *please* don't."

His smile faltered, and his forehead creased. "Why not?"

Hope racked her brain for an appropriate response. Nothing she could think of sounded kind. She didn't want him to feel like she wouldn't welcome his texts—if he was texting *her*, rather than her sister's phone. What if he sent sweet messages, or maybe even steamy ones recounting their time in the coat closet? Nothing Hope could say to her sister would explain her way out of *that*.

Panicked, she blurted out the only thing that seemed reasonable. "Because I'd rather hear from you in person."

Brent's grin widened. "Is that so?"

The blood instantly drained from her face. Oh, no. That hadn't come out right *at all*. At this rate, he'd show up at her window wanting to revisit the coat closet, and that would be very bad. No matter how good it sounded.

Stop thinking like that!

She forced herself to laugh. "I just mean, so much of our relationship has been long distance." She assumed. "Wouldn't it be better to communicate in person as often as we can? It *is* our wedding week…"

His eyes positively sparkled with desire. "That it is. Good night, Jackie."

Oh, but the things his heated gaze did to her.... Hope all but fled down the garden path, knowing without a doubt she was in very serious trouble when it came to Brent Albright. And worse, she didn't want it to end.

• • •

Ava and Meredith peppered her with questions the second she caught up with them outside the carriage house.

"Where did you disappear to for so long?" Meredith asked with a suspicious gleam.

"I promised not to say a thing," her mom declared, all the while looking like she was itching to do just that.

Meredith gave her an exasperated look, then centered her attention squarely on Hope. "You... and Brent?"

"All right, okay. I kissed him," she admitted. "It wasn't, like, planned or any—"

"In the coat closet," Ava interjected. "Under the stairs."

Meredith surveyed Hope's face as they walked along, and Hope tried to avoid her stare. "Has this happened before?"

"Huh?"

Meredith nudged her. "You kissing Brent?"

She grimaced. "Only slightly."

"Weird. Jackie and Brent were never that physical. I mean, she mentioned they'd kissed, but I've never seen Jackie looking quite like *that*."

Hope gaped at Meredith, then her mom. "Like what?"

"All pink," Ava said.

Meredith and Ava exchanged worried glances.

"This is a very messed-up situation," Meredith said.

Ava perused Hope again and nodded. "Yes."

CHAPTER FOURTEEN

Brent took Jackie's hand as they headed down the driveway for their morning walk. He'd suggested this mild form of exercise to help stretch out her muscles, since she was still too sore from yesterday to run again. She was normally so athletic—he was surprised the shorter route had caused her issues. Then again, the first part of it *had* basically been uphill.

Now he was regretting not sneaking down to the carriage house the previous night. He might have been able to give her painkillers. Or a massage.

He'd nearly gone, feeling certain that's what she was hinting at. But then, Jackie had never been that bold with him, and certainly not when family and friends were nearby. Had he misinterpreted it? Maybe let their kisses go to his head?

He shook himself free of those thoughts. The woman he loved was struggling. He wanted her to be happy and not in pain, like she seemed to be right now as she hobbled along beside him. "You sure you're okay?" he asked her for maybe the tenth time.

"Yeah, yeah. I just woke up a little stiff."

"Maybe you should take a dip in that hot tub later?"

"Mmm. That's a good idea."

"Maybe I'll join you?" he suggested, and she laughed.

"Not with my mom staying in the carriage house, you won't."

Rats. "Oh yeah. I forgot about that."

Jackie was finally loosening up about being in Blue Hill. He was happy about that, but he was even happier about how he and she had grown closer. They were learning things about each other and sharing intimate thoughts. And when she'd let down her guard last night in the closet…

Oh, man.

The woman had nearly set his body on fire.

Brent had never known Jackie to kiss like that. She'd practically devoured him with her fiery-hot kisses. Thinking of it later, he'd become so stoked about their upcoming honeymoon that he'd had to take a cold shower before bed.

Though they'd dated for over three months, he and Jackie hadn't slept together. She'd said she wanted to wait until after they were married, and, especially given their circumstances, Brent had understood. So he'd been totally caught off guard by the vixen under the stairs.

Not that he'd minded.

Not in the least.

Now, every moment leading up to their wedding night felt like a slow-burning fuse on a loaded stick of dynamite. He'd never experienced these feelings before or understood how desperately a man could ache to be with a woman. Physically. Emotionally. The whole nine yards. Brent couldn't wait to make love to Jackie and show her how deeply he cared. But he was a patient man, and Saturday was only three days away.

"What are you thinking about?" she asked as they ambled along the quiet country road with morning birds chirping.

"About Saturday." He lifted her hand to his mouth and kissed it. "I can't wait to make you my bride."

"And you'll be my groom."

"Yes," he said in low tones. "Won't that be fun."

"Brent." She swatted his arm at his innuendo.

"There's nobody out here but us," he said. "Besides that, I didn't say anything too lewd."

This caused her to laugh, and he enjoyed the sound of it. Pretty much everything felt great about being around Jackie.

Her eyebrows knitted together, and she seemed to be worrying about something.

"What are *you* thinking about?" he asked her.

"The wedding dress comes today," she said. "I was just wondering about how it's going to fit."

"Absolutely perfectly, I'm sure," he said. "Will I get a sneak peek at it?"

"No, Mr. Groom, you will not," she teased lightly. "Haven't you heard? It's bad luck to see the bride in her gown before the wedding day."

Brent affectionately squeezed her hand. "I'm so happy we're getting married. You're going to make the very best wife."

"And you're going to make an excellent husband." Her eyes sparkled when she gazed up at him. "It's exciting, in a way," she said. "Thinking of the future and the possibilities it holds."

"It is exciting. I know we haven't discussed this in detail, and we probably should have…" He hesitated a moment, growing uncomfortable, but if he didn't bring it up now, he needed to sometime. "But when you hinted that that you didn't want children—"

"I what?" She frowned and then said, "Oh, yeah. That. Maybe we should discuss this later?"

"Later?"

"Like on Friday? It's a pretty heavy topic."

"That's the day before the wedding. Things will be so busy then. Don't you think it would be best to discuss this while we have a quiet moment alone together?"

"What made you decide to bring this up now?"

"I noticed Sofia hasn't been drinking any alcohol since she's been here," he said, reflecting on his observation. "And William's been in an awfully happy mood. It made me start to wonder if maybe there's something they're not telling us. Like maybe there's a new little Albright on the way."

"That would be amazing for them."

"It would, yeah." The warm glimmer in her eyes only made him surer of his position. "When you and I talked about kids before, I honestly didn't have a strong opinion."

"And now?"

"Uh. How can I say this?" He ran a hand through his hair, feeling awkward about asking for this. He wanted to respect Jackie's wishes, but since his thinking had changed so dramatically, he was hoping that maybe hers had, too. "Something's changed. There's this new vibe between us. I don't know how or when it happened, but it has something to do with us being here.

"Maybe it's being in Blue Hill," he went on, "and the place where I spent so many happy childhood summers. Maybe it's being around my parents, who have their own fairy-tale marriage, and seeing the love between Sofia and William, too. Even my Grandmother Margaret and Grandpa Chad share a certain connection. It may not be evident on the outside, but—way down deep—I suspect they love each other very much and always have."

"I think you're right about your grandparents," she answered. "Your parents and Sofia and William, too. They're all so different, and still such great matches."

Brent stopped walking, so she did, too.

"Just like us." His voice grew husky when he took her in his arms. "I know you must feel it. This overwhelming attraction between us. And it's more than attraction. It's deeper than that. You and I got along great before. We had similar interests and goals. We were perfect together on paper, and yet..." He hugged her tighter. "There was something missing inside." He gazed down into her big dark eyes and nearly lost his bearings. Then her smile brought him home. "The *something* we seem to share now."

"You're the sweetest guy." Her voice trembled when she said it. "An absolute dream."

"If you still don't want kids, I'll learn to live with that, because the most important thing in my life is having you in it. But if you think you ever might reconsider..."

A tear leaked from her eye, and he stroked it back with his thumb.

"Hey. What's wrong?"

After a beat, she drew in a shaky breath, then

said, "I can't imagine anything more magical than making babies with you."

"For real?" He felt like a man who'd just won the lottery, and this stunned him a little because he'd never known how badly he wanted kids until now. But not just anybody's kids. Jackie's kids. His and hers together. Brent had not one shadow of a doubt. The woman he held in his arms was going to make a phenomenal mom.

"Then, sweetheart," he said, cradling her face in his hands. "We'll make it happen."

She tilted up her chin and said something that confused him. "If only we could make this real."

"It is real, darling," he said, bringing his arms around her. Then he held her up against him, deciding to show her just how real it was.

His lips brushed over hers, slowly at first—until she whimpered. Then he deepened the pressure of his kiss until she ran her fingers through his hair, begging for more. They stood there lost in each other as tiny droplets speckled their cheeks and clothing. Finally, thunder rumbled above them, and the skies opened up in a torrential downpour.

"Oh no," she cried, but she was laughing. "It's raining. So hard." The sky had morphed from powder blue to an angry gray haze beneath rumbling thunderclouds.

He took her hand. "We'd better make a break for it."

Then they raced back toward the house as the rain came down in droves, splashing up against the gravel drive and splattering their clothing, but neither one cared.

• • •

"Suck it in. Suck it in," Meredith urged, and Hope drew in another deep breath, the sides of the beautiful bridal gown pinching at her waist as Meredith cinched the ties of the lace-up back tighter.

"Careful," Elsa said. "We don't want to tear it."

Sally studied her thoughtfully. "We could maybe camouflage that part that doesn't quite come together." She turned her brown eyes on Hope. "How long is your veil?"

"That could work," Sofia agreed.

"I've got it." Margaret snapped her fingers with a victorious smile. "Spanx."

"Spanx?" They all stared at her, and Margaret nodded proudly.

"I've got some right here in my dresser."

Margaret pranced to her dresser and produced the promised body armor. A few minutes later, in the bathroom, Hope was distressed to learn that it fit. It also did help slim her waist some.

"Okay," she said, emerging into the bedroom, where the rest of the women waited. "Let's try again." Sofia and Sally scooped up the dress and carefully settled it over Hope's head as she held up her arms.

"Inhale," Meredith said in commanding tones, and Hope did as she pressed her palms to her waistline.

Yank. Ava tugged at the laces, and the back of the dress came together. Well, almost all the way.

"Maybe we should try that veil idea?"

Bile churned in Hope's stomach. She would never pull this off.

"Here it is," Sofia said, carrying it over. She settled the veil on Hope's head and adjusted it while Meredith secured it with bobby pins underneath so they wouldn't show.

Ava tied the bow at Hope's waist, and Sofia dropped the lower portion of the veil. It draped down Hope's back, landing a few inches above her waistline and concealing the slightly gaping back section of the dress.

"Success!" Ava grinned, and the others did, too.

"Oh, Jackie," Sofia told her. "You look like a fairy princess."

"Just beautiful," Sally said.

Hope frowned, worried about how she looked from behind. She peered over her shoulder into the mirror.

Ava discreetly shook her head as Margaret murmured, "Lovely."

Meredith beamed at her. "That dress fits you like a glove. You look beautiful."

A very snug glove, Hope thought, feeling stuffed inside it. But, when she turned back around and gazed at her reflection in Margaret's dresser mirror, she saw that it was true. She really did look beautiful. The gorgeous gown had a lace appliqué bodice with pretty long sleeves, and its organza skirt flounced out like a puffy white cloud around her. The shimmering material crinkled when she moved.

Hope held up the hem and tiptoed to the full-length mirror on a swivel stand in the corner to study her image. She turned and peeked over her shoulder one more time at the stunning lace-up back. The veil really did cover up the gaping portion pretty well. Through its gauzy fabric, it was pretty tough to tell what was laces…and what was Spanx.

"Ooh," she said, noting the color in her cheeks. "Nice."

"Better than nice," Meredith countered. "Spectacular."

"Ooh. Let's try it with the veil down," Sally said, admiring its inlaid lace appliqué that matched the lace on the dress. "How are you going to wear it for the ceremony?" she asked. "Veil forward or flipped back?"

"Not sure yet." With her standing here in this wedding dress, it was pretty hard not to imagine Brent actually being her groom. Not to want that. So badly.

In an alternate universe, yeah… That would be something.

"What about your hair?" Meredith asked. "Up, or down like you have it now?"

Hope was embarrassed to be liking this so much, but the truth was, she was loving being fussed over. Who knew when she'd ever have a real wedding of her own? So she might as well enjoy this fantasy moment. "I think up would be good." She smiled at Meredith. "Don't you?"

"Absolutely." Meredith seemed to be getting into this, too. So did her mom. Weirdly, it almost seemed that they were half wishing *Hope* was the one marrying Brent. But that was maybe all in her head.

"I've got more bobby pins in the bathroom,"

Margaret said. "I'll go grab some and be right back."
When Margaret returned, Hope removed the veil,
and Meredith styled her hair in a loose chignon at
her nape with wisps spilling forward.

Sofia added the veil again, and Meredith pinned
it in place. Hope's heart thudded at her reflection. It
was hard to believe the gorgeous bride in the mirror
was really her.

She bit her bottom lip, wishing with all her might
that this was more than make believe, yet she knew
that it wasn't. She'd tried texting Jackie after returning from her walk with Brent, in part to assuage her
building guilt. There seemed to be no good solution
to this trap she was in—none at all. If only her sister
hadn't continued delaying her arrival, Hope
wouldn't have gotten in so deep with Brent and his
family. Maybe Jackie didn't deserve any of them after all. But, in that case, she reflected sadly, neither
did she.

"Hey," Sally said gently. "No pouty frowns. You
look amazing."

"Wait," Ava said suddenly. "Shoes." She
rummaged through a box on the bed and pulled out
a stunning pair of high-heeled mules that looked
like glass slippers. They were accented with ivory
lace and had cross-straps over the ankles, which tied
in the back with silky cream-colored bows. "I want
these shoes," Ava said, handing them to Hope.

"You never know," Elsa teased. "Your day could
be up next."

Ava actually blushed. "I might be a little past
those opportunities."

"Bosh," Margaret contended. "Never."

"If you're going to toss a bouquet," Meredith joked, "your mom and I might have to fight for it."

"Fine by me," Sally said, chuckling. "I'm not interested for a while."

"Are you seeing someone, Meredith?" Grandmother Margaret asked her.

Meredith heaved a sigh. "Yeah, lots of someones, but they're only clients—and all of them are for somebody else."

"Hope's still single, too," Elsa commented. "Maybe she'll catch the bouquet."

"Er…I'm not so sure she has anyone on the horizon, either."

"That's what catching the bouquet is for," Margaret said with a wink. "I caught the bouquet at my best friend's wedding. Chad and I married eighteen months later."

"Grandmother," Sally said warmly. "You're such an old softie."

Though she never would have guessed this at first, Hope conceded it was true. She exhaled a bit, and the fabric of her dress pinched. Hope was a bit heavier than Jackie, and every ounce mattered in an outfit like this. All those yummy baked goods back at the carriage house hadn't helped her figure, either. It was lucky this wedding gown was the lace-up kind and the laces were long enough to be let out enough to accommodate her frame. It still wasn't very comfortable, but at least she'd gotten it on.

"I know it looks a little snug," she said self-consciously.

"Not one bit," Sofia said. "You look radiant."

"It's true," Meredith chimed in. "Extra pretty.

Almost glowing." She sent Hope a knowing look, then said sneakily, "I'm sure you'll glow *even brighter* on your wedding day."

"Extra pink," her mom chimed in unnecessarily, and Hope wanted to die of embarrassment. Fortunately, nobody but Meredith had any clue what her mom was talking about.

"Um, right." Hope surveyed the room, catching her mom and Meredith exchanging secretive glances. "Thanks, everyone." She couldn't help but wonder what her own wedding gown would be like one day. She could only hope it would be just as pretty as this gorgeous ivory one with the lace-up back.

"Let me snap a few pics," Sofia said. "So you can post them." She glanced around the room. "Do you have your phone handy?"

Hope swallowed hard. Not this again... "My phone?"

Before she could truly panic, Meredith pulled her cell phone from the back pocket of her jeans. "Why don't you take them on mine?" she said to Sofia. "That way I can edit the best ones for Jackie and send them to her."

"You're such a great maid of honor," Elsa said.

Meredith tapped her temple. "Always thinking." When the others weren't watching, she winked, and Hope wanted to hug her for her quick save.

After a few glamor shots, Sally surprised Hope with a sweet hug. "I'm so happy you're becoming my sister. Growing up, I always wanted one, and now I'll have two." She smiled at Sofia, then looked back at Hope.

Hope hugged Sally back, feeling extra terrible about deceiving her. Brent had said she could so easily read people. But Sally obviously couldn't read her. Or maybe the scarier thought was that she could, and Sally could tell Hope was honestly in love with her brother.

Would Sally feel that same connection with Jackie once she got here on Friday? In one way, Hope wanted that for her sister—for her to blend in as seamlessly with the Albright family as she had. But, in another, those same thoughts made her gut clench and her heart ache. Especially when she was thinking of Brent.

Their kiss in the rain this morning had been so romantic. And, for that fantasy moment, she'd wanted so badly to believe what Brent was telling her about everything being real.

She stared back in the mirror, seeing herself outfitted as his bride, and she knew it was all a lie. A lie that would be ending very soon, unless she died of heartbreak first.

Meredith handed her a tissue, and Hope realized she'd been crying. The other women probably mistook her tears for tears of joy instead of worry and regret. Either way, she was embarrassed to have gotten emotional. "Could I have a moment with Meredith?"

Everyone murmured their agreement and gave her warm smiles.

"She's just so happy," Meredith said as they were leaving. "About her big day."

"Girlfriend," Meredith said when the others had gone, and Hope sobbed harder, because her sister's best friend was being so kind. "Are you all right?

Hope dabbed her eyes with the tissue. "No. What am I'm going to do?"

Meredith pulled her in for a hug and patted her back. "Hang tough, *chica*. Hang tough. Friday will be here soon."

• • •

Brent and Derrick stopped at the co-op in town to purchase potatoes and corn on the cob for that night's clambake. He'd tried texting Jackie to see how the dress fitting was going, but he guessed she was too busy to answer. That was okay, though. They'd have plenty of in-person time later, just like she'd requested. He hoped at least some of that would be one-on-one, because he was enjoying discovering this new side of Jackie. A passionate side that was clearly not opposed to *private* displays of affection. And one that didn't shy away from connecting on the deeper level he'd always craved.

He and Derrick stopped at the fish shop, where they had lobsters, littleneck clams, and a variety of fresh seaweed called rockweed on special order. In true New England tradition, they'd bake the seafood and vegetables outdoors in the firepit.

After this morning's rain, the skies were still gloomy and gray. As they drove back to their grandparents' house, they chitchatted about the wedding and Jackie. Even the weather.

Since neither one had mentioned the elephant in the room—Meredith—Brent decided to bring her up. He didn't need tension between his best man and Jackie's maid of honor on his wedding day. Maybe if he had a man-to-man chat with his little brother, he could preempt that.

"So," Brent began cautiously. "The wedding party's almost all here."

"Yeah, all except for Jackie's sister." He glanced at Brent from where he sat behind the steering wheel. "Any updates?"

"Jackie called her this morning but couldn't get through. She left a voicemail, though. I'm hoping for good news."

Derrick frowned with concern. "Me, too. Poor woman. She's had this bug all week?"

"Since Saturday, apparently. She thought she was getting better, then had some kind of relapse."

"The week of her sister's wedding. That rots."

"I know. It's my wedding week, too."

"Lucky man."

"Derrick, about Meredith—"

"What about her?" His tone sounded snappy.

"She *is* Jackie's best friend."

"Yeah, and so?"

"So, do you think you could hold your fire? Just for a few days."

"*My* fire?" he asked combatively. "You've got to be kidding me."

"She's our *guest*, Derrick. An Albright family guest."

"To ask her, you'd think she's the queen."

"Unfair."

"No?" Derrick shot him a daggered look. "First, she rams into my SUV—and claims it's my fault.

Next, she insults my job at the table."

"Yeah, she probably shouldn't have done that." Brent issued a conciliatory yet reasoned response. "But maybe you shouldn't have insulted hers first?"

"Come on, man. The woman took an immediate—and intense—dislike to me. How was I expected to handle that?"

"With dignity and calm?"

"Funny."

"I wasn't trying to be. I'm serious."

Derrick flicked on his turn signal and glanced at Brent. "I get along with everybody. You know that."

"Normally, yes." Brent paused a beat before asking: "So, why not her?"

Derrick set his chin. "She's…challenging."

"So then, rise to the challenge." Brent shrugged.

"What?"

"Please, Derrick. I don't ask you for much, but I am asking for this one thing: a totally uneventful and happy wedding day."

Derrick considered this a moment, and then his shoulders sagged. "Sure, of course. I'll see what I can do to get along with *Meredith*."

• • •

"All things considered," Meredith said as they packed the bridal gown and accessories away, "I think the fitting went okay."

"Yeah," Hope said. "Apart from the fact that I got all weepy in front of everybody." After a few sniffles and reassuring hugs from Meredith, she was feeling better about things. It really was just a few more days until Jackie would be here.

"Nobody thought anything of it," Meredith told her. "They just figured you were being sentimental."

"It's hard not to be sentimental when you're playing a fake bride."

"I can only imagine." Meredith daintily picked up the wedding shoes and slipped them into their box. "But I honestly wasn't kidding. You really do look dynamite in that dress."

"Yeah, but it won't be me who's wearing it on Saturday."

Meredith flipped her long, dark hair over her shoulder. "He's really gotten under your skin, huh?"

"Only in the best possible way."

"I'm sorry, Hope. Sorry that everything's so twisted. But, seeing the two of you together, I'd say he's equally into you."

"Yeah?" she asked, daring to dream.

"Maybe if you explain to Jackie what's happened—"

Hope was shaking her head before Meredith even finished. "No. She'll totally flip."

"You're probably right about that. And anyway, then you'd still have the problem of telling Brent and his family. My gut says none of them will take this very well."

"I agree. One hundred percent." Hope's shoulders sagged. "It's just two more days, and then Jackie will be here."

"She'd better," Meredith said. "Or I'm going to wring her neck."

"Yeah, you and me both." Hope stared at her, feeling like she didn't deserve this compassion. She was Jackie's bestie, after all, and here she was, being so kind. "Thanks for all of this, Meredith."

"All of what?"

"For being a friend when I need it."

"Believe it or not, I do understand," Meredith told her. "I know what it's like to love someone when the odds are impossible."

"That happened to you?" When Meredith's eyes misted, Hope decided not to press her on it. "Oh no. I'm so sorry."

"It's all right," Meredith said. "Life moves on. It will move on for you, too."

Hope's cell phone buzzed on her dresser. "Wait," she said, checking the screen. "That's Jackie calling now."

"Great," Meredith said. "I'll go help Sally gather wood for the fire and let you take it. But, Hope," she said before leaving. "Maybe you should tell her?"

"Oh, no. I couldn't."

"She's going to figure it out soon enough. If I were her, I'd rather not be blindsided."

A frown tugged at Hope's lips. She frankly could no longer stand the thought of Brent marrying somebody else—anybody else. Much less her sister, who clearly didn't love him and was possibly conflicted about the commitment herself. "I know you're right. It's just… This is going to be tough."

Meredith gently patted her shoulder. "You don't have to tell her today, but I'd suggest filling her in before she gets here. She at least needs to know."

• • •

Hope spoke into her phone as Meredith closed the door. "Jackie. *Finally*. How's it going?"

"I'm still wrapping up the Martin wedding," Jackie said. "But things will be all set by the close of business tomorrow. I fly out of Nantucket first thing Friday morning and will be in Blue Hill by lunchtime."

"Super. I wish it was sooner."

"I know you do. Me, too. I saw the latest update," she said, changing the subject. "By the way, you look *great* in the dress."

"I'm sure you'll wear it even better," Hope said as heat burned in her eyes.

"Is everything all right?"

"Sure. Why wouldn't it be? This is a horrible thing we're doing to the Albrights, Jackie. All of them, including Brent."

Jackie huffed. "Yeah. I know. Don't believe I haven't thought about that, but one thing led to another, and—"

"We should have stopped it. I mean, I should have. In a way, this is all my fault."

"You *were* the honesty-is-the-best-policy spokesperson."

"I know," Hope said, breaking into a whimper. "And I've let everyone down."

"Let's try not to have negative thoughts right now," her sister insisted. "Brent and I made a deal, and I intend to make good on it, just like he and I planned."

Hope's chin trembled. "Sometimes plans change, though."

There was a pause. Then, "What are you talking about?"

"It's Brent. I *like* him."

"Sure you do," her sister said. "Everybody does. Brent's a very nice guy. I wouldn't be marrying him otherwise."

"You never loved him, did you?" Hope asked, her voice quaking. "Not even the tiniest little bit."

"What Brent and I have is mutual, Hope, and mutually decided on, okay? Please don't go second-guessing me now. I've got enough stress on my plate."

"Oh, right," she said wanly. "Like I don't."

"Fine. You're stressed out, too. And I'm very, very, very sorry about that. But I'll be there soon, and everything will be all right."

Somehow, Hope was beginning to doubt that. "I've got to know. Is your not being here really about the Martin wedding, or is something else going on?"

"I don't know what you mean?"

"You're not having doubts? Getting cold feet, maybe, because if you are—"

"No, absolutely not. Come on, Hope. What do you think? That I can't make up my mind? I told you about Rodney and how he treated me."

"Yeah, but a rebound marriage is no way to go."

"This is not a rebound marriage, okay?" Jackie said, beginning to sound irritated. "Don't think I haven't thought all of this through. I have. A gazillion times. I'm actually offended you'd think any differently. And even suggest the cold-feet thing. Who on earth put that in your mind?" She gasped. "Meredith?"

"Meredith's great," Hope said without directly

answering. "She cares about you."

"Unbelievable," Jackie said. "Just when you think you have a friend."

"She *is* a friend. To both of us."

"Really?" Jackie snapped. "Since when?"

This was going downhill fast. "So, um, about Brent…"

"What about him?" Jackie sounded so combative Hope was suddenly afraid to go there.

"Uh, it's just that you'd better get here soon. Promise me, Jackie."

"Of course, I promise, but what are you getting at, Hope? Why are you being so weird?"

"Things keep happening. Things that I can't stop." Hope's face burned hot at the thought of Brent's steamy kisses.

"Oh yeah? Like what?"

"Like Brent trying to text you," she said, thinking of another problem.

"Yeah, that part's been bananas. He's sending all these mushy texts, which is *so* unlike him. *Tonight was awesome. Can't wait to see you.* Why is he sending these, anyway? Are things really going that super?"

Hope rubbed the side of her neck. "I've…made some headway. As you! Totally you, Jackie. That's who Brent thinks I am, remember?"

"Huh. Well, anyway," Jackie continued. "Some of his messages haven't made any sense. Why would I need an umbrella next time, and what's the joke about the cozy coat closet?"

Hope's heart hammered. "Uh. Don't know. Maybe it's an inside joke?"

"Between who?"

"You and Brent."

Jackie seemed to dismiss this in an instant, focusing on something else. "The sailing photos were cute, though. Loved those."

"Oh, good." Hope waited a beat. "So, have you answered? I mean, at all?"

"No, because I wasn't sure what some of them meant. Except for the last one. That was pretty self-explanatory."

"What was it about?"

"He was asking about the dress fitting."

"You should say that it went fine."

"Okay, I'll do that." She sighed. "Because obviously it did."

"The dress is not my size. It was tailor-made for you, which is why you need to get here to wear it."

"I know. Okay. I hear you. Don't be like a broken record, Hope. I told you I'd be there, so I will."

"Great. Tomorrow."

"Yeah, tomorrow. Please just stop."

Hope's voice shook when she said, "I only want what's best for you, you know."

"Well, good," Jackie answered, "that's good, because I can tell you what that is. It's Brent."

CHAPTER FIFTEEN

Later that night, the group stood around the smoldering firepit, drinking wine and beer and enjoying the savory smell of baking shellfish. It was cooler than Hope had anticipated, and she'd only worn a thin cardigan over her T-shirt and leggings. She didn't even realize she'd been hugging her arms around herself for warmth as she chatted with Sofia until Brent slipped up behind her and draped a jacket around her shoulders.

"You looked a bit chilly," he whispered. "Better?" His dark eyes glimmered in the fire's glow, and Hope caught her breath.

"Yeah, thanks. That was really thoughtful of you."

"My pleasure." He gave her a peck on her cheek, and her skin warmed beneath his kiss.

"He's practicing," Sofia said as he left to gather more firewood. "His good husbanding skills."

"Husbanding's not a word," Sally said, strolling up beside them and holding a beer.

"It is now," Sofia said.

Hope snuggled into Brent's jacket, sliding her arms through its sleeves. The lightweight windbreaker carried a hint of his outdoorsy cologne, and she loved being wrapped in his scent. She zipped it up, happy contentment surging through her. She felt closer to Brent wearing his clothing, and anything that made him seem a part of her life filled her heart with happiness. She told herself not to fret over the fact that it was fleeting and to simply enjoy the present.

She saw Meredith across the lawn speaking animatedly with Ava, Elsa, and Margaret. William was helping Grandpa Chad retrieve drink refills from the house, and Derrick knelt by the firepit, poking at the coals occasionally with a long, charred stick. Hope saw him glance briefly at Meredith. Then he shook his head and returned his attention to the fire.

Meredith gestured with her wineglass, laughing at something Elsa said, then—seemingly against her will—her gaze trailed to Derrick. When he glanced up, she looked away, and Hope couldn't help but smile.

"Lots of tension between those two," Sofia whispered.

"You know what they say," Sally teased. "Where there's smoke, there's fire."

Hope giggled at their guessing. "I don't know, you guys. Seems like ice cubes might form in an inferno first."

Sofia and Sally chuckled.

"They're not a bad pair." Sofia took a sip of ginger ale. "All animosity aside."

Sally shrugged. "Opposites attract."

Hope lifted her wineglass toward the others. "Here's to—"

"Please don't say opposites." Sofia giggled.

Hope twisted her lips. "I was about to toast to attraction."

Sofia watched William fondly as he emerged from the house, carting three cold beers. "Hmm, yeah."

Hope took in their beautiful surroundings, thinking about how lucky Jackie was to be marrying into all of this. The sad thing was, Jackie didn't understand the full value of her fortune, because she hadn't been here this week getting to know everyone like she had. Meredith came up beside her and whispered, "I'm starved. When's dinner?"

"There're hors d'oeuvres in the house."

"What?" Meredith looked like this was the greatest news she'd ever heard. "Nobody told me."

"Let's go get some," she said softly, and Meredith nodded.

As they loaded their plates from the spread on the kitchen counter, Derrick strolled into the room and opened the refrigerator. "Ladies," he said, pleasantly enough.

"Looks like you're doing a great job with that fire," Hope told him.

Derrick extracted a bottle of beer from a shelf and shut the door to the refrigerator. "Thanks. I like working with fire."

Meredith arched her eyebrows at him. "Me, too."

Derrick uncapped his beer and studied her. "Is that right?"

A sly smile crept onto Meredith's lips. "Fiery clients. Some of them can be real bears."

Derrick actually laughed. "Bet those guys are hard to fix up."

"It's not the guys. Generally, it's the women."

Derrick choked on his swig of beer. "Who… would have…thought…that," he said, wiping his mouth with the back of his hand.

Hope rolled her eyes and chuckled. They were

trying so hard to be civil. "I'm excited about the clambake," she said. "It's been eons."

"Me, too," Meredith chimed in. "I've only been to one."

"Yeah?" Derrick asked her. "Where are you from?"

"Grew up in North Carolina, but I was born in Miami. My parents landed there by way of Puerto Rico."

"You speak Spanish?" he asked.

Meredith shrugged. "A little. You?"

"*Una cerveza, por favor.*" Derrick raised his beer bottle, and Hope could tell that Meredith was working very hard not to smile.

"Not bad," she told him. "You'll do just fine surviving in many bars."

She locked on Derrick's gaze, and Hope could practically hear the electricity crackling between them.

"Anywho," Derrick finally said, breaking away. "I'd best get back to tending that fire."

When he was halfway through the kitchen door, Meredith shouted, "Bye!"

Derrick turned slowly on his heel, speaking over his shoulder. "Catch ya later, Mer."

Hope wasn't totally sure, but she thought his eyes sparkled when he'd said that. She fanned herself with her free hand. "Looks like Derrick didn't leave the heat by the firepit."

"What do you mean?" Meredith asked, trying to look nonchalant.

"Was it my imagination, or was there some kind of vibe going on between you?"

Meredith pursed her lips, then, after a beat, said, "It was your imagination."

"O-kay," Hope said, giggling. "If you say so." She smiled at Meredith. "I'm just glad to see you and Derrick getting along."

. . .

Later on, the group sat around the firepit, enjoying the remnants of their delicious meal. The mood was jovial yet mellow as shadows stretched over the gently rolling waves, and sporadic glimpses of moonlight danced behind the clouds.

"Supposed to clear up tomorrow," Grandpa Chad said, lifting a forkful of potato. "Later in the day."

"Let's hope it stays that way," Margaret said. "For the wedding."

Everyone lifted their glasses and said, "Hear, hear."

Her mom leaned toward her. "Have you mentioned '*Eres Tú*' to Brent?"

"Mentioned what to me?" Brent took Hope's hand in his and gave it a tender kiss. "Keeping secrets from me, darling?" he asked, searching her eyes.

Hope wanted to die and go to heaven, but only if she could take Brent with her. Then she realized that was unfair. He didn't deserve to pay for her sins. Only she did. "Why would I do that?" Hope took a quick sip of wine to soothe her nerves while her mom explained.

"I've prepared the most beautiful song to sing at your wedding."

"Oh?" Brent asked, looking surprised, because he'd seen the karaoke video, too.

"It's in Spanish." She turned toward Meredith, who sat to her left. "Do you know the song '*Eres Tú*'?"

"No." Meredith shook her head while digging into her lobster. "Is it new?"

"Ancient," Hope replied, and everyone but her mom laughed.

"That's a very generous offer, Ava," Brent said. "But I'm afraid I've deferred all wedding planning to my beautiful bride."

"Um, thanks," Hope said.

A grin tugged at Brent's lips, and he turned away, saying something to Sally, who was next to him.

Ava sat up a little straighter in her chair. "Maybe at the reception?"

Hope was actually growing exasperated at her mom's persistence. Fortunately, she could pass the baton on dealing with that to Jackie when she got here, along with several other things. Not that she was thrilled about passing on Brent.

Derrick was engaged in conversation with William and Sofia, who sat near him. Hope didn't miss that the lovebirds held hands or the fact the back of William's hand pressed lightly against Sofia's belly as it rested in her lap.

Hope's heart fluttered for them and the happy anxiety they must be feeling. They apparently hadn't told anyone else yet, and Hope had vowed to keep Sofia's secret. Some of the Albrights probably suspected. Brent had hinted he did during his and Hope's walk in the country.

Hope tried not to imagine herself having children with Brent again, but her mind went down that wistful road anyway. Brent was so kind and caring. Fun-loving and generous, too. He'd make a really great dad. Hope could just feel it.

What if Jackie never gave that to him?

As people finished their dinners, thanks were issued to the Albright boys for cooking the fantastic meal and to Elsa for preparing the yummy cobbler, which had been served with ice cream from a local dairy to top it all off. It had grown late, with folks lingering around the fire, and the group was beginning to look weary from the fun exhaustion of the day.

"We should probably start cleaning up," Margaret said, standing. "We all need our rest for tomorrow."

"We're taking Brent away," William said with a chuckle. "Only we won't say where."

Brent rolled his shoulders back. "Best prepare myself for anything, in that case," he said, and everyone laughed.

Hope frowned, not understanding.

Margaret patted Hope's shoulder as she strode past her. "Don't worry, dear. It's going to be loads of fun."

CHAPTER SIXTEEN

"Rise and shine."

Hope groggily opened her eyes to find Meredith standing beside her bed and holding out a coffee mug. She was dressed in a nautical-looking outfit and wearing a quirky sailor hat and boat shoes. Ava, who was dressed similarly, stood in the doorway. Their outfits were all clearly part of a gag, but what was the joke, exactly? Whatever it was, they wanted Hope in on it, because her mom paraded into her room next holding an outfit that looked nearly identical to Meredith's for Hope to wear.

"It's time for your getaway," Ava said as thunder boomed outdoors.

Heavy rain pounded against the roof of their small cottage as Hope sat up in bed. "Where are we going in *that*?" she asked, referencing the weather.

"Grandmother Margaret has a plan," Meredith informed her with a bright grin.

Hope propped herself up against the headboard with pillows and took a sip of coffee from the mug Meredith handed her. She eyed the others curiously. "Have the guys already left?"

"Oh, yes." Ava waved her hand. "Hours ago."

Hope checked the clock on the nightstand, seeing it was nearly ten o'clock. She couldn't believe she'd slept so hard—or so late. "I guess I missed breakfast?" she asked with a grimace.

"Nope." Meredith grinned and motioned toward

the kitchen, then whispered behind her hand. "The others are out there, so you're Jackie."

Seconds later, Sally appeared in the doorway with a bountiful breakfast tray, complete with a small carafe containing more coffee. Hope spotted a selection of tasty-looking pastries, including a divinely puffy chocolate croissant, sliced fresh fruit, and butter and jams. "You guys," Hope said, feeling her eyes mist. "Thank you."

"You're our Princess for the Day," Elsa said, also appearing alongside Margaret, who grinned broadly. Sofia stepped past them and placed a sparkling toy tiara on Hope's head. It said "Princess Bride."

Hope cupped her hand to her mouth, then touched her crown. "I love it. I really do."

She noticed all the others were dressed as if they were going boating, too. "We're not…actually going out on the water?"

The women raised their eyebrows at one another, all repressing smiles.

"You'll want to wear non-skid shoes," Margaret said. "As well as your slicker."

"Well, okay," Hope said, feeling game. Although she sincerely hoped life vests would also be involved. She took a bite of the flaky croissant, and the warm chocolate melted on her tongue. "This is *amazing*."

Meredith giggled and picked up a napkin, leaning toward her. "You've got chocolate all over your face."

For the life of her, Hope felt as if Meredith was warming to her. And she had to be in a bind, trying to both support her new friendship with Hope and remain loyal to Jackie. Above everything else, though, Meredith appeared to value real love. Which made total sense. She spent her entire career focused on arranging it.

"Do I?" Hope laughed. "It was worth it."

• • •

Brent had no clue what his brothers had planned, but since his dad and grandpa were coming along, he suspected things wouldn't get too out of hand. And they basically didn't.

When William removed his blindfold, he found himself in Derrick's rustic cabin.

"What are we doing here?" he asked with a happy laugh. Streamers were everywhere, and a signed draped across one of the wood-paneled walls proclaimed "Bachelor Party." He stared at Derrick. "When did you do all this?"

"There was no 'emergency' at the boat school." Derrick chuckled. "I was getting ready."

"Aww." Brent affectionately hugged his baby brother. "Thanks, man." Through the sliding glass doors, Brent saw rain beating against Derrick's deck and the attached dock. Like Grandpa Chad, Derrick kept his bigger boat at the marina, though he had some smaller crafts he kept stowed away in an outdoor building here.

Brent saw that Derrick's round kitchen table had been laid for a card game. "Poker?"

Chad eagerly rubbed his hands together. "Prepare to lose your shirt."

"Not so fast, Grandpa," William said. "I might be

taking home the winnings today."

While they never played for much money, the family group often tossed some spare change into the pot to make things more interesting.

Derrick strode into his kitchen, where he had bags of chips and pretzels lined up on the counter. "I laid in the snack foods," he said. Next, he pulled open his refrigerator door. "And stocked up with tons of subs and pickles."

Brent's eyes warmed. "Sounds like you thought of everything."

"Don't forget the entertainment," Parker quipped, and Brent quirked a doubtful eyebrow.

"Not that kind of entertainment." Derrick laughed and slapped Brent's shoulder. He lifted the remote off the coffee table and turned on the enormous wide-screen television he had positioned between two side windows with a partial view of the water. "Streaming ESPN. All day long."

Brent chuckled in understanding. "Sounds like my perfect day."

"Plus, the pièce de résistance…" Derrick proudly pulled a heavy cauldron of something from the top shelf of the refrigerator and set it on the stove. "Homemade chili for supper."

William smirked playfully. "You have been a busy bee."

"We also have gifts." Grandpa Chad nodded toward a stash of colorful bags on a table near the corner.

"I feel like it's my birthday." Brent laughed.

"It's better than a birthday, mate." William shared a grin. "You're getting married."

"To somebody wonderful, too." Parker handed Brent a package.

"You want me to open it now?"

"Might as well get it over with," Parker said.

"Yeah," Derrick teased. "The suspense is killing me."

They all settled into the casual living room furniture made of sturdy oak and lined with thick brown and maroon cushions. Brent opened the present from his dad, which was a small box that had been set way in the bottom of a bag filled with tissue paper. He lifted the lid of the box, finding a key. "What's this?"

"The key to a small flat in Brooklyn."

Brent's jaw unhinged. "Dad, that's way too extravagant."

"You'll be up in the city quite a bit on business. I thought it might be nice to have your own place to get away to. Especially if you want to bring Jackie along."

"But, I can't let you—"

"It's already done." Parker's blue eyes shone. "Your mother and I discussed it. While we'd naturally love to have you and Jackie stay with us anytime, when you're working in the city, you may want to keep your own schedule."

"And have your privacy," Derrick said, nudging him.

"I don't know what to say. Thanks."

"It's a very small place, an efficiency," Parker explained. "In a brownstone in Prospect Heights."

"That's a really great neighborhood," William commented.

Parker nodded. "A colleague of mine was about to put it on the market, so he cut me a deal without the real estate commission."

"Are you sure?" Brent asked, still feeling bowled over.

"You can think of it as a wedding gift, if that makes you feel any better. One for both you and Jackie. I've got pictures on my phone. Would you like to see?"

Brent said of course, and everyone admired the sleek, upscale urban loft.

He hugged his dad. "Thank you. This is really too much."

"You won't need to get as excited over mine," Grandpa Chad said, handing him a heavy bag. Inside it, Brent found a thirty-year-old bottle of scotch.

"Oh yeah, I will," Brent answered with a grin. "Thanks, Grandpa. I can't wait to try it."

William went next. Brent opened the package, finding a selection of very fine Cuban cigars inside. "Why, thank you," Brent said, placing a fully wrapped one between his lips. "Thank you very much."

The other guys chuckled, and Derrick gave him the final bag.

"You didn't have to," Brent said. "You did all of this." He gestured around the room.

"Maybe you should see it first?"

Brent dug into the bag and pulled out a pair of boxers. He hooted when he saw they were adorned with little top hats and bow ties and flirty red lipstick marks, as well as stenciled lettering reading: *Hot Groom*.

"Nice," Brent said, still laughing. "I'm sure Jackie will appreciate these."

His dad doubled over with laughter. "That's the best gift."

"I agree," Grandpa Chad said, chuckling.

"Now I'm jealous nobody gave me a pair of those for *my* wedding," William groused, and that made everyone laugh harder, because William was basically the most conservative among them.

"Thanks, guys." Brent smiled around the room. "This is very special."

"What do you say, everyone?" Derrick asked. "Are we ready for me to deal?"

They settled in at the kitchen table.

As his brother shuffled the deck, Brent grinned at his family. "This is all really great. I wonder what the ladies are up to?"

. . .

Hope rode in the car with Sally, her mom, and Meredith. Ava and Sofia were ahead of them, leading the way through the downpour. Before they'd left the main house, the others had loaded lots of heavy bags and coolers into the vehicles. Hope had no idea where they were going—she only hoped they were headed someplace dry.

A short time later, after several twists and turns along winding roads hugging the water, they pulled into a marina. "We're not going sailing today, are we?" Hope asked, slightly aghast.

Sally laughed. "Grandmother Margaret gets seasick, so that's not happening." She peered through her window at the gloomy gray sky. "Besides, it's not the best day for it."

"It is okay for other things, though," Meredith said mysteriously.

"What other things?"

Ava pursed her lips and stared out the window. For the life of her, it looked to Hope like her mom was trying extra hard not to laugh.

They eventually parked in a gravel parking area near the boat slips. Hope studied the others in the SUV with wonder as the rain came down in droves. "So we *are* going sailing?"

"Not sailing," Sally said. "Just on the boat." As she climbed from the driver's seat, she issued a reminder to the others inside. "Don't forget to put up your hoods."

The group giggled and chattered happily as they made their way onto Grandpa Chad's enormous rig in carefully measured steps. Sally and Margaret hopped on first and helped the others by holding out their steadying hands. The bags of supplies and coolers were passed over as well, until finally everyone—and everything—was aboard.

"We best get down below," Margaret called as raging winds whistled.

Once inside the cabin of the boat, Hope was surprised to feel safe and warm. The cozy space was cheerily lit and just large enough to accommodate all of them comfortably.

"This is so sweet," Hope said, taking in the miniature kitchen and compact living area. There were open doors at both ends of the room, and each revealed part of a large platform bed. "We're not…

er, sleeping in here?"

"Heavens no," Margaret said.

Meredith grinned. "We're having a pajama party back at the house."

"That sounds fun," Hope answered, thinking it really did. "What about the guys?"

"They'll be gone overnight," Sofia said in cryptic tones.

Hope worriedly bit her lip, telling herself her concern was for Jackie. But, truthfully, some of it was for herself. "They won't be doing anything... naughty?"

Elsa chuckled lightly. "No worries about that."

"Then again," Margaret said, "with Chad along, you never know."

Ava laughed and unzipped her raincoat. "This is so cute in here. And stable. I can barely feel the—" The ship rocked to one side, and she grabbed onto a countertop, appearing suddenly white. "...water."

"The boat's securely moored," Margaret told her. "If things get too bad, we can always head back."

"No, let's not," Meredith said. "I mean, not unless we have to. I've never been on a boat before. This is very cool."

"Yeah," Ava agreed. "Jackie, you should snap some photos." Everyone agreed that was a super idea, especially before things got too out of hand. When they'd finished swapping Hope's phone around, Hope eyed Margaret, remembering something. "I thought the water bothered you?"

"The ocean bothers me," she explained. "Very deep water with no land in sight. Being moored at the dock is as far as I venture."

"This is a great idea," Ava said. "I'm so sorry Hope's not here to join in the fun."

Hope frowned, thinking of her sister. "Yeah, me, too."

"Okay." Sally unzipped a cooler. "We have booze."

She pulled out a chilled bottle of prosecco, and everyone cheered.

"*And* party games," Meredith said mysteriously.

"We've brought lots of great eats," Margaret said. "Plenty to drink, too. That small stove over there is ideal for making up tea or coffee. There's a French press kit in the cupboard, along with some mugs."

"That's living well for sailors," Meredith teased.

Elsa's smile brightened. "The Albright men enjoy their simple pleasures.

Meredith ducked her chin with a blush, and Hope wondered if she'd been thinking of Derrick and what sort of pleasures he might enjoy.

"Hey," Sally said. "It was my idea to bring the French press aboard."

"That's true, granddaughter," Margaret said. "I give you full credit."

"Do you sail much?" Meredith asked Sally.

"Not as much as I once did. Grandpa Chad used to take me all the time. Sometimes with my brothers, sometimes not."

"Sally sails better than any of them," Elsa said. "Except for Derrick, of course."

"We can all hold our own on the water." Sally uncorked the prosecco and held up the bottle. "Who'd like a glass?"

Several hands shot up, and Sofia said quietly, "I'll

just take some sparkling water."

All eyes turned on her, and Elsa asked gently, "Sofia?"

She puffed out a breath, appearing elated yet timid all at once. "All right, you guys. It's true. I'm pregnant."

"Oh, Sofia!" Margaret cried happily. "Congratulations."

"It's very early." Her shoulders sagged. "William and I were waiting to tell."

"Don't worry, sweetheart." Elsa hugged her shoulders. "We'll keep it a secret." She warmly studied her daughter-in-law. "And will pray for the very best."

Sofia's lips trembled. "Thank you."

After the others hugged and congratulated her as well, Meredith and Sally asked who all was hungry, deciding to serve lunch.

Hope couldn't believe the spread the others had prepared. There was cheese, prosciutto, and melon. Fresh bread and crackers…and hard sausages. A selection of delicious roasted nuts and marinated olives, too. And chocolate—there was so much chocolate, including yummy truffles and chocolate-covered cashews, and individual chocolate mousse tarts, as well as some delicious lemon tarts.

"How thoughtful," Sofia said when Sally poured her some non-alcoholic sparkling cider. "How did you guess?"

"Your failure to indulge in wine at dinner was a big tip-off." Sally smiled and whispered, "So happy for you."

"Okay," Meredith said once they were all settled

in with their drinks and plenty of delicious things to eat. "Shall we do presents first or play some games?" She was clearly viewing her role as maid of honor seriously and taking charge.

"Presents, too?" Hope asked, chewing happily on a huge slice of bread and a thick wedge of brie. "You've all already done too much."

Meredith gave Hope the side-eye, staring down at her food. Hope was clearly being out of character as Jackie, and somebody might notice.

"Oh yeah, ha-ha. I've decided to ease up a little bit on the carb thing," she announced to no one in particular. "At least for the next few days."

"And why not?" Ava said. Then she added a little too emphatically, "It's *your* wedding week, after all."

"So true," Margaret said. "And a girl only gets married *once*." She paused in sipping her prosecco. "Optimally, anyway." She apologetically eyed Ava, the lone divorcée in the room. "Sorry, dear."

Ava answered gracefully. "It's fine."

"Maybe we should play a game while we finish eating?" Sally suggested. "Let's give Jackie time to finish her food before opening gifts."

Meredith dug a large stack of notepads out of her tote bag and handed one to each person, along with a pen.

"What are these?" Hope asked.

Meredith grinned wickedly. "Dirty Mad Libs."

Hope widened her eyes at the group, then stared abashedly at Margaret.

"Don't worry about me," the older woman said. "Trust me. I've seen—and heard—just about everything."

Twenty minutes later, they were rolling with laughter at the lurid tales they'd each concocted by soliciting verbs, nouns, and adjectives from one another to fill in the blanks of their absurdly scandalous stories. Every single one of them had blushed at least once when reading her selection out loud, and Hope gave everyone bonus points, particularly the older women, for being such good sports about the game.

"Oh, my," Margaret said, still chuckling. "I can't remember when I've laughed this hard." They were raising such a ruckus on the boat they scarcely heard the rain any longer.

"Now that we're all loosened up," Meredith said, wiggling her eyebrows. "Maybe we should try one more?"

"Meredith?" Hope eyed her. "What are you up to?"

"Nothing," she said, but her grin gave her away. "Nothing at all."

Sally peeked inside the bag she was holding and guffawed. "Okay, then. Let's see if this group is up for it."

Hope's heart beat harder. "If it's really lewd, maybe we shouldn't—"

"Oh come on, Jackie," Sofia said. "We're all over twenty-one."

"Some of us much more than others," Grand-mother Margaret agreed.

Meredith grimaced and pulled the game box from the bag. "Pin the tail on the donkey, anyone?" She opened the box and lifted out a large folded piece of felt with a crossbar at the top, which held suction cups so the item could be stuck to a wall. Hope had no idea what it was until Meredith turned the fabric around.

Sally's eyebrows shot up. "That's not a donkey," she said, giggling. "That's the torso of a man."

Sofia blushed. "A very *naked* man."

"Yes." Margaret sagely surveyed the design, which was cartoon-like yet nearly anatomically correct. "But he's missing something very important."

"I've got that!" Meredith exclaimed, digging into the game box for an envelope. "Each one is Velcro," she said, her cheeks bright red.

Hope buried her face in her hands. "You didn't."

Meredith bent forward to whisper in her ear. "Like Granny said, this hopefully only happens once." She held up the silky purple eye covering that served as a blindfold during the game and waved it in the air. "Who wants to play?"

Elsa pursed her lips, then said, "I'll wait for someone else to go first."

Meredith looked around. "Sally?"

Sally started to stand, but Margaret intervened. "I'll take a crack at it," she said, stunning the others. Before she took the blindfold, she tilted her empty prosecco glass toward her granddaughter. "Another splash?"

"Sure, Grandmother." Sally's cheeks bloomed red. "No problem."

Nobody could believe it, but Grandmother Margaret actually won the game. Sofia whispered lightly to Hope that she thought she saw Margaret peek under the blindfold, but nobody honestly cared. They were all having so much fun. This was

the most amazing party Hope had ever been to. So
many generations, all getting along. Her mom
seemed to be having a really great time, too.

"This is quite a family you're marrying into," her
mom said happily, sitting beside her. Meredith had
packed away the man game, and they were on to
presents. Hope didn't know how four hours had
flown by, but somehow they already had.

"I know. They're really awesome. But, hey. So are
you."

"I'm sorry if I embarrassed you." Meredith
handed Hope a stack of presents, not really looking
regretful in the least. She actually appeared pretty
pleased with herself because everything had gone so
well.

"I'll just have to get you back sometime."

"Ha-ha," Meredith said brightly. Then people
started chanting for Hope to open her gifts. She was
half worried Meredith had given her something
really shady and was relieved to find a pretty
wedding-night negligee in the package instead. The
rest of the gifts were just as nice. Sofia supplied
scented soaps and bath salts. Sally gave her a pretty
travel purse for her honeymoon, while Margaret
gifted her with a pretty silk scarf from Italy. Elsa
presented her with an elegant gold-chain bracelet
with a small gold anchor on it. "To remind you of
our fun day here," she said, warming Hope's heart
when they hugged. Ava proffered her present last. It
was a stunning silver frame that she suggested might
hold a favorite pic from her wedding.

"This has been so wonderful," Hope said with a
sigh, thanking the others. "I don't know how I could

ever top this day."

Elsa's eyebrows rose. "How about with ice cream and a pajama party?"

"And pizza," Sally said.

"And chick flicks." Sofia grinned. "Can't forget those."

"Will we really all sleep in the house?" Hope asked, charmed by the idea of an adult sleepover.

"We've got plenty of sleeping bags in the attic," Margaret said. "We can sleep in the den."

Elsa viewed her worriedly. "If you'd like to take the sofa…"

"Bosh, Elsa. I'm not that old."

"No." Elsa giggled, her eyes on the wall where the man game had been. "Apparently not."

CHAPTER SEVENTEEN

Hope's eyes popped open when she heard the first car door slam shut. Then there was another, and another.

"My goodness, it's the boys," Margaret cried, scuttling in from the kitchen. She held a mug of coffee and wore her hot pink robe with fluffy pink slippers.

"Ack. What?" Meredith sat up abruptly, her face caked with Mother of Earth Mud Mask, which she'd apparently failed to remove before going to bed. Hope propped herself up on her elbows, nearly upending a half-empty bowl of popcorn, and stared around at the disarray. Streamers dangled from the ceiling while partially deflated balloons hovered near the ground. An open box of half-eaten donuts rested on an end table, and the case from the old VHS tape Margaret had located very late at night rested on the coffee table. She claimed to have purchased it by accident some time ago, mistaking its contents by the title. Little snippets of the film came back to Hope, all involving a male dancer with a blond mullet who looked like Rod Stewart on a bad hair day. He'd gone through four wardrobe changes and stripped down to nearly nothing.

Sofia pushed back the eye covering she'd been wearing, and Hope saw it wasn't a regular eye mask at all, but the one from their man-part game. "Wha-what's going on?" she said, looking dazed.

Ava sat up and rubbed her eyes, goggling at the mess.

Sally tugged her pillow over her head and moaned, "Five more minutes."

Hope could relate.

Before she could process much else, there were footsteps in the front hall and the sound of the front door closing. Meredith scrambled out of her sleeping bag and bolted toward the French doors. She threw one open and shrieked again. "Who are all those people?"

Hope craned her neck to see a crew of guys setting up a huge white tent while others carried in chairs. Eleanor Bell followed closely at their heels, barking out orders while waving her tablet. That's when she remembered Eleanor saying something about logistics and getting the "hardware" in place early.

"The wedding planner's here," Parker announced from the doorway to the library. He stopped short, staring at Elsa, who blanched when she noticed him eying something on her head. A cardboard man-part adhered to her hair, and it was sticking straight up, protruding from her crown like an X-rated antenna. She reached up and snatched it off, shoving the offending item beneath the flap of her sleeping bag.

Elsa smoothed down her braid and managed to say with dignified calm, "What are you guys doing back so early?"

Meredith stood frozen on the threshold to the outdoors, torn between dashing for the downstairs bathroom—and possibly past the men—or streaking through Eleanor's brigade in her PJs and mud mask.

When Derrick appeared beside his dad, she made a hasty decision and fled down the porch and across the grass, muttering something high-pitched and in Spanish.

Derrick watched, awestruck, as she trailed away, presumably toward the carriage house. He walked over and shut the door just as William and Brent entered the room.

Margaret had clearly forestalled Chad in the hallway, because Hope heard her say, "Not back there, dear. Not everybody's decent."

William surveyed the scene without comment and dipped his chin. "Morning, ladies."

Hope's face burned hot as Brent strode to the coffee table and picked up the empty video box entitled *Dirty Dancing*.

"Did Patrick Swayze moonlight?"

Sally, who was wide awake by now, shot to her feet and clubbed Brent on the shoulder with her pillow. Feathers spilled out of it on impact, sending little white puffs everywhere, joining the ones already on the sofa...matching loveseats...and all over the floor.

"Go on. Get out of here," she snapped playfully. "No boys allowed."

William pursed his lips, resisting a grin, while Derrick set his hands on his hips and just said, "Huh."

Brent held up a hand as Sally continued to pound him. "All right, all right. We're leaving." He chuckled, holding out the video box. "Who should I return this to?"

Sofia and Ava attempted to appear guileless, and

Hope tugged her sleeping bag up to her chin. Grandmother Margaret returned to catch Brent still holding *Dirty Dancing* as Grandpa Chad thudded his way upstairs. "Oh, for heaven's sake," she said, shaking her head at her grandson. "Give that to me."

• • •

When Hope and Ava entered the carriage house, Meredith was in the shower.

"You can go next, Mom," Hope told her. "I'm going to touch base with Jackie."

"Tell her she missed a great party last night. Wait." Ava paused, looking mortified. "You didn't upload any of those pictures to Instagram?"

Hope shot a teasing look at her mom. "Only the G-rated ones from the boat."

Ava gave a relieved smile. "Yesterday sure was something. Who knew the Albright women were so much fun?"

"Yeah." Hope laughed and headed toward the coffeemaker. "Coffee?"

"Make two cups for me," Ava called, bounding down the stairs.

Hope set the coffee to brew, then stepped out onto the deck overlooking the water. The sky still looked gloomy, but tomorrow was supposed to be a pretty day. It was after ten, so she hoped Jackie was headed to the airport. She speed-dialed her number and Jackie answered after one ring.

"Hi, Hope."

"Are you at the airport?"

"Headed there soon." A huge rumble roared in

the background like a billion tumbling bowling pins.

"What on earth was that?"

"Thunder," Jackie said, sounding winded. A loud *zip* indicated she was closing her bag. "It's been pouring here all morning."

"We got that yesterday."

"I hope it's clearer today."

"It is, and it's supposed to be even better tomorrow."

"My wedding day," Jackie said on a dreamy sigh. "I can hardly believe it."

Hope didn't doubt that. She'd been the one here doing all the prep work.

"How was the bachelorette party?"

"Memorable."

"Oh yeah? You only posted a few updates on Instagram. What was the deal with the boat and the sailor hats?"

"I'll tell you more about it when you get here. What time do you expect that will be?"

"I've got a noontime flight, which puts me into Boston a little past one. Blue Hill's four, four and a half, hours from there. Build in an extra thirty minutes for me to pick up the rental car."

Hope gasped. "You won't get here until six?"

"I said I'd be there for the dinner. Isn't that at seven?"

"Yeah, but what about the rehearsal?"

"My earlier flight was canceled, and the next scheduled one was all sold out, with people scrambling to leave the island before the storms."

A dead weight settled in Hope's stomach. "Oh no, Jackie. What if you don't—?"

"Hush. Don't even say it. Do you want to curse my travels or something?"

"No, of course not." Hope bit her bottom lip. "I'm just worried—that's all. The ceremony's in the morning—at eleven a.m. Then there's the big fancy lunch and reception."

"I'll be there for that." Jackie actually sounded annoyed that Hope would doubt her. "All right?"

"And tonight?"

"Hang on. I heard a horn." There was a brief pause, and Jackie returned to the line. "That's my car to the airport. Gotta dash."

"Text me from the runway."

"What?"

"To let me know you're taking off."

"Okay. No problem. I'll see you soon." Her tone softened. "And thank you, Hopie."

"You don't need to keep thanking me," Hope said, feeling like she'd gotten the better end of the deal. She'd come to love Brent and become enchanted by his family. Sadly, those benefits were double-edged swords. Because now Hope understood how hard it was going to be to lose them. "Just don't be late, okay? I honestly don't think I can do this for one more day."

She ended the call and wiped back the single tear that had streaked down her cheek.

"Honey?" Ava said, stepping through the sliding glass door. "Are you okay?"

Hope sniffed and tried to collect herself. "Yeah, Mom. Just fine."

"Is Jackie on her way?"

Hope nodded, and her chin trembled.

"Oh, sweetheart." Ava pulled her into a hug. "This is so very hard for you, isn't it?"

Hope met her mom's gaze, all teary-eyed. "How could it not be hard, Mom?"

"You're right." Ava hugged her again and patted her back. "The whole situation's terrible. You're the one who should be marrying Brent, not Jackie."

She lifted her head off her mom's shoulder and stared at her in surprise.

"You kids are falling for each other," Ava said. "Have fallen. It's written all over your auras and maybe in the stars."

"Well then, those stars have left us star-crossed," Hope said sadly. She pulled out of her mom's embrace and wiped her cheeks with the back of her hand. "And maybe that's what I deserve. But not Brent."

"When Jackie arrives, maybe you should explain things."

"To Brent? And his family?" Hope asked in shock. "That would blow this wedding apart."

"Yes. It could at that." Ava furrowed her brow. "But wouldn't that be better than Brent marrying the wrong sister?"

Hope inhaled sharply. "That's just it. Brent didn't ask me to marry him. He asked Jackie, and if this weird twin swap had never happened, he'd still be marrying her anyway."

"Then he never would have known what he's missing, would he?"

• • •

Later that afternoon, Brent knocked on the carriage house door, looking gorgeous in a coat and tie. Hope had dressed in a pretty white off-the-shoulders sundress with a flouncy hem that hit above her knees. She wore casual flat sandals with it and had partially pulled back her hair. Meredith and her mom were still changing for the rehearsal. Hope pressed open the screen to find Brent smiling at her while holding a beautiful bouquet of fresh flowers. "These are for you," he said, "from Grandmother's garden."

"Aww. How sweet."

"Sally's gathering wildflower bouquets for the bridesmaids, but I handpicked these myself just for you."

Heat warmed her cheeks.

"It's hard to believe tomorrow's the day."

"I know," she said, accepting the flowers and wishing it could be her holding the bridal bouquet tomorrow instead of Jackie. "Can't wait."

His eyebrows arched. "Have you heard anything more from Hope? Did she make her flight?"

"Yes. Thank goodness. She texted me from the runway that she'd gotten on the plane." Hope worriedly glanced at the time on the kitchen clock. Nearly five o'clock. "She should have landed in Boston by now and be on her way."

"Maybe you should call her to check in?"

"What? Now? I don't know, Brent. She's probably busy picking up her rental car."

"Might be good for us to update the others. Everyone's been asking about her."

"Yeah, yeah. Of course."

Hope's heart hammered as she set down the bouquet and nabbed her phone from where it lay on the kitchen counter. Half of her desperately wanted Jackie to answer, but the other half didn't. Especially with Brent watching her.

After three rings, Jackie answered, clearly out of breath. "Can't talk now." She sounded like she was juggling things. Suitcases, perhaps. "I'm headed back to the airport."

"Back?"

"I was on standby for the six o'clock flight."

"What do you mean? I thought you'd boarded the plane."

"We sat on the runway for hours, Hope." She turned her back on Brent when Jackie said her name. "*Hours.* Until people started complaining that the airline was violating federal regulations or something. The captain kept waiting on the all-clear from the tower, but it never came. Finally, they cancelled the flight."

"Oh, no."

"Oh, yeah. I wasn't going to call you until I was sure of this one."

"What do you mean, sure?"

"There's a chance that this one won't go through, either."

Hope stroked her heart-shaped pendant, her head suddenly woozy. This couldn't be happening. It couldn't. "What about—alternatives?" She was about to ask about a boat when she recalled that Brent was listening.

"Ferry service has been suspended for today. On account of"—thunder boomed loudly—"the storms."

"Please don't say it."

"I know, I know," Jackie wailed, and then her voice shattered into sobs. "Don't you think I feel terrible about this?"

Hope held up her hand, and Brent read her signaled need for privacy, stepping out onto the deck.

"Jackie," Hope said in hushed tones. "You can't bail on me now. You have to be here."

"I'm try-trying…" Jackie blubbered and blew her nose. "So, so hard. I never thought it would come to this, Hopie. Never dreamed it would go this far. At first I was afraid—"

"Afraid of what?"

"Marrying Brent. The decision was so hasty, and I was honestly still stung from Rodney."

"Oh, no. You mean Meredith was right? This was a rebound thing?"

"Since when have you gotten so cozy with Meredith that she's spilling all my secrets?"

"Since you decided not to show up for your own wedding week."

"Okay, all right. Sheesh. You don't have to be so mean. I already feel like the worst person on earth. Next to you, probably. I'm sure you feel even worse."

"Thanks, Jackie. Thanks a lot."

"And anyway, it's not all about Rodney."

"Let's hope not."

"Brent seems pretty wonderful. You've attested to this yourself. And he offered me something, Hopie. Something immeasurable. The kind of life I've always wanted."

Hope glanced through the sliding glass doors at

Brent's rugged profile framed by the backdrop of the bay, thinking that this was the sort of life she'd always wanted, too. Only she'd never known about it until this week and meeting Brent.

"It's just that, after we got our marriage license at the courthouse, I started getting nervous that I was making a—"

"Wait a minute. What did you say? Marriage license? What marriage license?"

"You know, the little piece of paper you sign at the courthouse that says you're legally wed? We had to take care of that a few weeks ago before Brent's business trip."

A lead weight settled in Hope's stomach. She was in a far worse fix than she'd understood. "You and Brent are already legally married?"

"Only on paper," Jackie hastily added. "Nothing really counts until the ceremony."

"What? Why didn't you tell me?" Hope's head reeled. She'd been falling in love—and making out—with a married man? *What?*

"What does it even matter if I get there in time?"

Hope anxiously fiddled with her hair, wrapping a strand of it around her finger. She couldn't possibly tell Jackie she'd already kissed Brent. Much less that she'd fallen head over heels for him. "You're right. I know you're right."

"Hang tight," Jackie continued in a panic. "I'm going to do everything I can to fix this. Let's just pray that flight at six goes off."

"And if it doesn't?"

Jackie paused in trepidation before replying. "There won't be another one until tomorrow."

Hope felt faint. "You're not saying you'll miss the wedding? Your own wedding, Jackie?"

"Let's not go there," she answered nervously. "We don't want to jinx anything."

• • •

By five o'clock, the gray skies had cleared, and a beautiful orange haze settled over the bay. Soft winds blew, and the setting sun dodged departing clouds, sending shimmering halos of light across the water. The view was breathtaking from the spot on the lawn where Eleanor had situated the altar, which was constructed from gauzy fabric draped from the enormous limb of a sturdy oak at the side of the yard that hugged the flower gardens.

Hope was embarrassed by the fluttering in her belly and the way her pulse raced as she stepped forward toward Brent, holding her homemade bouquet. She kept telling herself it was supposed to be Jackie partaking in this practice ceremony and not her. Yet she couldn't help but believe that Brent wouldn't be gazing at Jackie the same way he looked at her—like he was staring happily into his future.

Sally, Meredith, and Sofia stood off to one side, with Derrick and William on the other. Since the weather had improved and was predicted to hold for tomorrow, Eleanor's crew had established seating for the immediate family and their twenty expected guests in the space between the back porch and firepit area. The chairs were strategically placed at an angle so as to provide a view of both the nuptials and the bay beyond the altar. Her mom, Parker,

Elsa, Grandpa Chad, and Grandmother Margaret were all dressed nicely and seated in the front row.

Hope couldn't imagine a more idyllic spot in which to get married. Jackie was so incredibly lucky to be marrying a guy like Brent. When she arrived in Blue Hill, Hope was going to have to step aside and let her do just that. As much as she wanted to blame Jackie for this duplicitous situation, Hope now saw that this entire fiasco was legitimately her fault.

When she'd told Jackie that no, she wouldn't impersonate her, she should have stayed firm on that. She'd had dozens of opportunities to tell Brent and his family the truth since then, but she hadn't. And, in her guilty heart, she knew why. She'd been attracted to Brent from the beginning, and when he'd appeared equally attracted to her, she couldn't bear for the fantasy to end.

"So, this is where you'll stand." Eleanor gripped Hope's shoulders and gently scooted her over. "Be sure to keep your body slightly turned toward the groom."

Brent winked, and Hope's face heated all over. Keeping her eyes on the groom definitely wouldn't be an issue if she were the one marrying Brent. *But that's going to be Jackie's job tomorrow*, Hope reminded herself again and again and again. She peeked at her watch, privately fretting over Jackie's flight, and Eleanor raised an eyebrow in disapproval.

"This will only take five more minutes," she said. "We're not going to run through the vows."

"We're not?" Brent asked.

"It's best to keep that part special. You, of course, know the basic drill. The minister will ask you if you take Jackie to be your wife, and her if she takes you to be her husband. You'll exchange rings." She shot a look at Brent. "You have those?"

"Of course." He cocked his chin at Derrick, who patted his jacket pocket.

"Got them right here."

"Excellent, then." Eleanor briskly patted Brent's shoulders. "That's all there is to it." She carefully scanned the heavens. "Looks like the weather's cooperating, too."

Brent smiled at Hope. "Sounds like we're all set."

"Sounds like cocktail time," Derrick said with a grin.

"I'll drink to that." Meredith grinned back, and Hope marveled to herself once again at how well they were getting along. She was also impressed by Meredith's and her mom's ability to keep her secret. She'd told them about Jackie's latest delay, and both had groaned.

Eleanor nodded her goodbyes as the parents and grandparents stood from their chairs. "Won't you stay and enjoy a drink with us?" Grandpa Chad asked graciously.

"No, thank you. Best not." Eleanor packed her tablet away in her oversize purse, and Hope experienced a new burst of panic. What if that six o'clock flight did get canceled and Jackie couldn't get here in time?

"Er...Eleanor?" she asked her quietly and out of the others' earshot. "About tomorrow..."

"Yes. What about it?"

"It's just that I'm terribly worried. Worried that my sister might not make the morning ceremony.

She's experiencing weather delays in air travel."

"Now, that is a shame," Eleanor said, not completely appearing concerned about it. "I always liked Hope."

"Exactly. I mean, me, too. I love her, of course, and naturally want her here."

"Sometimes these things can't be helped. Sorry." Eleanor fished her keys from her bag and strode toward the drive in a perfunctory manner. Hope chased after her, her anxiety levels rising.

"If she can't… What I mean is, if Hope can't make it somehow. I was wondering if there's possibly any way to delay the wedding?"

Eleanor turned on her heel. "Delay?"

"Only by a couple of hours," Hope explained. "Perhaps put it off until afternoon, if necessary? The reception food's hearty. It could just as well work for dinner."

"I don't think so," Eleanor said. Her gaze swept over Hope. "You of all people would understand how the logistics of a wedding are set in stone. The violinist has another engagement later in the day. So does the minister." She waved a hand in frustration. "And don't even get me started on the catering issues."

"But—"

"No buts about it, I'm afraid." She gave Hope a sympathetic look, but Hope suspected her compassion was fake. "The show must go on, as they say."

"The show," Hope repeated, recalling her earlier acting role as Jackie and thinking about how much huger the consequences were now. "Sure."

Hope's phone emitted the alert tone, signaling she'd received at text, and Hope dashed for her clutch, which rested on one of the rear chairs. She heard Eleanor start her engine as she stared down at Jackie's message and her entire world caved in.

All flights canceled for tonight and tomorrow. We'll have to swap in Boston. Will email a plan. So sorry, Hopie. You're a champ.

...

Ava, Meredith, and Hope went to freshen up in the carriage house before the group departed for dinner. That's when Hope dropped the bombshell on the other two regarding Jackie's latest text. "I'm sorry, guys," she said wearily as they entered the kitchen. "But I'm afraid I've got bad news."

Meredith gasped. "Don't say it."

"Jackie's not going to make the wedding."

Ava completely paled, and Meredith raked her hands through her curls. "*Ay dios mio*, I told you not to say it. No, no, no. This can't be true."

"How can this be?" Ava asked. "What happened?"

"Those really bad storms haven't lifted. Nothing's landing in Boston. Boat service out of Nantucket's been suspended, too."

"So, what's going to happen?" Ava's mouth hung open. "*You're* marrying Brent?"

"He's already married," Hope spouted in a rush. "On paper—to Jackie."

Meredith slapped her forehead. "The marriage license. That's right. I remember Jackie saying something about going to get it, but that was weeks ago."

Ava perplexedly eyed Hope. "Oh, dear."

"Is this what Jackie wants?" Meredith asked, sounding incredulous. "For you to act as her during the ceremony?"

Hope nodded, feeling faint. "We're making the switch in Boston. At the airport, before Brent and Jackie leave on their honeymoon.

"Hope—wait." Ava held up her hands. "This is too much."

Hope felt like this great big snowball had been rolling for so long she was about to get crushed under its enormous weight. "Everything's all ready to go, Mom. The preparations...the caterers...the clergy. And—this time—the delay really isn't Jackie's fault. She couldn't help the weather."

Meredith sighed and crossed her arms. "So, you're going through with it? The reception, the wedding night, everything?"

"Er, probably not *everything*. I'll find a way to navigate the wedding night and day."

Ava and Meredith swapped incredulous looks.

"Seriously," Hope said in her defense. "Would either of you want to tell them? Talk to Brent and all the Albrights and tell them the truth right now?"

"No." Meredith's shoulders sagged, and then she frowned. "Not really."

"Oh, dear," Ava said again. "Oh, dear. Oh, dear. Oh, dear."

Meredith blew out a hard breath and held up her

hands. "This is nuts, but I'm here for you. Here for you and Jackie."

"What about Brent?" A tear glistened in the corner of Ava's eye, and seeing her mom get emotional made her feel emotional, too.

"If I'd never come to Blue Hill, he would have married Jackie anyway. He already made his decision, Mom. A long time ago."

Ava sighed dejectedly. "I suppose that's true. I only wish…"

"Wish what?"

Her mom's eyes glimmered. "That things had worked out differently."

"Yeah. Me, too."

• • •

Later, at the restaurant, Hope stared around the room at all the happy faces, thinking about how close she'd gotten to everyone. Now, she was deceiving them all in a most unforgiveable way. But what was her alternative? Ruining the special occasion they'd all worked extra hard to support? That would prove a major slap in the face, and Hope understood she couldn't do that to any of them — above all to Brent.

Maybe this would all be okay. Jackie and Brent were legally married, anyway, and that's precisely what Brent wanted. This wedding week in Maine was about showing their commitment to each other and creating happy memories with the family for everyone to look back on. Hope wouldn't rob them of those moments of joy.

It would be selfish of her—and heartless.

Tougher to keep up the ruse until she met up with Jackie in Boston and they switched back. But—for the benefit of Brent and his family—that's what Hope was steeling herself to do.

She forced a bright smile and turned to Brent. "I love chicken parmigiana," she said, responding to his comment about her menu selection. "So, I thought… Why not?"

"Why not, indeed." Brent toasted her with his glass, and she clinked her glass to his. "I can't believe this is really happening. Just think. By this time tomorrow, we'll be husband and wife. In the way that you wanted, sweetheart. With the vows, the rings…"

He stared down at her ring finger. "Grandmother Margaret's ring. Did Meredith bring it?"

Hope forced a pouty frown. "I'm so sorry. She tried. But the jeweler had…"

Meredith, who was sitting on Hope's other side, leaned toward Brent. "A death in the family."

"Oh, no."

"Very sudden." Meredith nodded. "They closed for the rest of the week."

"What rotten luck."

Hope's face steamed as she took a swallow of wine. "Yeah. Terrible."

Derrick, who had seen them toasting, held up his glass. "I think a toast is in order," he said, "to all of those who've gathered here from near and far to join in this happy occasion. Including those of us who arrived a bit late." He tipped his glass toward Meredith, and her eyebrows twitched.

"You know what they say," she announced

brightly, holding up her wine. "Better late than never."

"Hear, hear," Grandpa Chad called, saluting Meredith and also Ava.

"It's true," Elsa chimed in. "We're just so glad everyone could make it." Her face fell in a frown. "Except for Hope." She turned guilty eyes on the wedding couple. "We're all so sorry about that. Do you think there's any way she still might get here?"

Hope's shoulders sagged. "Things don't look good. There's a nor'easter blowing up the coast, and flights into Boston are grounded."

Sally frowned sadly. "If she can't make it, no doubt she'll be here with us in spirit."

"In spirit." Ava nodded, staring misty-eyed at Hope, then at Brent. "Yes, yes. That's true."

"Is there any way to delay the wedding?" Parker asked. "Hold off for just a couple hours to buy Hope more time?"

The women communally shook their heads. "I'm sorry, dear," Margaret told her son, "but Jackie's already checked with Eleanor. Rescheduling the event at this late date is impossible."

"That seems a shame," William said, and Sofia rubbed his arm in solidarity.

"Then let's all send good vibes Hope's way," Derrick said, regaining the floor. He raised his tumbler high. "Here's to Hope. To her health and speedy travels. And if she can't make it by tomorrow, here's hoping she'll be able to join us at our next happy occasion."

"To Hope," everyone cheered, clinking glasses all around.

Hope barely managed, her voice rasping hoarsely past the lump in her throat. "To Hope."

As appetizers were served, Brent took her hand under the table. "Don't worry, baby. Everything will turn out all right."

"That's a Beach Boys song," she bantered, trying to keep things light, although her heart thumped wildly and she simultaneously felt sick to her stomach. Suddenly, the chicken parmigiana didn't sound so appealing anymore.

"Maybe it should be our song, hmm?" His dark eyes glimmered, and heat crept up her neck, fanning across her face. "We don't have one, you know. It's not too late." His lips tipped up at the corners, and she couldn't help but think about how wonderful it felt to kiss them. And what a despicable thing she'd done. Kissing her sister's husband. She was determined not to let it happen again. Even if tomorrow was her fake wedding day.

"We can ask the DJ to play it at the reception," Brent persisted. "Maybe even for our first dance?"

"Isn't that song supposed to be special between the bride and groom?"

He traced her mouth with his thumb and whispered huskily, "Why can't we make it ours now?"

Hope's pulse raced. "I…can't think of any reason not to."

"Great." He squeezed her hand and turned to the group, proudly announcing their plan. "Attention, please. I'm very proud and happy to announce that Jackie and I have selected our couple's song. 'Don't Worry Baby' by the Beach Boys."

"Aww, how sweet," Meredith exclaimed.

"An oldie but a goodie," Derrick joined in, and everyone agreed.

"No one should be worried on their wedding day," Sally said, hoisting her wineglass.

"That's true," Margaret said.

"Smooth sailing from tomorrow on out," Parker promised with a fatherly gleam in his eye, and Hope wanted to vomit. She was such a horrible person, duping them all. She flagged down a waiter and asked him to bring her some sparkling water, which arrived right before their meals did. Thank goodness. She took several soothing bubbly sips.

After everyone was served, Meredith clinked the side of her water glass with her spoon. "Before we begin," she said, standing, "I wanted to thank everyone here for your hospitality. While I know the real toasting and roasting"—she winked at Hope, and the group tittered— "will take place tomorrow during the reception, I wanted to use this occasion to say how happy I am to see my best friend on earth becoming a part of such a wonderful family." She smiled admiringly at them all while pointedly avoiding Derrick's spot at the table.

Several people said *aww*, and Elsa dabbed the corner of her eye with a napkin.

"So, here's to an amazing wedding tomorrow. And to two people who were meant to be together." Meredith lifted her wineglass high. "To a long and happy marriage for both of you."

CHAPTER EIGHTEEN

Hope awoke to the sound of dishes clattering in the kitchen, and she smelled coffee brewing. Meredith and her mom were up making breakfast: her wedding-day breakfast. *Yikes.* Hope lunged for the phone on her nightstand, praying for an eleventh-hour reprieve. Maybe she'd heard from Jackie that she was on her way. Maybe everything would be all right after all. But, when Hope reviewed her messages, she saw the most recent one from Jackie had come in at two a.m. She'd heard her phone ding and read the text blurry-eyed. Something about the email being sent.

She flipped to her email app, opening the early-morning missive from her sister. It explained in detail how they'd meet up at the Boston airport outside gate security. They'd do a brief wardrobe exchange in the ladies' room, and then Jackie would go off on her honeymoon with Brent, as expected, and Hope could go on home. Her heart sank when she realized they might actually pull this off and that her sister would stand to benefit from the progress she'd made in Blue Hill, including with amazing Brent.

Then a stunning thought occurred to Hope. What if Brent hadn't been able to tell that she wasn't Jackie because he hadn't known Jackie well enough — but that he could sense it when the "Jackie" he'd be reunited with in Boston seems so different from the one he'd gotten to know? *Know and love*, Hope couldn't help think with a whimper.

"Good morning, Dancing Queen," Meredith said, waltzing into the bedroom with a coffee mug. Hope sat up in bed, turning her phone facedown on the duvet.

"Thank you." She forced a smile. "Coffee's just what I need." *Plus a double-shot of confidence. And maybe a sanity check.* She took a sip of coffee, her nerves on edge.

"I know you're upset," Meredith said kindly. "All of us are."

"I've never been in such a bind. But the Albrights…" Her voice wavered, and Meredith sat on the edge of her bed, taking her hand.

"They're pretty special, I know."

Hope's eyes burned hot. "Especially Brent."

"You've really come to care for him." Meredith smiled. "More than care. Right?" She handed hope a napkin, and Hope wiped her damp cheeks.

"He doesn't deserve either of us, you know?"

"Maybe not—but Hope?"

"Huh?"

"I do understand why you're doing what you're doing."

Hope sniffled. "Yeah? Why?"

"It's because you're a good person, deep down inside. You don't want to hurt anyone. You're trying to help your sister and don't want to ruin the wedding for the Albrights. But, most of all, I suspect, you don't want to disillusion Brent."

"This would kill him, Meredith. Break his heart. And I can't—"

Meredith raised her chin with one hand. "So, then don't."

"You can't imagine how conflicted I feel."

"Actually," Meredith said glumly. "I can."

• • •

Brent opened his eyes, then squinted them shut as bright light poured in from the partially opened blinds on the window.

"Up and Adam, Adam Ant," William said, uttering the expression their grandpa had used to rouse them during those childhood summer mornings when he and Brent had shared this room in the house.

Brent sat up partway, and his head throbbed when he gazed at William, who was surrounded in a sunny haze. "Darker, please."

William chuckled and handed Brent a mug of coffee before striding to the window and tilting the blinds upward. "How much wine did you have at dinner, man?"

"Not a ton, but maybe too much."

"It's a good thing Derrick was our DD."

"Yeah," Brent replied. Derrick had only had that one drink, even if he'd had the harder stuff. He set his feet on the floor and took a swig of coffee, which made him feel slightly human again. That's when he remembered it was his wedding day. A happy grin spread across his lips in spite of himself. "Thanks for the jo, bro," he teased lightly.

"Is it helping?"

Brent nodded and took another long drag of the

steaming java.

"Good."

Brent took a moment to peruse the room, his eyes adjusting to the faint natural light. "It seems eons ago we were kids here."

"It *was* eons ago." William laughed and took a seat on the twin bed that used to be his. "Those were some good times, huh?"

Brent reflected on those carefree summers, when the most pressing things he had to do were build fires for clambakes and go sailing with his grandpa. "Yeah, when we were little it was cool. Back before we became teenagers and started getting those summer jobs. Then, college came along…"

"And life." William sighed happily. "Not that life is bad now."

Brent smiled. "From the looks of things, you and Sofia have got it pretty good."

"It's great being married," William promised. "You'll love it."

"Oh yeah?"

"Yeah."

Brent checked his phone on the nightstand, seeing it was nearly nine o'clock. " Eleanor will be arriving soon, and I need to shower and shave. Thanks for the wake-up call."

"Someone had to do it," William joked. "So we drew straws."

"Shut up. I bet Derrick isn't even here yet."

"You're right. He's not."

"I'm excited for you and Sofia," Brent said. "About the baby." William had confided in his brothers, dad, and grandpa during their card game because he'd never been able to pull off a poker face. Particularly about something so personal and important.

When Brent had guessed the truth, William had spilled. Later, Brent discovered that the ladies had learned the happy news from Sofia on the boat, so the whole family was abreast of the information and fully on William and Sofia's side, emitting positive vibes.

"Thanks. We're excited, too."

"It's going to go great," Brent told him kindly. "You'll see."

William's eyes sparkled. "Sofia and I have a request."

"Oh? What's that?"

"If things go as planned, and well... We're hoping..." William took a deep breath and pressed ahead. "Hoping that you and Jackie can be our baby's godparents."

Brent's eyes warmed. He'd never felt so honored. "That would be amazing." He swallowed past the sore spot in his throat. "I'm sure Jackie would think so, too."

"She's a special woman," William said. "You're lucky to have her." His smile sparkled. "Of course, that goes both ways."

Brent laughed and drained the rest of his coffee. "Thanks. Yeah, I feel pretty lucky. Jackie's so much more than I hoped for. I mean, she really makes me happy. Really gets me. You know? I didn't think that it was possible for me to have what you and Sofia have. What Mom and Dad have. Even Grandpa and Grandmother."

William wiggled his eyebrows. "Love works in mysterious ways."

"Sure does."

"I'm really sorry about her sister, though," William said. "I can't imagine how I might have felt if you or Derrick hadn't made my and Sofia's ceremony."

"I know. The entire situation rots. I wish I'd met Hope earlier, but this thing with me and Jackie happened pretty fast."

"Don't I know it," William said, but his tone was lighthearted. "All of us knew it." Next, he confided quietly, "And, honestly? A few of us were concerned."

"And now?"

William stood and swatted him on the shoulder. "Now I'm worried for Jackie."

"Ha-ha." Brent smirked at his brother, not minding the playful ribbing.

"You two will do just fine. Everyone loves her." He chuckled. "She's prettier than you."

Brent set his mug down and lifted a pillow, preparing to lob it at William, who ducked behind the door.

"Bro."

William peered back into the room.

"Have you got another minute?"

"Sure." His brow creased. "What's up?"

Brent waited while William took a seat on the other twin bed, then said, "We've never really talked about this Grandpa thing."

"About Albright Enterprises, you mean?"

Brent nodded. "Yeah, that."

"Look, Brent. I'm really cool with it. I've got my job, and it's all good."

"But did you want it?" Brent was ashamed he'd never asked.

"At one point, I might have thought…maybe. But there are other things that matter to me more."

"Wow, William. You're just so perfect all the time. Even graceful about this."

"I am far from perfect. Just ask Sofia."

"Why her?"

"Because she knows all my flaws."

"Like what?" Brent joked. "You don't always floss your teeth?"

"Funny. Sure."

"I mean it. Tell me one thing. Anything. Give me something to work with to make me feel less…"

William worriedly met his gaze. "Less what, man? You can't mean to tell me you're… No. No way. My rich and successful little brother is *not* jealous of me."

Brent arched his eyebrows. "One thing. Come on, man. Give."

William chuckled out loud. "Okay, all right. But you can't breathe a word."

"Cross my heart," Brent said kiddingly.

"I've always been jealous of Derrick."

"No way."

William set his chin. "He's so stinking creative. I mean, really. He's amazing with his hands. I could never do what he does."

Brent considered this a minute. "Who knew? Derrick."

"And Sally," William admitted.

"Sally?"

"She's the genius in our family. Always got straight As."

"So did you."

"Yeah, but I had to work for them. She never did."

"You don't know that's true."

"Sure I do—because I asked her."

Brent chortled, imagining his sister's retort. "Of course she told you that. Sally wants to think she's better than the rest of us guys."

"Couldn't have been easy growing up with only brothers."

"We were nice ones, though."

"Yep. That's true." William pursed his lips and said, "And then there's you."

His brother could have bowled him over. "Me?"

"You always had all the girls, man. I was just tall and gangly."

"Come on, you had girlfriends." Brent stopped himself. "I mean, one—before Sofia."

"Ah, but you had plenty." A sly smile crept onto William's lips. "You even stole one of mine."

"What? No."

"Laurin Turner," William stated.

"Who?"

"She wasn't even in your grade at school. She was in mine."

"Wait a minute." Brent chuckled. "Are we talking elementary school? That's really reaching."

"She was my first love." William shared a wistful look, though he was clearly playing around. "But she was in love with my baby brother."

Brent searched the recesses of his brain. *Laurin. Laurin.* "The one with braids who lived down the street from us?"

"That's the one." William's eyes held a mysterious twinkle. "I tried to send her a love note, you know."

"You did not."

"Did so."

"What did it say?"

"It was pretty straightforward. Just 'William plus Laurin' with a little heart drawn after her name."

"That's sweet."

"Yeah, except she asked me what that blob meant."

"Blob?"

"I told you I wasn't artistic."

Brent chuckled. "Aww."

"And then, she told me there was only one Albright for her: you."

"I had no idea."

"Maybe she was hoping I'd fix you up."

"Sure, man. Sure," Brent said, laughing.

William stood and walked toward the door. "In any case, you'd better hurry up and get dressed. You should probably grab something to eat, too. The caterers are already here commandeering the kitchen and setting stuff up, so you'll have to move fast."

Brent nodded at his brother. "Thanks for all of that."

"No worries. Just don't go blabbing my secrets."

"You know," he said as William turned. "You're going to make a really great dad."

William smiled over his shoulder. "Thanks, man. So are you."

• • •

Sally held in Hope's waist as Meredith laced up the
wedding gown. The fit wasn't too, too bad. Just
slightly snugger than on Wednesday. Thank
goodness for Grandmother Margaret's shapewear,
which helped.

They were in her bedroom on the second floor.
The men had congregated in Grandpa Chad's study
behind closed doors, and Hope knew they all sported tuxedos. She foolishly couldn't wait to see Brent
in his, knowing he'd make a dreamy picture. Her
heart pounded at the idea that he might consider
her appearance dreamy as well. She couldn't help
but wonder about Jackie and Brent and what they
might each be feeling on this day if things had been
different.

If it had been Jackie here in Hope's place this
week, would the bride and groom be just as excited
about getting married as Brent and Hope felt now?
Would there be butterflies in Jackie's stomach at the
thought of holding both Brent's hands while gazing
into his eyes and saying "I do"? Hope just didn't
know, so she willed herself not to think about it. She
was only torturing herself, in the end. It was best to
focus on procedure while trying to divorce herself
from her emotions, because it was her emotional self
that was most likely to trip her up.

When Hope, her mom, and Meredith had entered
the main house, Sally had met them in the foyer and
hurried them upstairs to where Sofia, Elsa, and
Margaret were already beautifully dressed and

waiting. The navy blue bridesmaids dresses worn by Sofia, Sally, and Meredith had fitted bodices and an off-the-shoulder look on one side, which tied up in a silky bow on the other. They all wore cream-colored pumps, pearl necklaces, and silk flowers in their upswept hair.

Brent's grandma wore a pale blue silk suit, while Ava had donned a pale rose slip dress that hugged her figure, hitting right above the knees. Elsa wore a powder blue tunic and sleek cream-colored slacks. This was the first time she'd seen Elsa wear her hair down, and it tumbled past her shoulders in silky yellow waves.

Hope wore pearl stud earrings and her gold-heart necklace. She briefly considered taking it off but opted to keep it on as some kind of weird good-luck charm. And today, she needed all the good luck she could get.

"Everyone looks so pretty," she said, glancing around at the group.

"None of us outshines the bride," Elsa said, admiring Hope's refection in the mirror. Color dusted Hope's cheeks, and her eyes appeared extra dramatic, probably due to the heavy eyeliner, mascara, and eye shadow that Meredith had applied.

Meredith had insisted on giving Hope a makeover in the carriage house after breakfast, and Ava had urged her to go along with it to get her more "in character."

As if Hope wasn't deeply imbedded as Jackie already.

Though Hope didn't typically wear this much makeup, she conceded the effect was stunning—in the right sort of way for a bride on her wedding day. She actually looked radiant and not overly clownish, which she'd at first feared she might.

"It's true," Ava said. "I've never seen you looking so beautiful." Then she pulled her daughter in for a hug and whispered, "Everything's going to be fine."

But Hope knew that it wouldn't.

This was supposed to be the best day of her life — or really, Jackie's.

She was so mixed up, she didn't know what to feel.

Elation? Confusion? Fear? The tiniest glimmer of hope?

Meredith gently rubbed her back. "Hey, you," she said softly as Hope struggled to hold in her building tears. Hope peered at her, and she mouthed firmly, "*You've got this*."

Hope gathered her nerve, then blinked back the moisture in her eyes and forced a big smile, turning back toward the others. "So?" she asked, doing a mini pirouette in her gorgeous wedding dress. "Do I look okay?"

Sofia beamed. "You look incredible."

"Like a dream," Meredith said.

Ava pulled a tissue from her purse on the bed and dabbed her eye. "My first baby getting married," she said with a sniff.

"I couldn't have wished for a nicer granddaughter-in-law," Margaret said.

Elsa smiled. "Nor I a sweeter new daughter."

"Aww, thank you." Hope blushed hotly. "I couldn't have asked to join a nicer family, that's for sure." And she really meant that part. If only it could be her marrying Brent for real—that would be like the most amazing dream come true.

But dreams didn't come true for people like Hope. Especially when they committed horrible, unforgiveable sins like this one.

She told herself not to let her mind go down that road and to focus on the positive. Her sister and Brent were going to have a wonderful marriage because Brent was going to work hard at it.

Jackie would, too, if she knew what was good for her. Hope was going to do her best to make sure of that.

Sally strode to the window, which looked over the back lawn. "Yep, getting crowded already. The chairs are nearly full."

At least this was finally happening, so it would all be over soon.

Then Hope could get on with her ordinary life and try to pretend this never happened.

• • •

Hope clutched her bouquet tightly in both hands and approached the path leading to the altar. While the floral arrangement was gorgeous, she liked the handpicked flowers that Brent had given her for the rehearsal even more.

She saw him standing between the minister and Derrick under the large oak tree, and his image took her breath away. Brent was even more devastatingly handsome in a tuxedo than she could have imagined, and she'd been imagining him a lot.

The sun was behind her as she inched forward

with Eleanor at her elbow. "Wait just one sec," Eleanor whispered as the violinist played the prelude and Sally, Sofia, and Meredith took their turns walking down the aisle, holding yellow rose bouquets.

Once they'd assumed their places on the minister's left side, the violinist changed tunes. Unexpectedly, though, she didn't begin a string edition of "Wedding March."

She started in on a heartfelt rendering of "Don't Worry Baby" by the Beach Boys. Tears sprang to Hope's eyes when she realized what Brent had done. He'd requested this just for her. Eleanor held her back while the musician finished the sweet refrain, ending on a high note.

Hope gathered her reserves with a sniff, telling herself not to be foolish. *None of this is real*, she repeated in her head. *It's all make believe.*

After a short pause, "Wedding March" began, and wedding guests turned their heads in Hope's direction. Eleanor lightly tapped her arm, and she began her unsteady promenade toward the altar, people standing from their chairs while the strains of the music played on.

As Hope passed folks by, they sent her admiring glances before turning to smile at the groom. These were mostly extended family from Brent's side, and Hope didn't recognize most of the faces.

Her gaze swept past Grandpa Chad and Grandmother Margaret in the front row next to Ava. Elsa and Parker were seated there as well, and there was a nice-looking middle-aged man with a solid jaw next to Parker. Hope took him to be the family friend Margaret had said was like a brother to Brent's dad and an uncle to Parker and Elsa's children.

Two women vaguely resembling Elsa were located nearby, each with her husband, and every single face Hope encountered was lit up like morning sunshine.

Then she turned her eyes on Brent, and he blew them all away with his stunning smile and sexy dark eyes that beheld her with adoration and wonder.

This isn't real, she told herself again, repeating the mantra over and over.

Not real. Not real. Not real.

Hope sucked in a breath as the minister motioned for the guests to be seated.

Make believe.

The musician completed her song, leaving the sonorous sound rising in the wind.

Hope's stomach did flip-flops, and her legs felt like jelly as she scooted beside Brent, basking in his warm glow of love and affection, and she felt instantly bolstered by his presence.

Not real. Not real.

Hope's heart pounded as every ounce of her being wished this wasn't make believe.

She stole a glance at Meredith, who shot her a panicked look, like she was having last minute doubts.

But this was all too real, and it was too late to stop it.

The bridesmaids looked so beautiful.

Derrick and William looked awesome in their tuxedos, too.

But no man on the scene compared with Brent.

"Beloved guests," the minister began. "Family and friends of the bride and groom, we've gathered here today on this gorgeous Saturday in June to unite Jackie Webb and Brent Albright in holy matrimony…"

The ceremony proceeded with Derrick reading William Shakespeare's "Sonnet 116" and Meredith reciting the love poem "i carry your heart with me" by e. e. cummings, impressively from memory. During the exchange of vows, Hope's voice warbled when she said, "I do."

Not real. Not real. Not real.

The minister requested the rings, and Derrick took them from his pocket, handing the matching gold bands to Brent. He passed the larger one to Jackie and winked. "I love you," he mouthed in a whisper, and Hope's lips trembled.

"I love you, too," she whispered back, her head and her heart very nearly exploding from the painful truth. Because she did love him with her whole being, and at the moment her heart was breaking in two. Then, Brent slid the ring on her finger, promising to love her forever, and her heart shattered to bits.

When it was her turn, she was crying so hard, she struggled to get out the words.

Meredith stepped forward and handed her a delicate linen hanky, which she'd apparently had at the ready. Hope dabbed at her eyes and blew her nose so loudly it honked.

There was muted laughter from the crowd, but it was good-natured.

Everyone here was pulling for them. Rather, for Brent and Jackie.

This last thought only made Hope cry harder, and Sally scrambled toward Grandmother Margaret, who held out a tissue from the first row. Sally quietly scuttled back to Hope, passing it over, and Hope gave her a grateful nod, swiping at her streaming tears.

Finally, it was Hope's turn to slide Brent's ring on his finger, repeating her pledge, as the minister urged her along.

"I give this ring." She inhaled sharply. *Not real. Not real. Not real.* "...in token and pledge..." *Ouch, this is hard.* "...of my constant faith..." *Make believe. Totally made up.* "...and abiding..."

She choked back a sob, and Brent encouragingly patted her hand. "Abiding...love," she finished on a gasp.

She shoved the ring on his finger with a determined push and looked up to find his dark eyes shimmering.

"By the authority vested in me," the minister began.

Not real. Not real.

"Before God and these witnesses..."

My soul is doomed. Toast.

"...I now pronounce you husband and wife."

The kindly older man with silver hair smiled at them both and said to Brent, "You may kiss your bride." Then he winked at Hope. "And you may kiss your groom."

There is no way out of this nowwww.

Brent pulled Hope into his arms, and the crowd

hollered with their approval. *Not real. Not...* His mouth homed in on hers, and Hope's legs went weak. *...real.*

Then he kissed her really, really well, and the entire ceremony seemed about as real as it could get. Hope whimpered into his kiss as he held her closer, and the guests clapped and cheered, standing from their chairs.

He pulled back and grinned. "We did it."

Hope stared back at him wide-eyed and forced a shaky smile.

"Yeah," she said on a dazed sigh. "We *did*."

CHAPTER NINETEEN

Hope and Brent had barely completed their recessional when a waiter glided over holding out a tray loaded with bubbling champagne flutes.

Brent plucked one off the tray and handed it to Hope. "Sweetheart."

She took a huge sip as Brent did the same. The momentary reprieve ended when they became mobbed by wedding guests surrounding them—each wishing to offer up their heartiest congratulations.

"Jackie." Sally scurried toward her with open arms and pulled her into a hug. "Congrats. I'm so thrilled to have another sister-in-law." Then she smiled and said sweetly, "Gorgeous ceremony. I hope you don't mind, but I snapped a few candid pics and tagged your account on Instagram."

"What? Already?"

"Only of the best parts," Sally replied, grinning. Next, Parker squeezed his way forward, tugging along a blond man who looked about his age, but with a tanned complexion and a chiseled face. The Albrights had said Gavin was ex-military, and his buff frame suggested that he kept in shape. "Jackie," he said cordially. "I don't believe you've met Gavin Tate."

Hope extended her free hand to shake his. "Gavin. Great to meet you."

"Welcome to the family." His warm smile indicated he believed himself to be a part of it, and

Hope understood why. "Congratulations on your wise choice."

"We believe Brent's chosen wisely as well," Parker said, and Hope gave him a hug.

"Thank you," she said as he hugged her back. Elsa snaked through the crowd to embrace her next, and Ava was right on her heels. Brent's attention had been drawn off by the friendly group of aunts and uncles on Elsa's side, so Hope introduced her mom.

"This is my mother, Ava Webb," she said to Gavin, who sported a handsome grin.

"You hardly look old enough to be the mother of the bride," he said smoothly.

She preened like a big old peacock. "Flattery will get you everywhere," she teased.

Gavin shook her hand. "Delighted."

Brent turned behind her, glancing over his shoulder. "Ah, there you are," he said with a twinkle. "Come on over and meet my aunts and uncles."

Hope cast a wary look at her mom, hoping she wouldn't get carried away. Ava soaked up attention from complimentary men like a dry sponge dunked in water. "I, er…sure," she replied as her mom gave her a little wave. Then Brent hooked his arm through hers and began introducing her to the rest of the guests, starting with Elsa's two sisters and their husbands.

• • •

Brent couldn't believe how well the reception was going. Then again, his expert wife—the wedding planner—had been in charge of it. Brent's mind drifted over the word *wife* again, and he couldn't help but grin. What a wonderful word that was, and he'd be using it from here on out with Jackie. She was radiant in her bridal gown. It fit her just right, outlining her perfect figure, but it was her joyful spirit that shone the brightest. He'd honestly never seen her looking prettier. What a totally amazing week this had been, culminating with this life-altering occasion today. *Married. Woo.* It was still hard to believe the term applied to him.

William walked over and patted his shoulder. Brent was taking a breather from socializing and had stepped back to observe the festivities on his grandparents' back lawn. Wedding guests milled about, holding champagne or other refreshments, and everyone was chatting happily under the midday sun. Fortunately, the weather was mild. Not too warm and not too cool. With a full sun in the sky and a light breeze blowing, it felt just right.

"So, how's it feel?" William asked him, stepping closer.

"Honestly?" Brent's mouth twitched at the corners. "Pretty darn good."

William followed Brent's gaze, perusing the lively party. "Some people say being married takes getting used to. But it doesn't." He shook his head and sipped his champagne. "Not really."

Brent chuckled. "Things sure seem to have worked out for you and Sofia."

"Yeah." William's eyes instantly went dreamy. Brent wondered if that's how he looked, too, when he gazed at Jackie. Like a totally hopeless, lovesick puppy dog.

"So tell me about Bermuda," Derrick said, striding over to join his brothers. "Are you taking the shorts?"

"Sure, Derrick. Yeah, the Bermuda ones. They're down to my knees," Brent joked.

"Maybe the only shorts he'll be wearing are those boxers you gave him."

"William," Brent muttered in mock offense. "I'm scandalized."

"He *is* a married man." Derrick motioned with his champagne flute. "He knows whereof he speaks."

"Oh yeah?" Brent said, razzing his little brother. "When's your turn?"

Derrick's gaze happened to be on Meredith as she went prancing by, arm-in-arm with Sally, laughing and whispering something to her as they shot glances at Hope standing by the tent. "I'm sorry," he murmured absentmindedly. "What did you say?"

Brent and William raised their eyebrows at each other, and both guys started cackling.

"Oh no," Derrick said, obviously getting their drift. "No, no, and *no*."

"She's very pretty," William said in a reasonable fashion.

"Not seeing anyone, either." Brent grinned at Derrick. "From what I hear."

Derrick tried to blow them off by taking another sip of his drink. "And she calls herself a matchmaker," he said, pretending that he was disgusted with the idea.

William nudged him. "Maybe she just hasn't found the right match."

• • •

Hope felt like she'd scarcely seen Brent at all during the past hour, but Sofia told her not to worry. That was very typical during wedding receptions. The bride and groom were the stars of the day, and all the guests wanted to visit with them. There'd be plenty of time for privacy between them tonight, she'd said with wiggling eyebrows. Privacy was the one thing Hope didn't want to contemplate enjoying with Brent right now. *If things were different*, she thought, watching him sadly as he crossed the lawn. *But they're not.*

Eleanor came to speak with Hope, telling her that it was lunchtime, and Hope was glad for the opportunity to sit for a while and slip out of her heels. Even if they did make her legs look dynamite, these shoes were killing her.

Once everyone was seated with their food, the waitstaff circulated, refreshing drinks and serving ice water. After a short interlude while people got settled, the toasting began. Derrick stood first, extracting a folded piece of paper from his tuxedo jacket pocket, but Ava preempted him by shooting to her feet.

"Oh, Derrick," she shouted, waving her napkin. "One quick interruption if you don't mind."

Hope's pulse pounded. Ava wouldn't. She couldn't.

Then her mom pulled a small boom box out from under the table, and Hope realized with horror that she was going to.

Oooh, here she goes…

"Uh. Mom." Hope stood weakly, bracing herself against the table with her arms.

"You don't have to thank me, sweetheart," she said, glowing cheerfully. "Let this be my gift to you." She nodded at Brent, who stared at her, gob-smacked. "To you and Brent."

All eyes watched expectantly as Ava turned on her music player, and a full orchestra broke into a swell, hitting dramatic peaks and valleys with each new chord. Ava touched her thumbs to her shoulders and shut her eyes in some apparent form of meditation. An instant later, she flung her arms wide as if figuratively embracing the room.

Como una promesa, eres tú, eres tú
Como una mañana de verano

Meredith stood in shock as Ava belted out the lyrics in Spanish, sending Hope a questioning look, and Hope knew Meredith had her back. All she had to do was give a sign and Meredith would do whatever it took to remove Ava from the floor.

"Wait," Brent said in mild shock. "Is your mom *actually* singing '*Eres Tú*'?"

"She's not bad," Grandpa Chad mumbled, and Hope sank back into her chair, stunned. Ava's vocal skills had improved some since cousin's Debbie's wedding. Then she hit a crescendo, and Hope grimaced, deciding that they hadn't improved all that much. She leaned forward and set her elbows on the table, massaging her forehead as the song went endlessly on and on. At least now she'd have an excuse for the fake headache she was going to tell Brent about later.

And now, the refrain. Oh, ouch. Hope peered through her fingers, relieved to find all the champagne flutes still standing. Thank goodness her mom hadn't shattered any glass.

Brent soothingly rubbed her back between her stiff shoulder blades. "It's really all right," he said in a whisper. "It's coming to an end soon."

And it would have, too. If Gavin Tate hadn't hollered out during the applause that ensued, demanding an encore.

• • •

Later that afternoon, the area under the tent with the twinkling lights was converted to a dance floor. Brent's gaze washed over Hope as he held her in his arms and they had their first dance. "This is a great song. I'm glad we picked it."

Hope caught her breath, swept up in the fantasy of being his bride. "Yeah. Me, too."

They took another turn around the dance floor, with Brent leading her expertly in his arms. "You're a very beautiful bride," he told her.

"And you're a totally hot groom."

He chuckled at this, evidently pleased. "Maybe you'll find out how hot later."

Her cheeks steamed when she found herself wishing that she could.

But that was wrong.

More than wrong.

Twisted.

"I know there's still the bouquet toss," he said.

"And the cake. Uh, er…cupcakes."

"Yes, and those." His eyes twinkled. "But, between now and then, maybe we can slip away?"

"Oh, Brent. I don't think…"

He pressed his forehead to hers, his nose nudging hers. "Remember our coat closet?" he asked in a husky whisper.

"Yeah," she said, her voice featherlight. In spite of herself, she couldn't help wanting his kisses. They were so incredibly wonderful, after all.

"How about we revisit it?" His lips brushed over hers, and Hope's head spun.

"I…I don't kno—"

He nibbled on her lip, and she murmured her assent without even meaning to.

"Mmm-mmm."

"I know, sweetheart," he said, holding her closer. "I know."

Then he led her around the dance floor one final time as their onlookers broke out in polite applause.

Moments later, Brent tugged Hope along, pulling her by the hand. "Brent. Really, we shouldn't. Can't…"

He raised a devilish eyebrow and steered her into the hall. "Oh yes, we—ack."

Brent froze with his hand on the doorknob and goggled into the darkened coat closet under the stairs, where Ava and Gavin were engaged in an amorous embrace.

Hope did a quick body scan, relieved to see they both had all their clothing on. Although Ava's hem *did* look slightly hiked up, and Gavin's tie was askew.

It was bad enough that she and Brent had caught them making out, but she supposed it could have been worse. Knowing Ava, a lot worse.

"Mom!" Hope yelped.

"Uncle Gavin?" Brent said in mild shock.

Ava cupped a manicured hand over her puffy red lips. "Oh, hi, kids." She pulled a guileless face and stared at her daughter. "Is it time to toss the bouquet?"

• • •

By the time the bouquet toss came, it was after nine o'clock and Hope had been on her feet for almost ten hours. She was gratefully barefoot now, having kicked off her shoes shortly after the dancing—and her and Brent's discovery of Ava and Gavin in the closet. Ick.

She could barely stand to think about it. Why oh why was her mom so constantly out of control? She'd promised Jackie she'd tried to rein Ava in, but she might as well have been charged with roping a bucking bronco. Ava definitely marched to her own tune. She sang to it, too. Hope tried not to grimace while recalling Ava's serenade.

She was still on tap as the bride and had a duty to appear perky—for just a few more minutes, anyway. Then she could go upstairs and crash. Though from the look in Brent's eyes, he clearly had other ideas in mind.

He took her bouquet-free hand and gave it a kiss. "Let's get this part done so we can retire." His tone dipped toward sultry, and Hope staged a yawn.

"Good plan," she said, willing herself to look innocent-eyed. "I'm beat."

Hope peered over her shoulder at the wedding guests gathered on the lawn. Night had fallen, and shadows stretched long across the grass from the muted lighting on the porch, which included strings of tiny lights wrapped around its columns and complementing the dripping lighting display hanging from the surrounding bushes and trees.

When combined with the twinkling lights adorning the tent, the entire backyard looked like a whimsical wonderland. The sound of the surf gently splashing against the cliffs only added to the magic, as did the glint of the nearly full moon against the darkened water.

Hope stood on the highest step of the wrap-around porch with her back to the others. A small gaggle of women had collected at the foot of the stairs, all of them shifting awkwardly on their feet. Meredith was among them, and so was Sally.

Though Sally kept trying to creep away, Grandmother Margaret shoved her back into the fray. Hope was grateful at least that her mom hadn't inserted herself in the group. Yet, that begged the question of where Ava currently was. Hope's head pounded as she willed herself not to think about it. Especially as Gavin appeared *missing in action*, too.

"Are we ready?" Hope asked when Eleanor gave her the go-ahead. Even she looked eager to get this done with. It had been an extra-long day for Eleanor as well, and the caterers had begun packing up after setting out a large coffee tureen, cups, and supplies.

Hope was aware there'd be remaining food left out for nibbles, and the bartenders had left chilled buckets of drinks at the ready for any late stragglers to self-serve later.

People behind her roared, a few of them sounding more inebriated than others. Hope had never possessed truly great aim, but she aspired to landing her bouquet on Meredith.

Who better to be the next bride than a woman intent on creating *happily ever afters* for others?

Sally wasn't angling for marriage herself, and Hope didn't know the other hopefuls well, having only just met them. So, Meredith it was. Assuming Hope could make a straight shot.

The countdown began behind her.

Three. Two. One.

But when it was time to let go, Hope just couldn't. There was too much at stake to leave this to chance, so she spun on her heel and lobbed her bridal bouquet right at Meredith, who caught it as it hurtled toward her like a speeding bullet.

She stared down at the flowers and then up at Hope, her face beet red, and everyone cheered. Everyone but Derrick, Hope couldn't help but notice, as he set his beer bottle down on the side of the firepit and quietly stole away.

"Looks like that does it," Brent said, sweeping Hope off the top step and into his embrace. "Now, folks, if you'll excuse us."

Onlookers whistled and cheered as Brent bent low, scooping Hope into his arms.

"Brent!" she cried, kicking her heels. "What are you doing?"

"Carrying you upstairs," he said with a sexy grin. "Thanks, everyone, for coming!" he shouted across the lawn. "Stay as long as you want!"

· · ·

Hope stared at Brent, wide-eyed, as he carted her through the den. "You're not seriously going to carry me all the way upstairs?"

"Oh, no?" he said with a determined air. "Watch me."

Hope panicked over what was going to happen next. He was taking her up to their bridal suite, where he was expecting them to get to know each other—as man and wife.

Think. Think. Think.

She had to do something to ward off his attempts to take her to bed.

All the kissing had been bad enough. She definitely wasn't crossing *that* line.

Aha. Their early flight might be good to bring up.

"What an exhausting day... Exhausting but great." She staged another yawn. "Shame about that morning flight. I suppose we'll have to get up early."

His eyes glimmered in a predatory fashion. "Yeah, but we can always nap on the plane," he said, and she bit her lip.

Okay, that tactic failed. She had to try something else.

Brent reached the upstairs landing, and the door to the bridal suite lay dead ahead.

No time like now.

Hope dramatically dropped her arm against her forehead. "Oh. *Ooh.* Oh, oh-no."

His brow creased as he opened the door. "Sweetheart, what is it?"

"I think I might be coming down with another headache."

"Poor baby." He frowned. "Did it come on suddenly?"

"Yeah. No. I mean, I felt a little twinge earlier. It's probably been brewing all day."

"I wish you'd said something earlier."

"I didn't want to ruin the party."

Brent carried her over the threshold, and Hope moaned miserably.

"You really are feeling terrible, aren't you?" He set her down on the bed with a concerned look. "Maybe you should lie down for a while."

"Yes. *No.*" She started to recline, then immediately popped back up, hopping off the bed.

Brent and beds were a bad mix. *Bad, bad, bad.*

"What I mean is, I better take some meds first."

"I have acetaminophen in my suitcase," he offered.

Hope's suitcase sat on a stand in the corner. "That's okay," she said, rummaging around inside it. "I have a prescription. The only thing is..." she said, thinking fast. "It makes me really, really sleepy."

She pulled a face, and Brent's eyebrows rose. "Oh."

She could tell he was trying to figure out his next move. He poured her a glass of water from the pitcher on the table. There was wine and a cheese plate, too. She grabbed gobs of stuff from her suitcase, like her toiletries bag and more comfortable clothing.

She was designing a plan.

Arghhh. Hope wanted to kill Jackie for putting her in this predicament.

She also wanted to have her own head examined for going along with it.

She'd married her sister's fiancé. Well, actually—on paper—her husband.

Downright married him—with rings, I dos, and everything.

Not to mention that fiery kiss.

One way or another, Hope was going to survive this.

Somehow, Jackie and Brent would, too.

Then it would all be okay. Sure it would.

Still, in the back of Hope's mind, a gazillion doubts were crowding in.

How could things be okay, when Brent had fallen in love with her instead of her sister? What about the mess Hope had made by falling in love with him? And not just him—his entire family? Nobody could ever know the truth. Not with the tangled web she and Jackie had weaved.

The only way to get out of this now was to power through until tomorrow.

Somehow. With Brent.

And without having him land in the same bed.

Hope's tension spiked.

Oh, sure. That's sounds totally doable.

Brent tried to hand her the water, but she dashed away from him. "I think I'll go and change first."

"O-kay." Poor Brent almost looked like he'd been experiencing whiplash. Good thing he hadn't been privy to the manic thoughts in her brain.

She glanced around the room, wondering where the bathroom was.

He seemed to read that thought, at least, because he pointed to a door. "That way."

CHAPTER TWENTY

Brent sat in a chair by the table, feeling a little stunned. He'd poured himself a glass of red wine and served himself a few chocolate-covered strawberries for no other reason except that they looked delicious. He honestly wasn't hungry, but he figured he should eat something in case he needed the energy later. This *was* their wedding night, so he was hoping that things would improve so he and Jackie could enjoy it. If it didn't, though, they would always have Bermuda, and then—happily—the rest of their lives.

She'd only been gone five minutes when Jackie returned, still wearing her wedding dress.

"Is something wrong?" he asked when her pretty lips took on a pout.

"It's the laces," she said, motioning behind her. "They must have knotted somehow. I'm afraid I can't get the bow undone."

"Ah," he said, standing. "No worries. I'm happy to help with that."

She shuffled over to him, turning her back, and anticipation skittered through him. Given where everything started, this was some surprise, being in love with his wife. And it wasn't one-sided, either. He'd seen the look in Jackie's eyes during the ceremony. There was no faking real love like that. She was crazy about him, and he was crazy about her. Not only that—they were married.

Brent carefully untied the bow at the waistline of her lace-up dress, thinking this felt awfully sexy. Him slowly undressing his bride. He was bummed about her headache, though, so he would hold those thoughts for later.

The knot beneath the bow was really snug, but he gradually worked it free; then, one by one, he began loosening the laces.

Okay, he had to be careful here, because this was a very exciting dress.

Especially as it had begun revealing telling glimpses of what lay underneath.

Like…

Brent blinked in shock. "What…what is *that*?"

She was wearing some kind of industrial-strength girdle. It looked prehistoric. Like something his grandmother might wear.

"Oh." She spun on her heel with an embarrassed flush, gathering up her dress. "Just a little wedding dress undergarment. All the brides wear them." Then she hurried into the bathroom, leaving Brent's sexy fantasies doused in a hearty dose of ice water.

• • •

After a while, Brent heard the bathroom door pop open. He looked up from the laptop that rested on his knees and slammed back against his chair. Jackie had emerged in sweatpants and a sweatshirt, and her entire face was caked in shiny green goo.

His head spun as he tried to recall if he'd actually downloaded their boarding passes to his phone, but at the moment his short-term memory was shot. "Wow." He tried for something more, but all he got the second time was the same word, uttered more vehemently. "*Wow*." He downed a sip of his wine, then asked, croaking, "What *is* that?"

"Mother of Earth Mud Mask." She smiled, and her whole face crinkled into deep grooves, making her look like a very ancient Gila monster.

"I...I see," he responded, willing himself not to judge. All women supposedly kept beauty secrets. Of course, he'd heard about this. He'd just never expected to see them. Certainly not on his wedding night. "Well, um...will that help your headache?"

"Oh, yes. Very much. The mask is aromatherapeutic."

"Aroma...?" Brent exhaled sharply. "Okay. Whatever helps you feel better." He peered at her, wanting to make sure that was really his wife in that disguise. Apart from her bright, beautiful eyes, her face was nearly unrecognizable, and her extremely baggy clothing hid her nice figure. Why was she wearing so much of it? It was actually a little warm in here. "Did you get a chill or something?"

"Chill? Right. Yes." She twisted up her lips, and he wondered when the long red tongue was going to flick out and zap up a fly. Which was a really disgusting image for a wedding night. He rubbed the side of his neck, ashamed of himself.

"That sometimes happens with these headaches." She gave an exaggerated frown. "I'm totally freezing." She threw back the duvet on the four-poster queen-size bed. "I think I'll get under the covers and warm up."

Under most circumstances, a groom would view this as an invitation to climb into bed with his bride and help things get toasty. At this point in time, Brent didn't expect that was the right move. Displaying his "Hot Groom" boxers might not go so great right now, either. "Uh…all right. I'll just sit here and watch, then."

"Watch?" She gaped at him like he'd said something creepy.

"Watch out—for you. To be sure you…don't need anything. I won't be *watching* watching, naturally." Brent dropped his gaze to his computer. "I'll just check up on Albright Enterprises company stock or something."

She climbed under the covers, and Brent marveled at the fact she wasn't broiling. "Aren't you tired yet?"

"Nope. Not yet." Brent took another swallow of wine. He pantomimed scrubbing a hand over his face. "Do you…have to wear that thing all night?"

"The mask?" She sat up, resting on her elbows. "No. I'll wash it off later."

Inwardly, he cheered. "I'll just wait until then."

Her eyebrows arched, and Brent worried that he'd hurt her feelings.

"Not that it's any kind of problem, but I was just wondering… Do you go through this routine every night?"

"Oh no, this is definitely a one-off."

Brent let out a relieved breath. "Great. I mean, that's fine. Just…just checking."

She settled into the pillows. "It doesn't bother you?"

"Not if it helps you," he said, refilling his wine-glass. "Can I get you anything?"

She lifted her head to beam at him, and portions of the mask cracked, giving Brent the impression of a very old woman, like the one who rode the broom in *The Wizard of Oz*.

Brent jumped in his seat in spite of himself.

"Maybe a goodnight kiss?"

"Wait. You're not getting up till morning? I thought you had to wash off the mask?"

"Oh. Right," she said all frowny-faced. "I guess it depends on how I feel." In the next second she perked up. "I'm sure I'll feel better tomorrow."

"That…that's good, because we're leaving early."

"I'll be ready," she promised.

In his wildest dreams, Brent couldn't have predicted a wedding night as bizarre as this. "All right." He stood and cautiously approached the bedside, leaning over her. Then he shut his eyes and gave her a very quick peck on the lips. "Good night, sweetheart."

"Good night, Brent. It really was a marvelous wedding. So memorable."

He stared at her askance and hobbled back to his chair. "Yeah."

"Do you mind if I turn off this light?" she asked, indicating the one beside the bed.

"No, by all means. Go right ahead."

As she did, she shot him a sympathetic look. "Don't worry, baby. Everything's gonna be all right."

He couldn't help but smile. "Yeah. Bermuda's going to be fantastic," he replied, extremely anxious to get there.

. . .

Brent woke up six hours later to his phone alarm's beeping. He must have hit snooze twice, because it was already five thirty and he and Jackie had to leave in fifteen minutes. His back ached, and his neck was stiff. He massaged the side of it, noting he'd slept in the armchair by the table. At some point during the night, his laptop had slid off his lap, and it now stood closed on the floor beside his feet.

He still wore his tuxedo slacks and the pleated shirt, although he'd apparently yanked off his bow tie, since that rested besides his empty wineglass on the table.

The bottle of red wine was half gone.

"Jackie," he said in a whisper. "Jackie, you've got to get up."

She sat up and yelped like a surprised zombie in a B-rated horror flick. "Brent. What are you…?" She glanced quickly around the darkened room, then brought her palms to her face, which was caked in now-fully-dried green mud. "No *way*," she said, gaping at the clock. "It's morning?"

"Yeah, and we're going to miss our plane if we don't hurry."

She studied his outfit with remorse and glanced at the chair. "Were you up all night?"

"Only part of it," he said. "How about I go downstairs and brew some coffee while you grab a shower?"

"A shower sounds great," she said, scrambling out of bed. "Coffee, too."

"How's your headache?" he asked.

For an instant she looked like she'd totally forgotten about being ill, which was a good sign. She had to be feeling better.

"Great. I mean, gone. Completely." She blew out a breath. "I'm as good as new."

"I'm so glad." He smiled, thinking that their honeymoon might be salvageable after all. If they didn't have to run out the door, he'd seriously consider tempting her into a romantic morning. But no. "I'll be back with our coffees in a flash." He cracked open the door to the hall. "Wheels on the road at six."

"Wheels on the road! Thanks, Brent."

CHAPTER TWENTY-ONE

Brent had always believed that Jackie was a morning person, but he'd apparently been wrong. Maybe it was just the stress of this last week—and their wedding—taking its toll on her. She'd barely said two words to him during their drive from Blue Hill to Boston, and he'd done all the driving.

Mostly, she'd been distracted and playing around on her phone. He'd really liked those brief few days when they'd gone without technology. Maybe he could suggest a reprise for Bermuda? "You've been awfully busy," he said, trying not to sound annoyed.

"I'm sorry." She looked up, appearing regretful. "It's Hope. I just wanted to fill her in."

Now he felt bad for being annoyed. It was natural she wanted to check in with her sister. It must have been heartbreaking to not have Hope at the wedding. "How's she doing?"

"Finally better. Almost completely. She says the airline delays were probably a blessing in disguise. She had another minor relapse last night."

"Oh no."

"She's going to be fine," Jackie said. "She went to the doctor earlier and will check in at urgent care later this morning just to be safe."

"Good. That's good. She can update us before we board the plane, then."

"Yes."

She kept madly typing away, her fingers thumping against the tiny keypad.

"Looks like you're writing a whole novel."

"Nope." She smiled sleepily, and Brent could tell she still wasn't totally awake. Perhaps they could grab more coffee in Boston before heading to their gate. "Just the story of our love."

That sounded terribly sweet to him, and he said so. "It's got kind of a ring to it."

"Ha-ha, yeah." She kept typing and glanced up only briefly. "I'm sending some photos, too. You know, group photos and a few couple shots."

"Great idea."

"She wants to know what she missed." From the constant buzzing indicating her replies, he surmised Hope was pretty enthusiastic about it.

"It's a shame she couldn't make it."

"Yeah, but you'll meet her soon."

"When?"

Jackie bit her bottom lip, which was a new habit of hers he'd noticed. She'd only started it this week. "Um, maybe after we get back from Bermuda? Hope has the summers off, so we could go down to Durham sometime."

"That would be fun." He set his gaze back on the road. They were on I-95 now and approaching Boston, so traffic was getting thick. "Or she could come see us."

"Yeah, that, too." She turned off her phone with a flourish. "There. All done."

He glanced at her phone lying dark on her lap. "It's funny how those things have taken over our lives."

"It's true. They can be a pain but necessary."

"Not necessary," he told her. "Maybe a plus." He centered his hands on the steering wheel. "We seemed to get along just fine without our phones those first few days."

Jackie laughed. "I loved our picnic. Even the trek through the mud."

"That was a bit dicey. What with that gigantic stick-worm chasing us."

Jackie laughed again. "Right." She dumped her phone in her purse. "It was kind of fun not being distracted by phone calls, emails, and such."

"The Internet and social media, too."

"Yes, all of that," she agreed.

"Sometimes I wonder what life must have been like in the old days."

"Which old days?"

"Well," he said, "Grandmother Margaret and Grandpa Chad's day. Back when there were only three television channels—"

"Four, counting PBS."

"Yeah." He chuckled at her attempt at accuracy. "Did you know that my grandmother still communicates with some of her friends by snail mail?"

"How archaic," she teased.

He shot her a grin. "When's the last time you wrote a real letter?"

"On paper, you mean?" She settled back against her seat, adjusting her shoulder strap. "Last month."

"Liar."

"Hey! Our wedding invitations went by snail mail."

"That was an exception. An event. I hardly think

that counts."

"Oh yeah, Mr. Smarty Pants? When's the last time *you* sent a snail mail?" Before he answered, she jumped in. "Business correspondence doesn't count."

"Hmm."

"See? You can't remember."

"I would have if it was important."

"That's exactly it," Jackie said. "There's something so much more serious about snail mail."

"Do tell."

"I mean it. Nobody jokes around or says 'LOL' in a handwritten letter."

"Maybe you just haven't read one in a while?"

"Ha-ha."

Brent smirked. "Or written one, either."

She swatted his arm. "When I have something important to say, I'll write one."

"Are you sure?"

"Yes," she said smugly. "Absolutely." Her face lit up as she stared out the window and up at the sky. "Look. There goes an airplane. And another."

"We're almost there," he said with a grin. "Get ready for Bermuda."

• • •

Hope walked beside Brent at a brisk pace, pulling her rolling carry-on bag behind her as they entered the airport. They'd left his SUV in the long-term parking lot and taken a shuttle to the building. Though she'd spent a large part of the trip here catching Jackie up on particulars and coordinating their meet-up, she'd truly enjoyed her lighthearted banter with Brent. He was so easy to talk to, even when they were kidding about something as mundane as snail mail.

She fretted over his interest in meeting "Hope." Naturally, he was simply being a caring husband and trying to be a good brother-in-law, but she couldn't help but wonder what would happen the next time they saw each other. Would he experience any spark of recognition in seeing her? Or would he remain so completely convinced that she'd been Jackie that he'd never guess a glimmer of the truth? She was glad this whole charade would soon be over, because she couldn't endure playing her sister for one more day—or night. It was too painful.

Poor Brent. She'd really put him through the ringer on his wedding night. There'd been no prospect of romance at all. She supposed he and Jackie would work that out in Bermuda. The sad part was Jackie didn't know Brent any better than she had before, while Hope felt like she knew him inside and out. She'd come to understand how thoughtful and caring he was—secretly romantic and adoring, too. He clearly adored her, at least.

She could only wish he'd love Jackie just as much. Okay, maybe she *wanted* to wish that, and she tried really, really hard to believe that's what she wanted. Only it was exceedingly difficult to do when she had such deep feelings for Brent herself. Selfishly, the last thing she wanted was for Brent to look at Jackie the way he'd looked at her during their ceremony and so many times before that during their wonderful week in Maine.

This was such a messed-up situation.

They passed a donut shop on the main concourse, and Hope stopped walking. It was one of the landmarks she was supposed to look for, and she was to meet Jackie in the nearest ladies' room, which was supposedly just a few yards away.

Brent frowned and glanced at his watch. "Do you want a coffee or something?"

"No, um… I…" Her gaze darted down the corridor, and she spotted the sign she was looking for. "Just think I need to stop in the restroom."

"Yeah, of course. Probably a good idea to do before we go through security. The lines could be long."

"Yes." She gazed up at him, her heart pounding. He had absolutely no clue that this was goodbye. If she could drag this out and spend five more minutes with him, she would, but that would probably only make things more painful. As it was, they'd gotten a late start in Blue Hill, and finding a free parking space at the airport had been next to impossible. They were already running behind. Jackie would probably already be waiting in the restroom.

"You can go ahead," he said when he saw her hesitating. "I'll wait here."

Her pain must have been obvious on her face, because his dark eyes filled with worry. "Jackie?"

"Brent…" She pressed her lips together when they trembled. "I love you."

"I love you too, baby," he said warmly. "You never need to worry about that."

Heat prickled the backs of her eyes, and then—on impulse—she did it. Hope wrapped her arms around him and kissed him goodbye. It was a deep kiss, too. One filled with passion and longing and the heart-wrenching sorrow of letting go.

"Hey," he said, teasing her. "Maybe you should take bathroom breaks more often." He scanned her face when tears leaked from her eyes. "I was only kidding, honey. Hey," he said when she turned away. "Is everything all right?"

Hope sniffed and wiped back her tears. "It will be. Soon."

She started to drag her suitcase away, and Brent reached for its handle. "You can leave that with me if you want."

"No. I…" She drew in a deep, shuddering breath. "I'd better take it."

"O-kay." He frowned. "Are you sure nothing's wrong?"

"I'll be back in a flash," she promised, forcing a smile.

Then she spun around and dashed toward the ladies' room.

• • •

Hope darted into the restroom. Before she got far enough to find a stall where she could break down in peace, Jackie sprang at her in the small anteroom with sinks and mirrors. "Hopie!" she cried, hugging her so tightly Hope could barely breathe. "You made it!" She released her and frowned at her undoubtedly shattered expression. "But…why are you crying?"

"This. Us." Hope's voice shook. "Everything."

"Okay, fine. But let's not have a guilt attack now. We don't have time." Other women crowded in, trying to use the sinks and hand dryers as they partially blocked the way. Jackie scooted her aside so people could step past them. "Look at you. You're a wreck. What did those people *do* to you in Maine?"

"It's not *those people*, Jackie." She yanked out several paper towels from the dispenser and wiped her face. "They're the Albrights, and each of them have names. Including Brent," she said on a sob.

Jackie braced her by the shoulders. "We're going to get through this. It's almost done." She considered Hope's outfit and frowned. "Is that the best you could do for your honeymoon?"

"Jackie, come on."

"I mean it." She appeared aghast. "Flats?"

"You better wear them, too, if you know what's good for you," Hope insisted. "That's all Brent's seen you in all week."

"Not at the wedding?"

"Not then. No, of course not."

Jackie peered into the adjoining room and its row of individual stalls. "Let's get two right next to each other, and we can switch outfits. We can pass them underneath." Jackie sucked in a gasp, apparently noting that her carry-on was brown and Hope's was blue. Not only that, she had a checked bag and Hope didn't. "The suitcases. Do you think Brent will notice?"

"Depends on how observant he is. After all..." She leaned toward Jackie and whispered. "We're counting on him to think of you as me."

"I think you've got that mixed up," she said annoyingly. "You're the one who's been playing me."

"Yeah," Hope muttered morosely. "Until I started playing myself."

"What?"

"Never mind; doesn't matter."

"Maybe we shouldn't risk it," Jackie said. "Let's swap suitcases with me taking some of your clothes. You can take my checked bag back to Durham for now." She heaved an exasperated sigh, evidently agitated that she'd have to downsize her wardrobe. "Did you seriously not wear heels?"

This entire episode was so surreal, Hope felt like she was functioning on autopilot. In a large way, she felt numb. Like she'd gone from experiencing excruciating pain to sensing absolutely nothing. Maybe this was depression, because she suddenly cared about very little except for getting home to her duplex in Durham and crawling under the covers.

If she was lucky, she'd get to stay there for days. Weeks, even. All alone in the total darkness. Moisture warmed her cheeks, and she realized she was crying again. The sooner they got this done, the better. The most horrible part was, it wasn't only about her upended emotions—it was about what they were doing to Brent. Deceiving him in the most terrible, unforgivable way.

"Come on," Jackie said, nudging her into the next part of the restroom. "Two stalls just opened up."

"Fine, okay." Hope pulled herself together and went through the motions of swapping outfits with Jackie. Fitting into Jackie's skinny jeans was no small trick. "Don't you have anything looser?" she asked, calling under the stall. "Something with an elastic waistband?" Brent wasn't going to see Hope in it, anyway. She just needed something to wear for the trip home. Jackie shoved a pair of black leggings under the stall door.

"Try this."

Hope wriggled into them.

"Better?"

"Yeah, thanks." All at once, she felt like a teenager again—like she and Jackie were in on some stupid youthful scam. Yet they weren't so youthful anymore. They were both grown women who should know better. She yanked Jackie's top over her head and settled it around her hips, deciding the look was okay. She was not wearing Jackie's high-heeled sandals, however. She reserved the right to keep at least one pair of her own shoes for more comfortable traveling.

"Do you have a belt?" Jackie asked, evidently finding Hope's jeans too roomy.

"Here," Hope said, thrusting one through the opening.

They exited the stalls, examining each other. Looking at Jackie was almost like staring at her reflection—only there were those subtle differences between them that only they and their mother knew about. "Not bad." Jackie looked herself up and down, then stared at Hope. "This will probably do."

"Cool." A teenage girl with spiky black-and-purple hair and an eyebrow bar gawked at them. "Are you two twins? I don't think I've ever seen any so old."

"Uh…thanks," Hope said to the double-sided compliment.

"Yep," Jackie said smartly, tugging Hope along. "We're ancient." When they were near the restroom door, she screeched, "Eeep. The ring."

She stared down at Hope's finger, and Hope tugged off the wedding band, goggling at the engagement ring that Jackie wore. "You'd better remove that and hide it. Brent's seen me without it all week. He thinks it's at the jewelers getting resized."

Jackie nodded and slipped the ring into a small zipper pouch inside her suitcase. "There," she said, once she'd seated the wedding band on her hand. "That does it." She shot a cautionary look at Hope. "You should probably stay in here another five minutes just to be safe. I'll get Brent out of here and moving toward security ASAP."

The restroom lights swirled around her. "Okay." She leaned against a wall, afraid she might faint.

Jackie cast her a sidelong glance as she stepped toward the door. "You going to be all right?"

Hope nodded, her stomach churning.

"I'll text you from Bermuda to let you know we made it." She rushed back and gave Hope a quick hug. "Love you."

"Yeah, I…" All around her, Hope saw sparkly silver stars. "…love you, too." She blinked to clear her vision and then walked to a sink, where she splashed cold water on her face again and again and again. Finally, she realized it was also hitting her neck and the front of Jackie's top. She'd pretty much soaked herself. But if it hadn't been water, it might as well have been tears. Hope braced herself against the sink, then stared at her disheveled image in the mirror. Her hair was a wreck, and her eyes were bloodshot. The gold heart pendant dangled from a thin gold chain around her neck.

She recalled her conversation with Brent when he'd asked about the necklace. She'd told him the truth when she said she'd bought it as a gift for herself, because she wanted to believe herself loveable, even if nobody else could love her. The cold truth now was that, at this particular moment, Hope didn't love herself. On the contrary, she loathed who she'd become and what she'd done to Brent. And not just to him. To his whole family.

And Meredith. Dear, sweet Meredith, who'd been so very kind and doggedly loyal. Hope had dragged her into this, along with their poor mom. Even if Ava had gotten to sing at the wedding, in retrospect, she probably didn't believe the stress of it all worth it. Hope had made a mess of everything. But she hadn't acted alone. Jackie had been complicit in this. She'd aided and abetted the entire operation, and today she was planning to benefit from it—without giving a thought to the potential devastation they'd caused.

While Hope was probably the worst culprit, Jackie wasn't blameless. The two of them were bad news. Shameless. One just as recklessly unthinking and callous as the other. Neither one deserved a guy as amazing as Brent. What's more, he certainly didn't deserve either of them.

Hope's pulse raced, and her head cleared when she understood what she had to do. She had to fix things. Set them right. Even if—by doing so—she risked blowing them apart.

She couldn't let Brent blindly go to Bermuda with a woman he believed to be someone else—the person he'd bonded with and come to love in Blue Hill.

Hope had to stop him.

She had to stop Jackie, too.

She had to stop them both—before they reached airport security.

CHAPTER TWENTY-TWO

Jackie returned from the restroom looking like a different person. Seriously. A different person. Her makeup was no longer smeared, and she wore a bright smile, and yet…there was something different about her. "Feeling better?"

"Uh-huh, yep. So much."

Brent squinted and looked closer. Nope. It was Jackie, all right. Except… "Did you do something different with your eyes?"

"My eyes?" she asked, appearing alarmed. She smoothed back her hair, which was in a ponytail all of a sudden. "What do you mean?"

"They, uh…" Brent shook his head, deciding he was mistaken. He'd know his bride anywhere. And here she was. "It's nothing."

"Oh," she said, batting her eyelashes. "The new eyeliner. Is that it? I just applied some in the restroom."

Brent didn't know much about women's makeup, but he did understand it could have a transformational effect. "That's it. You've enhanced your beautiful eyes."

"Aww, sweet," she said, swatting his arm in a supposedly familiar gesture that somehow just felt—wrong.

Brent rolled back his shoulders, deciding he was imagining things. He'd probably feel better once they boarded their plane and were on their way to the sunny Caribbean. "Did you still want coffee?"

"Coffee?" Her gaze darted toward the donut shop. "No, thanks. We'd better move along."

He stared down at her neck, noticing it was gone. "Your necklace. That's what it is. You're not wearing it anymore."

Jackie clasped a hand to her neck. "Oh. Well. I decided to take it off."

His forehead rose. "Why?"

"I, um…just thought." She fiddled with her ponytail holder. "It would get in the way."

"The way? Of what?"

"Might set off the alarm."

"What?"

"In security."

"Oh, sure." He doubted that very seriously, but he didn't want to belittle her fears. "Good thinking. It might."

She grinned, and her pretty face set off some kind of weird alternate-reality kick. He'd know that gorgeous profile anywhere, but in a strange way, it seemed alien.

Not entirely alien but distant. Like he knew it, of course, only not intimately.

This was nuts. He was psyching himself out. "I kind of got used to seeing you in it."

"Oh. Did you?" She smiled, but her smile looked a little tight. "That's nice." She craned her neck to see up ahead of them beyond the throngs of passengers streaming out of a hallway leading to the gates. "It's crowded. It's a good thing we're going on through."

"Wait!"

Brent froze in his tracks, and a cold shiver darted down his spine. The woman shouting behind them sounded just like Jackie. Only Jackie—was here. He stared at her as the voice called again.

"Brent! Jackie!"

The color drained from Jackie's face, and he had a really bad feeling something terrible was going down.

He slowly turned around to find Jackie's mirror image staring at him. The only difference was she was dressed in other clothes and wore her hair down. "What?"

"Hope!" Jackie yelped, startled. "*What* are you doing?"

"What I should have done from the start," she said on the verge of tears. "I'm sorry, but this has to stop. And it stops right here—with me. All my life, I've been the big sister, but I've let you push me around. But not anymore. There's too much at stake. I'm no longer covering for you or fixing your stupid mistakes. I'm *done*."

Brent's gaze swept over her and then over Jackie. Then did it again. Had Hope come to see her sister off at the airport? In Boston? No, wait. That didn't make sense. And why was she so incensed? "Are you—?"

"Hope, yes."

"Hope." Jackie shook her head emphatically. "*No*."

He raked a hand through his hair. "I'm afraid I don't understand what's going on."

Jackie shot her sister a pointed look and grabbed Brent's arm. "We'd really better go."

"And just leave your sister? Here?"

He gazed into Hope's eyes and then down at the necklace.

Brent's heart thumped, and then it thundered.

"You're not Jackie," he said in measured tones.

"No." Her voice warbled. "I'm not."

"But I am," Jackie said, waving her phone in his direction. "And there's still time to catch our plane."

His head spun, and then his stomach flipped in the worst possible way.

For a fleeting instant, he was positive he was going to throw up.

"Are you telling me," he asked quietly, "that the two of you—"

"Swapped places," Hope said miserably. "Yes."

Brent stared off into the distance. Through one of the airport's plate-glass windows, he saw a plane taxiing out to the runway. "For how long?" he asked, unable to look at either of them.

"The whole week," Hope said.

Brent caught his breath and held it as his pulse thrummed in his ears.

"The whole week. I see." He turned his gaze back on Jackie. "So, you were never there?"

"I could...couldn't," she stammered. "The Martin wedding—"

Brent gaped at her. "You're kidding me?" Then he laughed at the absurdity of it all. "Okay, where are the cameras? You ladies have got to be punking me, right?"

When neither one responded, he knew that they weren't.

"For the love of everything holy." Brent blew out a hard breath. "So you weren't sick?" he asked Hope.

She hung her head in shame. "I was there with you the whole time."

He glared at Jackie. "And you were in Boston?"

"No. Nantucket." She reached for him, but he pulled away. "It's not as bad as it soun—"

"Not as bad?" he asked, his voice rising. When onlookers turned their way, he made an effort to tamp things down. "You let your sister pretend to be you," he said in a hoarse whisper. "And not just for any old thing. For our *wedding*. Wow."

Everything was starting to make sense, with lots of pieces falling into place. No wonder he'd discovered a whole new side of Jackie. That whole new side was linked by DNA. "Jackie" hadn't been Jackie at all, but Hope, her twin.

"Listen," Jackie said gently. "It's not like we're really not married. We are. From the courthouse in Boston."

"Yeah? How can I be sure that was you and not"—he sent Hope a dismissive look—"her?"

"It was stupid, I know," Jackie said feebly.

"Stupid doesn't even begin to describe it."

"Brent, there's still time," Jackie said. "Time for us to salvage this thing."

"Oh no, there's not."

"But what about your grandfather? His business?"

"Great." Brent angrily pursed his lips. "This is all really great." He set his eyes on Hope. "You know what you've done is going to devastate my family."

Her chin trembled. "I'm sorry."

"I'm afraid, this time, sorry's not good enough." He wheeled back on Jackie. "When were you planning to tell me?" When she didn't answer, he added incredulously, "Never?"

Brent had faced a lot of intense situations, but none of them were as wretched as this. He felt like someone had poured gasoline all over his soul and then set a match to it.

"You know what?" He held up his hands. "I'm done. You two ladies go to Bermuda together, if you want. Live it up. Have a great time scamming the locals." He grabbed his suitcase handle. "Oh. And don't forget the tourists. They're easy game."

"Great, Hope. This is just great. Thanks one whole heck of a lot." Jackie's whole body shook, and it looked like she was about to break down crying, too. But they would be crocodile tears, as far as Brent was concerned. She was already walking toward security.

He couldn't believe it.

The heartless woman was actually going to Bermuda. Fine.

Before he could leave, Hope raced up in front of him, blocking his escape.

"I know you don't believe it," she said with big, sad eyes. "But I wish I hadn't done it. I wish I'd never lied about who I was. But, Brent? I need you to know—I wasn't lying about one thing. The feelings I developed for you."

"What is this, Hope? Some kind of mind game?"

"No, I'm telling the truth."

"The truth," he said searingly. "That's a good one."

Tears leaked from her eyes. "I know I may have pretended to be Jackie, but everything I said and did was real."

"Down to the story about the necklace?" he asked, eying it harshly.

"Yeah, down to that."

"Well then, I'm glad you have it. Hope. At least someone's going to be your Valentine." It was a low blow, but she deserved it. She and her sister were without a doubt the most despicable people he'd ever met.

"I can understand why you hate me," she said, and in that moment, Brent's heart ached because he understood that he didn't. He was furious at her for her deception. But hate her? No.

He gazed into her eyes, searching for a glimmer of truth in her soul. For that incredible woman he'd come to know so intimately and love.

And she was there. He could feel her.

He wished to goodness that he didn't, because that made matters even worse.

"I've got to go."

Then he turned and walked away.

He had no idea whether she'd try to get a last minute ticket and board that plane with Jackie. But he didn't care.

He did get that he needed time to process things.

He also knew he wasn't ready to face his family. Well, not all of them, anyway. So he took out his phone and called Derrick to ask if he could come up to his cabin for a couple of days.

"Yeah, man. Of course." Derrick hesitated a beat. When he spoke, his tone was tinged with worry. "I thought you were supposed to be on your honeymoon?"

"There's not going to be any honeymoon."

For a moment, Derrick didn't answer, and then he finally said, "I'm sorry."

"Yeah. Me, too."

CHAPTER TWENTY-THREE

Hope sat on her futon next to Iris, who'd brought over a big plate of brownies. Double chocolate chunk with walnuts. Hope hadn't been able to resist them.

"You know, you're ruining my figure with all these treats."

"Hush, child," she said, her dark eyes twinkling. "You're in as great a shape as always. Besides that, haven't you heard? Stress burns calories."

Iris had dropped by four times since Hope had returned from Boston with serious ambitions of going into extended hibernation. It was pretty hard to sleep with Iris constantly coming over with something new and delicious to eat. She claimed she was trying out recipes for her church bazaar. There was going to be a big baking competition Labor Day weekend, and she badly wanted to win.

"I think this is your best recipe yet." Hope crammed another brownie in her mouth, thinking it was a close call between the brownies and Iris's Zesty Lemon Bars, which she'd made from scratch, using real lemon zest.

It had now been a whole week since the aborted honeymoon fiasco, and she'd not yet heard from her sister. She hadn't tried texting her, either. If Jackie'd honestly gone to Bermuda, Hope wasn't sure she wanted verification that her own flesh and blood could be that unfeeling. While she understood about not wasting the ticket or the accommodations, indulging in the vacation anyway just felt wrong.

"You don't know for a fact that she went there," Iris said, smoothing Hope's furrowed brow.

"How do you always know what I'm thinking?"

"I don't. But I've got good instincts." Iris took a sip of coffee. "You could always call her, you know."

Hope shook her head. "I'm not ready."

"What about your mom?"

"I don't think I can face her yet, either."

"You think she's with Gavin?"

Hope shrugged. "Maybe, if she's lucky. Mom knew the truth about what was going on. No doubt Gavin's on the Albrights' side."

"Who says anybody has to take sides?"

"Come on, Iris. You yourself said the whole situation was unforgiveable."

She waved her hand. "That's only because you shocked me at first." She laughed self-effacingly. "And I don't shock easy."

"I really do feel awful about everything."

"I know you do."

"You want to know the worst part?"

Iris waited patiently.

"I love Brent."

Hope's heart felt bruised, like every one of its chambers had taken a solid beating. It was hard to know how it was functioning anymore, but she was still there, and day after day, when she opened her eyes, she only felt more terrible about things instead of better.

"I'm sorry, child. Things will get better in time."

"And if they don't?"

"Maybe you should reach out to him?"

"I know how that would go over. Not well at all."

"You don't have to decide today," Iris told her. "Why don't you see how you feel tomorrow?" Iris drank a little more coffee and then said as an aside, "Did you know Dave and Barry are doing a pop-up?" she asked, mentioning the ponytailed guys who lived next to Hope.

"No. What?" She viewed Iris with surprise. "What kind?"

"They're junk metal artists, it seems."

"Really?"

"I know you've seen their trash bins out back."

"Yeah, but I thought... Well, I wasn't sure what I thought."

"That they were throwing out tons of trash? Destroying the environment? Heavens, no. They've been collecting things that other folks have discarded."

Hope thought on this, realizing she'd never actually seen even one dumpster rolled to the curb on trash pick-up day.

"Dave and Barry throw *nothing* away. I mean, nothing. They compost all their refuse and recycle everything else."

"How do you know all this?"

"They let me use some of their compost for my garden."

"Iris," Hope asked cagily. "Are you growing anything illegal?"

"No." She chuckled. "And if I were, I wouldn't tell you."

Hope hugged her friend. "I love you."

"I love you too, child."

"What day's the pop-up?"

"Next Friday night."

"We'll have to go. Will you be my date?"

"You know I will," Iris said, appearing pleased.

• • •

Brent folded his Bermuda shorts and tucked them in his suitcase. He actually had bought those shorts for Bermuda. What a total geek he was. Not to mention a super gullible guy. But that was okay; he'd learned his lesson now. *Burn me once…*and all that. He was a fast learner.

"You don't have to go yet, you know," Derrick said from his chair at the kitchen table. He'd made a pot of afternoon coffee and was nursing his second cup.

"Thanks. I appreciate that, but I've taken you up on your hospitality long enough."

For the past seven nights, he'd slept on his brother's sleeper sofa. It was comfortable enough, but Derrick had a day job and would probably appreciate having some evening time alone. Brent was sure it had gotten old, hearing the whole sordid tale three times.

He'd gone over the story those two additional times because he kept finding himself leaving out important details. Like that bit about Hope's necklace. Now that he'd exorcised himself of the information and dumped all his angst on his long-suffering brother, it was time to go. Lest he force Derrick to suffer longer.

"When are you going to tell the parents?"

"Don't know. Maybe never."

"Come on, man."

"Okay. All right. Sometime soon. Maybe once I'm back in Boston."

"You could run into her there."

"Jackie? Sure. But I don't have to see her to get the marriage annulled. I researched it online, and it should be straightforward enough. We both just have to sign the paperwork, but we don't have to be there at the same time. I doubt very seriously that she'll fight me on it."

"Here's what I don't get," Derrick said. "Why did you want to marry her to begin with?"

Brent hung his head, knowing it had been for all the wrong reasons. That was something he'd come to terms with. While Hope and Jackie had abused his good nature by deceiving him and his family, Brent couldn't pretend he was perfect. He'd been willing to marry a woman he didn't honestly love in order to get ahead professionally. His grandpa's hotel business somehow seemed a whole lot less important to him now.

"It was dumb, Derrick. Really dumb. I thought that—by being married to Jackie—things would be easier for me."

"In what way?" Brent could practically hear Derrick's keen mind working. "You mean business-wise? No way." His jaw dropped. "You mean Grandmother Margaret was right?"

"I've been thinking a lot about it," Brent said. "And maybe William's the right one to take over for Grandpa Chad. He's got financial training and needs the stability. He hasn't got tenure yet, and that's not guaranteed."

"Plus, he and Sofia have a baby on the way," Derrick added. "Do you think he'd even want that?"

"I'm not sure, but I have a hunch he might."

"What about you?"

"I'll think of something." Brent closed his suitcase. "I always land on my feet."

"What about Hope?"

"What about her?"

"Are you going to do anything?"

"I don't know."

• • •

The following Friday, Hope was getting ready for the pop-up when her phone rang. It was the first time she'd dressed up nicely to leave the house, and she'd decided it was time. Running to the grocery store in her sweatpants and Dancing Queen T-shirt didn't count.

After the pop-up, she and Iris were going for drinks downtown. Hope was meeting some of her teacher friends there and wanted to introduce her to them. Iris was the closest thing to family she had in the area, and she valued her friendship greatly.

Hope walked to the kitchen table and picked up her phone, and her heart skipped a beat. She hesitated only a fraction of a second before answering. "Jackie?"

"Hi Hope," she answered, sounding exhausted. "How *are* you?"

"Okay. And you?"

"Not great," Jackie said. "I haven't slept in weeks."

"These past two weeks? How was Bermuda?"

"Bermuda? Are you kidding? I didn't go."

Hope was stunned. "But I... We saw you walking toward security."

"I didn't know what I was doing," Jackie said. "I was confused."

"Yeah," she said sadly. "Me, too."

Jackie sighed. "So. Have you heard from Brent?"

"Me? No. You?"

"I don't really expect to." Her sister sighed. "I tried calling him."

"Yeah? What happened?"

"It went straight to voicemail."

"I'm sorry. Did you try texting?"

"I wasn't sure what to say."

"We did a horrible thing, Jackie. I mean, I did. Mostly it was me."

"Hopie," she said softly. "I read all your messages. The text messages you sent before we met up. I looked through the photos, too. Maybe a dozen times. The ones that you sent, and also the pics that got uploaded to Instagram."

"I'm sorry if they upset you."

"No, that's not it. It was more like...they surprised me. There was something going on, wasn't there? Something between the two of you?"

"I swear. I never meant for—"

"It's all right," she said. "I'm not judging you. Brent's a really great guy."

"He is."

"He just wasn't the guy for me."

"You mean because of the marriage of convenience thing?"

"I mean because of everything. The two of you together in those photos, Hope? Especially during the ceremony? It's like…you *glowed*. It sounds clichéd, but it's true. If I didn't know better, I would swear those pictures were of a real couple on their wedding day—a couple who loved each other very much."

Hope fell silent a moment, digesting what her sister was telling her. "So, you're not mad that I…?" She rubbed her hand over her face. "Okay. Yeah, it's true. I did fall for him, but I swear I didn't mean to."

"I don't think it was one-sided."

Hope's heart hammered against her rib cage. "Even if it wasn't, it's too late now."

"Have you tried contacting him?"

"Oh no, I couldn't. If he won't talk to you, I'm extra sure he wouldn't talk to me. You might have committed sins of omission from afar, but I stood right there in front of him and told a bald-faced lie. Several of them, actually. And not just to him. To everybody in his family, too." She waited a moment before asking, "Have you talked to Mom?"

"Yeah, she's pretty devastated about everything. She kind of knew things would go south, but she was really hoping they wouldn't. She's worried about you, too, Hope. She said you're not taking her calls."

"I'm about to head out somewhere, but I'll give her a call when I get home."

There was a lull, and then Jackie spoke. "Mom says she saw it, too. That thing between you and Brent—whatever was happening. She didn't want either of us getting hurt, but now we both have. She feels especially bad about the Albrights. She's going to send them a potted plant as an apology."

"That's nice of her. I hope they don't throw it out."

"Yeah."

"What about Meredith? How's she taking all of this?"

"Meredith's still not totally over things but says she'll get there eventually."

"Uh-oh."

"She really didn't like deceiving Brent and his family, and she especially didn't like being put in the middle, but she does understand what a difficult situation it was. Especially since it snowballed so quickly, like many bad schemes do. In spite of everything and how it ended, she still says she really likes you and hopes you'll find happiness with the right person someday."

"That's sweet. I really like Meredith, too. I hope you two can make it up."

"We already have. We're going to the movies on Tuesday."

Hope couldn't help but wish that everyone was so forgiving, thinking of Brent. But, in her very lonely and practical heart, she knew she'd never get that lucky.

"Anyway," Jackie said, wrapping up their conversation. "I just wanted to call and check on you and, well, say… I'm sorry. I'm sorry, Hope. Sorry that I dragged you into this."

Hope wanted to say she was sorry, too, and she was, for hurting so many people. What she wasn't sorry about, though, was getting to know and care for Brent. No matter what her future held, she'd had the good fortune to experience that little bubble of happiness with him during that glorious week in Maine.

"Thanks for saying that. And thanks for calling. I'm sorry about the big mess we made of things, too. And especially sorry I started it by letting them believe I was you. I thought I was helping at the time, with Grandmother Margaret and all. But now I can see that the best way to help is by being our true selves."

"No more pretending," Jackie said. "Those days are *history*."

"Over and done with."

"Love you, Hope."

"Love you, too."

· · ·

It took Hope another three weeks to work up the nerve to write her letter. It took her six days after that to get the courage to send it. There was so much she needed to say, and she wanted to take pains to say it carefully. Hope didn't know if anything would come of her missive, but she suspected nothing would. In any case, she didn't anticipate receiving a response.

Her summer break was drawing to a close, and she hadn't heard one word from Brent. Not that she blamed him for his silence. If she were in his shoes, she would have probably reacted the same way. Hope guessed, at this point, he had to have told his family the truth about what had happened, and they were all likely thinking her a terrible person.

At least she'd repaired things with Jackie. She'd reestablished contact with her mom as well.

Something positive had come from Ava's time in Blue Hill, though. Miraculously, Gavin hadn't ditched Ava. Even upon learning the news. According to him, the sins of the children shouldn't be visited on their mothers or something like that. Gavin also wasn't concerned with gossip or inserting himself in other peoples' affairs. What mattered to him was the spectacular attraction he felt with Ava.

They'd been a long-distance item for a couple of months now and were planning a trip to Peru soon, which was somewhere Ava had always wanted to go. Both Hope and Jackie were glad their vibrant mom had found some later-in-life happiness and that a tiny glimmer of good had come out of that calamitous wedding week.

Hope kissed the back of the envelope for good luck, then slid it through the slot in the mailbox outside the post office. As she drove away, her heart felt lighter. She could never completely make amends for her mistakes, but at least she'd be able to walk away from those days in Blue Hill with a clearer conscience, knowing she'd done the right thing.

CHAPTER TWENTY-FOUR

Brent sat at his desk in his brownstone, going through his financial data in his accounting software program. His independent consulting business had really taken off, and he'd be hanging out his shingle soon: opening an official office. He'd perused several potential rentals and had found a nice space in the Wharf District that suited him perfectly. It was close to shops and restaurants, so it would be a fun place to work. The rent was a little high, but the visibility couldn't be beat. Besides that, business had been good enough that Brent could afford it.

His family had taken the news about Hope and Jackie pretty hard. No one could believe it, and everyone was extra stunned because they'd loved Hope as "Jackie" so much. She was funny and sweet...smart and caring... How could any of them have guessed?

Brent sure hadn't. Although, upon reflecting later, he understood there'd been subtle signs. Hope's extra-light suitcase was the first big tip-off. Then there was her wardrobe, that flattering haircut, and her extra-warm smile... The reminiscing wasn't helping at all, so Brent decided to snap out of it. Best to focus on work, like he'd done these past several weeks.

With his business training and background, Brent was well suited to become an entrepreneur, and William actually had been glad to assume the reins at

Albright Enterprises. Brent hadn't fully understood that William had been hurt he'd been passed over for consideration by their grandfather. William was, after all, the oldest, but somehow Grandpa Chad never figured him first in line for the job. Not until Brent pointed out how perfect William would be at it, with his very sharp intellect and the diplomatic skills he'd honed during years spent in academia.

Things were going well with Sofia's pregnancy—she'd passed through the danger zone of the first trimester with flying colors, and all was on course for a healthy delivery.

William and Sofia still wanted Brent to be their baby's godfather, and he couldn't very well say no. The truth was, he was honored they'd selected him for the role. While Brent's family wasn't Catholic, Sofia, whose background was Dominican, had been raised as one, and William had converted before their marriage.

Brent's phone rang beside his computer, and he picked it up.

"Grandmother," he said, noting the caller. "What a nice surprise. You and Grandpa still in Maine?"

"Yes, till after Labor Day, although this time of year I tend to regret the decision."

Brent chuckled. "So how's Blue Hill?"

"Hot and buggy." She sighed. "It's August. How is the consulting going?"

"Really well. Several of my old contacts have come through for me. And, you know, word of mouth. I think my reputation precedes me."

She laughed at his stab at humor. "Let's hope it's in a good way."

"You know you can count on me, Grandmother."

"I always have." She paused and then pressed ahead. "There's something I need to tell you."

Brent, who'd been absentmindedly flipping through some charts on his screen, stopped, giving his grandmother his full attention. "Go on."

"It's about Hope, actually."

"Hope? Webb?"

"I got a letter from her yesterday and decided to sleep on it. After some thought, I think you need to see it."

Brent's heart pounded as they ended their call with his grandmother agreeing to forward Hope's correspondence. A memory came back to him in a flash, and he recalled being in his SUV with Hope on the way to the Boston airport.

She'd claimed people only sent snail mail when it was important. In any case, she stated that she would once she had something important to say. What puzzled Brent was why she'd decided to say it to his grandmother instead of him.

He'd have to wait three more days and for the mail to be delivered to find out.

• • •

Hope left her teacher training seminar at the county office building feeling invigorated. The school district planned motivational and educational meetings for its teachers each year. There were additional annual kickoff events hosted at the individual school level. Hope was glad to be returning to her job. She needed something to do each day besides hide under the covers and eat Iris's brownies.

"How was your summer?" Jessica asked as they walked toward their cars with their teacher bags and purses slung over their shoulders. Jessica was about Hope's age, maybe a few years older.

"Okay. How was yours?"

The woman held out her ring finger, displaying a pretty diamond solitaire. "*Good*."

Hope stopped walking to hug her. "How exciting! You have to tell me all the details."

"I will. Maybe at lunch?"

Hope had quite a few teacher friends but was always happy to make one more. Jessica taught science, so they saw each other occasionally for cross-curricular planning but they'd never been close. Surrounding herself with more happy people seemed like the right idea. Besides that, she liked Jessica a lot and admired her as a teacher. Students totally loved her, and her classes were always over-enrolled.

"I'd love to do lunch. When were you thinking?"

"How about that last teacher workday before our student open house? A bunch of us from the science department are getting together. No reason we can't include some of you math nerds, too."

"Ha-ha, thanks."

"I mean it," she said brightly. "If there's anyone else you can think of who you'd like to have join us, that would be super. We're meeting at that fun outdoor Mexican restaurant, and, you know, the more the merrier."

• • •

Brent lived in one of those rare places where the mail was still delivered on foot and pushed through a slot in the front door. Each day, when he heard the mail arrive, his blood pumped harder, and he found it impossible to concentrate until he'd picked it up and fanned through it. He'd hadn't expected the forwarded letter from his grandmother to arrive the day after talking with her, but he'd looked for it the next day. And the day after that…

Finally, it was here.

He set the rest of his mail on the entry table and walked into the small living room with a turret-style window. He'd furnished his place in modern decor, which was quite swanky to look at but honestly not that comfortable. He sat in a hard-backed chair, examining the envelope. It was addressed in his grandmother's hand with her Blue Hill return address, and the envelope was thick. He guessed because she'd tucked Hope's original letter and envelope inside.

Brent broke the seal on the outer envelope, surprised to find his fingers shaking. Two months. It had been more than two months since he'd seen her standing there crying in the Boston airport, and they'd never officially said goodbye. A lump welled in his throat when he considered that maybe that was what Hope had done in her letter. Said farewell to all of them.

He unfolded the piece of stationary that was decorated around the edges with blueberries. It looked like something one might find in Maine, and Brent wondered if she had bought the paper during her time in Blue Hill. Maybe on her girls' day out with the rest of the women.

He stared at Hope's carefully crafted script written in blue ink pen. The letter was dated two weeks ago, and he wondered whether the letter had gone adrift in mail delivery or whether Hope had written it earlier and then waited to send it.

Dear Mrs. Albright, it began.

You probably think it's bold of me to contact you this way, and I'll totally understand if you decide not to read this letter. I sincerely hope you will, though, because there's so much I have to apologize for and say.

Someone wise once said that sometimes "sorry's not good enough," and now I know that's true. There's no way to undo my deception of your grandson and your family, and I speak from the heart when I say if there was a way I could take everything back, I would.

Brent once told me you still keep up with your friends by snail mail, and I think that's so special, because writing things by hand requires a personal touch. It takes time and patience and much more dedication than is required for dashing off an email or a text. I'm telling you this to say that—in writing this letter—I'm acutely aware of the colossal errors I've made.

One of the largest was letting you down, once you'd been brave enough to trust me and embrace me in your family. Had things gone differently, you and I might have become friends. It breaks my heart that I've destroyed your confidence in my character, because nothing that I did or said when we were together (apart from wrongly pretending to be Jackie) wasn't real.

When I first heard you doubted Jackie's true feelings for Brent and her motives in marrying him, I didn't understand your concerns. In some extremely misguided way, I thought I was building a bridge between your family and mine by stupidly playing the role of my sister.

Please rest assured that I never falsified my emotions with you or anyone else in your family, including Brent. I know this sounds difficult to believe and may be hard to understand, but I didn't just come to love Brent during my week in Blue Hill. I came to love each and every one of you. I'd never felt so welcomed or included in my life. Being a part of your warm and wonderful family, if only for a week, was like a dream come true for me that I'll never forget.

I hope in time you'll be able to forgive me. But if you can't or won't, I'll definitely understand. Also, please try to forgive my sister, Jackie. If there's anyone at fault for the enormous hurt we caused, I'm far more to blame than she is.

Finally, I wanted to address the wedding day and thank you for everything you did to help make it memorable. I'll never forget that time spent with you and your family, and I will forever regret losing the love of your wonderful grandson.

Before my week in Maine, I'd never met anyone like him. I didn't even believe that sort of person was *possible—someone so warm, tender, and caring. Intelligent, thoughtful, and kind. Brent has all the qualities to make someone the perfect husband someday, and I have no doubt that he will.*

Brent deserves all the happiness that life can bring, as do all of you. And so, I close this letter in sorrow but also in love. My life will go on, as yours will, but there will always be a piece of my heart left behind in Blue Hill, Maine.

Sincerely,
Hope Webb

Brent stared down at the page in his hands, and his eyes burned hot. His heart ached, and he felt all churned up inside. It wasn't until he saw the small pockmarks of moisture hitting the stationary that he realized he was crying. And he hadn't wept in years.

CHAPTER TWENTY-FIVE

Hope sat at the sunny outdoor restaurant under an awning with her teacher group, a dozen of them clustered around a long wooden picnic table with benches. It was Taco Tuesday, and they were taking advantage of the discounted eats, which everyone appreciated on their teachers' budgets. Most people were drinking iced tea, but Hope was drinking water because the only kind of tea they served was sweetened. She'd been trying to eat more healthily these past few weeks and had begun freezing the goodies Iris brought her so she could enjoy them in moderation later.

She hadn't lost a ton of weight but was already feeling better. Cutting out a lot of sugar and processed foods helped. The floral skirt and top she'd worn today fit really well, and the color of her scoop-necked shirt matched her pretty yellow flats. She had her necklace on, as she always did, and now it served as a double reminder. Both to be good to herself and also to stay true to herself—while being honest before others.

A waiter appeared to refill her water just as the person across from her said, "Hey, does anybody know that guy?"

"If I weren't engaged, I'd want to," Jessica said. "He's smoking hot."

Hope turned to see who they were looking at, and her heart caught in her throat. It couldn't be, but it was Brent. He stood there, scanning the crowd, wearing a black polo shirt and jeans and holding a wildflower bouquet. Hope blinked hard, quite certain she was imagining it. Then his eyes settled on hers.

"Whoa," Jessica whispered. "He's *your* friend?" She gave Hope a playful nudge. "I thought you had a boring summer."

Brent tilted his chin, and she got unsteadily to her feet. "If you'll…uh…excuse me," she said to the others before walking toward him in a daze.

"Brent?"

"I'm sorry if I'm interrupting. Iris told me I could find you here."

"Iris?" she asked, gobsmacked. "But how—"

"Your return address was on the envelope, and she was gardening outside."

Hope licked her parched lips, her mouth feeling sandpaper dry. "I don't understand."

"I read it, Hope. Your letter. Grandmother Margaret sent it to me."

Her cheeks burned hot.

"I'm sorry if you didn't mean for me to see it, but I'm glad that I did."

"I didn't think you'd ever want to hear from me again."

"I didn't, either." His mouth tipped up in a lop-sided grin, and Hope's heart thumped. "Until I did."

He held out the flowers. "These are for you, if you'll accept them. Along with my apology."

She numbly took the flowers, still wondering if she was dreaming. But as she lifted the fragrant bouquet to her nose, its sweet scent assured her that everything that was happening was very real. "What do you have to apologize for?"

"For not digging deeper," he said. "Looking beyond how things were on the surface to how they are inside."

"And how are they inside?" she asked, barely daring to hope. He raised a hand to her cheek, and her whole world went topsy-turvy.

"I think you know," he said huskily. "What happened in Maine was wrong." He searched her eyes. "But, at the same time, incredibly right."

Hope's heart pounded because she so desperately wanted to believe. Believe that he was saying what she'd wished he might. That he'd fallen for her, too.

"I'm so sorry for everything," she said. "For lying to you—and your whole family—about who I was. None of you deserved that, most especially not you."

"I'm not so sure about that." Brent's forehead rose. "I've been doing a lot of thinking ever since I read your letter. At first I was angry with you—at you and Jackie both. Then, in time, I understood that I should lay some of the blame on myself."

"On you? But why?"

"I was the guy who proposed to a woman I didn't love. A person I didn't even *know*, Hope. Someone I couldn't tell from her twin, for crying out loud. So, what kind of man does that make me? I'll tell you what kind. Somebody pretty imperfect."

She stared up into his heady dark eyes. "You seem pretty perfect to me."

"I know that's what you believe, but it's important for you to understand that I played a role in this, too." He took her in his arms. "In a strange way, you did me a favor and kept me from marrying the wrong sister. I mean, there are things that are great about Jackie, but she's not the woman for me."

Hope's heart beat even harder as she absorbed his words. "There's something I need you to know," she whispered. "I wasn't pretending. Not about how I feel."

"That's what I figured." He smiled. "And I'm glad. Because, Hope?" He held her closer, smashing the flowers between them. "I wasn't pretending, either."

Her heart melted as she met his swoony gaze.

"You know what I think?" he asked, his eyes sparkling. "I think we should try again."

"In Blue Hill?"

"No, in Durham." He considered her carefully. "Or in Boston. I've got a new day job in consulting now, so I'm my own boss."

"How great. But what about your grandpa? Albright Enterprises?"

"William's taking over all that."

"Is that what he wants?"

"It's what he and Sofia want." His smile grew. "They're having a little girl and naming her Julia."

Hope's whole soul welled with happiness. "That's wonderful!"

"So, what do you say?" he asked, jiggling her in his arms. "Will you date me?"

"Are you kidding?" She let out a joyful laugh. "Yeah."

"No pretending this time," he said seriously. "No more lies."

"I promise."

His lips brushed over hers, and her skin tingled. "I think we might have a future, Hope Webb."

"I do. I mean, I do, too," she replied with a blush.

He chuckled at her reaction. "You might want to save those words for later."

"How much later?"

"Let's take this slow." His mouth met hers in the world's deepest and most soulful kiss until hoots and hollers broke out from her teacher friends, as well as other patrons in the restaurant.

"I'll take it any speed you want," she answered shyly. "Just promise me one thing."

"Yeah? What's that?"

"Take me on another picnic?"

"Oh, sweetheart," he said with a laugh. "Don't you know? I'll take you anywhere in the world you want to go."

"But probably not to Bermuda," she joked.

"No," he said, chuckling. "Probably not there."

"That's okay," she said, angling for another kiss. "I hear it's overrated, anyway."

EPILOGUE

Hope snuggled down in the double-size sleeping bag beside her new husband. She couldn't believe he'd booked them this suite in an ice hotel! The walls were carved into exquisite ice sculptures, and the bed was remarkably cozy, considering it was essentially a block of ice covered with a wood board and a comfy mattress. Flames flickered in the glass-encased gas fireplace on the far side of the room, giving the space an ethereal appeal.

"This honeymoon's been like a dream."

"You're telling me."

Brent tugged her nearer, and her cheek brushed against his morning stubble, filling her mind with memories of all the exciting skin-to-skin contact they'd enjoyed last night. While the temperature in here was below freezing, she wasn't chilly in the least. Brent's body heat warmed her through and through.

She wore fuzzy flannel pajamas, and he had on his sweatpants with a long-sleeved tee. Both of them wore hats, like they were on an adventurous outdoor camping trip, yet they were sheltered inside this amazing structure. Hope couldn't believe this was real and not a fantasy. She never could have imagined such an unusual and unique honeymoon locale.

"What made you pick this place?" she asked, gazing up at him.

He smiled, and lines crinkled at the corners of his swoony dark eyes. "It was about as far from Bermuda as we could get."

"Yeah, that's true." She giggled, because he'd surprised her so thoroughly with this winter-wonderland getaway. They'd been ice-skating and snow rafting and had had all sorts of fun playing in the beautiful Canadian snow. "There's definitely no need for bikinis here."

"Except for in the hot tub," he said with a sexy growl.

She laughed, loving him so much. "Yep. Except for in there."

Despite their best intentions in taking things slow, once they'd started dating, their relationship had evolved quickly. Because they hadn't been lying about their backgrounds, wishes, or likes in Maine, they already knew tons about each other. Hope couldn't quell that little flutter in her belly every time they got together, and the dreamy look in his eyes said Brent experienced the same deep attraction to her.

By Christmas, they were already talking about marriage, but then they became conflicted about how to move forward. Considering they'd already had one pseudo-wedding, it felt weird to plan another. They weren't so sure about asking their families to sit through a second one, either. So, in early January, Brent arrived at the inspiration that they should elope to a justice of the peace. They'd done that in Durham three days ago exactly. Iris and Hope's teacher friend, Jessica, had served as their witnesses.

Hope intended to keep teaching at her school, and Brent had decided to relocate his consulting business to the Research Triangle area so they could officially move in together as husband and wife. They'd already done a little browsing online and had picked out a few cute homes to visit when they returned to North Carolina.

Hope couldn't wait to buy a little house with Brent and begin making it their own. Of course, she'd miss Iris, but—wherever they settled—Iris wouldn't be that far away and could always come visit. Or Hope could visit her. Jackie also had been really supportive of Hope and Brent's elopement and future plans. She'd started doing yoga and meditation, both of which seemed to help mitigate her high-anxiety nature.

Their mom was doing great, too, as were all the Albrights, who'd generously forgiven Hope and Jackie for their deception, because they were good people with very big hearts. In Hope's eyes, the biggest heart of all belonged to Brent. She wrapped her arms around him, holding him close.

"Thank you for doing this," she said. "Planning this fab honeymoon. Everything."

A pretty solitaire sparkled on her ring finger next to the gold wedding band Brent had placed on it. When they'd exchanged vows in the courthouse during their private ceremony, her heart had brimmed with joy. She couldn't wait to get started on their new life together and see where it led.

"I'm so glad that you're happy." He kissed the top of her head. "I'm happy, too."

"I love you, Brent."

His eyes sparkled. "Not half as much as I love you."

"Oh yeah?" she challenged. "Wanna bet?"

He laughed warmly and kissed her. "How about we call it even?"

"All right." She grinned and laid her head on his shoulder, feeling peaceful and adored. Of all the potential husbands in the world she might have landed, she only wanted him, and she was happier than ever to be his one and only bride. Even if things had started out a little rough, they'd turned out okay in the end.

"So you're kind of into me, huh?" she asked in a flirty way.

"One hundred percent."

"That's good." She held him closer. "I'm glad that it's mutual."

"Yeah." He shot her a loving smile that spoke volumes. "Me, too."

Turn the page to start reading the charming
and heartfelt small-town romance

Accidentally Family

A Pecan Valley Novel

SASHA
SUMMERS

CHAPTER ONE

Today was always going to be a life changer, Felicity knew that. Watching her firstborn walk across the graduation stage, smiling ear to ear, was one of those slow-motion moments, a blur of happy times, milestones, and pride. Her daughter, Honor, was done. Eighteen. A high-school graduate, ready to spend the night celebrating with her friends.

Which was exactly as it should be.

This, now, leading her two kids into the emergency room, was not.

"How serious was the accident?" Honor asked, holding tightly to her hand.

"Honor," Nick, her sixteen-year-old, snapped. "You heard as much as she did."

It had been one of those times she'd wished her phone wasn't synced to her car. How could she have known the hospital was calling? How could she have known Matt, her ex—the kids' father—had been in an accident? A *serious* accident. They'd all just assumed Matt had ditched, as was the trend.

"Hold my hand, Nickie," Honor mumbled thickly, reaching for her little brother's hand.

Nick didn't say a word, but Honor didn't have to ask again.

The way her kids relied on each other was one good thing to come out of her messy divorce. They weren't just siblings anymore. They were best friends. Best friends who had no idea what was happening. It was possible Matt's replacement family was here—in the waiting room—families did that when things like this happened.

Coming face-to-face with his fiancée, Amber; her megawatt smile; and her killer legs wasn't going to make this any easier. Neither was meeting Matt's son, Jack—the baby Nick blamed for destroying their *happy* family. As much as she'd like to think Nick could keep it together, there were no guarantees. When it came to his father, Nick was equal parts hostility and resentment. The potential for reality-television drama in the hospital waiting room was a real concern.

But if the last two years had taught her anything, it was that a smile was normally the best accessory. Even when the last thing she felt like doing was smiling. Like now.

"Is that Dr. Murphy?" Nick asked.

Felicity glanced at the man at the nurses' station. At well over six feet, Graham Murphy stood out. Seeing his tall, broad back encased in green hospital scrubs was a relief. While the two of them hadn't been close the last few years, Graham and Matt had been best friends through med school and partners when Matt still had his OB/GYN practice here in Pecan Valley. "Graham?"

"Yes?" Graham Murphy turned to face them, instant recognition easing his features—briefly. His brown gaze searched hers. "Felicity." That was all. Her name, without a hint of emotion.

But he was having a hard time making eye

contact with the kids, and that said so much. If Matt was okay, he'd say so. Wouldn't he? He'd offer some sort of reassurance. A smile. Something. The shock of the phone call was quickly turning into something substantial—and cold.

"I got a phone call? About Matt." Maybe he didn't know anything. Maybe—

"I'll take you to him." He cleared his throat, drew in a deep breath, and spoke. "He's going to surgery. His jaw is broken, so talking isn't comfortable. He's in bad shape, a lot of pain, but he held on to see you. Keep it positive—good thoughts, that sort of thing, okay?"

Honor was nodding, tears streaming down her face. Felicity wiped them away, pressing a kiss to her cheek.

Nick. Poor Nick. She hugged him close, his tall frame rigid and unyielding in her arms. Since the divorce, Nick's anger had grown every time Matt missed a game, concert, birthday, or holiday. While she understood, she worried Nick's fury would consume whatever affection he still felt for his father.

Graham looked at her, then nodded, leading them past the nurses' station and into the emergency room. He stopped beside the last door off the hall.

"What's best for him? One at a time? All together?" Honor asked.

"Together." The word was all Nick could manage.

Graham squeezed Nick's shoulder and went inside. "They're here, Matt."

Felicity went first, doing her best not to react to

her ex-husband's appearance. But it was hard. His face was swollen and misshapen, a white gauze ice pack taped to his jaw. He was covered with several blankets, one looked like an inflated packing sheet, and each breath he took was labored and watery. He looked wrecked, in every sense of the word.

Honor immediately headed to her father, but Nick hung back.

"No crying," Matt said, the words slurred. He pressed a kiss to her forehead. "So beautiful. S-sorry…missed it. Graduated. I'm so proud. And I love you, baby girl."

"Don't talk, Dad." Honor kissed his cheek. "Mom recorded it all. You can be bored with it later—when you're better."

Matt nodded, the movement stiff. "Good." He was hurting; she could hear it, see it. "Nick?" The word a plea.

Nick crossed the room, hands shoved in pockets, jaw muscle working. "I'm here, Dad."

Matt reached up, his hand shaking so bad that Nick had no choice but to cradle it in both of his.

Felicity saw her boy's chin quiver, saw him wrinkle up his nose, the way his breathing hitched. He'd held on to his resentment for so long, he wasn't about to lose control now. But seeing him struggle hurt—so much.

"I love you, son." Matt spoke clearly, enunciating carefully. "I love you both so much."

"We love you, too, Dad," Honor said, kissing him again. "You just concentrate on healing thoughts. Good stuff. Fast cars and ice cream and puppies and—"

A nurse came in, effectively shooing the kids away while pulling the rails up on his bed. "It's time, Dr. Buchanan."

"One second," Matt said. "Felicity."

Felicity jumped. "Yes?"

Matt waited until they were alone before speaking. His gaze pinned hers, and his voice wavered. "Amber's dead. Jack." His face crumpled. "And Jack..."

Her heart stopped. "Matt, I—"

"He's alone, Felicity." His blue eyes bore into hers. "Please..." He pressed his head back into his pillows, closing his eyes. "Take him." It was a gruff whisper. "Love him."

She stepped closer, hating the crush of air from her lungs. "He needs *you*, Matt." She leaned over him. "You're his father."

His gaze burned. "I'm a doctor; I know what's happening. This is it." He spoke calmly, even as his eyes glistened. "I'm asking you to care for my son."

"Matt..." Felicity stared at him through horrible, painful tears. "Fight. You hear me?"

"Please, Filly." He grabbed her arm. "Please."

She squeezed his hand. "I promise I will. You promise you'll fight."

He nodded once, relaxing against the mattress.

"We're going now, Dr. Buchanan." The nurse brushed past her, kicking off the brake on the hospital bed.

Felicity trailed behind, numb.

"He will be okay," Honor said, taking her hand. "He's so fit and healthy. He's going to be fine."

Felicity squeezed her hand, unable to shake the

dread seeping into her bones. She wanted to believe that was true. But the look on Matt's face… "How long will the surgery take?" she asked Graham.

"It depends. A while." He glanced at his wrist-watch. "I can call you if you want to go home?"

Honor shook her head. "We're staying, right, Mom?"

She nodded. "Nick?"

Nick was still staring at the doors they'd wheeled Matt through. "We can stay."

"Want to see Jack?" Graham asked.

"Jack?" Felicity frowned. "He's here? Matt said they were leaving him home with a babysitter." This wasn't a place for a baby. Especially now. Her heart ached for the little boy. For Amber. And for Matt.

Graham stared at her. "Jack…he was in the car, too."

Felicity stared at Graham, sinking further into despair. "He was?"

"Oh my God." Honor covered her mouth, bursting into tears then. "Is Amber with him? Poor little guy's got to be freaking out."

Graham looked at her but didn't say a word.

"Is he hurt?" Felicity asked.

"He's in a coma—sustained some head trauma," Graham said. "His right femur is broken and there's a lot of scrapes and bruises. But children are amazingly resilient."

"Amber can sit with him." Nick shoved his hands into his pockets, shooting a look at Honor.

"No, she can't." Felicity shook her head.

"Yes, she can," Nick argued. "He's her kid. Her

problem. Not yours."

"Nick, he's your brother," Honor argued.

"No, he's not," Nick shot back.

"Nick." Felicity faced her son. "He is your half brother." She touched Nick's cheek. "And he needs us right now. Amber died in the crash." She pulled Honor close, trying to hug them both—but Nick stayed stiff. "That little boy has no one in the world except your dad. And us."

Nick stared up at the ceiling, shaking his head.

"I could use some coffee," Graham said. "Anyone else?"

"Yes, please, Graham. Thank you." Felicity looked at the man who'd once been one of her closest friends. "And thank you for being here."

"Jack's around the corner." Graham nodded. "Nick, walk with me?"

"Come on, Mom." Honor held her hand out. On her daughter's face she saw everything that was churning inside of her. Fear, determination, sadness, and the need to *do something* so the horror of the night wouldn't bring her to her knees.

• • •

Graham glanced at his daughter, Diana, sitting in the corner of the hospital cafeteria. The thick black eye makeup she wore ran in tracks down her cheeks, her chin rested on her knees, and her ear-buds were—as always—plugged in. She was mad at him—as always. This time, he'd been the asshole who was stopping her from having a life. Meaning he wasn't letting her drive five hours away with a bunch of kids he didn't know to listen to a band called Broken Souls.

She saw him, saw Nick, and wiped her cheeks. His first instinct was to go to her, to hug her, to comfort her. But she'd already told him what he could do with his instincts. *Nothing like hearing your daughter tell you to screw off to warm the cockles of your heart.*

"Coffee?" he asked Nick.

Nick shook his head, pacing back and forth while Graham fed coins into the coffee machine.

"Soda?" he asked.

Nick shook his head again, rolling his shoulders.

"Candy bar?"

Nick stopped, leveling him with a hard look. "I'm good."

He doubted that. And while the boy had every right to be upset, something told Graham it went deeper. Before his wife had died, before Matt had deserted his family, before his and Matt's practice had disintegrated, he'd known Nick well. Holidays, birthdays, summer cookouts, vacations—the Murphys and Buchanans had been close. And then life had taken a rapid nosedive, his world splintering into pieces so small there was nothing recognizable left. He glanced at Diana again, her too-skinny frame turned away from them as she held on to this latest grief with every fiber of her being.

She believed she was a 'magnet for bad-luck'. From her grandparents to her pets to her mother, Diana's life did appear to be one long strand of miserable pearls. And now, tonight.

Accidentally Family

A Pecan Valley Novel

SASHA SUMMERS

Available now!

AMARA
an imprint of Entangled Publishing LLC